Edward Hull

Mount Seir

Sinai and Western Palestine, being a narrative of a scientific expedition

Edward Hull

Mount Seir
Sinai and Western Palestine, being a narrative of a scientific expedition

ISBN/EAN: 9783337294823

Printed in Europe, USA, Canada, Australia, Japan

Cover: Foto ©Andreas Hilbeck / pixelio.de

More available books at **www.hansebooks.com**

MOUNT SEIR,

SINAI AND WESTERN PALESTINE.

BEING A NARRATIVE OF A SCIENTIFIC EXPEDITION.

BY

EDWARD HULL, M.A., LL.D., F.R.S.,

DIRECTOR OF THE GEOLOGICAL SURVEY OF IRELAND,
PROFESSOR OF GEOLOGY, ROYAL COLLEGE OF SCIENCE, DUBLIN.

WITH MAPS AND ILLUSTRATIONS.

Published for the Committee of the Palestine Exploration Fund by

ALEXANDER P. WATT,
2, PATERNOSTER SQUARE.

1889.

Inscription.

PREFACE.

THE outcome of an Expedition is a book; and in the preparation of this narrative, which has been a labour of love, I have many friends to thank for their assistance. But I must here confine my special acknowledgment to two composite bodies, namely, the members of the Expedition, and the Committee and Secretary of the "Palestine Exploration Fund," who have endeavoured to meet my wishes in every way.

For the defects which may be found in the book itself, I can only plead the pressure on my time from many engagements.

THE AUTHOR.

DUBLIN,
10th October, 1884.

CONTENTS.

CHAPTER I.

CHAPTER II.

CHAPTER III.

CHAPTER VIII.

CHAPTER IX.

CHAPTER X.

CHAPTER XIV.

CHAPTER XV.

CHAPTER XVI.

CHAPTER XVII.

CHAPTER XVIII.

CHAPTER XIX.

CHAPTER XX.

CHAPTER XXI.

CHAPTER XXII.

CHAPTER XXIII.

APPENDIX.

LIST OF ILLUSTRATIONS.

NARRATIVE OF AN EXPEDITION THROUGH ARABIA PETRÆA, THE VALLEY OF THE ARABAH, AND WESTERN PALESTINE.

CHAPTER I.

"OUTWARD BOUND."

THE work of the Palestine Survey, which had been partly completed in Moab by Captain Conder, R.E., having been interrupted through the opposition of the Turkish Government, the Executive Committee of the Palestine Exploration Fund determined to undertake a geological reconnaissance of Western Palestine and the Jordan Valley, in accordance with the programme of work to be done under the auspices of this admirable Society. The Topographical Survey of Western Palestine had now been completed and published, so that the time seemed ripe for investigating the physical phenomena of Western Palestine, the Valley of the Jordan, and of the deep depression in which lies the Salt Sea.[1] An offer to undertake this exploration having been made to me by Colonel Sir Charles W. Wilson, on the part of the Executive Committee of the Palestine Exploration Fund, I consulted with some friends regarding the nature of the countries to be traversed, climate, and other matters ; and having received sufficiently encouraging replies, I gladly accepted the offer, and began preparations for carrying it out :—the Lords of the Committee of Council having been so good as to grant me three months' special leave of absence from my official duties in Ireland.

I had long taken a deep interest in the physical history of Palestine. I had read nearly everything that had been written on the subject,

[1] I prefer this name to that of the "Dead Sea," a name of much later origin, and originating in a misconception. The name "Salt Sea" (Gen. xiv, 3) is peculiarly appropriate to an inland lake of such intense salinity, and was in use at the time when the Pentateuch was written. The Arabic name for this lake is "El Bahr Lut," the Sea of Lot.

B

including the great work of M. Lartet, the geologist attached to the expedition of the Duc de Luynes, and had even gone so far as to deliver a public lecture on the physical history of the Jordan Valley and the Salt Sea in the theatre of the Royal Dublin Society.[1] Little did I think, when delivering that lecture, that I should have an opportunity in a few months' time of testing the correctness of my views by actual observation on the spot! Such, however, was the case; and within a few weeks I was busily engaged in my preparations for departure for the East.

It was of first importance to choose suitable companions. The Committee kindly allowed me to select an assistant; and I gladly accepted the offer of my son, Dr. E. Gordon Hull, to accompany me in that capacity, and, also, as honorary medical officer to the party. Major Kitchener, R.E., then in Egypt, was nominated by the Committee to undertake the topographical survey of the Wâdy el Arabah, and region to the north as far as the shores of the Salt Sea, so as to join up the triangulation with that of the Ordnance Survey of Palestine;[2] and Mr. Armstrong, formerly Sergeant-Major R.E., who had taken part in nearly the whole of the previous survey, was appointed his assistant. It is scarcely necessary for me to say with what pleasure I received the tidings of the appointment of Major Kitchener as my colleague. I was aware of his great experience in the work of the Palestine Survey, of his knowledge of the character and customs of the Arab tribes amongst whom we were to travel, and of his ability to converse in their language. All this inspired an amount of confidence of ultimate success I should not otherwise have felt, and the result proved that my confidence was well founded. In matters connected with our dealing with the Arabs I readily deferred to his judgment, which I always found to be judicious, while he often acted as spokesman in our negociations with the Sheikhs.

It was, also, a matter of much importance to the safety of the party, towards the attainment of our objects, that great prudence should be exercised in dealing with the Bedawins;—at least we supposed so. The unhappy murder of Professor Palmer, Lieut. Gill, and their companions,

---

[1] An abstract of this lecture appeared in *Nature*, March, 1883.

[2] The Palestine Survey Map, published on a scale of ⅜ of an inch to one statute mile, includes the western shore of the Dead Sea as far as Sebbeh; from this point the southern boundary runs along Wâdy Seiyal, Wâdy el Milh, Wâdy es Seba, and the Wâdy Ghuzzeh, to the shore of the Mediterranean Sea, south of Gaza.

by the Bedawins of the Tíh, was still fresh in our memories, and sometimes caused a cold thrill when I thought thereon.   Some of my more judicious friends, when speaking with me on the prospects of my journey, accompanied their congratulations and good wishes with gentle hints to beware of the treacherous Bedawin, and " to remember the fate of Palmer." They little thought, kind souls, how they were adding to my own mental anxiety, which I trust I did not allow any one to share, or even suspect. I kept it under lock and key, along with Besant's narrative of that horrible tragedy, and insisted, in reply to my friends, that the circumstances of Professor Palmer and myself were entirely different (which was undoubtedly the case), and that in the capture and execution of the murderers the Bedawins had received a lesson which they would not readily forget.   Such was also the view that my friend and counsellor, Sir Charles Wilson, had endeavoured to impress upon me.[1]

As will be seen in the sequel, both the scope and area of the Expedition were considerably enlarged as time went on.   In the letter of Mr. Glaisher,[2] F.R.S., Chairman of the Executive Committee in which the route and objects to be kept in view were definitely laid down, it was stated that we were to proceed overland to Egypt, where we should be joined by Major Kitchener, and from thence strike into the desert of Sinai, which we were to traverse as far as the head of the Gulf of Akabah.   From thence we were to proceed northwards along the whole length of the Wâdy el Arabah, to the southern end of the Salt Sea, and proceeding along the western shore as far as Ain Jidi (Engedi), turn up into the tableland of Judea to Hebron, from whence the officers of the Engineers were to return to Egypt, while the other members of the Expedition were to proceed to Jerusalem, and organise another expedition into the Jordan Valley, Moab, and Northern Palestine.   It will thus be seen that a tour of unusual extent and interest was placed within our reach, including countries and places second to none in importance from their sacred associations, their historical antecedents, and the physical conditions under which they are placed. The Committee also took care that everything should be done for the

[1] The matter is very fully gone into in Mr. Besant's " Life of Professor Palmer." There can be no doubt, as we afterwards learned on the spot, that Palmer's death was planned by the agents of Arabi Pasha, and that the Arabs, who were to a man on Arabi's side, were only carrying out the orders they had received from Egypt.

[2] Of date 7th July, 1883.

comfort and safety of the travellers. The Egyptian Government, through the Foreign Office, offered an escort as far as Akabah, the limit of Egyptian territory; but as we had no reasons for apprehension from the Arabs in the Sinaitic peninsula, we did not think it necessary to avail ourselves of the kindness of Cheriff Pasha, who had offered through Major Kitchener to give us every assistance in his power. The district where an escort of soldiers was likely to be of use lay between Akabah and the Salt Sea, and here the Egyptian escort would have been unable to accompany us.

The party as it now stood consisted of four; but it was obviously desirable that it should include a naturalist, who should make notes and collections of the representative fauna and flora of the district to be traversed; and of a meteorologist, who should also make observations on the temperature, rainfall, and aneroid determinations of the levels of special points along our route. I therefore cast about in my mind for volunteers having the necessary time and qualifications to undertake those departments of research, and was most fortunate in both instances. Mr. Henry Chichester Hart, who joined us in the former capacity, had been personally known to me for several years as an ardent investigator of the flora of Ireland, having made several reports on the botany of special districts of that country, under the auspices of the Royal Irish Academy. He had also acted as Naturalist in the expedition of Sir George (then Captain) Nares, R.N., to the Arctic regions, which had penetrated as far north as 83° 14′ lat. To these antecedents Mr. Hart added an uncommon power of enduring bodily fatigue; and he proved a most agreeable addition to our party, owing to his imperturbable good humour, and the extent of his knowledge on natural history subjects. Mr. Reginald Laurence, Associate of the Royal College of Science, Dublin, who accepted my invitation to act as Honorary Meteorologist to the Expedition, had also been my personal friend for several years, and from my knowledge of his antecedents and ability, I felt sure he would prove the right man to complete our quorum; and in this I was not disappointed. Never, I feel sure, were six persons more happily associated in an undertaking of this kind. Throughout our whole tour the utmost good feeling prevailed amongst the members; each took an interest, not only in his own department, but in those of the others, and tried to assist in them as opportunity offered. My son, having had considerable practice in photography, undertook to bring home photographs of the district through which we were to pass, and through part of which no photographer had as yet penetrated. Our Expedition was thus tolerably complete in all its branches.

The previous expeditions sent out by the Society had been managed by the officer in command, either through a dragoman or with the natives direct. As, however, the present journey was through a country unknown to any of the members of the party, and among tribes of indifferent reputation, it was thought best to make use of the facilities provided by Messrs. Cook & Son, whose agents and dragomans in Cairo are well acquainted with the Desert and the Sheikhs of the various tribes. Consequently, an arrangement having been come to with the London office, we were enabled to travel without trouble as to tents, food, attendants, escort, or camels, everything being done for us, perhaps the more efficiently on account of the personal interest taken in the Expedition by the head of the firm.

Several days were spent in London by all the members of the party in making preparations. Theodolite, compasses, aneroids, thermometers, photographic apparatus, guns, revolvers, ammunition, geological hammers, maps, suitable clothes, stationery, and many other articles had to be provided, packed, labelled, and despatched. Mr. Armstrong was to follow in a few days by steamer from Marseilles, and join us in Egypt. My son and I met the Committee in Adam Street for a parting consultation and farewell, which was very warmly given us by the Chairman, Mr. Glaisher. On the day following we all dined with my brother-in-law, the Rev. H. Hall-Houghton,[1] at the National Club, Whitehall, and on Saturday we took our seats for Dover in the train at Ludgate Hill Station, Mr. Cook being on the platform to see us off, and wish us "a good journey." We crossed the "silver streak" during an interval of comparative tranquillity, and in a boat, fortunately, other than the "Calais-Douvre," so reached Paris in the evening, without having had to undergo the usual passage experiences.

We left Paris for Milan by the "through train," *vid* Basle, on Sunday evening. Our train was to have been in connection with another leaving Basle about noon, but as we approached this city our progress gradually approximated to a walking pace. With a view, doubtless, to reciprocity, as we got impatient the train slackened speed, with the not unexpected

---

[1] Mr. Hall-Houghton is a member of the General Committee of the Palestine Exploration Fund, and was present at the meeting of the Special Committee on the previous day.

result that we were late for the train into Italy. The day was wet and cold, and in order to pass a part of it in motion we took the next train to Lucerne, hoping for a change. But this beautiful city was draped in sombre garb. A canopy of cloud shrouded from our view the mountains, while a ceaseless drizzle damped our desire for sight-seeing. Some of the party, however, visited the remarkable "glacier garden" near the city ; and after dinner at the hotel we were glad to find ourselves again in the train, notwithstanding the disappointment of being obliged to cross the Alps at night. But though night, all was not dark. As we ascended the mountains towards the St. Gothard Tunnel the canopy of cloud melted away ; and about midnight the moon and stars shone forth, illuminating the snow-clad heights on the one hand, and throwing into still deeper shade the ravines and frowning precipices along which we threaded our way. On issuing forth from the tunnel on the Italian side, and as break of day approached, we found the sky clear, and we descended into the plains of Lombardy amidst a blaze of sunshine, which cheered our spirits ; and under such circumstances we drove through Milan, visited the cathedral, and in the afternoon took our seats in the train for Venice which we reached after dark. It was a new experience for all of our party but myself to find ourselves seated in a gondola, and piloted along through the canals, shooting numerous archways, and gliding along the dark, mysterious walls of houses, churches, and palaces, to the steps of the Victoria Hotel, where we were soon comfortably housed, to await the departure of the P. and O. steamship "Tanjore" for Egypt on the following Thursday.

We endeavoured to put our time to good account, and see as much of the "Queen of the Adriatic" as possible. I found that my former visit had in no way lessened the pleasure of a second, and I saw and heard much that had escaped me previously. Engaging the services of a very efficient guide, who informed us that he had accompanied Mr. Ruskin when collecting his materials for "The Stones of Venice," we made a very full examination of the Palace of the Doges, the Duomo of St. Mark, and other sights of this wonderful city. In the evenings we sipped our coffee under the colonnade of the Piazza, listening to the music of a very fine military band, or gazing with wistful eyes into the brilliantly lighted shops, so eminently calculated to elicit the last lira from the pocket of the beholder. Though we made some purchases, I fear our stay in Venice did not add materially to the wealth of the city. We recollected there were bazaars in the Eastern cities we hoped to visit with objects of still greater novelty than those even of Venice.

Owing to the quarantine regulations, the "Tanjore," Captain Briscoe, was unable to come up to the Grand Canal, so we left Venice in a steam launch, in which we were conveyed down through the lagoons to the place in the bay where our good ship rode at anchor.   We passed several islands and forts, amongst others one built by the Genoese in the fourteenth century, and several, rising from the lagoons, erected by the Austrians in 1859-60. These lagoon islands are in some cases of vast extent, and are covered by the waters of the Adriatic when the wind blows strongly from the south.   In 1875, on the 5th of January, a south wind banked up the waters of the Adriatic till they overflowed most of the islands, and for two days the Piazza of St. Mark was submerged to the depth of four or five feet.

We found the "Tanjore" crowded with passengers when our contingent had come on board.   These included General Sir Evelyn Wood and party returning to Egypt, and several persons bound for that country, as well as for Cyprus and India, whose company we enjoyed till we reached Port Saïd.   In the evening we weighed anchor, and steamed down the nearly smooth waters of the Adriatic, often out of sight of land, but sometimes with distant views of the coasts and islands of Italy on the one hand, and of Dalmatia on the other.   One of the islands, called "The Half-way Rock," rises as a sharp ridge, apparently of limestone, from deep water.

Early on Saturday morning, we entered the harbour of Brindisi as far as the coaling depôt of the P. and O. Company, and we had all to turn out of our berths pretty early in order to pass muster before the medical officer, who was pleased to give us "a clean bill of health," without a very strict *diagnosis* of each case.   On this and a subsequent occasion I had an opportunity of observing the absurd nature of quarantine regulations. Like the passport system, that of quarantine only seems to give to travellers gratuitous trouble and expense, without accomplishing the object for which it is supposed to be instituted. How this was illustrated in our own case will be noticed in the sequel.   In the case of the "Tanjore," it was so long since she had left Egypt (from which the cholera had almost disappeared) that any case on board would have manifested itself long ere she had entered the Venetian waters ; yet she was not permitted to enter the harbour, and her passengers coming from the west and north of Europe, where cholera had never entered, were subjected to inspection on reaching Brindisi ![1]

We spent Saturday and Sunday in this port, awaiting the arrival of passengers and mails for Egypt and India. The time was agreeably occupied in visiting the town and surrounding country in company with one or two friends, amongst whom I may be allowed to mention the name of Mr. Sinclair, R.E., Secretary to the Governor of Cyprus, Sir R. Biddulph. Both the plants and animals of this neighbourhood indicate an approach towards those with which we were afterwards to become familiar in Egypt. The low cliffs of the shore, formed of yellow tufaceous limestone, abound in shells of late Tertiary age,[2] some identical with those of the adjoining waters, while the ground swarmed with bright green lizards, beetles, and ants ; butterflies, wasps, and flies also floated about in the air, giving abundant occupation to Mr. Hart in collecting specimens and noting their habits. One peculiar species of wasp here lays its eggs in little balls of mud, in which the larvæ may generally be found.

The sub-tropical vegetation of the district is remarkably rich. Here the graceful date-palm waves its plumes aloft, amidst groves and gardens of olives, figs, oranges, vines, mulberries, and stone-pines. The eucalyptus has been introduced and planted extensively along the roads, while the hedgerows are formed of the bristling lines of the large cactus (prickly pear) and aloes. The cotton-plant is cultivated in ground which can be irrigated, while oleanders, myrtles, and foreign plants adorn the gardens.

The town itself, the ancient Brundusium, visited but scarcely seen by thousands of travellers annually, is of much interest, from its position and history. It stands on an inlet of the Adriatic, and the harbour, of great importance in Roman times, is capable of holding large ships. The harbour is connected by a causeway with a fortification, or castle, standing on the summit of a cliff to the south of the town, and in a commanding position. This is now used as a prison, and the inmates are usefully employed in a variety of reproductive works, such as carpentry, smiths' work, tailoring,

---

[1] That Egyptian cholera comes, not from India, but from Mecca and Midina, and is generated amongst the thousands of pilgrims who annually are collected for several days within an exceedingly limited area, where they are subjected to the effects of breathing foul air, drinking corrupted water, and living in filth and privation, will be conceded upon reading the " Rapport sur la dernière épidémie de Choléra à la Mecque," in the *Gazette Médicale d'Orient,* September, 1883, by M. le Dr. Abdur-Rassack.

[2] Pliocene according to Collegno's map.

&c., at which we found them busy when visiting the place on the afternoon of our arrival. There is a ditch and wall, with towers and gates, erected by the Emperor Frederick Barbarosa, probably on the site of more ancient structures, and amongst the remains of Roman work are two marble pillars, one of which is broken, at the end of the Appian Way.

The country inland consists of an extensive plain, about 200 feet above the sea, richly cultivated in crops of maize, wheat, and cotton, with farm-steads surrounded by gardens of olives, figs, and vineyards. This plain is traversed by the high roads to Rome and Naples, and several ancient fountains, doubtless coming down from Roman times, still afford water for thirsty men and animals by the wayside. The plain, formed of shelly limestone, beds of marl, clay, and sand, was at a very recent geological period the bed of the sea, and its uprising has added thousands of square miles to Italian territory.

On Sunday morning Captain Briscoe held Divine Service in the cabin, and read the prayers and lessons with due solemnity and effectiveness; and at 3 o'clock on Monday morning we steamed out of the harbour.

We soon passed from the deep indigo-blue waters of the Adriatic to those of the Mediterranean, which are of a greener tinge, not unlike those of the Atlantic. The voyage was very agreeable, and we only once came in for bad weather, which did not last very long. The view from the deck of the "Tanjore" on Monday towards the north-east was always striking, even at the distance from the land at which we sailed. The bold and rocky mountains of Albania stretched away for miles from left to right; beyond which, at a distance of over thirty miles, might be seen the mountains of Greece ;—the sun lighting up the peaks and scarped terraces of the white limestone of Epirus ; the Island of Corfu lying in the fore-ground. Towards evening the coasts of Cephalonia and Zante came in sight.

Awaking next morning, we found ourselves approaching Crete (Candia), and now a stiff gale was blowing from the north-east. Rain also was falling, and we began to feel tolerably miserable. The breakfast table was not quite as fully occupied as usual, and some of us found it con-venient to retire to our cabins before we had had time to partake of a hearty meal. However, about "tiffin" time the wind moderated, and we returned to the deck to watch the scenery of the island, along whose coast we were sailing at a distance of about twenty miles. The Island of Crete (as is well known) is mountainous; the peaks of Mount Ida, rising to 7,674 feet, were on this day cloud-capped. The sides are cut into deep ravines,

clothed with a slight forest vegetation. The sunshine effects were sometimes very beautiful, the higher elevations being so brightly white as to
resemble the snow-clad summits of the Alps. Towards evening the sky
presented a grand spectacle. Overhead the stars shone forth from the
dark blue vault of heaven ; from time to time the clouds which hung over
Crete were illumined by brilliant sheets of lightning often bursting forth
from behind the mountains like the flames of a volcano in active eruption ;
while brilliant meteors occasionally streamed across the heavens. This
scene lasted several hours. The beauties of the sky were so enticing,
and the air so balmy, that it was with regret we turned into our berths
late at night.

CHAPTER II.

EGYPT.

Land now disappeared from view, and we bid farewell to Europe ; the blue ring of the horizon was unbroken during the next day. After sunset I went to the bow of the ship to watch the effect produced by the medusæ when tossed up in the foam of the ship's prow. It is a sight full of beauty. Each sheet of white foam, as it was cast aside by the ship's side, was lighted by a thousand silver sparks caused by the phosphorescence of these pretty little creatures, quite invisible to the eye by daylight. I was told that sometimes dolphins may be seen disporting themselves amidst the shoals of medusæ, but on this occasion we were not so fortunate as to see any. On the 1st November we entered Port Saïd at 10 a.m., and for the first time touched the shore of the African continent ; I trust, with thankful hearts for all the mercies we had received.

Slowly we steamed up the harbour towards our anchorage, passing a line of steamships of several nations, chiefly British. On passing an Egyptian man-of-war we received a salute (presumably in honour of General Sir E. Wood, but the question has not been decided !) the men standing all along the bulwarks with hands horizontally extended, looking like so many human crosses clad in white, or like shirts hung out to dry. Soon after, a state barge came alongside to take Sir E. Wood and his party off for Ismailia. It was unfortunately completely filled, so that there was no room for us—doubtless a matter of profound regret to the General, who took his departure amidst much shaking of hands and waving of handkerchiefs. Leave-taking now became general all round. Our passengers broke up into parties for their respective destinations ; and at length we tumbled overboard into a boat and rowed for land with the gloomy prospect of a night sail up the canal in a passenger steam-barge amidst a crowd of unsavoury Moslems. Our baggage was carried to the hotel by porters, whose powers of endurance seemed little short of those of mules or camels. Mountains of heavy baggage, calculated, one would have supposed, to crush them to the earth, were piled on their backs. All hands helped the men to their feet, and off they started for the Custom House amidst the shouts and gesticulations of their comrades. We were, however, spared the annoyance of unpacking our baggage ; the Director-General of Customs having, through Mr. Cook's agent, sent instructions to pass all our baggage and effects unexamined.

During dinner we made a discovery which relieved us of our difficulty. We learned that a P. and O. steamer was to leave Port Saïd at 4 o'clock for Alexandria, and we resolved to take passage in her, and by this way to go on to Cairo. The "Dakatlieh" was airy and not very full of passengers, and after the close packing of the "Tanjore" we felt very comfortable indeed. We had a good night's rest, and were up betimes to view the African coast, evidences of which first appeared in the distant lines of feathery palms. We had been coasting for many miles off the Delta of the Nile, and all along our track the waters of the Mediterranean had changed their ordinary deep green into a lighter tinge, in consequence (as I was informed by Mr. Le Mesurier, of the Egyptian Railway Department) of the influx of the Nile waters.

It is unquestionable that the Nile carries down large quantities of mud into the Mediterranean, which is taken up by the prevalent eastward current, and finds its way into the harbour of Port Saïd, where dredging operations have constantly to be carried on at heavy cost in order to keep the channel of the required depth. The Damietta branch of the Nile may, from its position with reference to Port Saïd and the ship-canal, be considered the more immediate cause of the silting up of the canal bed.

This source of expense and danger to the navigation Mr. Le Mesurier proposes to meet in the following way[1] :—It will be observed on referring to a map of the district, that between the harbour of Port Saïd and the Suez Canal on the one side, and the Damietta branch of the Nile on the other, lies the great inland lake of Menzaleh, through which the canal has been carried, chiefly by dredging, for a distance of twenty-seven miles. The portion west of the canal still remains under water, but that to the east is now dry. This western portion, covering an immense area, Mr. Le Mesurier proposes to convert into a great precipitating basin for the Damietta branch, the effect of which would be *ultimately* to convert

---

[1] The project I only give in outline, as kindly communicated to me by Mr. Le Mesurier himself, during our stay on board the "Tanjore."

this tract into a vast field for agricultural purposes, while the waters which would pass off into the Mediterranean, being to a great extent deprived of their silt, would cause *immediate* relief to the harbour of Port Saïd, and that part of the canal which opens into it.   This is a grand scheme, calculated to be of benefit both to the agricultural and commercial interests of Egypt.   I can only express the hope that Mr. Le Mesurier may have the happiness of seeing it one day put into execution.

On approaching Alexandria, a pilot came on board to steer us through the intricate channel by which the harbour is entered ; and on rounding the point of the large breakwater, we came in view of the city and its harbour[1] all at once, a view calculated to afford both pleasure and surprise, —pleasure at its beauty ; surprise, that a harbour and city so recently the scene of a tremendous bombardment, should, at first sight, present such slight traces of the conflict.   In front lay the city, built on a gradually-ascending slope, and in the background to the left the elevated and fashionable suburb of Ramleh.   On the left of the harbour, the Fort of Pharos, partly in ruins, the lighthouse, and the Palace of Ras-el-Teen, white and glistening in the sunshine, and surrounded by pleasant gardens. On the right, the barracks, fortifications, lighthouse, and other public buildings : and in the distance, the noble column known as "Pompey's Pillar."   The harbour itself was gay and busy.   Ships of many nations lay at their moorings, both merchantmen and passenger steamships ; while the beautiful yacht of the Khedive swung at anchor in the centre. The surface of the water swarmed with smaller craft and barges, amongst which was one to convey on shore Her Majesty's Consul, Mr. Cookson, who had made the passage with us from Port Saïd, and whose acquaintance we had the pleasure of making.   He kindly insisted on sending us ashore in his barge, and told off his *khawass* to accompany us to our hotel, and afterwards to conduct us over the palace and fortifications.   Owing to this kind action on the part of Mr. Cookson, we were enabled to see the principal sights of this ancient city to the best advantage ; nor did this gorgeous, but most amiable, official leave us till he had seen us off in the train for Cairo in the evening.

We found much of the city in ruins—ruins caused by the mob, not by British guns ; and, as much uncertainty prevailed as regards the future of Egypt, restoration and rebuilding were proceeding but slowly.   It

---

[1] The city has two harbours—the western, or Eunostus, and the eastern, or New Port. We entered the western harbour.

only required the British Government to make the announcement that at least a contingent of our troops should be allowed to remain in Egypt for the preservation of order to induce capitalists to come forward and commence building. But this the Government had hesitated to do, and confidence in the future was consequently shaken. Who that knows Egypt can doubt that a permanent protectorate, supported by a sufficient British army, would prove a blessing of incalculable value to the country?

No object in Alexandria interested me more than the noble monolith known as "Pompey's Pillar." The name is misleading, as one naturally associates it with that of the great Roman general ; but, as the Greek inscription shows, it was erected in honour of Diocletian during the prefecture of Pompeius, in the year 302.[1] But whatever its origin, its immense size and beautiful proportions strike the beholder with admiration. Like most of the Egyptian monoliths, it is of red porphyritic granite, 73 feet in length, with a circumference of 29 feet 8 inches, highly polished, standing on a pedestal, and surmounted by a capital 16 feet 6 inches in diameter, giving a total height of very nearly 100 feet to the monument. It may well be doubted whether a monol th of this description belongs to the epoch of the Roman occupation. It is far more likely that its origin dates back to that period of very ancient Egyptian art which gave birth to the obelisks, the Sphinx, and the Great Pyramids. Its original birthplace was amongst the granite quarries of Upper Egypt, and whether hewn fresh from the native rock, or taken from some more ancient structure, it was a work of no small skill to transport it from its original site and erect it upon the elevated platform of solid limestone from which it is visible for miles in almost every direction.

It is to be hoped that Pompey's Pillar will defy the cupidity of foreign states. Within a few years the two companion monoliths of the ancient city have been carried away : one to adorn the banks of the Thames, the other those of the Hudson. Who that visits the modern cities of Europe, and witnesses the monuments of ancient Egyptian art, of which that country has been stripped, in order that *they* may be adorned, can restrain a sigh of regret at the spoliation of the land where art of the grandest conception had its birthplace and its maturity while that of Greece and Rome was still in the future?

[1] The inscription is given in Murray's "Handbook for Egypt," Part I, p. 132.

We left Alexandria in the afternoon, in company with an officer of the army of occupation, and travelled along a route, to us, new and full of interest. The railway at first passes along enormous mounds of broken pottery. And here I may mention that in the East, often when all traces of buildings have disappeared, fragments of pottery remain to attest the former existence of buildings. The reason of this is that pottery is almost indestructible. Houses, temples, churches, may have been laid in ruins, the materials broken up and carried away, but a "potter's vessel" when once broken is useless for any purpose ; no one cares for it, and it is left to add to the accumulations which take place at every town or village.

Soon we emerged on the Garden of Egypt, the fertile Delta of the Nile, without which, indeed, Egypt would be but a rocky or sandy desert penetrated by a deep gulf, as the Egyptian priests informed Herodotus was its original condition. Interminable fields of maize, cotton, sugar-cane, and other produce cultivated by the fellahin, succeed each other, irrigated by means of little water-wheels, sometimes worked by men, sometimes by bullocks, the water carried in narrow channels made by the feet, and allowed, when required, to flow over the beds containing seed ; all probably very much as in the time of Ptolemy, if not even earlier. Groves of the date-palm, with enormous clusters of golden fruit, rose aloft above the level of the Delta, or formed small clumps near the villages.

The cultivation of the palm, and of other fruit trees, was largely extended by Mehemet Ali, who made a decree promising remission of a certain amount of taxation for each tree planted. This had the desired effect. On producing a certificate of having planted so many trees the fellahin had his taxes reduced. Some time after, when the work of plantation had been accomplished, the decree was repealed, and a tax was put on the trees—a financial operation of questionable probity, but beneficial to the Government and to the cultivator, who enjoyed the fruits of his labour.

We passed several towns and villages of the fellahin ; of the latter nothing can be conceived more miserable as human abodes, and in comparison with which a village in Connaught might be considered worthy of admiration. The houses consist of small mud cabins huddled together, in which men, women, and children share the space with dogs, fowls, and pigeons. The cow or donkey does not require shelter at night in this part of the world ;—so is excluded from the family circle.

We crossed two branches of the Nile, each about as wide as the Thames at Kew, the water of which was as usual turgid. The water had fallen to 6 feet below its maximum, which it reached about the middle of October. The origin of the fine sediment which the Nile always carries in suspension, as well as of the rise and fall of the waters themselves, is now fully understood since the publication of Sir S. Baker's remarkable work.[1] Briefly stated, the origin is somewhat as follows :—The Nile below Khartoum consists of one undivided stream ; but at El Damer, about 170 geographical miles lower down, it receives the waters of a great tributary, the Atbara, descending from the highlands of Abyssinia. This river undergoes the most extreme transformations. During the early months of the year the waters are so reduced as sometimes to form only a series of great stagnant pools, in which are collected in very close quarters all the aquatic inhabitants, consisting of fishes, crocodiles, and huge tortoises. The banks, through a long line of country at the base of the mountains, are formed of masses of mud and silt, easily undermined, and liable to fall into the waters on the rise of the river. About June tremendous thunderstorms, accompanied by deluges of rain, break on the Abyssinian highlands. The waters of the Atbara rise with extraordinary rapidity, and descend with a roar like that of distant thunder, giving warning of the approaching deluge. Soon the channel is filled up with the flood, the banks of mud are undermined, and fall down in large masses into the waters, where they are speedily broken up and converted into silt, the finer portions of which being carried along finally enter the Nile, and impart to its waters much of the turgid character for which they are known in Lower Egypt.[2] The river now becomes a great fertilising agent, and when allowed to flow over the cultivated fields imparts the necessary moisture ; so that, under the influence of a powerful sun, two to three crops can be annually gathered off the land ; giving rise to an extraordinary amount of natural wealth. That this sediment originally caused Lower Egypt to be reclaimed from the Mediterranean Sea was known to Herodotus, who calls this country " the gift of the Nile."

Arrived at Cairo one of the first arrangements to be made is for a visit to the Pyramids, always a memorable event in any man's life. After all

[1] " Nile Tributaries of Abyssinia," p. 52.

[2] A good deal of sediment is also brought down by the Bahr-el-Azrek, or the Blue Nile, some of the sources of which also are found in the Abyssinian highlands. The White Nile also is a source of sediment.

FIG. 1.—VIEW OF THE MOKATTAM HILLS AND SUBURBS OF CAIRO, FROM THE WEST BANK OF THE NILE.

that has been written upon these grand monuments of Egyptian art it might appear presumption to attempt to add even a small quota of information ; still, at the risk of such an imputation, I venture to give a brief account of my own impressions.

The drive out from Cairo is very charming. Having crossed the river the road runs along its bank for several miles under the shade of overhanging branches of the Nile acacia, and fine views of Cairo and of the range of the Mokattam Hills behind are obtained. Here we happened to meet the Khedive and his retinue on returning from his morning drive, and further on we turned in at a gate leading past the palace built for the Prince of Wales, through groves of oranges, lemons (just beginning to ripen), fields of maize, sugarcane, and cotton. Another turn brought us to the causeway, which runs in a straight line westward towards the base of the platform on which the Pyramids of Cheops and Ghizeh are built, and from which the first view of them is obtained. The first view will probably disappoint the traveller, for (owing to the transparency of the air) the distance is greater than he supposes ; consequently the structures appear smaller than is really the case. The avenue itself is three miles long, in a perfectly straight line, over-arched by acacia trees, whose shady boughs, laden with large fruit-pods, afford a grateful shade from the sun's rays.

The best view of the Pyramids is obtained from a part of the causeway road, about half a mile from the platform on which they are built. From this point the four principal Pyramids are seen ranged in line ; that of Cheops, or "the Great Pyramid," in front ; that of Ghizeh next, and two much smaller ones in the rear. In the background is the ridge of sand which marks the line of the desert, stretching on either hand for miles.

It is well known that these great tombs of Egyptian monarchs are built on a platform of the nummulite limestone, which has been partially levelled for the foundations, but has never been entirely cleared from the accumulated rubbish. This platform of solid rock marks the limits of the Nile Valley. On driving up to the summit of the platform you are immediately beset by a crowd of importunate Arabs, who have mastered sufficient of your language to make you understand that independent action is out of the question, and that you may as well resign yourself submissively into their hands. Having done so, and decided whether you will ascend to the summit or descend into the vast interior,

C

you get breath to cast your eyes upwards along the face of this jagged mountain side, *as it now appears,* and to appreciate in some measure the vastness of its proportions.

The Pyramids you behold are, however, very different from those of the time of Herodotus. In the first place you perceive that the Great Pyramid is truncated, instead of ending nearly in a point like its neighbour, that of Ghizeh. Again, you observe that the apex of Ghizeh is cased in smooth stone while the whole exterior of the Great Pyramid is formed of step-like rows of masonry. It was not thus that the Egyptian architect handed over his great work to his monarch ; for in 1837 Colonel Howard Vyse discovered two casing stones in position, which may now be seen. They are blocks of limestone, 8 feet 3 inches long and 4 feet 11 inches in perpendicular height,[1] and indicate that the whole exterior was encased by polished blocks, giving it a perfectly smooth and glittering surface, well calculated to protect the building from injury, and to give an aspect of finish and completeness very different from that which it now presents.[2]

The act of vandalism which has deprived the Pyramids of their outer casing was perpetrated by the Caliphs, who carried away the stones to build the mosques of Cairo ; the result being that the general appearance of the exterior gives one the impression that these most ancient of buildings are rapidly disintegrating and destined to fall to pieces in the course of ages. This is no mere fancy. Let any one examine closely the condition of the outer walls, and he will find that they are penetrated by cracks and little fissures in all directions, along which the stone is crumbling away. These are due, I believe, to the expansion and contraction occasioned by the great changes of temperature between day and night; and the consequence is, that when a thunderstorm breaks over the district, as sometimes happens, the loosened pieces are washed down, and fresh surfaces for the sun to act upon are exposed. In course of time, therefore, the Great Pyramid, as well as that of Ghizeh,[3] must become a ruin ; and for this the only remedy is re-casing.

[1] Murray's "Guide," Part II, p. 246.

[2] It is stated by Abd-el-Lateef that the casing stones were polished and covered with inscriptions.

[3] The upper part of Ghizeh is still cased with its original polished blocks, hence its apex terminates in a platform so small as to appear from below almost pointed.

All our party but myself elected to ascend the summit—I to visit the interior, in hopes of recognising some of Professor Piazzi Smyth's marks and determinations ; so, delivering myself into the hands of four Arabs, I dived into the dark passage.   This is an undertaking which (as Miss Martineau observes) no one should attempt who is at all of a nervous temperament.   You soon begin to repent of your choice when you find yourself within the dark walls, descending deeper and deeper, two savages before and two behind.   Occasionally they stop, and put the question, "How you feel, sir ?" to which, of course, you reply, "Oh, quite well !" Inwardly you *feel* quite the reverse, but it is no time to allow the slightest hint of timidity to escape.   At length, after an indefinite descent, and another equally indefinite ascent, you find yourself in the great interior called the "King's Chamber," dark and oppressive, notwithstanding the flickering of the candles which your guides carry.   And now they take advantage of their opportunity : they demand *bakhsheesh*, produce various "*antiqua*," generally shams, and strive to make you purchase on the spot. Making a virtue of necessity, I promised bakhsheesh all round, and that I would make certain purchases upon getting to the open air, it being manifestly impossible to examine these articles with the aid of their gloomy light.   This satisfies my tormentors, and after a hasty glance all round, we commence our outward descent, and at length emerge into the dazzling light of day.   My guides again produce their "*antiqua*," demand their *bakhsheesh ;* but now it is *my* time to make terms.   Seating myself on a stone, I proceed to select what I wish, and to name my own price ; and finally, with a franc each for *bakhsheesh*, send them about their business.[1]

Meanwhile my companions had descended from the summit of Cheops, and were engaged in discussing with their Arab guides "the great bakhsheesh question."   My ambitious colleague, Mr. Hart, however, was not satisfied with the ascent of one pyramid ; and, taking advantage of his opportunity, while the backs of the Arabs were turned, gave them the slip and was soon scaling the sides of Ghizeh, the top of which he safely reached. What, then, was the surprise of the guides on beholding one of the Englishmen from this elevated position calmly surveying the landscape !

[1] There are three execrable words which were constantly cropping up during our journey, and of which travellers should beware, viz. : "bakhsheesh," " antiqua," and " quarantina."   The language would be improved if these were expunged from its vocabulary.

They could scarcely credit their senses ; but presently, giving vent to their feelings in unutterable Arabic, they proceeded towards the pyramid in hot pursuit, and on reaching the little platform on the summit surrounded my imperturbable colleague, gesticulating violently and overwhelming him with imprecations.   Above all things they could not believe that he had scaled the slippery polished cap of the pyramid in the boots in which he stood.   So, in order to satisfy them on this point, he proceeded to descend as he had gone up, and safely reached the bottom along with his bare-legged tormentors.   It was afterwards explained that the Arabs were answerable with their heads for any mishap to travellers visiting the Pyramids, but it is probable that "the great bakhsheesh question" was really the most potent cause of their dissatisfaction on this occasion.

The Pyramids are built of nummulite limestone—not hewn on the spot, but brought from quarries situated at the base of the hills ten miles above Cairo, on the right bank of the Nile.   The quarries are of vast size, as I was informed by Dr. Schweinfurth ; and one may there see tokens of the care exercised in selecting the stone, soft portions being left, the harder cut out for blocks.   The lines drawn by the overseer for the workmen are also visible on the walls.   The blocks were transported on a sloping causeway to the water's edge, floated across, and then hauled up a long similar causeway, still in existence, on the opposite side to their destination.

The Sphinx is, however, sculptured out of the native rock, and the horizontal lines of stratification are too plainly visible.[1]   The head is of harder material than the neck, which is formed of softer and whiter strata. Every one must regret the defacement which this grand work of Egyptian art has undergone ; but knowing the custom of Mohammedans to deface all objects which they consider idolatrous, it is not difficult to trace the cause for this act of barbarism.[2]

The so-called Temple of the Sphinx must excite the admiration of every beholder.   It consists of a series of vast rectangular chambers, cut out of the solid limestone, with recesses for tombs.   The walls are lined with massive blocks of the red granite of Syene, beautifully cut and polished, each fitting closely to its neighbour.   One of the walls lies

[1] Our witty, but not very accurate guide, Mark Twain, says the Sphinx is made of granite !

[2] As witness the defacement by breaking off the nose of the greater number of the statues in the Museum of Antiquities, Constantinople.

exactly north and south, so that when the shadow of the sun is coincident therewith it is noonday.

In this temple (as I was informed by one of the guides) Professor Smyth spent much of his time when engaged in making the measurements for his well-known work.[1]

When passing through Alexandria we had the pleasure of making the acquaintance of that indefatigable traveller and excellent geologist, Dr. Schweinfurth, to whom Mr. Hart had a letter of introduction. Having arrived at Cairo just after ourselves, he kindly offered to accompany us on a visit to the Mokattam Hills, at the base of which the city is built, and from which the stone for the construction of the houses and public buildings has been chiefly obtained.

This range of hills, though of no great elevation (600 to 700 feet), forms a fine background to the city, as well as to the Valley of the Nile, owing to the abrupt and scarped face it presents towards the north and west. It is composed of beds of the nummulite limestone, remarkably fossiliferous, both nummulites, shells, echini, and even fossil crabs being abundant. The quarries are of great extent, and the stone beautifully white, or slightly yellow, and capable of being chiselled into fine mouldings and architectural forms. From the summit of the ridge, which had been the sanitary camp of the British troops during the outbreak of cholera, we enjoyed an extensive view, and one full of variety and interest. To the right, at our feet, lay the capital of Egypt, with its streets, palaces, mosques, and churches, interspersed with gardens and groves of trees ; and in the foreground, standing on a projecting platform, the citadel and the mosque of Mehemet Ali, with its exquisitely graceful minarets. To the left, and washing the eastern base of the hills, stretched the green and fruitful plain of the Nile ; the great river itself carrying its channel from side to side, and crossed opposite the city by the bridge we had passed over the previous day. Looking across the valley, the horizon towards the west is bounded by the yellow ridge of the desert sands, in front of which, as if to mark the boundary between the region of verdure and that of drear sterility, are planted the Pyramids, in grand procession, headed by the greatest and oldest ; those

---

[1] "Our Inheritance in the Great Pyramid." However much, in this hypercritical age, one may feel inclined to doubt some of the conclusions at which this author has arrived, every one must admire the labour and enthusiasm with which he endeavoured to work out a great problem.

of less stature and of more recent date bringing up the rear throughout a tract of many miles up the river side. Away towards the north might be seen the plain of the Delta, with its green illimitable fields, and frequent groves of palms. From no other spot, perhaps, can the mind become so fully impressed by the fact that to the Nile, and the Nile alone, does Egypt owe all she has of fertility and wealth. Beyond is the desert of sand, a sea-bed without its animate forms, lifeless and waste. Dean Stanley has well observed, that the Nile, as it glides between the Tombs of the Pharaohs, and the City of the Caliphs, is indeed a boundary between two worlds.[1]

Under the guidance of Dr. Schweinfurth we were able to see the most satisfactory evidence that at a very recent period, and while the shells of the Mediterranean and Red Seas were still unchanged, all the great plain we have been contemplating was submerged to a depth of over 200 feet. At about this level the limestone rock is bored by *Pholades*, and shells now living in the neighbouring seas are to be found imbedded in sand and gravel which then formed the shores ; while the coast-line was defined by the cliffs, which rose some 400 feet above the waters. The sand-beds with large *Clypeasters*, which occur south of the Pyramids, indicate the position of this sea-bed on the opposite side of the Nile Valley. How great has been the change since then ! But long ere the foundations of the Pyramids were laid, the sea had receded to a level perhaps not very different from that at which it stands to-day.[2]

On ascending towards the summit of the ridge we visited several enormous caverns sufficiently large to shelter an army, which occur on both sides of the valley, and at an elevation of about 500 feet above the sea. These caverns are hollowed in the limestone rock, and evidently not by human agency. They afford a suitable retreat for the rock pigeons, which we started from their nests. Dr. Schweinfurth considers these to be ancient sea-caves ; and if this be so the land has been still further submerged within a very recent period. On the summit of the plateaux we reached one of the entrenchments of the army of Arabi Pasha ; and at a short distance further, towards the east, the British

---

[1] "Sinai and Palestine," Edition 1873, Introduction, p. xxxiv.

[2] To this physical fact in the history of the Nile Valley I shall have occasion to allude further on ; and the detailed proof must appear in another place. It is only necessary here to give the general result. When we say that the sea has receded, this is owing to the land having been elevated.

station for making observations on the recent transit of Venus. The spot is marked by a block bearing the following inscription :—

CAPTAIN GREEN, R.E., 1883.

Next in interest to the Pyramids we may place the Museum of Egyptian Antiquities at Cairo, a collection of surpassing interest and variety, illustrative of ancient Egyptian art, collected mainly through the instrumentality of Mariette Bey. The museum stands by the banks of the Nile. It unfortunately happened that at the time of our visit the Director, to whom I had a letter of introduction, was absent, and the official catalogue had not then been published, but with the aid of either " Murray" or " Baedeker," and the inscriptions accompanying the objects themselves, the visitor need be at no loss.

In this place I may refer to the Nile oscillations. On the wall of Shepherd's Hotel is to be seen a map, or diagram, upon which is represented the oscillations of the water for each year as it comes round.[1] Those for the year 1882-3 were as follows :—

---

[1] There are generally three successive risings of the Nile waters, due to the influx of the floods from the Atbara, and the Blue and White Nile branches.

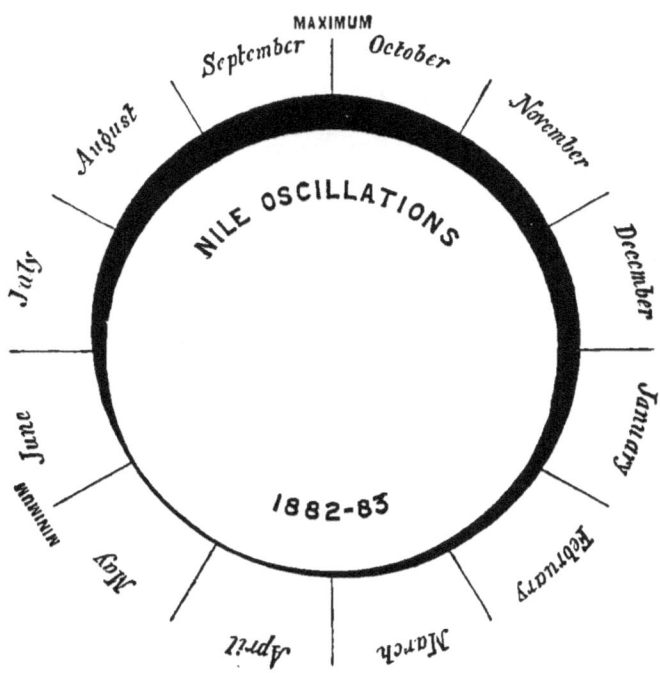

Elevation.		Months.
Minimum	.... {	May. June.
Slight increase	....	Latter part of June.
Rapid increase	.... {	July. Middle of August.
Slight increase	.... {	Middle of August. ,, September
Maximum		End of September.
Slight decrease		Middle of October.
Rapid fall	...{	End of October. November. December.

			Months.
Elevation.			
Gradual decrease	....	....	January. February. March. April.

On Monday, 5th November, our Arabs and camels mustered for inspection in an open space of ground not far from our hotel, and we went out to visit them and to have our first experience of bestriding a camel's back. There were about forty in all—some with saddles for riding, these being slight and young-looking; the others with nets and ropes for baggage. The men belonged to the Towâra tribe, of whom the head Sheikh, Ibù Shedid, resides permanently in Cairo.[1] I liked the faces of the men, which were open and good-humoured, and felt confident we should be perfectly safe under their charge ;—a confidence not misplaced by subsequent events. The Towâras occupy the whole of the Sinaitic promontory south of the Tîh plateau. They are divided into five branches, of which the Szowaleha is the largest; next the Aleygats, then the El-Mezeine, the Ulad Soleiman who live near the town of Tor ; and last, the Beni Wassel, a very small branch near the south-east coast.

The Towâras are a peaceable tribe, friendly to travellers, and had no part in the murder of Professor Palmer and Lieutenant Gill. Their Sheikh, on the contrary, was instrumental in bringing four of the culprits to justice, and accompanied Sir C. Warren into the desert to effect their capture.[2]

The negociations for our escort had been effected between Messrs. T. Cook and Son's agent at Cairo and the Abbot of the Monastery of St. Catherine. By him our men and camels were sent over to Cairo, from their home in the Wâdy Feirân, in order to receive their baggage loads, and to pass inspection ; and they had arrived outside the city the evening

---

[1] Not by choice, probably, but by constraint, as a hostage for the good behaviour of the tribe.

[2] It had originally been intended that we should have an escort of the Egyptian Camel Corps, which had been kindly granted by Cheriff Pasha at the request of Major Kitchener, of the Egyptian Cavalry, but the proposal was afterwards abandoned for very good reasons ; first, it could not accompany us further than Akabah, beyond which station the services of an escort were only expected to be of value ; and secondly, we felt there was no necessity, as we had full confidence in the good faith of our convoy.

before we saw them in the space near the hotel. In the course of the day
the whole procession with their loads passed in front of our hotel, and
afforded a sight probably not very novel to the residents, but to us not
only novel, but of considerable interest. The camels upon which we were
to ride were bestrode by their respective drivers ; then came others with
barrels of flour, barrels for water, the tents, five in number, rolled up into
the most compact dimensions ; boxes of provisions, our camel trunks, crates
with live turkeys and poultry, and other matters too numerous to mention
in detail. We were not again to see them until our arrival at the landing
stage near Ayun Mûsa, on the eastern side of the Gulf of Suez, to which
place we intended to proceed by rail and boat.

On the morning of 8th November we left Cairo by rail for Suez,
passing by Zagazig and Tel-el-Kebir, where Arabi Pasha had made, a few
months previously, his most determined, but ineffectual, stand against the
British arms. As far as Zagazig the country is richly cultivated, immense
fields of corn, cotton, and sugarcane succeeding each other mile after mile ;
while the station platforms were piled with great bales of cotton, com-
pressed and bound with iron-straps, for shipment to England and elsewhere.
Occasionally the Egyptian ibis, an elegant bird with white plumage, and
in form somewhat like a small heron, might be seen in flocks amongst the
cultivated fields, close to the teams of buffaloes while ploughing ; or at
other times perched on the backs of the buffaloes themselves, busily
engaged in clearing the ticks from these animals ;—a process which the
animals themselves evidently enjoyed.

After leaving Zagazig the country becomes more and more arid and
desert-like, till at length, on approaching Tel-el-Kebir, the sands set in
as far as the eye can reach on both sides. We noticed the ditch and
entrenchments of Arabi's army which were stormed by the British troops
under General Lord Wolseley, and a small camp of Egyptians still
occupied the ground. We also passed the burial-ground of the British
troops who fell on that memorable occasion, prettily planted with shrubs
and flowers, which were being carefully tended by gardeners. Tablets to
the memory of the officers and soldiers have been placed on the walls of
the English church at Cairo.

The route lay along the side of the "Sweetwater Canal," which carries
the waters of the Nile to Suez, Ismailia, and Port Saïd. This canal was
constructed by the Ship-Canal Company, and it occupies very much the
line of the ancient channel intended to connect the waters of the Nile

with those of the Red Sea. Beyond the tract influenced and irrigated by its waters, all was sandy desert covered by scrub, amongst which the only visible inhabitants were a shepherd and his flock. It was dark when we reached Suez, and on entering our hotel we learned that the steamship, the "Shannon," had arrived from England, and lay in the gulf awaiting the arrival of H.R.H. the Duke of Connaught, on his way to India.

Next morning, on ascending to the roof of our hotel, to take a glance at the surrounding country, we were struck by the bold aspect of Jebel Attâkah, which rises in the form of a lofty escarpment along the western shore of the Gulf of Suez a few miles from our position. In form and outline it seemed to bear some resemblance to the ridge of Jebel Mokattam behind Cairo, and to be in some measure, in a geological point of view, representative of it ; the strata were, in fact, easily visible from the roof of the hotel. We determined to devote the day to a visit to this fine range, and taking a sail-boat manned by four Arab sailors and a boy we dropped down the gulf. The wind was light, and sometimes failed us, so that the sailors had recourse to the oars, which they accompanied by a monotonous chant extemporised for the occasion, and, as we supposed, in our honour ; as we could distinguish the word "hawajah"[1] not unfrequently. At length, after three hours, we landed on a pier leading up to the quarries which were opened by M. De Lesseps for his buildings at Suez. From the pier we toiled up to the quarries under a burning sun (the temperature in the shade being 91° Fahr.), and were rewarded by finding the limestone rocks crowded with fossil shells, though generally only in the form of casts. Our return was enlivened by a steady breeze which sprung up from the north-west ; and as we were carried along we kept a sharp look-out for the flying fish, which from time to time leaped out of the water, and after skimming over the crest of the waves for some yards, disappeared. As we neared the harbour the sun went down behind Jebel Attâkah ; and soon after, the sky over the hills was all aglow, as if behind it were concealed a great city in conflagration ; the deep red of the west shading off through purple and roseate hues into the dark grey of the zenith. It is only in the East that such sunsets reward the beholder.

[1] Hawajah (or gentleman) is the Arabic word applied to Europeans.

CHAPTER III.

INTO THE DESERT.

THE day following, Saturday, 10th November, we were to bid farewell to Egypt and to civilisation—the day much desired—the beginning of our special work. It was a gay and beautiful sight as we slowly sailed down the gulf towards our landing place on the Asiatic coast. Away to the west, the broken ridge of Jebel Attâkah marked the shore of the African continent, and behind this, other headlands, separated by deep bays, carried the eye along the western shores of the Red Sea. The placid waters of the gulf sparkling in the sunlight stretched around, while towards the east the long line of the escarpment of the Tîh bounded the horizon several miles from the shore—its rich brown tints speckled with white softly shading into the rich chrome yellow of the desert sands below.

In the roads several large ships, gaily decorated in honour of the Prince, lay at anchor; we counted nine in all, most of them going south. The waters of the bay were beautifully clear, so that on approaching the shallows we could peer down to the bottom—generally formed of rippled sands—sometimes of coral rock—and observe the multitudes of dark purple echini, bristling with long spines, which decorated the floor. Amongst the echini, starfishes were less frequently to be seen, shells few or none.

On approaching our landing stage, as the shades of evening drew on, we noticed our Arabs and camels waiting our arrival, and in the distance the groves of palms and tamarisks which mark the position of "Moses' Wells." Along the shore on our left were the white tents of a quarantine station. Soon after we touched the shore, and selecting our camels, were on the march towards our camp beyond the palm-trees. On arriving we found our tents, five in number, pitched in a circle; that on the right the kitchen, aglow with the light of a lengthy stove, upon which sundry pots and pans were doing service; while Abu Miriam, the presiding deity, sat behind, wielding the implements of his art with a master hand, and with a result which we were soon after fully to appreciate. In half-an-hour we were seated around the table of the dining tent, in which was served up a most excellent dinner, commencing with soup and passing through various stages to the final custard pudding. This was not a bad beginning for our desert life ; and it occurred to us that "roughing it in the desert" was not such a terrible fate after all !

Our tents were spacious and prettily decorated inside with Eastern patterns. Each tent had its two little beds, a table with basin and water-jug, and two camp stools, while the floor was covered with carpets. Hooks fastened to the centre pole enabled us to hang clothes and other articles in a safe and convenient place. The baggage was piled in the centre of the camp. Near our tents were the camping places of the Arabs, who had broken up into groups round their little fires, the camels lying or standing around, and often giving vent to their feelings in deep groans. The men were preparing supper—some roasting or grinding coffee, others corn between two flat stones ; others, again, were chatting over their pipes. The scene to us was novel and interesting ; but only to be repeated day after day under varying conditions of time and place until both the novelty and interest had ceased.

Sunday, 11th November.—When we awoke this morning our camp presented a lively scene. The Arabs were busy at their coffee roasting, Abu Miriam at preparations for breakfast, which was being got ready in the dining tent. The sun was shining in a cloudless sky ; all was bright and cheerful. The cocks, hens, and turkeys had been turned loose, and kept up such a cackling and crowing that one might have imagined oneself in a country farm house at home. We rested this day in our tents—a plan we always adopted unless under special cases of urgency—and we had a short service at 10.30, at which all the members of our party were present. It is no small advantage in the use of the Church of England Service that it forms a link of union and of prayerful sympathy with so many Christians at home and abroad. This, I think, we felt as we read the Lessons for the day, and offered in faith and hope our prayers in words which, though familiar to our ears, are ever fresh and appropriate. The remainder of the day was spent in short rambles and preparations for an early start into the desert next morning.

Monday, 12th November.—At length we are in the Desert and "on the track of the Israelites," as nearly all travellers agree that the first camp of the host in the Wilderness was pitched at Ayun Mûsa.[1] It may here be well to state our usual marching arrangements, which were observed throughout as far as circumstances would permit. We generally rose a little after daybreak, breakfasted about 7.30; and while breakfasting the Arabs and servants were busy taking down the tents, loading the camels, and preparing for a start. A small luncheon tent was reserved to accompany the Dragoman, but as soon as the baggage camels were ready they started on their way. Soon after 8 o'clock we were in our saddles, and ere long left the baggage camels in the rear; but at noon the luncheon tent was pitched, and those of the party within reach gathered for lunch and rest. It often happened, however, that Major Kitchener or others of the party were too far apart to join in the noonday meal. During our halt the baggage camels would pass, so that on our arrival at the camping ground we generally found the tents set up, furnished, and all things in preparation for dinner, the usual hour for which was 7 o'clock. This meal was always looked forward to after a long day's march with zest, as the time when fatigues could be forgotten, hunger satisfied, and the events of the day discussed.

Should my reader have the curiosity to inquire how we satisfied our thirst, often in "a dry and thirsty land where no water is," I may be allowed in reply to state that the beverages we found most useful were, for dinner, claret and water, in the proportion of one of the former to two of the latter. Tea we found more refreshing even than coffee, which it gradually replaced; and for one member of our party, who was a total abstainer, it was an essential. Brandy we seldom touched, and only used medicinally. Cigarettes were a great consolation in a long march and after dinner; and the Arab guide always appreciated the offer of one of these little articles of luxury, which helped to relieve the dull monotony of a continuous tramp through weary miles of sandy or gravelly ground.

The route we were to take had been carefully considered by the Committee of the Palestine Exploration Fund, and Colonel Sir Charles Wilson had favoured me with the results of his knowledge and experience of the Sinaitic peninsula. By his advice we selected the road to Jebel Mûsa, by Serabet el Jemel, and the Wâdy Nasb, in preference to that by the Wâdy Feirân usually taken by travellers. By this route we should be able to examine the beds of limestone belonging to the "Desert Sandstone" formation, from which he and Mr. Bauerman had collected the only

[1] Wilson, "Ordnance Survey of Peninsula of Sinai," p. 150.

fossils which had hitherto been discovered in any of the strata older than the limestones of the Tih, and by which the geological age of the Desert Sandstone could be determined. It happened that some uncertainty still prevailed regarding the determination of these fossils, and the consequent age of the formation ; one authority having maintained that the strata were of Carboniferous age, another that they were of Triassic. Under these circumstances it was desirable that more specimens should be collected, and that if possible the age of this great formation—which, as Russeger supposed, extends from Nubia at intervals through the Sinaitic peninsula, and northwards into the valley of the Jordan—should be finally determined.[1] There were many points in the geology of the Sinaitic district requiring elucidation, and the geological map of the Ordnance Survey, published in 1869, required additions, especially in the district west of the Gulf of Akabah. We, therefore, determined to take a line of march from Jebel Mûsa to Akabah, which would skirt the borders of the Jebel el Tih, and take us through a district comparatively little known. From Akabah we were to take a course along the Wâdy el Arabah to the southern shores of the Salt Sea—making topographical and geological observations throughout— and thus to join up the triangulation of the Sinaitic peninsula with that of Western Palestine.[2] From the southern shores of the Salt Sea we were to work our way to Jerusalem by the western shore, Ain Jidi and Hebron ; and subsequently the geological reconnaissance of Western Palestine and the Jordan Valley was to be carried out. This programme embraced a region of great interest ; and would open a route for future travellers, which in its entirety had not hitherto been traversed ; although, in one way or another, the district embraced by it had been visited by various travellers. To what extent we were able to accomplish our purpose, and with what results, will appear in the sequel. As regards the scientific details, I shall only introduce them here when they appear likely to be of general interest, and when they are necessary in order to make the narrative intelligible.[3]

[1] The result of our examination was to show that there are two sandstone formations of very different ages, the upper of which alone represents "the Nubian Sandstone" of Roziere. This will be explained further on.

[2] The triangulation was entrusted to Major Kitchener, R.E., assisted by Mr. Armstrong, formerly of the Palestine Survey.

[3] It is intended to deal with the scientific details and conclusions in a work especially devoted to these subjects, to be published by the Committee of the Palestine Exploration Fund during (it is hoped) the year 1885.

Our course for the two first days, as far as the W. Gharandel, lay along an undulating plain, bounded on the west by the Gulf of Suez, and on the east by the escarpment of the Tih plateau.   It has been aptly named in the Bible the Wilderness of Shur, which, according to Mr. Poole,[1] means " The Wilderness of the Wall ;" for such is the appearance of the long escarpment which bounds the table-land of the Tih to the eastward, from the W. Gharandel to the Mediterranean.   This tract is broken by low-terraced hills, but is generally covered by sand and gravel containing sea-shells.   It is unquestionably to some extent the former bed of the Red Sea, when the land was submerged to a depth of at least two hundred feet lower than at present.   In some places four terraces at successive levels may be distinguished, indicating, probably, as many sea margins formed during the rising of the land.   One of these, about three miles south of Ayun Mûsa, is crossed by the road, and is 40 feet higher than that on which we had been riding.   Fragments of selenite strew the ground, often in great abundance.

On our way we espied a group of Egyptian vultures (*Neophron percnopterus*) perched on a bank about half a mile to our left.   These were the first living things we had seen during several hours, and we felt curious to ascertain the cause of their presence.   This was soon explained on our coming upon the carcase of a dead camel partly devoured.   Dead camels are seldom allowed to lie for any length of time unvisited by these, or other, birds of prey, who congregate from afar in districts where to the eye they are unseen.   I shall have a still more remarkable case to relate in a future page, but this was the first illustration we had of the passage, " Wheresoever the carcase is, there will the eagles (or vultures) be gathered together."[2]

On looking in a south-easterly direction from rising ground near our camp at Ayun Mûsa, we observed in the far distance a dark isolated hill, somewhat resembling the crater of an extinct volcano, and known as Tâset Bisher.

It lies in the line of the broken escarpment of the Tih plateau, but it was clear that at this place the escarpment is crossed by a valley descending to the plain from the interior, the isolated hill above referred to occupying a position at the southern entrance to the valley.   A little after noon of this day (12th November) we came more directly in front of this valley,

[1] Bible Dict. quoted in "Ord. Survey Sinai," p. 150.
[2] Matt. xxiv, 28 ; Luke xvii, 37.

which will henceforth possess a melancholy interest as the spot where the late Professor Palmer, Lieutenant Gill, and their attendants were murdered by the Arabs. I took a sketch of this spot from our midday camp. I have already referred to this lamentable event, which has been described by Professor Palmer's biographer in befitting language. We discussed the matter with our Arabs, who expressed their abhorrence of the foul deed, and when questioned as to the way it happened, the account they gave was to the following effect.[1]

The Arabs of the Tîh were on their way down the valley to Ayun Mûsa and Suez, in pursuance of an order from the agents of Arabi Pasha to kill the Christians, when they fell in with Palmer and his party on their way up the valley to negotiate with the tribes inhabiting the region of the Tîh. The result is known ; but our informant seemed to believe that it was in consequence of orders from Egypt.[2]

We camped for the night by the Wâdy Sudur. In reality there is no valley here, only a series of shallow watercourses spread over a space of a mile in breadth, and very little below the level of the plain. Generally these watercourses are perfectly dry, as on the present occasion ; but we were told by the Arabs that a fortnight previously a party of Bedawins were encamped at a spot amongst them, when suddenly a great torrent descended from the mountains, flooding the plains, and carrying their tents and goods down into the sea. The evidences of a recent flood were clearly visible to us as we crossed successive branches of this imaginary valley. Here, as elsewhere in the Desert, the floods which arise from thunderstorms, on reaching the plains often spread out fan-shaped over wide areas, but without wearing down definite channels.

Our march on the next day was one of the longest, extending over a distance of about 30 miles. During the early part of the day the terraces were numerous and distinct, and the beds of sand contained numerous oyster shells ; it was clear we were traversing the old bed of the Gulf of Suez. We passed several burrows of the jerboa, an animal about the size of a small rabbit, very shy and difficult of approach. These burrows continued at intervals throughout our course, as far as the borders of The Ghôr. Here also we met with beds of the pretty little desert melon

---

[1] Of course I do not vouch for the accuracy of this account, but I believe it to be a correct view of the case as understood by the Arabs of the Towâra tribe.

[2] As the spot had previously been visited by Col. Sir C. Warren, we did not consider it necessary to deviate from our route in order to do so.

(*Citrullus colocynthus*), with its long sprays and trefoil leaves spreading over the ground, of the freshest of green tints ; the fruit, about the size of a small orange, was in various stages, some green, others banded with yellowish tints.   This fruit is acrid to the taste, and only used medicinally by the Arabs.

During this long day's march, as at other times, I had ample opportunities of studying the manners and powers of the camel, and I may offer a few observations thereon in this place.   The animal I bestrode was the tallest of the party, and his name was " Ashgar."   He was a steady going old gentleman, and served me faithfully till we parted at Akabah.   But I feel sure he was incapable of attachment, except to his own driver, and that we parted from each other without regret on either side.

The motion of the camel is at first unpleasant to the rider, but he soon gets used to it.   He is thrown forward at each step, and his best plan is to let himself go with the movement ; any attempt to retain a steady upright position being useless.   The camel in walking has a slow majestic pace ; he holds his head erect, and though apparently looking upwards, he sees the ground beneath his feet perfectly well, and picks his steps in rocky or broken places with wonderful sagacity.   When walking the side feet overlap each other, so that the print of the hind foot is in advance of that of the forefoot to an extent of from 14 to 20 inches.   This gives him an immense stride, so that his rate of progress is much greater than the rider supposes when perched on his back.   A good dromedary will walk at the rate of four English miles per hour, or even more, but the average rate is less than this.   When receiving his load or his rider, he lies on his belly, the legs gathered under him, and during the process or even in anticipation of it, gives forth the most horrible moans or growls.   Anything more hideous than the voice of a camel when he is discontented can scarcely be conceived ; the tone varies from the grunting of a pig *in extremis*, to the last braying note of a donkey, or the deep growl of a lion ; and during the daily processes of getting ready for the march, the chorus produced by some thirty camels receiving their loads is something too horrible for description.   The great ordeal for the rider is to keep his place while the animal is getting on his legs.   Being seated on the saddle, the animal commences to rise by raising himself half way on his hind legs, when the rider is suddenly jerked forward, and has to keep a tight hold of the front pommel of the saddle in order to retain his seat ; next the camel gets up on his fore feet, and the rider is thrown back ; and lastly, the process is concluded by the camel bringing the remainder of his hind legs into the erect position. The reverse process need scarcely be described. As the camel walks along he occasionally takes a bite of some favourite plant ; but this often becomes very troublesome if the traveller is in a hurry to get on ; and besides this the plants often disagreeably taint his breath.

Each camel is provided with a driver, to whom he generally belongs ; and between them there is established a bond of sympathy, as they have probably been brought up together from childhood, at least on one side. The camel will sometimes obey no other leader, and if compelled by ill-treatment to do so, has been known to take his revenge on the occurrence of a favourable opportunity. My camel driver was a nice little fellow, of whom I got quite fond. His name was "Sala," and he was the son of a minor Sheikh of the Towâra tribe. His cousin, Khalil, was driver to Mr. Hart's camel, and as they both dressed exactly alike, were about the same height, and had somewhat similar countenances, I for some time took them for brothers. Khalil was rather the more active and stronger of the two. They were great friends, and when they were marching side by side, leading their respective camels, they carried on lively conversations, which I often wished I could understand. Sala wore a red and white turban, a white cotton shirt descending below the knee, girt round the waist by a broad leather belt, and a loose mantle gracefully thrown over the shoulder. He carried his long gun slung behind his back, a little antique sword by his side, his pipe in the left hand, and the camel rope in his right. Inside his mantle was a leather strap passing over the shoulder with cases for powder and ball ; and within the folds of one of his garments was carried his money, his flint, steel, and touch paper, and other small articles. The colour of his skin was rich bronze. He had a pleasant face, and large expressive eyes which would light up with pleasure on any little act of kindness being offered to him, or on having performed some act for which I expressed my thanks. He was always at his post in the morning ; the camel saddled, water-bottle and saddle-bags properly adjusted and ready for the early start. Good little Sala :—how many weary miles have you trudged untiringly with me over the sandy plain, or the almost interminable valley, without a murmur or appearance of impatience !

The sun had long set and the moon was shining out clear and brilliant, ere we reached our camp in the Wâdy Gharandel. This valley is one of the most fertile in the desert. It descends from the east along the base of a fine ridge of limestone fully 2,000 feet in elevation. To the west, bordering the sea, was the corresponding limestone ridge of Jebel Hammân, at the base of which break forth the warm springs of the Hammân Faroûn. The valley is dotted with tamarisks and a few palms, as well as with numerous herbs and shrubs; but except after rain is dry and sandy. Water, however, is close under the surface; and a short distance from our camp were the wells, whither our camels wended their way to slake their thirst after an abstinence of 24 hours, during which they had marched a distance of about 47 miles.

The Wâdy Gharandel is considered, with much probability, to be the Elim of the Exodus, "where were twelve wells of water and three-score and ten palm-trees," and where the Israelites encamped by the waters;[1]—a view in which I concur; nor can it be urged as an objection that there are fewer wells at present than those named in the passage above quoted. Water can easily be obtained in many of the dry valleys simply by digging a shallow well, and I have no doubt any number of wells with water might be dug along the line of the Wâdy Gharandel. After the long dry march of the Israelites southwards along the tract we had come during the last two days, it must have proved a most refreshing rest to the weary multitude to enter this leafy valley and find abundance of water.

While on this subject I may refer to one point connected with the Exodus which has not generally been considered. It is taken for granted that the physical geography of the Isthmus of Suez was at the time of the Exodus just as it is now; and if so, we might well ask, why was there any necessity for the performance of the great miracle by which the Israelites were delivered out of the hands of the Egyptians? Why, in short, could they not have crossed over on dry land, without the intervention of Almighty Power to cleave for them a channel through the waters, there being a long stretch of dry land to the south of the Great Bitter Lake?

It has been supposed that the passage may have been made through the waters of the Great Bitter Lake; but this is scarcely a fair interpretation of the text which states that the waters of the Red Sea were divided.[2] In the face of the remarkable topographical accuracy of the Book of Exodus, I am not prepared to admit that the term "Red Sea" (Yam Suf)

[1] Exod. xv, 27.

[2] Compare Exodus xv, 4 and 22. On this subject, see author's paper in *Quarterly Statement* for April, 1884, p. 137; also chap. xx, p. 185.

FIG. 2.—LAKE DEPOSITS OF THE WÁDY USEIT.

Terraces of white marl and silt, with gypsum (Lake beds) in the foreground. The limestone hill of Serabit el Jemel in the distance.
Looking, east and south.

can be applied to any of the lakes which lie along the line of the Isthmus. May we not rather suppose that at this period—upwards of three thousand years ago—the Red Sea waters *did* actually occupy the line of the present canal, at least, as far as the Great Bitter Lake, to a depth which would render them impassable to a host of emigrants?

I have already mentioned that the waters of the Red, and (I may add) the Mediterranean, Seas extended over the lands of Egypt and along the shore of the Gulf of Suez to a height of over 200 feet above the present level of these waters, at a time when the existing species of shells were already living. The process of elevation of this sea-bed over so large a tract was probably exceedingly gradual, and at the date of the Exodus the elevation may not have taken place up to the present extent. A strip of Red Sea water—not very deep—may at this time have stretched from the Gulf of Suez as far north as the Great Bitter Lake, forming to the host of Israel an effective barrier to their progress into the desert. The passage may have taken place to the north of the present head of the Gulf; if this be so, it fits in with the Bible history that the Wády Amárah, lying between W. Sudur and Gharandel, would be the Marah of the Bible, the water of which, rising out of the gypseous deposits of that district, would naturally be bitter.[1] This spot was three days' journey south from the supposed place of the passage of the Red Sea; and the next stage for a lengthened halt would be the Wády Gharandel, called in the sacred text "Elim," or the place of trees.

Evidences of the existence of ancient lakes throughout the district we were now traversing are not infrequent. The form of the ground sometimes of itself suggests this view, and it is confirmed by the nature of the deposits themselves. Between Wádies Amárah and Wardan, on the north, and Wády Hamr on the south, the hills of limestone assume the form of basins, sometimes connected by narrow necks with each other, or with outlets towards the sea. The deposits enclosed, and occupying the beds of these basins, consist of stratified gravel, sand, and marl, with gypsum and selenite. They are often of considerable thickness, and assume the form of minor terraces inside those of the more ancient limestone. Thus in the Wády Useit such deposits are to be seen forming extensive banks, and of a thickness approaching 200 feet (Fig. 2). A second basin, probably connected with the former, appears to have extended from the

---

[1] This spot, or another, viz., the spring known as Abu Suweirah, is thus regarded by Wilson, "Ord. Survey Sinai," p. 151.

flanks of Jebel Wûtah to those of J. Hammân Faroûn. I do not here propose to enter further into the details connected with these ancient lake-basins than to say that the lakes probably occupied these hollows amongst the limestone hills at a time when the land was depressed several hundred feet below its present position, and when the waters of the sea rose to a level somewhat corresponding to the outlets of the inland waters. Owing to this the waters were banked up; and we can conceive that, upon the gradual rise of the land, the outlets would deepen their channels, and ultimately the lakes would be drained. The large quantity of gypsum and selenite in these lacustrine deposits indicates, probably, that the waters of the lakes were unfit for the support of molluscous forms of life, of which I could find no traces in the deposits themselves.

Similar terraces have been noticed by Sir Charles Wilson in other parts of the peninsula ; and Dr. G. E. Post calls my attention to his determination of lacustrine deposits in the W. Feirân and extending into the W. Solâf for a distance of a whole day's journey.[1]

Having crossed the plain at the head of W. Useit we encamped for our noonday meal at W. Saal, near the base of Serabit el Jemel.[2] A brook ran through the valley, and some small palms and tamarisks greeted our eyes. After the hot ride and march we were thankful to lie down in the shade of our tent and partake of a good luncheon—

" O Melibœe ! Deus nobis hæc otia fecit."

The palm-tree in the desert is always a sign of moisture, and when met with is an object of interest and beauty. I asked our dragoman, Ibrahim, whether Arabs ever cut down palm-trees. He replied " No, but they are sometimes blown down by storms, or swept away by floods."[3]

"Do they ever plant them ?" I asked.

"Yes ; they put seed into moist places, let the plants grow two or three years, then take them up and transplant them. This is necessary, for they will not bear fruit unless they are transplanted. After the fifth year they bear fruit."

[1] "Sunday School World," Philadelphia, Oct., 1882.
[2] "The Fort of the Camel," probably so named from its form, which is some-what like a camel with its hump on the back.
[3] As in the case of the flood of 1867, witnessed by the Rev. Mr. Holland, when several Arabs and 100 palm-trees of the W. Feirân were swept away.

Dates are gathered at the end of October in these parts and in Lower Egypt ; at Alexandria they are later.[1]

Later in the day we passed through a tract in which there were excellent illustrations of the formation of terraces by torrent-action. The strata consisted of soft marly limestones and shales, and when horizontal were scooped out into terraces, with intermediate ravines ; when highly inclined, into a succession of escarpments and slopes. It was a waste wilderness of crumbling strata ; but full of interest to the geologist. The terraces of the Wâdy Hamr, on our next day's march, were also remarkable, and reminded me of the pictures I had seen of those in the Colorado region of America.

[1] We saw them on the trees about Alexandria the beginning of November.

CHAPTER IV.

DEBBET ER RAMLEH.

HITHERTO our course had lain through a region in which limestone was the prevalent formation, either rising into hills and escarpments, or forming the solid floor, and underlying more recent deposits. But now we were about to enter one composed of more ancient rocks, rising from beneath the limestone beds, and consequently producing a variety of scenery differing from that we had hitherto witnessed. The first of these older formations consisted of red and variegated sandstone, already referred to as the "Desert Sandstone," which with the "Nubian Sandstone" forms a wide belt of comparatively level country along the base of the limestone escarpment of the Tîh for a distance of about one hundred miles. Commencing on the west with the Debbet er Ramleh, and stretching eastwards along the line of the Wâdy Zelegah, W. Biyar, and W. el Ain, to the margin of the Arabah Valley, it terminates along the line of a great dislocation (or "fault") against the hills of porphyry, which there bound the Gulf of Akabah on the western side.

This extensive tract of sandstone, so rich in its colouring, so peculiar in its rock sculpturing, separates the limestone plateau of the Tîh on the north from the mountainous region of the Sinaitic peninsula on the south, which culminates in the rocky heights of Jebel Serbal, Jebel Mûsa, and Jebel Katarina, formed of gneiss, granite, and porphyry. We were now about to enter on the elevated sandstone district of Debbet er Ramleh ;[1] and, near the head of Wâdy Hamr, the spot where the limestone gives place to the sandstone can be clearly determined, as the latter formation may be observed rising from beneath the former on the northern slopes of this deep glen.

We camped for our noonday meal on the Ramleh Plain, over which were scattered beautiful little round pebbles of quartz, jasper, and agate, of divers colours. In full view was the limestone escarpment of the Tîh,

[1] Or "Plain of Sand."

which several miles to the north of our position stretched with a bold, nearly unbroken, front, from Jebel Wutáh on the west to Jebel Emreikeh on the east. Below us, towards the east, lay the deep depression of the Wâdy Suwig, and its branch the Wâdy Nasb. Beyond rose the dark terraces and scarped cliffs of the desert sandstone, sloping at a gentle angle northwards towards the base of the Tih escarpment, and through a gap we could distinguish in the blue distance the rugged outlines of Serbal. The heat was intense, as there was no shade, and the flies, as usual on such occasions, proved excessively noxious. Our tent was at an elevation of about 1,700 feet above the sea, but the thermometer registered 90° Fahr. in the shade, and this in the latter part of November! That evening we pitched in the Wâdy Nasb, one of the few spots where wells permanently supplied with water are to be found, and therefore a favourite camping ground.[1] Our thirsty camels, after getting rid of their loads, proceeded up the valley about three miles to the well. Major Kitchener, my son, and I also followed, weary as we were, in hopes of finding the fossiliferous limestone. The limestone we found, but not the fossils on this occasion ; and we were glad to sit down on the well side and get a draught of the cool waters. The presence of water here is doubtless due to the fissure, or fault,[2] which traverses this valley, and owing to which the sandstone is elevated to a higher level on the east side than on the west.

The next morning, accompanied by my son, I climbed the cliffs above our camp, and we were rewarded by the discovery of a good number of fossils—both of shells, corals, and echinoderms, in a rather imperfect condition, but which it is believed will serve to determine beyond question the geological age of this great formation—the "Desert Sandstone."

Later in the day we started along the Wâdy Suwig, which stretches in an easterly direction, skirting the granitic and sandstone districts, and leading us in the direction of Mount Sinai. The scenery was interesting,

---

[1] Professor Palmer gives an amusing account of his camping experiences in the W. Nasb, and of the entomological pests of the place, loc. cit. p. 195.

[2] This fault was first described by Mr. H. Bauerman, "Ord. Survey Sinai," with figure.

[3] Some of the fossils from the Wâdy Nasb Limestone collected by Wilson and Bauerman are decidedly of Carboniferous age, and are figured in the Report of the Ordnance Survey of Sinai. Those we collected bear out this view. I am glad to be able to state that Professor Sollas, of Trinity College, Dublin, has kindly undertaken to prepare an account of the fossils collected by our party. The results will appear in the Scientific Report of our Expedition.

from the numerous examples of castellated cliffs and isolated tors of the sandstone strata, perched on bases of granite or porphyry. Amongst the most remarkable of these are the two great pyramids, of which the larger is called Jebel el Malah. Of this, perhaps, the finest view is that obtained when looking south. They are formed of horizontal courses of red sand-tone resting on granite ; and that to the left has a quadrangular form, the faces of the pyramid being well defined.

Fig. 3.—Pyramids of Red Sandstone resting on granite and porphyry.
View from the Wâdy Suwig.

After winding for several miles along the sandy bottom of the Wâdy Suwig—often diversified by lovely green patches of the desert melon (*Citrullus colocynthus*)[1] and other plants—we at length came to the foot of Serabit el Khadim, a massive pyramidal mountain of red and white sandstone in horizontal courses, and perforated by numerous caves and fissures, the retreat of wild animals, and often of equally wild men. A large number of eagles were soaring about its cliffs ; but upon our approach

---

[1] Otherwise called "The Vine of Sodom" (Deut. xxxii, 32).

they rose higher and higher into the air, and performed their gyrations beyond the reach of our guns or rifles. Looking northwards, the cliffs of sandstone in the foreground are seen to be cut into forms resembling walls, buttresses, and sometimes isolated tors. These were in places lit up by the rosy tints of the western sun, or thrown deeply into the shade; while far in the distance to the north the white escarpment of the Tih bounded the horizon in the direction of El Nakel.[1] This mountain is now celebrated as the site of an Egyptian temple.[2] Turquoise mines have been worked from ancient times, and within the last few years Major Macdonald employed the Arabs in blasting the rock for these gems, having built himself a house and living in the midst of his workpeople.

Saturday 17th November.—We camped to-day in the Wâdy Kamileh at the base of some cliffs of sandstone bearing " inscriptions," but of so indefinite a character that to me they seemed well calculated to afford materials for equally indefinite speculation. In this place Palmer and Drake spent a Christmas Day; caught a *Cerastes*, and entertained the Arabs somewhat in the manner of the Egyptian magicians.[3] The locality furnishes a favourite camping ground for the Towâra as there is a perennial spring, and the overhanging cliffs afford shelter from the sun by day, and from the dew by night. Further on, the sides of the valley opened out and the sandstone cliffs on either side afforded interesting forms of terraces with scarped sides, projecting headlands, tors, and castellated masses.

We had been passing for several days through a district containing both large and small game; but except for the tracks in the sand, and a glimpse of some sand partridges, we might have been ignorant of the fact. Bears, hyænas, gazelles, ibexes, besides hares, jerboas, and other small rodents, are said, with much probability, to abound. It is wonderful how these wild animals manage to conceal themselves from the eye of man. Long before he sees *them* they see *him;* or scent him from afar;—and off they go. The bear and hyæna lie close within dens or under thickets; the ibex disappears over a precipice; the gazelle vanishes across the plain; the hare or partridge crouches close to the ground, which they exactly resemble in colour;

[1] Along this road Ibraham, our dragoman, conducted the late Lord Talbot-de-Malahide and his daughter.

[2] These remains were originally discovered by Niebuhr; for a recent account see Palmer's " Desert of the Exodus," p. 191, &c.

[3] " Desert of the Exodus," p. 250.

and the little jerboa drops like a shot into its burrow hole. I was reminded, when travelling through this country, of a tour I had made some years previously through the northern highlands of Scotland in a district where there were thousands of red and roe deer, but only on two occasions had we an opportunity of seeing a pair of antlers. This, however, was in early summer time, when these animals betake themselves into the high solitudes of the mountains.

CHAPTER V.

GRANITIC REGION.

WE were now about to bid farewell for a time to the region of sandstone, and to enter one composed of much more ancient formations, consisting of grey or red granite, porphyry, and igneous rocks; giving rise to scenery of a bolder and more majestic character, and for the most part destitute of that grotesqueness which frequently characterises the region of sandstone. Still, remnants of this latter formation were seen from time to time to linger on the summits of the granitic cliffs, especially along the northern sides of the Wâdies Berk, Lebweh, and Berrâh. One of these (Fig. 4), of which I have taken a sketch—and almost the last of these outlying remnants—will give a general idea of the form of these interesting ruins of a once more extended formation. It will be gathered from a consideration of the form and position of this outlying mass of sandstone that the older rocks, upon which the sandstone rests, originally constituted a platform over which the strata were deposited in continuous sheets, and over a horizontal area vastly larger than that which they now occupy.

We camped for our midday meal near the head of the Wâdy Berk, at an elevation of about 2,700 feet above the sea, amidst a waste and wilderness of crumbling rocks, consisting chiefly of red porphyry, which some distance back had burst through and ultimately replaced grey granite of older date.[1] Notwithstanding the elevation and the time of year, the temperature in the shade at 1.30 P.M. was 85° Fahr. The road (if such it could be called) consisted of a camel track amidst boulders and masses of shingle, often channelled by torrents. The scenery was wild and desolate in the extreme, but relieved here and there by little knots of

---

[1] The grey granite of the Sinaitic peninsula is marked and coloured "Metamorphic" on the geological map of the Ordnance Survey, 1869. But I was unable anywhere to see evidences of foliation where I happened to have an opportunity of examining it. A tabular structure is apparent in some places, but this is to be found in eruptive granites, such as that of the Mourne mountains in Ireland.

vegetation, amongst which the pretty ubiquitous plant (*Zygophyllum*)—beloved of the camel—with rose-pink or yellowish blossom, was conspicuous. This is "the erymth" of the Arabs, and is perhaps the most continuous of all the plants of the desert, as we met it at intervals all through from Ayun Mûsa to the vicinity of Jerusalem.

On descending into the W. Lebweh we were struck by the appearance,

Fig. 4.—Sandstone Tor, resting on a basis of granite and porphyry. Seen from the Wâdy Berûh.

near the centre, of great tabular masses of very red granite (pegmatite) and porphyry, traversed by numerous basaltic dykes, ranging generally in north and south directions. These rocks weather dull brown; so that until I examined them closely and broke off fresh faces with my hammer, I mistook them for sandstone. In composition they consist of red felspar and quartz; and masses of this type predominate, as we found afterwards all through the mountainous part of the Sinaitic peninsula. These rocks are everywhere traversed by dykes of dark basalt, so conspicuous as to attract the notice of our dragoman, and even of the Arabs. One of these dykes can be traced by the eye for at least a distance of two miles; and towards the east it enters a basin in the mountains called "Bahera el Harriah."

On Saturday evening we camped in the Wâdy Lebweh, at the foot of a conical tor of granite, and at an elevation of about 3,800 feet. The air was cool and bracing. Before dinner I climbed to the top of the tor, and as the sun approached the horizon enjoyed an extensive prospect all around. To the north in the distance was the table-land of the Tih, breaking off along a steep, indented line of light grey cliffs. Looking westward and southward across the plain at my feet, and through the gaps in the rugged sides beyond, I could descry in the distance the serried heights of Jebel Serbal, Jebel Mûsa, and the adjoining peaks, now coming for the first time into view, and giving promise of majestic scenery when we should approach nearer to them on the following day. Around, the granitic rocks, fissured and traversed by deep depressions, seemed crumbling into ruins ; and, as if in contrast to this display of nature in her wilder forms, just below was our little camp with its five pretty white tents, its busy inmates all astir preparing for the night, and close beside, the Arabs gathered around their little fires were preparing their evening meal ; our camels meanwhile were wandering in all directions over the plain in search of the tender herbs, and hopelessly (I fear) in search of water.

Next Sunday, the 18th November, might have been spent at rest, but there was no water, and we were obliged to move on. The morning was bright and sunny, yet bracing ; the dew was glittering on the herbage, and we were surrounded by wild and picturesque scenery. Our march lay down a valley, of which the granite walls contracted more and more till they terminated at the lower end in two huge massive buttresses guarding the entrance to the pass, one of which is called Jebel el Gebal, and rises about 1,500 feet above its base. It can therefore be imagined with what feelings of gratification we surveyed this scene from the backs of our camels. Nor did this feeling end here, for on issuing forth through the giant gates of the pass, Mounts Katarina and Serbal were sighted in the distance. We had got a glimpse of the peak of Serbal before, "but now" (in the graphic language of Palmer) "the whole mountain rose up in all its azure grandeur before us."

I have referred above to the beauty of the desert herbage. Few of those who have not personally traversed this region have formed any other idea of a valley in the Sinaitic peninsula except as a sandy or stony waste with a few plants and palm trees here and there where moisture is present. This, however, is far from being the proper view. The valleys are generally covered by dwarf plants throughout, ever varying by the disappearance of one kind and the appearance of another. Some are very persistent, others only local; while the thorny acacia (or shittim tree of Exodus), the tamarisk, the broom (or retem), and less frequently the date-palm, in some small degree compensate for the forest vegetation of more temperate climes.

At no time during our wanderings through the Sinaitic peninsula was I so much struck by the beauty of this desert flora as when we commenced our march down the Wâdy Berrâh on this Sabbath morning. The whole surface of the nearly level plain was gay with its peculiar dwarf vegetation, on which the dewdrops were sparkling like diamonds in the clear sunshine. The plants seemed to arrange themselves in little natural gardens, or individual bunches with gravelly spaces between ; each plant separately set in its place shows itself to the best advantage, and the eye wanders over a tract bedecked with leaves and flowers of various hues, from tints of green through those of yellow and pink to red. Amongst these the *Santolina fragrantissima*, of a delicate bluish green, and the *Zygophyllum simplex*, with its silky bracts of yellow, pink, and reddish hues, form the most abundant kinds. The latter plant, somewhat resembling in general appearance and size the heather of the British hills, is much more beautiful from the variety of colouring of the blossom. As the eye rests with pleasure on the desert garden, and beholds with wonder the decorative powers and processes of nature, one forgets for the time the absence of the green grass, of the daisy, the cowslip, the primrose, and other field flowers of home—and so the beholder goes on his way rejoicing.[1]

On descending from the narrow gorge of the Wâdy Berrâh, the range of J. Katarina rises grandly in front. This mountain out-tops the neighbouring heights—a giant amongst giants[2]; and shortly after, on looking to the right, the serrated ridge, sharp peaks, and deep clefts of Serbal

---

[1] If I recollect right, that curious little plant " the rose of Jericho " (*Anastatica hierochuudica*) was found here and there from the Sinaitic peninsula into the Jordan Valley. A list of the plants of the Sinaitic peninsula, drawn up by Sir J. D. Hooker from the collections brought home by the officers of the Ordnance Survey, will be found in the Report of the Ordnance Survey of Sinai, p. 247.

[2] The heights of the chief mountains, as determined by the officers of the Ordnance Survey, are as follows :—

Jebel Zebir	..	..	..	8,551 Eng. feet.
„ Katarina ..	..	..	8,536 „	„
„ Umm Shomer	..	..	8,449 „	„
„ Mûsa*	..	..	7,373 „	„
„ Serbal	..	..	6,734 „	„
Ras Sufsafeh	..	..	6,937 „	„

* The elevation as determined by Mr. Laurence with the aneroid, calculated from Suez, was 7,585 feet, and calculated from Akabah was 7,595 feet, both considerably over those of the Ordnance Survey, but less reliable.

appeared, dark and majestic, against the sky.[1] It was a scene not to be forgotten. We had full in view not only some of the finest mountains in this part of the world, but those which had witnessed the power and presence of Jehovah in a special and terrible manner amongst His chosen people. One could not gaze on such a scene without emotion almost too deep for utterance.

The Wâdy es Sheikh, which we were now traversing, is interesting from several circumstances. We find ourselves surrounded by low granite hills, with serried outlines and irregular forms. And we observe that they are penetrated by dykes of dark basaltic (or dioritic) rock, which from their greater hardness form the crests of the ridges, and project from the sides like broken walls. The general direction of these dykes is W.S.W. and E.N.E., but there are some which run transverse to these. These basaltic dykes are seen to cut through others of red porphyry, and which are, therefore, of older date.

Another feature of interest is the extensive grove of tamarisks which is found near the centre of the valley. We had not hitherto seen so large a grove, nor trees of this kind of such size, or so graceful in form. The drooping twigs were covered with flowers at the time of our visit; and from the numerous heaps of ashes lying about it was clear that the wood is used by the Arabs for charcoal. Young plants were, however, springing up in place of the old, and our camels enjoyed the opportunity of browsing on the green leafy sprays and twigs.

Towards the upper part of the Wâdy es Sheikh we met with terraces of marl, fine gravel and laminated sand, rising from 60 to 80 feet above the present bed of the valley. These terraces were originally much more extensive and continuous, but have been to a large extent carried away by the torrents which descend from the mountains. At the head of the W. Watiyeh these soft strata occupy the floor of a plain about half a mile across. There can be little doubt, I think, that these deposits, surrounded as they are in nearly every direction by higher ground, were formed over the bed of an ancient lake, or chain of lakes similar to those I have already described in the Wâdy Hamr and Wâdy Gharandel, further to the north-west. They have since been drained, owing to changes in the level of the country and other causes ; and are possibly referable to a period when rain was much more abundant than at the present day.

[1] An excellent view of this grand mountain, as well as of J. Katarina, is given in "Picturesque Palestine," edited by Col. Sir C. W. Wilson, Parts 18 and 19.

E

We now reached the foot of a lofty ridge of red granite and porphyry, rising to a height of 1,153 feet above the plain, crossing our path in a direction a little north of east, and forming a sort of outer wall to the mountainous district of Sinai to the south. Major Kitchener and others of our party climbed to the summit of this ridge, and planting the theodolite on the highest pinnacle, took angles to all the conspicuous points within sight. The ridge is traversed by a gorge—one of three passable ones—called El Watiyeh. It was one of the grandest I had ever seen ; the walls of red porphyry rising from 800 to 1,000 feet above the remarkably level floor of the pass itself. The effect is more striking from the intense redness of the porphyry, rendered deeper still, sometimes almost to blackness, apparently by the fierce rays of the sun, from which one is glad to get protection by keeping close to the shady side. The gorge bends to the right in a northerly direction ; and on emerging we found ourselves in an open space, and in front of a succession of granitic heights and intervening valleys by which the ascent to Jebel Mûsa is made.[1]

This remarkable ridge is found on examination to be a huge " dyke " or mass of porphyry and red granite protruded through the floor of grey granite, which seems to have been the most ancient and fundamental rock of this region. The junction and relations of these two important masses of plutonic origin may be clearly seen at the northern entrance to the gorge ; and half way through it will be seen that a basaltic dyke coincides with the general direction of the gorge itself.

On Monday evening, 19th November, we encamped in a plain about seven miles from the Convent of St. Catherine, and near a spring of water surrounded by palms and other plants. The elevation of our camp was found by Mr. Laurence—who made the determination from observations on the boiling point of water—to be about 4,880 feet. The air of the following morning was cold and bracing. Here we remained while visiting Jebel Mûsa and the neighbouring places.

[1] This was the road taken by Captains Wilson and Palmer, and the Rev. F. W. Holland, in 1869. Mr. Holland considers this locality to have been the scene of the battle with the Amalekites (" Desert of the Exodus," p. 52), but this view was not accepted by the other explorers, for reasons which appear sufficient. Wilson prefers the W. Feirân as the scene of action (" Ord. Survey Sinai.")

CHAPTER VI.

MOUNT SINAI

THE next day, Tuesday, 20th November, was a memorable one to our party, for it was that on which we made the ascent of Jebel Mûsa, the traditionary seat of the giving of the Law by Jehovah to Israel. So much has been well and eloquently written upon the character, scenery, and surroundings of this mountain that I shall content myself with a few personal observations.

I need scarcely say that the tradition above referred to has been almost universally accepted.[1] The late Professor Palmer arrived at the conclusion that the Lord descended on Jebel Mûsa (Mount Sinai) and there delivered the tables of the Law to Moses, who in turn delivered them to the people on descending from Rás Sufsâfeh.[2] This majestic cliff, rising nearly 2,000 feet at the head of an extensive valley well calculated to afford camping ground for the Israelitish host, from whence they could behold the display of Divine power, seems in all points to answer to the description given in the sacred text of the scene of these events. This view is also held by Sir C. W. Wilson, who points to the existence of the stream of Wâdy Sh'reich which descends from behind Rás Sufsâfeh as being in all probability that into which Moses cast the dust of the golden calf. The same writer, also, lays just stress upon the fact that the position of this rock answers well to the description of "the mountain that can be touched."[3] Leaving our camp early (for we knew that we had a long day's work before us), we marched up the wide plain of Wâdy es Sheikh, and, afterwards turning to the right, entered the Wâdy el Deir, when we came in front of the grand cliffs of Rás Sufsâfeh, rising abruptly from the plain,

[1] The only exception, perhaps, is that of Dr. Beke, who supposed one of the mountains at the head of the Gulf of Akabah to be Mount Sinai, and Mr. Baker Greene, *Quarterly Statement*, October, 1884.

[2] A good engraving of this mountain is given in Palmer's work, *supra cit.* p. 35, and also in "Picturesque Palestine." The grand cliff, however, in this latter appears somewhat more isolated from the mountain to the left than is really the case.

[3] "Ordnance Survey of the Peninsula of Sinai," p. 146.

and intersected by several deep clefts. In front was a little hill crowned by the tomb of some celebrated Sheikh, and away to the right an incongruous square structure, built for a summer residence of Mohammed Ali. I felt satisfied that here was the camping ground of Israel, and in front the "Mount of the Law." The spacious plain we had been passing through, covered with herbage, would have afforded ample space for the people with their flocks and herds, and the mountain masses in front, reverberating with the thunders of heaven, would have been well calculated to impress them with awe and reverence.

Turning again to the left the path leads up to, and past, the convent of St. Catherine, and thence, by an excessively steep and long ascent, to the base of the great wall of rock, upon the summit of which are perched the little chapel and mosque of Jebel Mûsa. To an ordinary pedestrian this wall would be inaccessible, as it rises as a sheer precipice before him ; but on looking to the right along its base, one perceives that the rocks are cleft in twain, and that the path turns sharply to the right, and passes through this cleft, between vertical walls on either side. After this there is a climb of several hundred feet, round by a partially artificial flight of steps to the summit above the great precipice. I mention this cleft, because on entering it I exclaimed to myself, " Can this be the cleft of the rock in which the Lord placed His servant when He made His glory pass before Him ?" Whether this be so or not, the cleft is remarkable as a natural feature, and from its wild and impressive surroundings.

Nothing can exceed the savage grandeur of the view from the summit of Mount Sinai. The infinite complication of jagged peaks and varied ridges, and their prevalent intensely red and greenish tints, have been noticed by Pococke, Stanley, and other writers.[1] The natural red tints of the granite and porphyry seem to have been deepened and intensified (as I believe) by the rays of the sun ; while in some places the rocks are blackened through the natural process of weathering.[2] Everywhere they are rent, fissured, and crumbling into ruins ; breaking off along steep walls, and traversed by dry ravines and almost waterless, therefore treeless, valleys ;—destitute of verdure as seen from this elevation. The whole aspect of the surroundings impresses one with the conviction that he is here gazing on the face of Nature under one of her most savage

---

[1] "Sinai and Palestine," Edit. 1873, p. 12.

[2] It is well known that the rays of the sun have the effect of deepening the colour of the felspar crystals of which the rocks are largely composed.

forms, in view of which the ideas of solitude, of waste, and of desolation contend with those of awe and admiration. The summit on which you stand is over seven thousand feet above the sea, but some distance to the south is the still loftier height of Katarina.[1] Beyond, in the same direction, the eye wanders over a succession of rugged mountains and deep ravines, forming the Sinaitic peninsula, and bounded on either hand by the deep depressions in which lie the Gulfs of Suez and Akabah. Distant glimpses of the table-land of the Tîh to the north, and of the mountains of Edom which bound the Wâdy el Arabah on the east, are also obtained. Having planted the theodolite on the flat roof of the mosque, Major Kitchener was able to take angles on several prominent points in the direction of our future line of march. The mosque and little Greek church are constructed from the materials of the ancient church supposed to have been erected by the Empress Helena. That it was a work of much beauty, and involving great labour and expense, is testified by the fragments of the ancient building in the form of the pedestal of a granite pillar, portions of a cornice, and other architectural fragments in white marble, or in red sandstone, which are strewn about ; all of which must have been brought from long distances, and carried to the summit of the mountain only by great labour.[2]

We came down from the mount by the Pilgrims' Road, more direct and precipitous than the former, and accompanied by a monk of the convent. Our eyes were gladdened in this dry and barren land by an actual running stream, descending along the gorge of granite cliffs from a little reservoir constructed in a natural basin close to "Elijah's Cave," and a remarkably tall cypress, which all travellers have noticed.[3] No one, who has not a firm step and a good eye, should try this path, as a sprained ankle, or possibly a broken leg, may follow a false step. Just as we came in view of the convent and gardens, we had a good illustration of the deceptive appearance, as regards size and distance, which all objects in this region assume, owing to the wonderful transparency of the air. It may be said, with truth, that,

---

[1] Climbed on the same day by Mr. Hart, after the ascent of J. Mûsa.

[2] While here we saw for the first time the little animal (*Hyrax syriacus*) called "the coney" in the Bible ; for a description of which the reader is referred to Tristram's "Fauna and Flora of Palestine," p. 1. The district also contains the ibex (*Capra bede*), or "wild goat" of Scripture, illustrating the passage, "The high hills are a refuge for the wild goats, and the stony rocks for the conies."

[3] A view of this cypress is given in "Picturesque Palestine," p. 113 ; some years ago, when Niebuhr visited the spot, there were two.

generally speaking, all objects in the landscape are twice the distance and twice the size they actually appear.   So now, on coming into view of the convent and its surroundings, in the valley below us, though these objects *looked* so close as to be only within two or three hundred yards off, they were all miniature representations, and so reduced in size that it seemed as though we were beholding a model of the reality.   The effect was extremely pretty.   We could see over the whole exterior of the building, with its high massive walls, loopholed turrets, and the church rising above the flat roof of the building.   Behind were the fruitful gardens, with the neat vineyards, beds of vegetables, and fruit trees, amongst which several tall cypresses rose high into the air.   All this we could see as if so close that a few strides would place us in their midst ; but it took us a good half hour to clamber down the cliff, and cross the slopes to the walls of the building, which is capable of affording accommodation for 200 inmates.

We remained three nights in the camp of the Wâdy es Sheikh.   Never shall I forget the discomfort of these nights.   I was attacked by a small insect,[1] almost invisible to the eye, which covered the body with little pimples of the most irritating kind, making sleep impossible, and life a burden.   The warmth of the bed rendered these bites almost intolerable ; and I had frequently to rise in order to sponge myself with cold water, or with diluted carbolic acid, which gave only temporary relief.   For some time I could discover no cause for this irritation, but the insect was at length discovered by the dragoman.[1]   Though loth to do so, I naturally attributed the presence of this insect to my Arab, whom I had allowed to ride on my camel while I was walking ; and orders were issued that the camel drivers were not, for the future, to ride on the camels of the travellers. This gave much dissatisfaction, but the comfort of the travellers was considered of more importance than the convenience of the Arabs.   Some time afterwards, when referring to the matter, I discovered who the real offender was.   It appears that during the first night of our camping a vagabond Arab arrived, and, the nights being cold, he took possession of my camel-saddle, with which he wrapped himself round, and thus passed the night, no doubt, comfortably to himself.   The legacy he left behind next morning was the insect.   My Arab was therefore really not to blame, and he was naturally indignant when the dragoman hinted that he was the offender,

---

[1] Called "Arab lice."   Not having preserved specimens for examination, I am unable to give the scientific name ; but I cannot doubt it was that which produced one of the plagues of Egypt.

and exclaimed, "If you find one of these ——— on my body or in my hair you may kill me!" All this I did not ascertain until Sala and I had parted for ever. I mention the matter here, in order that other travellers may avoid a similar fate by having their camel-saddles deposited within the tents at night.

We had now reached Jebel Mûsa, the most southern point of our proposed route, and henceforth our course took a north-easterly direction. In order to explore the district lying between the head of the Gulf of Akabah and the eastern margin of the Tîh, and connect the topographical and geological features with those of the Sinaitic peninsula, which had been so well worked out by Captains Wilson and Palmer, we took a course towards Akabah seldom traversed by travellers hitherto. We retraced our steps for some distance by the Wâdy es Sheikh, passed again through the gorge of El Watiyeh, and emerged on an extensive undulating plain, Elwi 'l'Ajramiyeh, which we traversed nearly due north to the head of the Wâdy Zelegah. Major Kitchener took a course more to the left, in order to determine the position of an important spring called "Ain el Akhdar," and rejoined us late in the evening at our camp, some distance down the Zelegah Valley. It is probable that a large portion of the plain we traversed during this day had formerly been the bed of a lake. It was covered with fine gravel, through which bosses of granite or basalt sometimes protruded. This lake may have been connected with that of the Wâdy es Sheikh previously referred to.

The upper part of the Wâdy Zelegah is remarkable for its geological features. The valley itself is excavated through beds of brown, red, and variegated sandstone, which are but slightly removed from the horizontal position, having a dip towards the N.E. of two or three degrees. These sandstone beds are sometimes deeply channelled; and form terraces, flat-topped tables, and sometimes isolated tors. The cliffs rise on either hand; those on the south of the valley giving origin to a scarped ridge called Jebel es Zerf. Through these sandstone beds the old foundation rocks, consisting of granite, porphyry, or greenstone, occasionally protrude; showing that the rocky floor, on which the sandy strata were originally deposited, was exceedingly uneven in form, rising into ridges or solitary peaks, or hollowed into furrows. An instance of this kind was observed about four miles below the head of the valley.

The Wâdy Zelegah was first explored by Laborde; afterwards by Palmer. It is about 20 miles in length, and its general direction is north-east to its junction with the Wâdy Biyar, when it bends to the east for several miles, and expands sometimes to upwards of a mile in breadth. The scenery along its course is striking. It is bounded by cliffs of coloured sandstone rising from 1,000 feet to 1,200 feet above the bed of the valley. The sides are often covered by enormous landslips, and by masses of rock brought down by the torrents; while small terraces of more ancient date, formed of alluvial material, are found in sheltered spots. The Cretaceous limestone, with numerous fossils, is continuous amongst the cliffs on either side; and as the dip of the formation corresponds very nearly with the fall of the valley, the same strata continue for long distances to form the boundary walls.

The floor of the W. Zelegah is decorated with dwarf shrubs and plants; and little groups of tamarisk are occasionally to be found, the tender fronds of which were eagerly devoured by our camels. Sometimes the ground is perfectly flat from side to side; and where sandy is covered by the circular or ear-shaped hills of the large black ant, and under many of the bushes the jerboa has its burrow-holes. These burrowings in the ground are dangerous both for horses and camels; and the camel of my son having placed his foot on one of these concealed holes it gave way, and the rider was sent flying over the camel's head in my sight. I was much relieved when he got up, and pronounced himself unhurt.

The Wâdy el Biyar descends from the escarpment of the Tîh, and uniting with the Zelegah Valley they both change their name, and at a bend towards the north are known as the Wâdy el Ain, so called from the fine perennial spring which bursts forth near its head. The terraces of alluvial materials which rise about 50 feet above the present bed, both in the valleys of Zelegah and Biyar, indicate the existence at a former period of rivers and floods far more extensive in their operation than those of the present day. On Friday evening we camped at the entrance to the W. el Ain, having made 21 miles during the day. Our camp, near the entrance to the Wâdy Mugrah, was about 3,000 feet above the waters of the Gulf of Akabah.

At about ten o'clock on Saturday morning, on turning a bend of the wide valley towards the east, we came in sight of the Jebel el Berg, a fine mountain, solitary and of quadrangular form, rising in our front to a height of about 2,000 feet above the plain. It is formed of horizontal courses of sandstone, and is accompanied by several minor heights of similar formation in outline, somewhat like the Egyptian Pyramids. The beds of sandstone are planted on a foundation of granite and porphyry. Another mountain—Jebel el Ain—somewhat similar in form and structure, is a conspicuous object from the valley of this name, and lies several miles further to the east. In this neighbourhood the beds of sandstone some-times assume tabular and castellated forms, illustrating the process of atmospheric weathering, and offering many a tempting subject for the pencil of the artist; but little time was at our disposal for indulging in essays with the pen or pencil.

CHAPTER VII.

WÂDY EL AIN.

WE were now about to experience a surprise for which we were entirely unprepared,[1] in the form of a magnificent gorge, resembling one of the great cañons of Western America. The road we were taking is seldom traversed either by travellers or by Arabs, and our guides were unacquainted with it. It is next to certain that the Israelites did not take this route, which from its nature would have been impracticable for a host of men, women, and children with cattle. Professor Palmer has happily identified the position of "Hazeroth" with that of Ain Huderah, which lies to the east and south of our course ; and the children of Israel, in journeying towards Ezion Geber, doubtless took the easier and more direct route, under Divine guidance, by the Wâdy Saal and Wâdy el Huderah ; and then descending, by the *lower end* of the Wâdy el Ain, to the sea coast of the Gulf of Akabah, continued along its margin to Ezion Geber. The upper part of the W. el Ain, as I have already stated, would have been impracticable for such a host. To us, indeed, it presented a spectacle of the grandest kind, illustrating the marvellous erosive power of water, when employed in cutting its channel through an indefinitely long period of time. (See Frontispiece).

Shortly after leaving our midday camp our eyes were greeted by the unusual spectacle of a grove of palms, following the course of a trickling stream of clear water issuing from the fountain which gives its name to the valley, and the first we had seen since leaving the Convent of St. Catherine. Following with some difficulty the course of the stream between narrow walls of granite, we presently found ourselves in a gorge about twenty yards in width, with walls rising to still higher altitudes, up to 600 feet or 700 feet, by estimation. The air was deliciously cool and fresh. Several kinds of birds darted about; and some plants, hitherto unrecognised, gave Hart abundant employment. My son got his camera

---

[1] Although the W. el Ain has been described by Ruppell and by Miss Martineau it will bear repetition.

into operation, and soon exhausted the stock of plates remaining for the
day's use. Every few yards brought us in front of still loftier cliffs of
granite, occasionally capped by pyramids and tors of sandstone, until at
about half-a-mile from our entrance to this grand cañon, and after winding
from side to side, we found ourselves confronted by inaccessible cliffs,
estimated by Kitchener and myself at 1,000 feet to 1,200 feet in altitude
above the bed of the brook.[1] A little further on, cliffs of sandstone were
seen capping the granite on the left; and at length, after numerous
windings, a lengthened vista opens out along a straight reach of about
three miles, nearly flat along the bottom, and bounded by steep slopes of
granite seamed by dykes and sheets of greenstone. At the end of this glen
we found our tents pitched on a terrace of gravel, slightly raised above the
bed of the now dry stream course. Little groves of palms, tamarisks, and
tall reeds were refreshing to the eyes, and afforded choice provender for
our camels ; and, behind our tents, at the base of the cliffs, our Arabs
rested in groups around their fires, chatting over the events of the day, and
preparing the evening meal.

There were not wanting proofs that this remarkable ravine, now
almost waterless, is sometimes the channel of a mighty river, which
sweeps down towards the sea in an impetuous flood, carrying everything
within its reach before it. Immense masses of shingle were piled up
within the entrant angles and protected places of the valley where eddies
would be formed ; while large boulders and masses of driftwood were
sometimes to be seen lying stranded in similar positions. One can well
imagine that after one of the great thunderstorms which burst on the
mountainous parts of the peninsula, and suddenly convert dry valleys into
impetuous torrents, this gorge of the El Ain must present a spectacle at
once impressive and terrible ; for it then receives the combined floods of
the Wâdies Zelegah, El Biyar, and numerous smaller tributaries. In such
a case, woe to the unhappy traveller who finds himself within the walls of
the grand cañon ; he himself may possibly escape by scaling the cliffs, but
his camels and baggage would be swept away beyond the hope of rescue.
On this account the Arabs seldom enter this part of the valley. To them
it remains mysterious and almost unknown ; and we may feel assured
that, to the host of Israel, it would have proved a dangerous and almost

[1] Mr. Armstrong made a survey of this gorge of the W. el Ain by a series
of compass bearings, and pacing from angle to angle of the gorge. It will be
found represented on the new map of the P. E. F. when published.

impracticable road, and one which under the guidance of God—who "led his people like a flock"—they were not likely to follow.

Sunday, 25th November.—We had morning prayers in the tent, and in the afternoon, while engaged in writing, word was brought "that the engineers were approaching." We had heard, when in our camp near Mount Sinai, that a party of engineers had arrived from England at Suez, and were waiting for camels to carry them to Akabah ; and we understood that they had come out to take observations along the line of the Wâdy el Arabah in connection with "the Jordan Valley scheme."[1]

Presently the baggage camels passed our tents at a rapid pace, and about an hour afterwards two gentlemen, with dragoman and servant, passed also. I had ordered coffee to be prepared with the expectation that the engineers would favour us with a call *en passant;* but with that reserve which is peculiar to Englishmen—and not one of their most agreeable characteristics—they refrained from any communication with our party.

Feeling satisfied that their object was to reach Akabah before ourselves and forestall us in securing camels, though we had a right to priority, I requested Major Kitchener to draw up a letter to the governor of Akabah with directions that he would secure the services of Sheikh Mohammed Ibn Jhad, and obtain the requisite camels. This letter I despatched the same evening by the hand of our conductor, Bernhard Heilpern, who started down the valley accompanied by an Arab, passed the tents of the engineering party at night, and reached Akabah on the second day ; and so well did he accomplish his task that, on our arrival, we received a message from Sheikh Mohammed saying that he was on his way from his mountain home to visit us, with the result which will be stated further on. Having thus taken measures to prevent our expedition being blocked, or at least being seriously delayed at its most critical stage, we prepared to resume our journey next morning.

Our course continued for several miles down the Wâdy el Ain, sometimes in view of a conspicuous mountain called Jebel el Aradeh, which rose between us and the sea, towards the north-east. This mountain was ascended by Kitchener for survey purposes, and Hart for botanical. It forms a landmark in that part of the country, and like most of the

---

[1] The scheme according to which it is proposed to flood the valley of the Jordan to the level of the Mediterranean, and to cut a canal between the inland sea thus formed and the Gulf of Akabah.

isolated hills consists of beds of sandstone and limestone on a granitic base. At length we came to the point where the Wâdy et Tîhyeh opens on the left into the apparently interminable Wâdy el Ain, and we gladly struck up the former in a direction somewhat circuitous, but generally making towards the north and east. We rested at noon by some wells in the sandstone rock, which was often encrusted with salt. The spot is pretty on account of the groups of palm trees. Through the rest of the day our course lay over a very broken line of country, diversified by deep depressions, terraced escarpments of limestone or sandstone, and ultimately we emerged on a wide plain bounded by fine escarpments of the former. The surface of this plain is dotted with plants; and in April is green with herbage, and occupied by several hundred Bedawins, who come here with their flocks and herds for pasturage, and to make butter;—now it was nearly deserted. At length, after a very long day's march of ten hours, we pitched our tents near the head of the Wâdy el Tîhyeh, at the base of a limestone cliff, and at an elevation of 2,400 feet above the sea.[1]

[1] These elevations were taken by Mr. Laurence with the aneroid, and worked out during the evenings.

CHAPTER VIII.

REGION OF THE TÎH.

WE had now entered the district of the Tîh plateau, as generally under-stood; but towards the south-eastern part of its extension its margin can scarcely be recognised. From the Wâdy el Ain northward and east-ward, the country is formed of a succession of scarped ridges and valleys, with but little symmetry or order of succession; so that it is impossible in this district to say within many miles where "the escarpment of the Tîh" really begins or ends. This disarrangement of the geographical boundaries is, I need scarcely say, due to geological causes. The strata, instead of preserving a regular order of succession, according to which the limestone ridge forming the margin of the Tîh succeeds a plateau of sandstone, as in the district north of Debbet er Ramleh, are here broken into, and displaced, by several large "faults," ranging both in northerly and easterly directions. Thus, the order of succession is disturbed, the strata are dislocated, sometimes repeated over again, and a series of scarps and valleys, transverse in direction to each other, are pro-duced. Even when we had reached the limestone district new ridges of considerable elevation were descried far to the north and west, and it was a question whether these ought not to be taken as the boundary of "the Tîh." As a geologist, however, I must hold that the Tîh begins with the limestone formation; though I doubt whether this ground of identification will be considered satisfactory by geographers. Another consequence of this irregularity in the contours is, that the southern drainage system is prolonged far inwards towards the north. Several of the faults, or lines of dislocation in the strata above referred to, were seen by us on our way, and as far as practicable laid down on the geological map which accom-panies this volume.

Desert partridges appeared to be numerous in the Wâdy el Tîhyeh.[1] Shortly after entering we noticed several harriers soaring above the

---

[1] Probably "Hey's Sand Partridge" (*Ammoperdix Heyi*).

right side of the valley, and presently the cause was revealed when a "covey" of the partridges were started by us amongst the rocks. They are a little smaller than the English partridge, and differ in colour and general appearance, being light reddish-brown on the back and speckled white and brown on the breast ; the beak is bright yellow. They seldom take the wing ; but when startled either lie close to the ground, which they greatly resemble in colour, or run up the banks or rocks with great speed, and try to hide themselves.

During our long rides we often beguiled the way with a song, a cigarette, or a scrap of conversation. Amongst all our party there was no one such an adept at the latter art as Ibraham, our dragoman. He was a strict Mohammedan, and had done haj (or pilgrimage) to Mecca ; and from having seen so much of the world could spin his yarn by the hour. Often I have been amused to watch him and Bernhard Heilpern riding side by side, the former keeping up a brisk conversation, to which the other had only to reply by an occasional grunt, or nod of assent. One day, after one of these *tête-à-têtes* (which were always in Arabic), Ibraham came to me, and says, "Mr. Bernhard, sir, he be very good man ; he want to improve the costumes (customs) of these Bedawins."

"Why," I replied, "does he want them to wear trowsers ? I fancy a Bedawin in trowsers would be no longer a Bedawin."

"No, sir, he wants the Bedawin to settle down and cultivate the ground, but Bedawin will not do that." (Ibraham always spoke of the Arabs with mingled contempt and pity.) "I say to our sheikh, 'You be very poor peeble here ; you have very little to eat and very little cloths. Why you no go to Cairo and get some land ; then you grow crops and get rich ?' (Sнеiкн). 'If I go to Cairo and take land I have to pay for it. If I lose my crops I have to pay all the same or go to prison.[1] If wicked Bedawin come and kill other Bedawin on my land, he go off, but I be killed, or go to prison for life. If wicked Bedawin steal a donkey of other Bedawin on my land, I have to pay for the donkey, or go to prison. I don't want to go to prison, or to pay for my land. *Here* (looking around) I have no master ; I be free. Nobody can put me in prison in the desert.'"

It is to be feared that with such strong arguments against settling down as an agriculturalist in Egypt before him, there is not much hope that the Arab of the desert will fulfil the hopes of good Bernhard.

[1] A Land Act is evidently badly wanted here!

Perhaps I may here relate another of Ibraham's tales. It is about the origin of the Dabour tribe ; "Dabour" in Arabic means "a wasp."

Once a pious Bedawin, seeing with pity the ignorant state of his friends around him, determined to make a journey to Cairo "to buy some Khoran," and so to teach them how to pray. So he collects together all his money and effects, and after a long journey arrives at Cairo. There, a stranger and unbefriended, he enters a coffee-house, where he meets a man to whom he recounts the object of his visit. "Very good," says the man, "how much money have you got?" "Four dollars," replies the Arab. "Well," says the other, "that is enough to buy some Khoran ; hand the money over to me, and to-morrow I will bring you what you require."

So the poor Bedawin hands over his four dollars, and his considerate friend appoints a convenient place where he may receive the Khoran next day. Accordingly at the time appointed the two meet each other, and the stranger pulls out a leathern bag tied at the mouth with a string, and says, "This is the Khoran, put your ear to it and you will hear the Khoran speak." So the Arab applies his ear to the bag, and hears, buzz—buzz—buzz. "Now," says the man, "take this home, and when you arrive call all your friends together, then put the Khoran on your head, and tie the string tight ; tell all your friends to say exactly what you say, and to do exactly as you do ;—and then they will know how to pray aright."

So in due course the Bedawin returns to his family and friends with "the Khoran," and having assembled them together around him, says : "Here is the Khoran, which will teach you how to pray. Now, when I put it on my head, you do what I do, and say exactly what I say." He then proceeds to open the bag very carefully and to insert his head therein, tying the string tight ; the wasps which the bag contained naturally resent this intrusion, and proceed to show their resentment in the usual way. So, presently, the Bedawin exclaims, "Oh, Allah, Allah, help, help !" All exclaim, "Oh, Allah, help, help !" The Bedawin, "Oh, I shall die !" All, "Oh, I shall die !" (oft repeated). He then falls to the ground, rolling and kicking about vigorously ; all follow his example. This goes on for a little time, and with a probable termination in accord with the poor Bedawin's exclamation, when "a sensible man" happens to pass by, and says, "What are you all doing, what is it all about?" So the people explain that their friend in the centre has got the Khoran on his head, and is showing them how to pray. "But," says the man of sense, "that

FIG. 5.—ESCARPMENT OF TURF-ER-RUKN. LOOKING NORTH AND WEST.

E. H!

Cliffs of Limestone resting on variegated sandstone. Plain covered by gravel and herbage. In the foreground our luncheon-tent pitched at noon. 28th November, 1883.

is not the Khoran, and that is not the way to pray." So he goes over to the Bedawin—now half dead with agony—and loosens the string of the bag, upon which out fly the wasps, and every one scampers away. The secret was out, and the poor Arab found out that he was "sold to the Egyptians!"

The man and his tribe were henceforth called "Dabours," and they inhabit a district of the Tîh between Nakel and the Gulf of Suez. It will probably be allowed that a dragoman, with an illimitable stock of such stories, must be a favourite on a long day's march !

We camped for the night in the Wâdy el Khiass (Valley of Thieves),[1] a wide valley in the district of the Tîh, but of ill repute, as its name signifies. It lies in fact on the border land of several tribes, and is thus more than ordinarily open to the incursions of those who do not respect the rights of property, especially in the matter of flocks and herds. As we were approaching the time when we should part with our escort, my son thought it a favourable opportunity for taking measurements of their individual heights of stature, breadth of chest, and length of arm, with the general result of showing that the Arabs of the Towâra tribe (at least as represented by our guides) are somewhat lower of stature than the British army standard. Their power of enduring fatigue, and bodily agility, would probably be found superior.

The next morning we were on camel back by 7.30. The air was very cold, the thermometer having registered 27° Fahr. during the night, and in an hour we reached a tableland about 3,450 feet above the sea level ; the highest point of our line of march in the region of the Tîh. Towards the east hills rose above us still enveloped in the morning mists ; but in the opposite direction the sun was lighting up an extensive range of white lime-stone ridges, stretching in a north-easterly direction, the upper surface of which corresponded to an imaginary plain at least 1,000 feet above our present level, but broken through by many glens and depressions, amongst which the early rays of the sun were playing with exquisite effect. In about two hours more we came in sight of the Wâdy el Arabah, with the mountains beyond. It appeared like a vast plain, bounded on the eastern side by rugged and dark mountains rising behind each other, range above range, to a great, but unknown, elevation. Near our midday camp (Nov. 28), we descended from the limestone ridge on to an extensive plain of the sandstone formation. The boundary of the two formations runs along the crest of a broken ridge called Turf-er-Rukn (Fig. 5), at an

[1] Wâdy el Khiass leads into Wâdy el Hessi.

elevation of about 3,600 feet above the sea level, often forming isolated tors, and tabulated headlands. The plain is covered with scrub, and strewn with pretty little round pebbles, formerly imbedded in the sand-stone rock itself. Here we noticed several individuals of a little animal, a batrachian, allied to the salamander (one of the group of so-called "Sand Lizards"), darting about over the hot sands. It is about 5 inches long from head to tip of tail, head flattish, and of a colour exactly resembling that of the sand over which it runs, except in the dusky bands over the lower part of the tail. It is very active, and when pursued makes vigorous efforts to escape amongst the prickly bushes of the desert. It probably feeds on ants and other insects.

We camped for the night on a pebbly plain, preparatory to our descent the next day into the great valley of the Arabah, which was to terminate the first stage of our survey. Our course had been very much that of the arc of a circle, the chord of which would lie from W. to E.; that is, from the head of the Gulf of Suez to that of the Gulf of Akabah. Henceforth it was to be northwards, along a tract of country not well known, and offering to us the prospect of much which would be interesting and new to science. On the day following, 29th November, we descended the eastern slopes of the Tih, by the Haj Road, amongst features and scenery of the grandest description, down to the shore of the Gulf of Akabah. At about noon we came in front of a massive serrated ridge of red granite and porphyry, which rose up, as it were, across our path, and stretched in a north and south direction for several miles. On reaching its base the road turns sharply to the right, and for some distance lies along a valley, bounded on the left by the porphyry, and on the right by contorted beds of limestone. The line of this valley coincides (in fact) with that of a great fault, the direction of which Mr. Laurence determined with the prismatic compass to be North 28° East. Along this line of displacement the limestone strata are brought down against the porphyry, as shown in the annexed section, Fig. 6, p. 68. The effect of this sudden change in the character of the physical features is most marked, and can scarcely fail to attract the notice of the most casual observer.

Descending to the foot of the mountains we crossed the level plain by the margin of the waters of the Tranquil Sea, and passing through the palm groves, which give the name of "Elim" to the spot, we made for our tents, which we found pitched near the fort, beyond those of the engineers.

Close by Sheikh Mohammed, with several of his relatives, was seated ; we saluted each other, and passed on.   Bernhard Heilpern had accomplished his mission, and the Sheikh had declared that he considered himself engaged to settle with us before coming to an arrangement with any other party.   He no doubt inwardly chuckled at the good fortune which had sent him at one time two sets of English travellers to fleece, and to outbid each other for the honour of his valuable services.

Sheikh Mohammed Ibn Jhad, head of the Alowín tribe, is a man of about sixty summers ; of full, rather common-place features, dark eyes, and beard tinged with grey.   He was clad in a rich scarlet cloak lined with yellow silk, a white shirt and girdle, yellow silken khefeyeh[1] on his head, and red leather boots.   He carried a large, rather antique scimitar, and a revolver was stuck in his girdle ; of course the long pipe was in his hand.   He spoke with animation, and much modulation of voice, from the *sotto voce* of confidence to the high pitch of expostulation.

His brother, Sheikh Ali, who afterwards became our guard through the Wâdy el Arabah, was of the usual Arab type, with sharp aquiline features, and dark restless eyes.   He was less gorgeously clad than his elder brother, and only chimed in occasionally during the conversation relating to our proposed route.   In one respect both brothers exactly resembled each other—they loved money much !

That evening the preliminaries were verbally agreed upon, in presence of the Government notary, who was to draw up a document for signature, in which the terms were to be distinctly stated, and the following evening was appointed for the execution of the deed.   The terms were to the effect that Sheikh Ali (as representing his brother) was to conduct us safely up to the entrance of the valley towards Petra and Mount Hor (Jebel Haroun), and one day's march up the Wâdy el Arabah beyond ; from which point we were to turn off to the left towards Gaza, to the south of the territory of the Tihyaha, with whom the Alowín were at feud. We were not to sleep even for one night at Petra ; or to delay longer than absolutely necessary in a district the inhabitants of which were, in the Sheikh's opinion, "very bad people."   We were to pay (as we supposed) 36 dollars for the right to pass through his lands, and so much for each camel per day.   The whole journey was to be completed in 15 days ; and

---

[1] A kind of kerchief with tassels at the four corners.   When worn it is doubled and bound on the head by a double chord or fillet.   The ends either hang down, or are drawn up, and fastened in the fillet by means of the tassels.

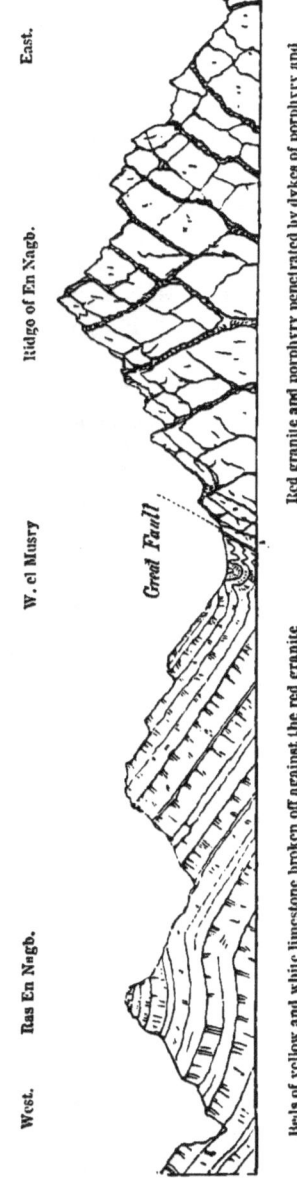

FIG. 6.—GEOLOGICAL SECTION ALONG THE HAJ ROAD ABOVE THE GULF OF AKABAH.

West.

Ras En Nagb.

W. el Musry

Ridge of En Nagb.

East.

Great Fault

Beds of yellow and white limestone broken off against the red granite along a line of fault.

Red granite and porphyry penetrated by dykes of porphyry and diorite.

the Sheikh undertook to have the camels and men ready for us early on
Monday morning.   When we met the following evening the document
was read out by the notary, but a little hitch occurred at the article
about the 36 dollars.   We had understood this was toll for the whole
party; the Sheikh asserted that he meant it was the sum for each of the six
"hawajahs," making 216 dollars.   A long and angry discussion took place
on this point; but as the Sheikh was firm, declaring that this amount had
been settled by the Government at Cairo as the toll for travellers, we
had to give in.   At length the document having been agreed upon, our
conductor produced the money bag, counted out the large silver pieces,
which the Sheikh placed in little piles before him on the floor, amounting altogether to a sum equal to £135 sterling.   Mohammed then proceeded to untie a corner of his inner garment, and from the folds thereof
produced the important seal, which alone could give efficacy to the
instrument.   It was a small seal of white metal engraved with Arabic
characters.   This the notary took, and having wetted a space on the
parchment impressed the seal with due solemnity.   Before leaving home
I had hunted out an old family seal, unused for many years, and had brought
it with me for an occasion of this kind.   This seal I now produced, and
it was also impressed on the document.   Finally, Bernhard Heilpern, as
representing Messrs. T. Cook and Son, signed his name.   We then broke
up; and recollecting that sharks abounded in the waters of the gulf close
by, I thought this fish a true representative of the man we had been
dealing with, and I took this opportunity of dubbing the head of the
Alowîn tribe by the style and title of " Sheikh Shark," the name by
which he is in future to be known.[1]

It will be seen from the above account of our agreement with Sheikh
Mohammed that the route was different from that marked out for us by the
Committee of the Palestine Exploration Fund, and which we had determined, if possible, to adhere to; namely, to make a reconnaissance down
the whole length of the Wâdy el Arabah to the shores of the Salt Sea.
This route Mohammed positively refused to undertake, on the ground that
his brother had killed a sheikh of the Tîhyaha, and that if he were to pass
through their territory, which lay north of the road to Gaza, we might be

---

[1] The late Dean Stanley states that he was treated by Sheikh Mohammed with
almost princely courtesy.   Probably so, if the Dean gave him everything he
asked for; or possibly he may not then have learnt how to bleed travellers.

attacked.[1] He therefore proposed the only alternative, that we should proceed across the Tîh to Gaza. This was a serious disappointment to us all ; for it not only would have extended our journey over a district we did not much care to visit, but would also have obliged us to leave un-explored an important portion of the Arabah Valley, and to make a gap in our surveys between the Sinaitic peninsula and Southern Palestine. How it ultimately happened that we managed to complete our survey of the whole valley of the Arabah down to the shores of the Salt Sea, and also to visit Gaza, will appear in the sequel.

It now remained for us to take leave of our Towâra guides, and to hand them the usual " bakhsheesh," or present, expected by all Arabs, whether well paid or otherwise, for their services.[2] Accordingly each of us presented our camel drivers with a sum equal to about five shillings, and 50 shillings were divided amongst those who had care of the baggage. The sheikhs received double the amount of the drivers. This seemed to give satisfaction, and wishing each other " ma'as salamah," we shook hands and parted.

[1] He stated that we (the travellers) would be in no personal danger, but that his Arabs might be killed, our camels carried off, and we left in the lurch.

[2] This is a detestable system, and should be discouraged by travellers, except for extraordinary services and good behaviour.

CHAPTER IX.

AKABAH.

AKABAH is a fort held by the Egyptian Government with a garrison of eight soldiers, and it is pleasantly situated near the eastern shore of the gulf of that name, and close to its northern bay. On descending from the slopes of the Tîh by the Haj Road, the head waters of the bay open out before the traveller, and an extensive grove of palm trees is seen to sweep round the head of the bay in a semicircle from left to right. These palms are probably indigenous; for the old name of Akabah was "Elim" or "Elath," which means a grove of trees; probably palms.[1] This is of special interest, because two species of palm here flourish. The date palm (*Phœnix dactylifera*, Lin.) and the doum palm (*Hyphœne Thebaica*, Mart), which instead of consisting of a solitary stem with leafy plume atop, bifurcates or branches repeatedly. The two varieties may be seen growing together directly north of the bay, and it is the only place where I have seen both.[2]

On the west side of the bay probably stood Ezion Geber (the "backbone of a giant"), mentioned by Moses in the same sentence with Elath, and, also, as one of the camping stations of the Israelites,[3] probably after having descended from the mountains of Horeb into the Wâdy el Arabah or Wilderness of Zin. The name, perhaps, was given from the great ridge of porphyry which, ranging from north to south, strikes the coast at Ras el Musry. No traces of this place remain, but in the time of Solomon it was an important port.[4] It is distinctly stated to have been "beside Elath, on the shore of the Red Sea, in the land of Edom." Its position therefore is beyond doubt; and from this place a great highway must have run up the valley to Kadesh Barnea and entering the hills by one

[1] Deut. ii, 8.

[2] The doum palm is common in Upper Egypt, and on the banks of the Atbara; Baker's "Nile Tributaries," p. 32. Professor Hæckel mentions its occurrence near the Arab village of Tor. "Visit to Ceylon."

[3] Numb. xxxiii, 35.

[4] 1 Kings ix, 26.

of the passes have continued its course northwards, probably by Hebron, to Jerusalem.[1] The waters of the gulf are beautifully clear, and the shore is formed of shelly gravel, consisting of pebbles of porphyry, granite, greenstone, and quartz, mixed with pieces of coral, and great numbers of shells, chiefly univalves, of which Hart collected altogether about 200 species. The rise and fall of the spring tides is about 6 feet, and the waters abound in fish, amongst which are "flying fish" and sharks. The presence of the latter renders bathing rather dangerous, and the habit is not much indulged in by the inhabitants, though not altogether perhaps from the presence of these voracious fish.

The average temperature of Akabah is high, and in summer the heat must be almost overpowering. The land at the head of the bay might be made a fruitful field if cultivated, as it is covered by rich loam, and water is so abundant below the surface that the Arabs have only to scrape holes a few inches deep in the gravel near the shore in order to give their camels drink. The palm grove here is the largest we had seen since leaving Egypt. Doubtless wheat, maize, olives, indigo, and cotton might be cultivated with success ; yet nothing is grown but the palm, which requires little culture ; and the lazy inhabitants prefer to lounge about, smoking their pipes, and doing next to nothing in order to turn to account the bounties of nature.

Notwithstanding our agreement with Mahommed, and the handsome sum of money he had secured, we learned on the day following (Saturday) that there had been a judicious distribution of gifts on the part of our neighbours to secure priority in the start on Monday. We therefore thought it prudent to invite the Sheikh into our tent on Saturday evening in order "to keep him straight," by the presentation of a gift "in token of our high esteem." I had brought out a small revolver, a pretty instrument of American workmanship, and at the suggestion of my colleagues had resolved to sacrifice it for the public good on this occasion. We all felt sure that the sight of such a present would at once convert the Sheikh from the position of a wavering ally to that of a staunch friend. During all this

---

[1] This may be the road described by Sir C. W. Wilson as "the road from Huila (Elath) to Petra, which appears to have run up the W. el Arabah and W. Gharandel by Dinna (Ain el Ghudyan). Regarding the position of Kadesh, I shall have more to say in another page. The Rev. F. W. Holland considered that the Israelites, after leaving Mount Sinai, marched northward by the W. el Atiych on the plateau of the Tih to Kadesh Barnea, without descending to the Valley of the Arabah. Rep. Brit. Assoc., 1878, p. 622.

time, he and his relatives were being housed in our luncheon tent and entertained at our expense, and we felt that, everything considered, we had the highest claim on his good offices. Accordingly, on his entering our tent after dinner, I made him a neat little speech through our interpreter, closing by the presentation of the revolver, which I felt sure would draw forth a reply overflowing with gratitude. What, however, was our surprise when the Sheikh, taking the weapon in his hand, examined it, and then deliberately laid it on the table. He then drew from his girdle a revolver of much larger calibre and somewhat similar make, assuring us that he had already more than enough of such gifts. A consultation was then held amongst ourselves, and we agreed to substitute two English sovereigns for the revolver, which I gladly reclaimed. This had the desired effect; and the Sheikh made a solemn promise that nothing should prevent an early start on Monday morning. It appeared, however, that his brother Ali was by no means pleased at the favours we were heaping upon Mohammed. He sent a private message, therefore, to us to request that we should give no more presents to his brother, but keep the rest for him !

Thus ended this eventful week, and everything being now arranged, we were in a position to pass the following day in a comparatively contented frame of mind.

The next day being Advent Sunday we had prayers in the tent, and just as they were concluded the distant firing of guns announced the approach of a large body of pilgrims returning from Mecca on their way to Tunis and Algiers. We ascended the hill behind our camp, and beheld a procession of 500 or 600 people with camels winding their way along the base of the mountains from the pass of the Haj Road, and deploying in the plain behind the Fort. It was a curious sight. Some were clad in bright garments, others in brown or black cloaks. In front was carried a large banner bearing the crescent, and there was one single horseman who made his way to the Fort. We presumed he was in command of the guard. Sheikh Mohammed with his attendants proceeded to receive the pilgrims, who were now under his protection, and they soon were busy preparing to camp for the night. Gordon took a photograph of the party.

We were early astir on Monday morning for our start up the Wâdy el Arabah, and on this day we had our first heavy shower of rain. Hitherto, day after day of more or less hot sunshine had succeeded each other ; but during Saturday the temperature had fallen (the maximum only reaching

69° Fahr.), the sky was cloudy, and towards Sunday evening signs of an approaching storm began to manifest themselves. Accordingly we made our preparations. Trenches were dug round our tents, the pegs were firmly hammered down, and we got all baggage under cover. Soon after retiring for the night we heard the booming of heaven's artillery amongst the mountains, and flash succeeded flash with much brilliancy. The rain came at first in heavy drops, and then poured down steadily. The tents, however, proved sound ; not a drop entered, and we rejoiced to think that the parched and thirsty ground would drink in the refreshing rain ; that plant-life would receive a fresh impulse, and cover the plain we were about to traverse with verdure and flowers. In the morning rain still fell, heavy clouds hung on the mountains, and we had to mount our new camels, and make our arrangements for a start, under a dripping sky.

We broke up our camp in a scene of indescribable confusion. Our new Arabs were quite unused to their work ; and it was excessively difficult to apportion the baggage to each camel, to have the tents taken down and packed, and to get the men to lade their own animals. The clatter of tongues was loud and incessant, above which those of the Sheikhs were the loudest. The roaring and groaning of the camels was hideous to hear ; our dragoman, Ibraham, was storming, and our conductor silent with despair. As I was setting out he said to me, "I trust we shall meet again to-night !" Glad to get out of this babel, we rode off ; but it was past eleven o'clock when the baggage camels were ready to start, owing, I was told, to Mohammed not having supplied the requisite number of camel nets.

CHAPTER X.

THE WÂDY EL ARABAH.

THE Wâdy el Arabah, which we were now about to traverse, is by far
the largest and most striking depression in Arabia Petræa. It is called in
the Bible "the Wilderness of Zin," and was traversed by the children
of Israel throughout a large portion of its extent ; first, according to
the views of some authors, when going up to Kadesh Barnea to take
possession of the Promised Land, and afterwards, when disastrously
driven back before their enemies, and doomed to wander in the great
desert of Arabia during a space of nearly forty years. They retraced
their steps, again, at the end of thirty-eight years, on the second visit
to Kadesh Barnea, and before the encampment in the plain at the
western base of Mount Hor, where Aaron died ; and lastly, when obliged
to circumvent Edom and Moab, on their way to the Promised Land by the
Jordan Valley.

The great valley of the Arabah was first brought to the notice of
Europeans by Robinson and Burckhardt,[1] who traced up the course of the
valley from the Gulf of Akabah to the Lake Asphaltites.   But it has also
been visited and described to a greater or less extent by subsequent explorers, amongst whom may be mentioned Laborde, Lord Lindsay, Dean
Stanley, Dr. Wilson, Professor Palmer, and, more recently, M. Vignes, in
connection with the expedition carried out by the Duc de Luynes.[2]   These
travellers have shown that this valley is the physical prolongation of that
great depression which, commencing at the north with the valleys of the
Litany and the Orontis, stretches southwards along the course of the
Jordan, the Salt Sea, and The Ghôr, through the El Arabah itself into the
Gulf of Akabah;—a depression justly pronounced by Humboldt to be the
most remarkable on the face of the earth.   This physical continuity is, as

[1] "Travels in Syria," p. 360–412.
[2] "Voyage d'Exploration de la Mer Morte."   3 vols. (Paris).

may be inferred, due to similarity in the physical conditions. Throughout the whole extent of the tract described, the strata of the earth's crust have been fractured and vertically displaced, so that those on the eastern side of the fracture have been relatively elevated, or (in other words) those on the western relatively lowered. This fracture is known amongst geologists as a " fault," and in consequence of the displacement above stated, the rocks and formations on opposite sides of this depression do not in general correspond to each other.

The existence of this great line of fracture along the depression of the Jordan Valley and of the Arabah has been recognised by Hitchcock, Tristram,[2] Wilson,[3] and Lartet,[4] who has in the clearest manner demonstrated the physical results of the displacement in the region of the Salt Sea and Jordan Valley. These observations I have had an opportunity of continuing throughout the whole length of the Wâdy el Arabah, and I have succeeded in tracing the line of this fracture from The Ghôr to the Gulf of Akabah, throughout a distance of about 120 miles.[5] The details of the geological structure of this tract will be published elsewhere ; but I may here state that the line of fault generally runs along the eastern side of the valley, and close to the base of the mountains of granite and porphyry, where its position has been determined at frequent intervals by the broken and disconnected stratification. The general direction of the fault is N. 10° E. A general section across the centre of the valley from west to east, such as that given in the adjoining page (Fig. 7), will serve to explain the relations of the formations on either side, and show the effects of the break and displacement in producing the striking contrast in the position of the formations, and in the character of the scenery, on opposite sides of the valley.

From this section it will be seen that the limestone (L) of the table-land of the Tîh, which comes down to the valley and forms its floor underneath the superficial gravel, is broken off against the granite and porphyry (G.P.) of the opposite side ; while the limestone itself is lifted vertically into

[1] Trans. Assoc. Americ. Geol., p. 348 (1841-42).

[2] "Land of Israel," 2 Edit., p. 320, et seq.

[3] Bible Dic., Art. "Arabah."

[4] "Geologie de la Mer Morte," p. 259, et seq.

[5] As shown on the geological map of the expedition. According to Robinson, Arabah is a Hebrew word signifying "a desert plain," or "steppe," and has come down to us with the prefix " El," as " El Arabah," as the great plain throughout its whole extent from The Ghôr to the Gulf of Akabah ("Bib. Res.," ii, 186).

FIG. 7.—GENERAL SECTION ACROSS THE W. EL ARABAH TO ILLUSTRATE ITS GEOLOGICAL STRUCTURE.

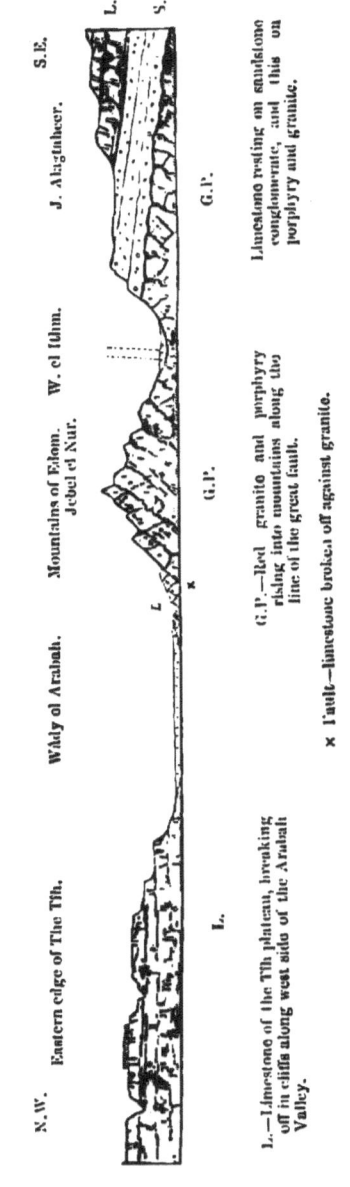

N.W. Eastern edge of The Tih. Wâdy el Arabah. Mountains of Edom. Jebel el Nur. W. el Ithm. J. Ahgtaheer. S.E.

L.—Limestone of the Tih plateau, breaking off in cliffs along west side of the Arabah Valley.

G.P.—Red granite and porphyry rising into mountains along the line of the great fault.

× Fault—limestone broken off against granite.

Limestone resting on sandstone conglomerate, and this on porphyry and granite.

the high plateau of Edom (L), the red sandstone formation (S) being interposed.

The great leading fracture above described frequently sends forth branch fractures to the right, which, in some cases but not always, follow the directions of the valleys. There are others also parallel to it; and amongst the most remarkable of these is one traversed by the Haj Road, on descending from the Tîh towards the head of the Gulf of Akabah, already described (Fig. 6, p. 68). This is the leading fracture on the western side, and enters the gulf near Ras el Musry. The ridge of reddish granite to the east of the fault is seamed by dykes of deep red porphyry and basalt, crossing each other at angles of about 60°, cutting the rock into "lozenge-shaped" sections, somewhat like the vertebræ of a backbone. The ridge stretches from Ras el Musry northwards for about ten miles. At its eastern base, by the waters of the gulf, was in all probability situated Ezion Geber, and it may be presumed that the name " the backbone of a giant," was taken from the ridge which rose so boldly and massively behind the walls of the city.[1]

When describing the coasts of the Gulf of Suez, I had occasion to refer to the evidence of the recent elevation of the sea-bed, so that gravel and sand, with shells and corals of species still living in the adjoining waters, are to be found at levels up to 200 feet above the present surface. This elevation is not local, and may be supposed to have influenced the whole region of Arabia Petræa, and therefore the shores of the Gulf of Akabah. Accordingly, accompanied by my son, I made careful search for shells in the gravels of the valley, and not without success. The bed of the valley, sloping from the sea-margin up to the base of the mountains behind Akabah, is formed of loose gravel, and in this we found, ere leaving our camp, examples of univalves, amongst which was a *Murex*, several bivalves, an operculum, together with pieces of coral. These occurred at a level of from 80 to 90 feet above the sea ; but it could be seen that the gravel in which they occurred sloped upwards to the base of the ridge at a height of about 200 feet, so that the ridge must be considered to have once formed the rocky margin of the gulf itself. The following

---

[1] According to this view Elath (Akabah) and Ezion Geber were at opposite sides of the gulf. According to the statement of Moses they were evidently close to each other, and therefore not likely to be on the *same* side of the bay. Antoninus Martyr of Placentia, describes Æla as a port at the head of the Red Sea, about A.D. 600.

day both Hart and myself found shells (*Cardium*, *Trochus*, &c.) and
corals near our camp, at an elevation of 130 feet, and there was no reason
to doubt that they might have been found even at higher levels up the
valley.   From this it was clear that during the time that the shores
of the Gulf of Suez were depressed 200 feet (or more) lower than at
present, those of the Gulf of Akabah experienced a like submergence.
This raised beach had also been recognised by Mr. Milne, who estimated
the rise of the land at 40 feet.[1]   From the above account, however, it
will be seen the real amount of elevation has been much greater.

Our course during the next two days lay along the Arabah Valley
northwards, during which we made short excursions to the right and left.
The mountains of red porphyry and granite, seamed by numerous dykes,
towered majestically on the right; and under the rays of the setting sun
were lighted up with rich tints of red and purple.   On the left the cliffs
of sandstone, surmounted by others of limestone, formed the abrupt
margin of the Tih plateau.   During this time we had opportunities of
becoming acquainted with our new escort, under the command of Sheikh
Ali.   It was soon apparent that our Alowín were inferior to the Towâra
(whom the former affected to look down upon as not true Bedawins at
all), both in physical development and in sagacity.   Generally speaking,
our Alowín were small in stature, nearly black, a half-starved, smoke-dried
set, clad in rags or dirty garments; in a word, a gang of ragamuffins!
My own camel-driver was a poor half-witted fellow, who gave me much
trouble, and was quite unreliable at a pinch.   He was a sorry substitute
for my well-built, intelligent, and lively Sala; though, to do him justice,
he was most anxious to please; and when, some days later, I had to get
him exchanged for another, he was dreadfully downcast.

The entrance to the Wâdy Redadi, about 12 miles north of the shores
of the gulf, is remarkable for the castellated and pinnacled forms of the
limestone cliff, of which Gordon took a photograph.   In this district game
of various kinds appears to abound.   Sheikh Ali told us that ibexes were
numerous amongst the mountains on the east side, and gazelles, hares,
and partridges were observed by most of our party.   The gazelles, however, were so shy that it was almost impossible to get within shot of them.
Hart noticed one undisturbed, and was preparing to stalk it, but just as
he was approaching within range his camel began to bellow, and he saw

---

[1] Quart. Journ. Geol. Soc., vol. xxxi, p. 9, *et seq.*

his gazelle no more! Laurence also had a close view of a magnificent eagle which he estimated must have been 8 feet from tip to tip of wing. But although it kept soaring above him for some time, it was ever out of gunshot. The bird was probably attracted by a lamb which was following our camp.

I may here give a general sketch of the geological character of the Wâdy el Arabah throughout its length, which will enable the reader the better to understand the sequel, and prevent unnecessary repetition.

Fig. 8.—Jebel Nachaleagh (or Jebel Umm Kâmel) and the Edomite Mountains near Wâdy Abu Berka, as seen from the western side of the Wâdy el Arabah.   Cliffs of " Desert Sandstone " resting on granite and porphyry, and repeated by faults.

I have already spoken of the general contrast between the two sides. The eastern side is the grander and more striking of the two, except close to the Gulf of Akabah, where both sides are formed of granite and porphyry, rising into bold and rugged ridges.   On the western side these rocks soon pass below beds of sandstone, followed by others of limestone, which break off in steep escarpments with grand headlands and bastions.

There is a slight dip to the northwards, which ultimately brings the limestone down into the plain opposite Ain Gharandel. Henceforth there is a double terrace on the western side, and the strata stretch away indefinitely into the high table-land of the Tîh. At distant intervals these terraces are broken into by winding valleys, which give access to the interior of the table-land. On the eastern side the mountains of granite and porphyry behind Akabah, intensely red in colour, so as to give rise to the name of "Jebel el Nur" (or mountains of fire), gradually decline in elevation northwards, and several outliers of the Desert Sandstone are seen capping the higher elevations of the older rocks towards the head of the Wâdy Turbân. Soon afterwards, as we proceed northwards, the sandstone formation descends to lower levels, breaking off in abrupt walls and precipices in the districts of the Wâdies Gharandel and Dalâghah, and forming the escarpment of Jebel Haroun (Mount Hor), which towers conspicuously above all the other heights. Farther in the distance to the east, the light grey and brownish ridge of Jebel Zibbeyagh, forming the margin of the limestone table-land of Edom, may be seen at an elevation of about 3,000 feet above the plain. The limestone begins immediately east of the Wâdy Mûsa, behind Petra, forming the upper portion of the ridge east of this celebrated valley. In this district, however, the Desert Sandstone sometimes forms a double or treble escarpment, owing to the existence of large faults by which the strata are successively repeated, as shown in the view of J. Nachaleagh (Fig. 8).

This general succession, modified by changes in the dip, and by faulting, is continued all the way northwards to the eastern side of The Ghôr, and along the shores of the Salt Sea. At the base of the escarpment are the red sandstone cliffs, sometimes resting (as at Es Safieh) on a foundation of older crystalline rocks, and extending up the flanks of the escarpment to an elevation of 2,000 feet above the Salt Sea. To these succeed soft sandstones of variegated colours, probably belonging to the "Nubian Sandstone" formation surmounted by the Cretaceous limestone of the table-land, which stretches far away eastward into the Syrian Desert, the haunt of nomadic tribes.

The surface of the Wâdy el Arabah is variously covered by loam, gravel, and blown sands, which are often piled up in great dunes covering large areas, and form a great obstacle to travellers. Occasionally the limestone rock appears in isolated bosses or ridges, as is the case along part of the watershed about 45 miles north of Akabah. There are no continuous

rivers throughout ; and the floods which from time to time descend from
the glens, which open out on either hand, are speedily absorbed, or
evaporated, on entering the plain.   It is hence difficult to conceive how
this great valley, which is sometimes seven or eight miles in width, especially
near its centre, could have been excavated and levelled down, unless the
action of the rivers and streams of the bordering hills had originally been
supplemented by the levelling action of the sea waves on the south, and of
the inland waters of a great lake on the north, of the watershed.   As I
have already shown, there is direct evidence that the waters of the Gulf of
Akabah· originally extended to a level at least 200 feet higher than at
present ; and I shall presently give proof that those of the Salt Sea were
at a level at least as high as those of the Mediterranean, or 1,300 feet
above the present surface of the Salt Sea.[1]   If this be so, it is highly
probable that at a still earlier period, when the whole region was being
elevated out of the ocean, the waters of the two seas met from either side
of the present saddle, from 45 to 50 miles north of the Gulf of Akabah.

Shortly before noon on the 5th December we reached the wells known as
Ain el Ghudyan (Fig 9), which have been identified, with very questionable
accuracy, with the position of Kadesh Barnea.[2]   The wells are situated on
some flat and marshy ground ; one of large size, at which the camels had a
good drink, the other smaller and surrounded by stone pavements.   We
were badly off for a supply of water for future use, but there was nothing
with which to draw, though the well was not more than 8 or 10 feet deep.
At length, after much disputation, and the promise of bakhsheesh, a tall

---

[1] The old terraces of gravel and sand, with univalve shells, which occur near the
spot of our camp of the 13th December, can only be referred in my opinion to the
action of the Salt Sea when at a high level, there being no barrier towards the
north.   The aneroid stood at 29·0 at this spot, and was very much the same as
at the margin of the Gulf of Akabah.

[2] The position of Kadesh Barnea is a subject of much uncertainty, but it
may be inferred to have lain somewhere inwards from the western margin of the
Wâdy el Arabah to the north of the watershed.   Mr. Holland came to the conclusion that this place was either at Ain Kadeis, at the western end of Jebel
Magrah, or at the eastern base of this mountain near the head of Wâdy Garaiyeh
(*Quarterly Statement*, Jan. 1884, p. 5).   Dr. Trumbull, following the views of the
late Rev. J. Rolands, and having personally visited the spot, concurs in identifying
Ain Kadeis (one of the alternative spots of Mr. Holland) as Kadesh Barnea ;
and names Jebel Madurah of that district as Mount Hor ("Kadesh Barnea,"
1884, p. 129, *et seq*.)   I am inclined to concur in the former identification, but
not in the latter.   See p. 188, *et seq*.

Fig. 9.—Ain el Ghudyan, in the Wâdy el Arabah. (*From a photograph by Dr. E. Gordon Hull.*)

Arab divested himself of his light garments, and jumped down the sides laughing and shouting. The waterskins were thrown down to him by the others, who joined in the chorus, and our water barrels were soon filled.

On Thursday, 6th December, we encamped near the centre of the Arabah Valley in an oasis of green shrubs surrounded by sandhills. The general features of the valley had quite changed. On the east the grand terraces of red sandstone of Jebel Zibbeyagh and Jebel Nachaleagh, surmounting their granitic foundations, rose to elevations of 2,000 or 3,000 feet, and along the deep depression of the Wâdy Gharandel formed massive walls, with horizontal courses of natural masonry. But on the western side the almost continuous limestone escarpment had sunk down and disappeared, and a great expanse of sandy plain stretched away for many miles towards the north-west, opening an uninterrupted entrance into the region of the Tîh. This expanse, however, was partially broken by a low ridge of limestone, at the end of which, at a distance of six miles, the solid line of the watershed stretched across the valley to the base of the eastern ridge ; and beyond, to the north-east, the broken heights leading up to Mount Hor bounded the landscape. We were at length about to reach the long wished for "saddle" of the Wâdy el Arabah, towards which we had been slowly rising day by day for four days ; and early in the afternoon our luncheon tent was pitched on the saddle itself, and we could look north-wards down the descent of the Arabah Valley towards the depression of the Salt Sea.

Wâdy Gharandel.—Throughout our wanderings we met with three valleys of this name. One entering the Gulf of Suez, two days' march from Ayun Mûsa ; another descending from the mountains of Edom, about 40 miles north of Akabah ; and the third descending from the table land of Moab, and entering the Salt Sea from the south-east. These valleys are all remarkable for their physical features ; and our camp on the 6th December was nearly opposite the entrance of the second of these, where it opens out on the valley of the Arabah. Near its entrance are some wells (Ayun Gharandel), which were visited by Laborde and Vignes. The valley itself was explored by my son, together with Messrs. Hart and Laurence. On passing by some low bluffs of loose sand we saw the entrance to the valley between cliffs of hard coarse puddingstone over 100 feet high, which rest on the limestone formation. This conglomerate is formed of blocks and fragments, chiefly of sandstone, porphyry, and metamorphic rock, derived from the cliffs further east. Here the valley

G 2

is pretty wide, and contains a fair amount of shrubs and acacias.   After winding up the valley for a mile in an easterly direction, it appears as if about to come to an abrupt termination.   A spring of fresh water wells out, giving rise to a considerable amount of verdure.   The cliffs are formed of red porphyry, which here rises up sharply against the limestone.   We have in fact crossed the main fault of the Wâdy el Arabah.   The porphyry is surmounted by other cliffs of the red Desert Sandstone.   Through this mass of rock a small stream has cut its channel, and the only way up the valley is by this narrow chasm, averaging about 10 feet across, and bounded by walls gradually increasing in height.   After passing up this for a few hundred yards, the chasm widens out somewhat ; and the sandstone cliffs gain an altitude of over 800 feet, forming a magnificent and almost perpendicular wall of rock, specially towards the north.   Some time was spent in this grand valley, which lays open the structure of the Edomite mountains almost to their centre.   Having taken some photographs the party returned, and reached the camp at the base of Jebel Haroun long after dark.

During the day, when crossing the numerous sand-dunes, it helped to pass the time to note the many and varied footprints often clearly impressed on their surface.   Of these the most numerous were those of the gazelle, which are somewhat like those of a sheep, but sharper and more closely compacted ; others of hyænas, and a few of large felines, probably leopards.   If one were to draw a conclusion from the great numbers of these footprints it would be that during the night the whole surface of the valley is alive with wild animals, which emerge from their dens and hiding-places in search of food and water.

After a long and fatiguing ride over very broken ground we camped in the Wâdy Abu Kuseibeh, near the entrance to the Wâdy Haroun, and at a distance of about five miles from the base of Mount Hor.

FIG. 10.—MOUNT HOR (JEBEL HAROUN) AS SEEN FROM THE WATERSHED OF THE WÁDY EL ARABAH, LOOKING NORTH-EASTWARD.

CHAPTER XI.

PETRA AND MOUNT HOR.

WE rose early next day to commence our short day's journey towards Petra. All around we beheld a sea of ridges and furrows of various rocks—and still more varied colours—tints of red, purple, and grey predominating, and we camped at the entrance of a grand gorge leading up into the heart of the Mountains of Edom, there to await the arrival of the Sheikhs of Petra, who we felt sure would not be long in making their presence known.

During our progress up the Wâdy el Arabah we had seen from time to time the English engineers whom I have already described as having passed our tents in the Wâdy el Ain, and whom we afterwards found camped at Akabah on our arrival there. We had had no communication, as they appeared to desire to avoid our company, and had forbid their dragoman (as we were informed) even to divulge their names. It may be presumed they were engaged in endeavouring to ascertain by the barometric process the elevation of the watershed of the Arabah above the Gulf of Akabah. On our part the observations of this same point would necessarily be more complete, as the level could be determined, not only by means of the aneroid, but by that of the theodolite, and also from both sides ;—that of the Gulf of Akabah and of the Salt Sea, the depth of which below the Mediterranean had been accurately determined by the Ordnance Survey of Palestine by actual levelling from the Mediterranean itself. It can therefore be stated[1] that the height of the saddle is nearly 700 feet; but even were

[1] DETERMINATIONS OF THE ELEVATION OF THE WATERSHED, W. EL ARABAH.

				Above Gulf of Akabah.
Mr. R. Laurence, 6 Dec., 1883, by aneroid ..	..	..	..	910 feet.
Do.	Do.	deduced from hypsometrical determination of elevation of Mount Hor ..	.. .. ..	390 ,,
			Mean	650 ,,
M. Vignes' determination, 240 métres	..	..	..	787 ,,
Major Kitchener and Mr. Armstrong's determination by triangulation ..	.. .. ..	.. ..	..	660 ..
			Mean of all	699 feet.

it less than this it is clear that it would render a ship canal impracticable except it was to be worked by locks ; but for this purpose a large and constant supply of running water from some still higher source would be required, and this is not to be found in the region on either side of the great valley. I therefore regard the proposal of a ship canal in the line of the Jordan Valley, and of the Wâdy el Arabah, as impracticable from a purely physical point of view, even supposing that the political and social obstacles could be overcome.

We now commenced our preparations for a visit to Petra, the ancient capital of the Nabatheans, and to Mount Hor, the sepulchre of Aaron. No more grand monument could be erected to the memory of a man honoured of God than that which nature has here raised up. For, amidst this region of natural pyramids, Jebel Haroun towers supreme, and from its summit Aaron was doubtless enabled to look across the great valley to the hills of Judæa, which he was only to behold from afar. Thus Jehovah, in passing sentence of premature death upon his servant for a public act of disobedience, left him not to die without honour ; and for ever after, the most conspicuous hill in all this country has been inseparably connected with his name, and stands as a monument to his memory.

Mount Hor is formed of reddish sandstone and conglomerate, rising in a precipitous wall of natural masonry, tier above tier, with its face to the west. The base of the cliff of sandstone rests upon a solid ridge of granite and porphyry, and the summit of the sandstone is somewhat in the form of a rude pyramid, on which is built a little white mosque, supposed to be over Aaron's tomb. This mosque was an object easily to be recognised for triangulating purposes. On the 10th December, Major Kitchener and Mr. Armstrong succeeded in planting the theodolite on the summit of the mount, and in taking several angles on other conspicuous points. The mount is flanked by two remarkable bastions of sandstone, standing erect on the granitic base, and somewhat in advance of the mural cliffs.

On our way up to the entrance to the Wâdy Haroun, the gorge by which Mount Hor and Petra are approached from the west, we passed numerous flocks of sheep and goats browsing on the shrubs of the valley. We had intended to push on up the gorge, and some of our party thought that they might be able unobserved to climb Mount Hor (as had previously been done by Professor Palmer), and thus steal a march upon the inhabitants of Petra ; but on approaching the entrance an obstacle presented itself which we had not expected. Our Sheikh Ali dismounted from his camel, and turning round to us protested by all that was sacred that, if any of us ascended Jebel Haroun without the permission of Sheikh Arari of Wâdy Mûsa, he would return back to Akabah. To do so, he said, would produce a feud between himself and his friend, the Sheikh of Petra, and he would not be responsible for the consequences. After much disputation it was agreed that we should pitch our tents near the entrance to the gorge, still on his (Sheikh Ali's) ground, and then push up the pass, and hold a consultation during lunch. So on we went, Ali breaking out from time to time in protestations. The gorge was very fine ; the rocks of marvellously varied forms and colours ; and soon it contracted to a mere torrent bed, above which the cliffs of sandstone towered aloft in great precipitous walls of several hundred feet. We wound our way over blocks of rock and masses of shingle amidst luxuriant bushes of the oleander,—not however now in flower, but laden with large fruit pods—along with which were several other plants and shrubs, such as the tamarisk and the ubiquitous broom. Amongst the rocks which form the sides of the valley may be recognised massive agglomerates of volcanic origin, formed of blocks of trap, granite, and porphyry ; much older, however, than the Desert Sandstone which rests upon them, and probably of the age of the dykes of porphyry or diorite which penetrate the granitic and gneissose rocks of this region.

We accordingly proceeded up the Wâdy Haroun to a spot where the path to Petra ascends the northern side, and where there are the remains of some ancient buildings. We discussed our future course of action, and came to the conclusion that it would now be useless to attempt to ascend Mount Hor unrecognised, as we had been informed that guards had been posted to prevent our progress. A messenger was accordingly despatched to Petra to request Sheikh Arari to send word upon what terms we could visit both Petra and Mount Hor.

On returning down the valley to our camp, about four o'clock in the afternoon, Sheikh Abdullah of Petra arrived, accompanied by several other horsemen, with the reply that the Head Sheikh of Wâdy Mûsa (Sheikh Arari) was absent in Damascus ; that on no consideration could we be allowed to ascend Mount Hor, and that to visit Petra each of us (i.e., the hawajahs) would have to pay thirty dollars. We replied that we must visit both Mount Hor and Petra ;—or neither ; and that the terms were so

---

[1] Lartet has recognised this agglomerate under the name of " Poudingue de Dj. Haroun," and apparently refers it to a much more recent age.

excessive we could not entertain them.   A long and angry discussion ensued, and the prospect of an arrangement seemed less and less imminent as time went on.   At this juncture Major Kitchener produced a document which he hoped would have a wholesome effect on the minds of these unreasonable people.   It was a Firmân, granted to him when Consul for Anatolia, by which he was authorised to visit all the Holy places of the Turkish Empire !   The document was explained to the envoys from Petra, who scrutinised it closely, probably without b coming much the wiser as regards its contents.   For a time this seemed to have some effect.   They retired for consultation, and we gave them till the next morning to propose reasonable terms to us.

I may here explain that these Arabs of Petra, though practically independent, and accustomed on all occasions to have their own way with travellers, still have a lingering respect for the Sultan as the head of the Mohammedan world ; and if this respect can be made to fall in with their pecuniary interests it becomes of paramount effect.

Next morning a parley was held ; terms were proposed by us and accepted.   They were then committed to writing, and the money was counted out and placed on the table.   The document was about to be signed when a new mine was sprung by the Petra Sheikhs.   "Bakhsheesh," they said, "must be paid for the Head Sheikh Arari, absent in Damascus." Now, as his share had already been included in the sum to be paid, this was too much for us to put up with.   We all exclaimed, "Helas ! "[1]   The money was returned to the bag by Bernhard Heilpern, and I declared the negotiation at an end.   Orders were then issued to strike the tents, and to commence our march down the valley.   The Petra envoys retired, decidedly crestfallen at this turn of affairs, and at the prospect of losing the good sum which was just within their reach.   But we saw that it was necessary to give these extortioners a lesson, and to show that all travellers were not to be trifled with or fleeced with impunity.   For the time, therefore, the prospect of a visit to Petra, and of triangulating from the summit of Mount Hor, seemed at an end.

The Petra horsemen who had momentarily departed up the Wâdy Haroun soon returned, and, joined by others, followed our party.   Presently they rejoined us, and humbly asked for bakhsheesh to remunerate them for the loss of their valuable time.   This we sternly refused.   After

---

[1] *I.e.,* "finished."

another conference they came up to Major Kitchener, asking us to return, and offering easier terms. We again declined, as we had no security that if we assented they would not again fall back on the old practice of deception. After we had proceeded about six miles from our camping ground in the morning, in the direction of the Wâdy el Arabah, the Petra Sheikhs became thoroughly alarmed. They saw we were really slipping from their hands, and probably asked themselves what account would they give of all this to Sheikh Arari on his return from Damascus? At length we came to a spot bounded by an amphitheatre of rocks and favourable for camping. It being Sunday we had not intended to make a lengthened day's march, as we only wanted to place ourselves and the Petra men at a good distance apart, and to camp on a spot well within the limits of Sheikh Ali's territory. The horsemen now came up, and said that if we would camp here for the night they would assent to the terms we proposed, and take us to Petra and Mount Hor on the following day. This, after some discussion, we agreed to, the terms being written out and signed before the tents were pitched; with the addition that, all demands for bakhsheesh were to be struck out, and that the money was not to be paid over until we had returned safely to the camp. This was unpalatable to the Sheikhs; but as we were in a position to dictate terms to them, and we determined to take every precaution to secure safety and success, they were agreed to.

I will here place, side by side, for the guidance of future travellers, the terms as originally demanded by the Sheikhs of Petra, and those ultimately assented to, and carried out. It will be their own fault if they allow themselves to be imposed upon, as has too often been the case on former occasions. We believe the Gates of Petra are now open on reasonable terms to those who have nerve and will to resist extortion; and the Sheikhs, sooner than lose their visitors and the money they may bring, will come to terms on the basis now established.

ORIGINAL DEMANDS OF THE SHEIKHS.	ALTERNATIVE PROPOSALS ON OUR PART.
First demand.—30 dollars[1] for each of the six travellers for Petra (Wâdy Mûsa) only. Mount Hor denied on any terms.	22 dollars for each of the six travellers for Petra, and 12 dollars for Mount Hor. (Refused.) Total, 34 dollars.

---

[1] The money is paid in majedies, a silver coin, six of which make £1 sterling, the value is nearly that of a dollar.

Second demand.—42 dollars each for both Petra and Mount Hor; and 6 dollars each for the use of horses which were to be compulsory on us.

Total, 48 dollars each.

We dec'ined to have the horses, as we already had camels. Also the terms as being still too high.

Third demand.—54 dollars each without the horses, and 5 dollars each for the Head Sheikh Arari.

We again declined to accept these terms.

Ultimate terms.—Assented to by the Petra Sheikhs. 22 dollars each for Petra, and 6 for Mount Hor. Also, 6 each for providing supper for the Sheikhs, and 6 each as a present to Sheikh Arari, in all 204 dollars; or £34 sterling.

It was also agreed to that no money should be paid till the return of the party in safety; and that if any sum should be extorted by the inhabitants of Petra during the visit the amount was to be deducted. These were hard terms according to the views of the Sheikhs, and in fact quite unprecedented. The reader who knows something of travellers' visits to the rock-hewn city will probably concur in thinking that they were sufficiently liberal, and that the arrangement regarding the time of payment was not unnecessary.

Thus was the morning of wrangling and turmoil closed in, at least, outward harmony and peace. Our camp was pitched in the centre of a recess amongst the sandstone cliffs, and close by the pass which opens out on the Arabah plain. The Arabs took up their quarters at the foot of the cliffs, forming little groups around their fires; and over their coffee and pipes discussed with abundant vigour the events of the day. I held Divine Service in the dining tent, selecting as the first lesson for the evening the account of the death of Aaron on Mount Hor, as given in Numbers xx. All retired early to rest, preparatory to a start next morning before daybreak.

Monday, 10th December.—All our party but myself were on their camels by four o'clock, the intention being to ascend Mount Hor, make observations, and afterwards go down into Wâdy Mûsa and visit Petra, where I hoped to join them. They were accompanied by one of the Sheikhs of Petra and Sheikh Ali. Major Kitchener took his theodolite; my son took his camera and a good supply of dry plates for photographing. Hart was very sanguine of a good ingathering of specimens both zoological and botanical, and supplied himself with preserving apparatus accordingly; and Laurence took charge of the thermometrical and barometrical instru-

ments. Not feeling equal to a double day's work, I contented myself
with a start two hours later for Petra, and accompanied by Sheikh
Abdullah and another sheikh from Petra, together with our dragoman,
Ibraham, I left the camp about six o'clock ; Bernhard Heilpern remained
to take care of the camp during our absence.

It was still dark when we set out ; and we had to thread our way over
the plain towards the east by the aid of a lantern carried in front of my
camel, and so for an hour we wended our way towards the entrance of the
Pass of Wâdy Haroun. Just as day began to dawn, *but before sunrise*,
I turned to take a look at the country behind. What was my surprise
on looking beyond the Valley of the Arabah to behold the whole table-
land of the Tih to the westward lighted up with remarkable clearness, the
plains and escarpments distinguished by lines and streaks of gold and white ;
so that it might have been supposed that we were looking towards the
direction of sunrise rather than of sunset, and that this region was lit up
under the first rays of dawn. I expressed my astonishment to Ibraham ;
but that worthy was equal to the occasion. Nothing could surprise this
man ; nothing was new to *him.* He assured me that it was always so, and
that in these parts the western lands receive the sun's rays before those of
the eastern ! The effect was doubtless due to the light of the morning sun
reflected from the sky.

On entering the ravine of the Wâdy Haroun above our camp of the
previous morning, a griffon vulture (*Gyps fulvus*) appeared soaring above
my head. It was a handsome bird, and with my glass I could scan its form
and colour. The body was grey, and the wings tipped with black. Soon
another appeared ; and presently, one after another, about a dozen came in
sight, flying low or clambering up the rocks. The animals had been gorging
themselves on the carcase of a camel of our party, which, from overwork
and probably insufficient food, had dropped down from exhaustion on the
previous day.

As we were wending our way up the gorge of the W. Haroun,
Abdullah and our dragoman kept up a lively conversation. Some time
after I inquired of the latter what it was all about, and he rehearsed it to
me as follows :—

Abdullah. Have you ever been on pilgrimage ?

Ibraham. Yes ! once to Mecca, and twelve times to the mosque at
Jerusalem (El Khods).

A. Where do you live when you are at home ?

I. Cairo.

A. Is Cairo comfortable (quiet)?

I. Yes!

A. Who rules at Cairo?

I. The English and the Khedive.

A. Where is Arabi?

I. A prisoner in Ind (India or Ceylon).

A. Is Arabi comfortable?

I. Yes! I believe so.

A. Has he his family with him?

I. Yes!

A. What has he got to live on?

I. An allowance of £2 a-day.

A. What are these hawajis (name for European gentlemen) with you?

I. Inglese.

Silence ensued, during which Abdullah was probably ruminating on the fact that these same Inglese were also the rulers of Cairo. Afterwards Ibraham went on to inform Abdullah that the English had several ships of war in the Suez Canal, and that they could easily march an army "with cannon" across the Tih to Petra should any ill-treatment be offered to the travellers.

Passing again the oleander bushes, the fresh green of whose leaves was pleasant to the eye, we came to the base of the lofty sandstone cliffs where we had lunched on Saturday; and now our path left the ravine, and we struck up the mountain side to the left. The climb was stiff and difficult; enough to try the strength and skill of camels and horses even of the desert;—but they did not fail. We soon got amongst some grand rock scenery. On the right a deep ravine, partially clad with verdure, laid bare the base of the precipices of granite surmounted by great mural cliffs of red or variegated sandstone, rising in tiers to heights of 1,000 or 1,200 feet.[1] Beyond these other terraces and tors of sandstone came into view. Here, indeed, the sandstone formation of Arabia Petræa displays itself in its grandest proportions and most varied forms; and the presence of oleanders, cypresses, and other shrubs along the beds of the ravines and little glens,

---

[1] The rocks here are traversed by several large "faults" or dislocations, along one of which the pathway winds for a considerable distance. See Geological Map.

adds to the beauty and freshness of the scenery.   The cliffs were perforated
with caves and holes, where eagles, hawks, and owls find safe nesting places ;
and possibly beasts of prey, a secure retreat during the hours of day.   To
the left rose the sandstone terraces, culminating in the summit of Mount
Hor.   They have a gentle "dip" or inclination eastwards towards the
Wády Músa.   Presently, on having crossed the "Nagb," a pass between
the Wádies Haroun and Músa, we came to some ruins of ancient
buildings ; and on the left the faces of the sandstone cliffs were sculptured
around doors, or entrances, into interior chambers.   These were the
suburbs (as it were) of the ancient capital of Arabia Petræa ; and, when we
came within view of a solitary column standing on the top of a ridge,
we felt that we had entered the city itself, with its ruined temples,
theatres, palaces, rock-hewn dwellings and tombs, and possibly Christian
churches.[1]

It is not my intention to attempt any description of this wonderful
city of the past, of which Laborde has left an excellent plan within reach
of all,[2] and which has been already well described by previous travellers.   I
will only here observe that the styles of architecture and sculpturing remind
us of Egyptian, Greek, and Roman works ; secondly, that in the destruction
of these ancient structures, there have been three kinds of agencies in
action ; for not only has the hand of man and the "hand of time"—as
represented by frost, heat, and tempest—been here, but the shocks of
earthquakes have evidently been a powerful factor in the work of demolition.
This is evinced by the peculiar characteristics of the damage done in some
places.   We see not only the stones of columns partially dislocated, and
turned out of their original positions, but also in the case of some buildings,
such as "the Great Temple," those of the walls partially thrust out from
their beds into the air.   Similar phenomena have been recognised as the
results of earthquake movements both in Italy and Egypt.[3]

When gazing, now at the stupendous walls of rock which enclose the
winding valley of Wády Músa, now at the architectural ruins, the work of
the hand of man, I became profoundly impressed with the conviction that in

---

[1] Petra was the seat of an Archbishop early in the 5th century, according to
Carl Ritter.   "Palestine and Sinai," Eng. Edit. 1866. Vol. I.   For a history
of this remarkable city, see Quatremère "Mem. sur les Nabathéens." Journ Asiat.
Soc. 1835, T. xv, p. 31.

[2] See Baedeker's and Murray's Guides.

[3] By Lyell in his "Principles of Geology," &c.

originating and executing these works, man himself had been but an imitator of nature ; that he had endeavoured to reproduce artificially those forms which the natural architecture here presented to his view was well calculated to suggest to him.   The noble cliffs and rock faces at the base of Mount Hor of themselves assume forms simulating artificial structures, such as temples, fortresses, or dwellings of men.   Here may be seen three grand natural façades of sandstone ranged side by side like a line of palaces, but severed from each other by intervening spaces ; and one cannot help conjecturing that the examples of natural architecture here, as well as at other places, displayed along the sides of the valley, had suggested to the early Edomites and Nabathean inhabitants the idea of imitating in art what nature has so prominently placed before them.

The colouring of the sandstone cliffs of Wâdy Mûsa should not pass unnoticed; it is wonderfully gorgeous, possibly altogether unique.   I have seen coloured sandstone formations in the British Isles and in Europe, but never before colours of such depth and variety of pattern as these.   The walls of rock reminded one of the patterns on highly painted halls, Eastern carpets, or other fanciful fabrics of the loom.   The deepest reds, purples, and shades of yellow are here arranged in alternate bands, shading off into each other, and sometimes curved and twisted into gorgeous fantasies.   These effects, due to the infiltration of the oxides of iron, manganese, and other substances, are frequent in sandstones to various degrees ; but nowhere, as far as my observation goes, do they reach the variety of form and brilliancy of colouring to be found in the Wâdy Mûsa amongst the ruins of Petra.

Little time was allowed for an examination of Petra, or the Wâdy Mûsa, as the days were short ; and, owing to the difficulty, not to say danger, of traversing the mountain path in the dark, it was necessary to allow ourselves time to get out of the Wâdy Haroun before sunset.   My companions had not joined me when I began to retrace my steps.   As it afterwards turned out, when the party reached the summit of Mount Hor, they found themselves in mist, which delayed the trigonometrical observations for nearly two hours.   Hence much precious time was lost, and their visit to the Wâdy Mûsa was consequently a hurried one.   We all reached the camp, however, in safety, our party about an hour after sunset, the other about four hours later.   Fortunately for them a brilliant moon shed its light on their path, and enabled them to avoid the pitfalls with which the road over the Nagb was beset.

The results of the day's work were very valuable. Major Kitchener and his assistant, Mr. Armstrong, were successful in taking angles on several prominent points, both backwards and forwards, along the line of the Arabah valley, and as far north as the hills overlooking The Ghôr. Mr. Hart found a considerable number of plants, amongst others three species of ferns, indicating a moister and more temperate climate than that we had experienced, and leading to the belief that in spring time the mountain side must exhibit a rich carpeting of flowers, such as crocuses, lilies, and amarillas, which were only now appearing above ground. Mr. Laurence took barometrical readings at the summit of the mountain, in addition to those of the hypsometer (an instrument for determining altitudes by the temperature of the boiling point of water). To myself the observations I was enabled to make on the geological structure of the Edomite range were of essential value in the construction of the geological map of that part of the district. We were all delighted with our visit to this most wonderful of cities, and congratulated ourselves on having accomplished it on terms far more favourable than those of previous visitors. I here give the altitude of Mount Hor as determined by the aneroid observations of Mr. Laurence.

Altitude of Mount Hor (Jebel Haroun).

	English feet.
Altitude by boiling point of water above camp (W. Kuseibeh)	3,340
„ aneroid above camp	3,320
Mean	3,330
Elevation of camp above Gulf of Akabah (about)	1,450
Height of Mount Hor above Gulf of Akabah	4,780
„ „ „ Dead Sea, 4,780 + 1,292	6,072

The elevation of Mount Hor, as determined by the hypsometer, was 4,260 feet, and of Petra 2,935 feet, and it is probable that these are more reliable results. The elevation of the former, as determined by Major Kitchener by triangulation, is 4,580 feet.

The next morning (Tuesday, 11th December), we broke up our camp for a march into the Arabah, but a scene, half tragic, half comic, was first to be enacted. Our conductor handed to the sheikhs the money and the *bakhsheesh* agreed upon, but still they were not satisfied. All night long the Petra envoys, Sheikh Ali, and others had kept up a protracted wrangle, and next morning the gale increased to a storm. We had strictly fulfilled the terms of our contract, and nothing would induce us to alter it by a hair's breadth. After the envoys had been paid they should have departed. We were on Sheikh Ali's ground, and they were intruders. We requested them to leave the camp, but they remained shouting and gesticulating, and demanding more money. We then requested Ali to eject them, but he dallied, and the confusion increased. Bernhard then told Ali that he was no sheikh at all, or " only a quarter of one," as he was unable to protect his territory from intruders, and his convoy from the insults of these Petra robbers! This was more than Ali could bear. In great fume he called his men to arms, and when I emerged from my tent in the morning I found the clansmen " standing to their guns"—in other words, standing in a row with their long flint locks resting on the ground, the men themselves scarcely able to conceal a grin of amusement. The scene was comical enough; the old guns would have been of little use, and I rather think that one of our revolvers would have been more than a match for a dozen of them. The display of force, however, was not against *us*, but against the Petra Sheikhs, who finding things beginning to look serious and that nothing more was to be got out of our "man of iron," Bernhard Heilpern, mounted their nags and rode out of the camp towards the hills; Sheikh Abdullah declaring that if he should catch Heilpern within ten miles of Petra he " would do for him;" and the latter, that if he should ever catch Abdullah within twenty miles of Jerusalem, he should do the like for him!

With such farewells we watched our Petra guides ride up towards their native haunts; we ourselves were soon on the march in the opposite direction towards the Great Valley, where we camped in the evening, glad to leave behind us such a den of thieves.

Jebel Magrah.   W. Garaiyeh.

Jebel Jeráfeh.

W. Jeráfeh.

A. Johnson, delt.

FIG. 11.—PASS BETWEEN JEBELS MAGRAH AND JERÁFEH. *(From a sketch by the late Rev. F. W. Holland.)*

View looking eastwards across the Jeráfeh Valley to the opposite Mountains.

CHAPTER XII.

INTO THE WÂDY EL ARABAH AGAIN.

THE Wâdy el Arabah, west of Mount Hor, becomes a great plain about 15 miles across. Under the circumstances in which we were placed a detailed survey of both sides became impracticable. Having a more certain knowledge of the west side than of the east, we accordingly devoted more of our attention to the latter, and worked our way northwards at no great distance from the base of the hills. The plain is here formed of sand and gravel composed of great varieties of stone, such as granite, porphyry, felstone, quartz, sandstone, and limestone. Near the west side rise Jebels Jerâfeh and Magrah, or Mukrah (Fig. 11).

The plain was occasionally strewn with blocks of porphyry, granite, and trap, with a few of sandstone of considerable size—some measuring 14 inches across, and occasionally sub-angular. Nevertheless, many of them, if not all, must have been carried down from the interior mountains by the torrents, and spread over the great plain by the vast floods which have left their channels as evidence of their occasional presence. It may be possible, on the other hand, that the presence of such large blocks may date down from a time when the waves of the retreating sea washed the bases of the mountains and caused the cliffs to crumble into pieces. In the afternoon we came upon the dry bed of a large stream, flowing northwards between banks of reddish clay, under which the limestone floor of the plain was sometimes disclosed ; and shortly afterwards, on reaching an elevation, the hills of Judæa and the basin of the Salt Sea came into view. This was hailed by cheers from our party, and a few hundred yards more brought us to our camp.

My readers may here be inclined to put the question to me, How does it come to pass that you were on your way down towards the Salt Sea, inasmuch as by the arrangement with Sheikh Ali, he was to take the party across the Desert of the Tîh towards Gaza instead of along the route towards the north into The Ghôr ?[1]   I feel that some explanation of this is due, and

[1] The Ghôr (or Depression) is the name for the deep basin in which the Salt Sea (Bahr Lut) lies.

H

I have deferred it to this point in order not to interrupt the thread of
the previous narrative. The fact was that our plans had undergone a
complete change previous to our expedition to Petra, and it came about
in this wise.

Sheikh Ali, amongst other qualities, not restricted to Arabs, was fond
of money. Like his brother, Mohammed, he was a devoted worshipper of
" the almighty dollar," and he had probably been pondering for some time
on the best means of adding to the treasures he was to receive from us
Englishmen by some special service. He was aware of our desire to
traverse the whole of the Great Valley down to the shore of the "Bahr
Lut," or Salt Sea, and of the disappointment it had been to us when his
brother Mohammed Ibn Jhad had declared his inability to forward us in
that direction beyond one day's march from the Wády Kuseibeh. Ali
however, had no such scruples ; and being now his own master, he resolved
to make a proposal which would have the twofold advantage of falling in
with our views and of putting some additional dollars into his own pocket.
On the morning of the 7th December, as we were approaching the watershed, he hinted to our dragoman, Ibraham, the idea that to reach the Salt
Sea in a direct line down the Wády el Arabah was not absolutely
impracticable ; and that having a great desire to forward our views, he
would undertake all the risks and dangers appertaining to such an exploit,
provided a sufficient inducement were held out to him on our side.

Ibraham was not long in communicating this intelligence to our conductor, Bernhard Heilpern, who at once entered into negotiations with
Sheikh Ali, and a sum of 100 dollars was ultimately agreed upon. We
were seated in our luncheon tent on the afternoon of the 7th December,
which was pitched on the gravelly terrace forming part of the watershed
of the Arabah, and, looking northward towards the hills overhanging the
basin of the Salt Sea, we felt how hard was our lot that our passage thereto
was barred ;--that our plan of a survey from end to end was beyond our
powers, owing to the fears, real or pretended, on the part of our Sheikh
and his brother ; and that the interesting series of observations on the
topography and geology of the great valley were now about to be abruptly
broken off. On the other hand, the prospect before us was one sufficiently
discouraging. There, to our left, lay the great limestone table-land of the
Tíh, which all travellers had condemned as for the most part monotonous,
dreary, and uninviting. Over this " Desert of the wanderings " lay our
journey towards Gaza of about ten days' march, where we expected to

arrive—if indeed our camels would have strength to carry us so far[1]—scorched, weary, and downcast at the interruption of our projects.

I was full of such thoughts when, on the occasion above specified, Bernhard informed me that he was about to communicate intelligence which would be a pleasant surprise. " I listened with all my ears," as he related his conversation with Sheikh Ali, and asked my sanction to the negotiation. This I had no hesitation in giving at once, without waiting for a consultation with my colleagues, and the matter was concluded. In the evening I had the pleasure of communicating the tidings to the rest of our party, and of witnessing their satisfaction at the good news. Thus it came to pass that on leaving the Wâdy Kuseibeh we were able to continue our march northwards towards The Ghôr ;—little thinking that, notwithstanding our reprieve, we were still destined at a future day to visit Gaza !

On Wednesday evening (12th December), we encamped near the springs called Ain Abu Werideh. It was a novel sight to see clear running water lined by thickets of young palms, tamarisks, willows, reeds, and bullrushes ; and the numerous well-trod paths leading to the banks of the stream, showing impressions of the feet not only of sheep, but of gazelles and other wild animals, indicated how much the water was appreciated by *them*. Still, it was saline to the taste, and reminded one of some of the mineral waters sold in England. About half a mile north of our camp we came upon an extensive swamp, lying between steep banks of sand, gravel, and marl, and grown over with trees, plants, and reeds. On looking down into this dense mass of vegetation one could not doubt that it was the haunt of wild animals, especially of wild pigs ; and Mr. Laurence, in exploring a part of the thicket, came upon the lairs of two carnivores, in one of which bones of a recently devoured camel were lying about. The sands above the banks were also covered in all directions by the *spurs* of various animals.

But a new point of interest regarding the physical history of this part of the Great Valley here presented itself to us. On every side I found myself confronted by banks of horizontally stratified materials, through which the streams had cut down channels, and thus laid them bare and open for examination. These banks were sometimes of coarse material,

---

[1] We had afterwards reason to thank Providence that we had not to traverse the Tîh to Gaza, as it became certain our camels had not sufficient strength for such a journey. One of them (as we have seen) actually died the day following of exhaustion.

such as gravel ; at other times they consisted of fine sand, loam, or white marl, with very even stratification, and contained blanched semi-fossil shells of at least two kinds of univalves, which Professor Haddon has kindly determined for me to be *Melania tuberculata*, Müll,[1] and *Melanopsis Saulcyi*, Bourg. (Fig. 12).[1]

From the position of these strata it was clear that they occupy the bed of a wide depression, gradually narrowing southwards, but opening northwards in the direction of the great basin of the Salt Sea. In that direction there was no solid barrier by which they could have been banked up so as to form lake deposits isolated from those bordering The Ghôr itself. That they were deposits of an ancient lake was to me perfectly clear ; but was I to suppose that they had been deposited under the waters of the

Salt Sea when they stood at the level of these terraces of marl, silt, and gravel? This was a question of so startling a kind that I hesitated for some time to reply to it, though my aneroid marked 29·9 inches — almost exactly that of the shore of the Gulf of Akabah ! We were therefore (approximately) at the level of this gulf and of the Mediterranean, or nearly 1,300

Fig. 12. —Shells from the ancient bed of the Salt Sea near Ain Abu Weridch.

feet above the waters of the Salt Sea itself. If therefore these deposits were those of the ancient sea-bed, its waters must have been at least 1,300 feet higher than at present. I reserved my assent to so startling a conclusion ; but before I left the district no shadow of doubt remained on my mind that this had indeed been the case.[2]

During the three following days we were frequently within view of a remarkable ridge, called Samrat Fiddûn, rising to an elevation of 844 feet

---

[1] Tristram mentions these shells as occurring in great numbers in a semi-fossil condit'on on the marl deposits by the Dead Sea (" Fauna and Flora of Palestine," p. 196). Both of these genera are also found in the fluvio-marine beds of the Isle of Wight, formed in brackish or salt waters.

[2] The deposits rise about 100 feet higher than that stated. I called Mr. Hart's attention to this interesting physical problem, and he quite concurred in the conclusion I had arrived at. The evidence will be given at greater length in another place.

above the sea, and only connected by a slight saddle with the heights which form the boundary of the Great Valley on the eastern side. This ridge is formed of red and grey granite, with dykes of porphyry, and from its summit Major Kitchener made a successful series of triangulations. Accompanied by Mr. Armstrong I examined an adjoining ridge of less elevation, at some distance to the westward of Samrat Fiddân, and was surprised to find its summit composed of gravel and boulders of granite, basalt, and porphyry, piled up in the manner of a moraine, or of a vast shingle beach. As the idea of ice action is here out of the question, I was obliged to conclude that we had before us an old littoral beach, belonging to the period when the waters of the Salt Sea washed the base of the adjoining ridge, and that the ridge itself is an old sea margin.[1] From its base the plain stretches across westward to the escarpment of the Tîh at a distance of six or seven miles, and the Great Fault of the Wâdy el Arabah ranges along the western margin of the ridge, by which the limestone forming the floor of the valley underneath the lacustrine deposit is " brought down " against the granite. The plain is traversed by the Wâdy el Jeib and its tributaries, along the banks of which occur terraces of breccia or conglomerate, sometimes calcareous, and formed of pebbles of porphyry, limestone, &c., sometimes resting on sand or silt. These beds have been recognised by M. L. Lartet as ancient deposits of the Dead Sea, of a period when the hydrographical conditions were very different from those of the present time.[2]

On Friday, 14th December, we pitched our tents near the entrance to the Wâdy Suweireh, north of the Samrat ridge ; and as Major Kitchener wished for time to survey the western margin of the limestone plateau beyond the Jeib, it was arranged to remain here two nights. We were now within a day's march of the edge of The Ghôr, and it was deemed a good opportunity to despatch a messenger to Jerusalem for horses and mules for our party, to meet us on our arrival at Es Safieh, in order to proceed up to the Holy City by the western shore of the Salt Sea and Ain Jidi,[3] according to the instructions of the Committee. There was only one Bedawin amongst our party who knew the road, and being aware of this

---

[1] I here picked up a porcupine's quill. Though these animals exist through-out a large tract of The Ghôr, they are so shy and nocturnal in their habits as to be seldom visible.

[2] " Geologie de la Mer Morte," pp. 171-3.

[3] The Arabic name for En-gedi (1 Sam. xxiv, 1).

he put a high value on his services. Twelve dollars to take a letter to the agent of Messrs. T. Cook and Son were offered and refused. He demanded fourteen, to which we assented. After this he said he was afraid to go lest he should be killed. We began to suspect that our Sheikh was tampering with him, as it was the interest of the former to detain us as long as possible in The Ghôr. Under this view I sent a polite message to Sheikh Ali to inform him that, if he attempted to detain our messenger, we should dismiss him and his men right off, and march down into The Ghôr, and place ourselves under the protection of the Ghawarneh. This had the desired effect ; the messenger no longer demurred, but required a companion. To this reasonable proposition we agreed, and also to divide sixteen dollars between them both. It was a splendid moonlit night when our Arabs started off on their long and somewhat perilous journey ; for it was just possible they might be captured by the Arabs of Palestine, and be taken for spies or robbers. Nor would this have been surprising, for a more villainous-looking savage was not, I feel sure, to be found in all the Desert of Arabia than was our messenger, Hassam. He was armed with a club which he said he carried to keep off "robbers." This being a term of wide application might be considered to include all who made themselves obnoxious to its owner. He was induced to part with it for a small sum ; and it is now in the possession of my son. One of the Sheikhs of the Hawatha, who "happened to drop in" at this time, gave them advice how to proceed, and soon they were off towards the western shore of the Bahr Lut,[1] each bearing a missive in duplicate to the Agent at Jerusalem.

On the following day some of our party made an excursion into the mountains to the east. We entered the Wâdy Suweireh, and ascending up its western side, crossed a remarkable gap (or nagb) into the Wâdy el Weibeh. Just at this spot is the junction of the red sandstone formation with the older rocks. The sandstone rising in a grand cliff on the left of the gap, and the granitic rocks on the right. Just as I was engaged in making a drawing of this remarkable geological feature, Sheikh Ali had reached the crest of the gap mounted on his camel. It was probably the first time he had looked down into the Wâdy el Weibeh, of which one day he might possibly be the lord. Whatever might have been his reflections, there he stood motionless as a statue, surveying the scene—certainly a grand one—in front of him. The opportunity was not to be lost. In a

[1] Lot's Sea, the name by which the Salt Sea, or Dead Sea, is known amongst the Arabs.

few seconds Gordon had set up his camera, and the form of the Sheikh and his surroundings were portrayed on the photographic plate ere he commenced to move away.[1]

The scenery of the Wâdy el Weibeh was indeed enough to impress a less observant man than Sheikh Ali. After passing through the Gap of the Wâdy Suweireh (or Valley of the Necklace), so called from the string of palm trees, we found ourselves on the edge of a wide plain, broken by several small ridges and furrows, beyond which rose a grand escarpment of yellow limestone, stretching from the great shoulder it presents to the

FIG. 13.—PASS INTO THE W. EL WEIBEH.

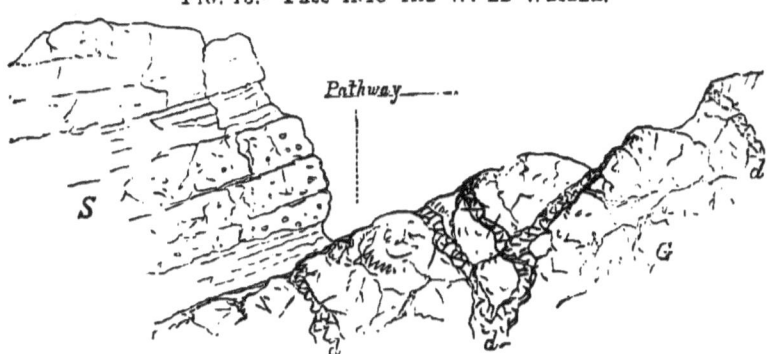

Cliffs of red and purple sandstone and conglomerate (*S*) resting on porphyry (*C*), penetrated by dykes of felstone and diorite. (*d*)

valley of the Arabah on the west, to the culminating scarp of Jebel Salamah on the east, a distance of some five or six miles. Parallel to and below the limestone escarpment, were several others of the sandstone formation, dipping below the former, and breaking off in steep, sometimes precipitous, cliffs, highly coloured with tints of yellow, brown, red, or purple. The valley itself was by no means destitute of verdure. Numerous small palms, shrubs, and plants decorated its surface, and set off the coloration of the sandstone cliffs to advantage. On *our* side the valley was limited by a dark ridge of granite, porphyry, and greenstone; and far away in the distance the horizon was bounded by the limestone tableland of Moab, which looked (from our position) as if decked with a forest

[1] In the photograph, however, the sheikh and his camel only appear like a speck; so deceptive as to size and distance are objects in this region.

vegetation ; but, as we are informed by the late Mr. W. Amherst Hayne, no trees, not even shrubs or bushes, exist over the whole of the great plateau of Moab, except at Jebel Attarus.[1] Perhaps, however, this observation does not apply to the *sides* of the plateau, which were within view from our camp.

We learn that the Bedawins from Petra are closing around us, and fires are visible in various directions. We think it as well to be on the move, and to get down amongst the friendly Ghawarnehs, by the shore of the Salt Sea. One sheikh has done us the honour to follow us from the Wâdy Mûsa, and demands " bakhsheesh " for the loss of his valuable time. He has planted his spear in the camp, and had supper ; but on the question of money he finds Bernhard Heilpern "a man of iron." "Why have you followed us ?" he asks. "Have you brought us letters from our friends, or despatches from Akabah or Petra ?" The sheikh has to admit that he has done nothing to earn the money ; and, deeply offended, he takes his spear, mounts his camel, and rides off, henceforth our enemy.

As we were retiring for the night, flashes of lightning were seen towards the south-west over the Tîh country. Presently the rumbling of thunder grew more and more distinct, and a little later the whole air was resonant with successive peals. One discharge burst forth just over our camp, and the reverberations from the adjoining mountains were so mixed with the direct discharges that the effect was that of a continuous cannonade. The whole storm passed over in about half-an-hour, and only a few drops of rain fell in our camp, but amongst the mountains to the right the rain had come down in torrents, as was shown by the numerous watercourses we had to cross the following day.

Disintegration of the rocks of the Wâdy el Arabah.—No one who has not seen it can fully realise the extraordinary way in which the rocks of this tract are breaking down and crumbling into dust. In Europe and the British Isles frost and ice are powerful disintegrators, and Col. Sir C. W. Wilson has observed the effects of frost in the higher elevations of the Sinaitic peninsula in dislodging large masses of granite ; but here there is neither frost nor ice. Still, not less rapidly, but, as I should judge from appearances, even more rapidly, are the agents of disintegration at work. On a large scale, it is true, the mountains and cliffs are solid : but their outer surfaces are generally completely rotten. Whether it be

---

[1] " Land of Moab," p. 390.

granite, porphyry, trap of any kind, or limestone, the result is the same. Sandstone is, perhaps, the least friable amongst the several varieties of rock. Let any one scramble up the sides of a hill formed of granite, porphyry, or limestone, and he will find everything give way under his feet. If the side be pretty steep he will experience the not very agreeable sensation of treading upon a heap of loose cinders. The stones have no cohesion; they are burnt, broken, gritty, and most unpleasant to tread on. I was often reminded on such occasions of the ascent of the slaggy cone of Vesuvius.[1] Again, let any one try to collect specimens of granite, porphyry, or other varieties of trap-rock, and he will find it often next to impossible to get one with a fresh fracture. He strikes with his hammer an apparently solid block, and he finds it break into small pieces, each surface of which (except that of the original exterior) is coated with dust which has somehow penetrated into little joints and fissures quite invisible to the eye. When my son and I were engaged in collecting specimens from the ridge of Samrat Fiddán, we had frequent instances of this kind ; and it was with much difficulty we could obtain specimens with fresh surfaces.

What, it may be asked, are the agents of disintegration in a region where frost and snow are unknown, and where the rainfall is small and fitful ? The answer, as it seems to me, is to be found when we consider the extraordinary diurnal ranges of temperature to which this region is subjected. During the day the powerful rays of a nearly vertical sun in a cloudless sky raise the temperature of the rocks to a high degree. They are sometimes almost too hot to be touched by the bare feet of the Arab, or the bare hand of the European. Thus they are baked and scorched to an extraordinary degree ; all moisture is driven out, and the material expands with the high temperature. Afterwards night ensues, and when the sun sets the rapid radiation of the heat into the atmosphere speedily reduces the temperature, which after midnight falls very low. A temperature of 85° Fahr. to 90° Fahr. in the shade, and 120° in the sun, falls during the night as low as 45°–50° Fahr. Expansion and contraction are consequently continually operating upon the outer portions of the rocks,

---

[1] Similar phenomena have been observed by Mr. A. B. Wynne in the districts of Kutch, and in the Trans-Indus salt region, where the atmospheric conditions, and some parts of the geology, are not unlike those of the district above referred to. See "Geology of Kutch," Mem. Geol. Survey, India, vol. ix, p. 22, and "Geol. of Trans-Indus Salt Region," *ibid.*, vol. xi, p. 17.

which are ready to split up and crumble away along the planes of bedding, or of jointage, whether visible or concealed, by which they are traversed. Then when a thunderstorm happens to come, with its deluge of rain, raising in a few moments a torrent which rushes down every dell, and converts waterless valleys into impetuous river-beds, the stones give way in all directions, and are swept down and spread over the plains to a distance scarcely credible. In such a way may we explain the striking results of atmospheric denudation in this region,—the formation of the lofty precipices, the grand escarpments, the jagged peaks, the long and deep valleys, and the presence of the alluvial detritus which overspreads the spacious plains.

FIG. 14.—TERRACES ABOVE THE DESCENT TO THE GHÔR.

Beds of white marl and silt, formerly the bed of the ancient Salt Sea (Bahr Lut).
About 1,050 feet above its present level.

We were now on the road traversed by Robinson, Palmer, and Drake. It was difficult to traverse, being formed alternately of the beds of torrents and of soft sand dunes piled up by winds from the south-west, and often rising high on the sides of the limestone cliffs on our right ; for here the limestone forms the flanks of the Wâdy el Arabah on both sides. On our left the great marly plain, the ancient floor of the Salt Sea, stretched away to the banks of the Jeib, and the escarpment of the Tih beyond. We passed several parties of the Alowîns, and of other tribes about Petra, returning with their little donkeys laden with corn, which they had purchased from the Ghawarnehs of Es Safieh, and were carrying home for the use of their families.

On crossing the Wâdy T'lah, a deep ravine, descending from the mountains on the right, and giving rise to a dense vegetation of tamarisks, thorny acacias, and bamboo canes, we found ourselves for the first time since leaving Petra amongst ruins of solid masonry, evidently the walls of a reservoir, constructed to receive the waters of the brook during floods. The north and south walls were 70 feet long, those east and west 85 feet in the interior. A little below was a pile of ruined walls, probably those of a dwelling, and beyond on the flat the outlines of extensive fields. Major Kitchener considered these ruins to have belonged to one of the numerous Arab cultivators, who, several hundred years ago, had occupied the district we were now traversing. Here there was evidence of an elaborate system of irrigation, and of a state of rural prosperity which has since disappeared, probably owing to the depredations of the mountain tribes. We were to have opportunities further north of witnessing similar instances where cultivated places had lapsed into a state of nature.

Standing on these ruins, and looking in a north-westerly direction across the valley, here about five miles wide, we beheld the terraces of white marl and silt, originally the bed of the Salt Sea, spread over a wide area, and bounded by the limestone cliffs of the Tih. Where cut into by river courses, these nearly horizontal strata form a series of tabulated terraces from 20 to 30 feet high (Fig. 14). We left the road in order to examine them, with the hope of finding shells, or some other relics of former aqueous life ; but our search was not rewarded with success, notwithstanding the occurrence of the univalves before referred to in the terraces near our camp at Ain Abu Werideh. Our elevation here was about 250 feet below the level of the Mediterranean, or 1,050 feet above that of the Salt Sea, now about 15 miles to the north of our position. Towards evening we camped on a terrace near the edge of the deep ravine, the Wâdy Butachy ; looking across which the eye rested with admiration on the grand escarpment of the cretaceous limestone surmounting the red cliffs and terraces of sandstone, which rise along the line of th Wâdy Gharandel, and range northwards along the eastern shores of the Salt Sea.

CHAPTER XIII.

THE GHÔR AND THE SALT SEA.

ON Sunday morning, 16th December, after fifteen days of toilsome travel since leaving Akabah, we found ourselves standing on the brink of that mysterious depression, in Arabic, called "The Ghôr," or basin in which lies the still more mysterious inland lake, usually called "the Dead Sea," but more appropriately "the Salt Sea." This latter name I prefer to the former; first, on the ground of priority,[1] and second, on account of its expressiveness, owing to the intense salinity of the water. By this name it was known in the days of Abraham, while its more modern name has been founded on the erroneous impression "that nothing can live in the vicinity of its saline and sulphurous waters,"[2] an impression disproved by Maundrell, Chateaubriand, and numerous more recent travellers.

The descent into The Ghôr, by a steep and slippery path, was most striking. In front to the north stretched a great plain, green with vegetation. To the right, in an open space, might be seen several large Bedawin camps, from which the shouts of wild men, the barking of dogs, and the bellowing of camels ascended. In the distance, but obscured by the haze, were the shores of the Salt Sea, a band of blue indicating the position of the waters; and on either hand of our pathway stretched the white terraces of the old sea-bed, indented by several deep channels, particularly those of the River Jeib, on the west, and of the Butachy and Gharandel on the east.

The banks of The Ghôr along the southern margin rise in the form of a great white sloping wall to a height of about 600 feet above the plain, and are formed of horizontal courses of sand and gravel resting on white marl and loam This mural cliff sweeps round in a semi-circular form from side to side of The Ghôr. The upper surface is nearly level (except where

[1] Gen. xiv, 3 ; Deut. iii, 17.

[2] "Survey of the Holy Land," by J. T. Bannister and Dr. Marsh, 1844. The Arab name is El Buhr Lut, or the Sea of Lot. Lartet mentions that small fish live in that part of the Salt Sea south of the Lisan.

broken into by the river channels), and from its base stretches a plain covered partly, over the eastern side, by a forest of small trees and shrubs extending northwards to Es Safieh, and partly by vegetation affording pasturage to the numerous flocks of the Arabs who settle down here during the cooler months of the year. It is impossible to doubt that at no remote period the waters of the Salt Sea, though now distant some ten miles, washed the base of these cliffs ; and a rise of a few feet would submerge this verdant plain, and bring back the sea to its former more extended limits.

From this position, also, the white terrace of Khashm (Jebel) Usdum, cleft by a thousand fissures, and channelled by innumerable furrows, is seen projecting from the sides of the loftier limestone terraces of the Judæan hills ; and towards the east similar terraces of whitish alluvial deposits are seen clinging to the sides of the Moabite hills, or running far up the deep glens which penetrate the sides of the great table-land. In these terraces, the upper surfaces of which reach a level of about 600 feet above the waters of the Salt Sea, we behold but the remnants of an ancient sea-bed, which must originally have stretched from side to side far into the area now occupied by its waters. We naturally put to ourselves the question, " Since this sea has no outlet, what has become of the materials which have disappeared ?"[1]

On descending towards the plain we came upon numerous flocks of black goats and white sheep, tended by women in long blue cloaks, the invariable colour of women's dresses amongst the Arabs ; and our way lay pleasantly through glades and thickets of small trees and bushes, green even at this time of year, but how much more so would they be in a few weeks hence after the winter rains. Through these our long train of camels wended their way, headed by Sheikh Ali, and cropping the tender twigs of the shrubs, till we reached the lower plain on which were pitched the winter camps of some hundreds of Bedawins. Presently, our party being observed from the camps, a group of merry children, with a few elders, came trooping up and arranged themselves along our line of march, regarding us with eager curiosity. It was the first group of Arab children I had seen, and a very pretty sight it was ; and as I passed along they returned my "sabâh-l-khair" with a hearty chorus of little voices which was very

[1] To this question I hope to give a detailed reply in another volume in which I propose to deal with the physical history of The Ghôr and of the Jordan Valley.

pleasant to hear. I afterwards learned that these children belonged to the tribe of the Alowîns and Hâwathas, all friends and relatives of our party, so we had cause for a hearty greeting.

We were soon, however, to meet with less welcome visitors. On proceeding some distance northwards we observed a small hill about a mile in front of us crowded with horsemen standing as sentinels, and evidently on the look out for us. Presently a Hâwatha, or Alowîn, horseman galloped up from behind, and after the usual salutations informed us that the horsemen in front belonged to Sheikh Arari of Petra (who, it will be recollected, was absent at Damascus when we visited that place), and that behind him was the Sheikh of Kerak (Canon Tristram's friend, I presume), who, as our dragoman, Ibraham, informed us, was "a very bad man, and was always at war with all the other tribes." Thus, this personage, with such a bad reputation, happened to be down just at our arrival (so we were informed) amongst the Ghawarneh, whose guests we intended to become while waiting for horses from Jerusalem, and we were aware that he was a deadly enemy to Sheikh Ali, who headed our escort! It appeared to us we were getting into a trap, of which the door was closed in all directions except that we had just come ; but to turn back was out of the question. After consultation it was decided to camp near the spot we were on, towards the eastern base of the hills, while Major Kitchener and Bernhard Heilpern, with some of the party, went ahead to ascertain on the spot from Sheikh Arari the real state of affairs, and his intentions towards ourselves.

Proceeding with our camels, we selected a spot for camping, and while the tents were being set up Mr. Armstrong and I ascended a little hill, from which we could witness the proceedings of Major Kitchener and those with him. They had reached the hill on which the horsemen had stationed themselves ; and presently we saw several of these leave the hill, and, descending into the plain, commence careering over it, then wheeling round, brandishing their spears, and performing sundry equestrian feats, as is the manner of Arabs. Soon afterwards the whole party came down from the hill, and accompanied by our friends, who were on foot, they approached our camp in little parties at the rapid pace of Arab steeds. It was a pretty sight, as the party were handsomely dressed and carried their lances aloft ; the horses, caparisoned with coloured cloths and tassels, were handsome, spirited little animals. The party consisted of Sheikh Arari, his relatives and special retainers ; and no doubt were "the flower" of Arab cavalry.

Presently some of the troop ascended the hill on which we were seated, and as they approached we rose to our feet and exchanged salutes, then shook hands all round. I said we were friends; they replied by placing their hands on their hearts. I then offered them cigarettes, and so we parted;— but only for a season.

It appeared that at the interview between Sheikh Arari and Major Kitchener, the former had demanded tribute for passing through part of his territory. His followers also put in a claim for bakhsheesh. The former claim we admitted; the latter we refused to admit. It was needful, however, to act with prudence, for we were practically prisoners at the discretion of this powerful chief, whose camp was only a mile distant from our own, and who could muster a large number of spears at his call. We therefore promised the Sheikh a sum equal to £5 if he would engage that we should not be molested during the rest of our journey to the territory of the Ghawarneh at Es Safich; to this he agreed, and he kept his promise. We all considered Sheikh Arari "a gentleman." Towards evening the spearmen mounted their horses and rode away, and we had evening prayers in our tent.

That evening we learned that the story about the Kerak men being amongst the Ghawarnehs was, in a great measure, an invention, certainly exaggerated; and we had some reason to suspect that Sheikh Ali was in league with the Petra Arabs, who were his relatives, to get us into a trap in order to extort money from us. He himself pretended to be very much alarmed at the report; but finally, on being pressed by us, he promised to start with us early next morning for Es Safieh, "even if he were to get his throat cut," as he said, passing his hand across his neck! We felt that the risk was not very great; so, accepting the proposal with a good grace, we presented him with a cigar, though our stock of tobacco was getting very short, and parted for the night.

On Monday morning, 17th December, we were up and off by times northwards towards the village of the Ghawarneh, as we wished to get a good start of the Petra Arabs, who, we feared, notwithstanding the promise of Sheikh Arari, might follow in pursuit, and perhaps take possession of some of our baggage, or possibly of the owners. Our route lay along the base of the hills on the east side of The Ghôr, and to the right rose the rugged mountains and cliffs leading up to the table-land of Moab, and penetrated by deep valleys or ravines.

We passed through several thickets of small trees and shrubs, generally more or less thorny, such as the *Zizyphus*, the *Seyal Acacia*, and the *Salvadora Persica*; all requiring care in order to avoid them. Amongst these were the "apples of Sodom" (*Solanum Sodomœum*), a small yellowish fruit of a solanaceous plant, growing to about eight feet high, with prickly branches and a flower of a blue or purple colour, exactly like that of a variety of potato. Amongst other plants was the osher tree (*Calotropis procera*), indicating truly tropical conditions of climate; also *Balanites Ægyptiaca*, *Retama rœtem*, *Morina aptera*, and oleanders.[1] Amongst the dense groves and clumps of small trees birds were fluttering about, ring doves (*Turtur risorius*), sometimes in flocks, together with bulbuls and finches. It was a lively and pleasant scene to one who had been traversing the *comparatively* lifeless tract of the Arabah Valley for so many days. But what was still more novel, were the evidences of human industry which we encountered as we approached Es Safieh. We passed over several open spaces where men were ploughing with a yoke of oxen; many trenches had been dug for irrigating purposes, and we were soon to witness the systematic manner in which irrigation is carried on by the industrious inhabitants of this part of The Ghôr.

Proceeding onwards in single file, we found ourselves within the village of the Ghawarneh. This had a most curious appearance, not unlike an extensive encampment of gipsies, such as may be seen in Hungary and along the banks of the River Danube. The tents, formed of dark cloth of camels' hair, supported on poles and rafters, were arranged amongst the thickets in lines or "squares," and tenanted by men, women, and children, together with sheep, goats, dogs, and poultry. As we passed along we heard the sound of the corn mills, or of coffee-grinding, the bleating of sheep, and barking of the dogs; but the attitude of the dark inhabitants was quiet and friendly, and they readily returned our salaams.[2] Having traversed the village we came to an open piece of ground surrounded by trees and bushes, and here we camped about noon.

The village of Es Safieh and its inhabitants, the Ghawarnehs, were visited by Canon Tristram,[3] who during his short stay does not appear to have been as well treated as was the case with ourselves during a sojourn of ten days.[4] Yet it must be admitted that he made good use of the time

---

[1] Mr. Hart has made a good collection of plants from this part of The Ghôr. Tristram has described this vegetation ("Land of Moab," p. 391).

[2] In the East it is the custom for the superior to greet the inferior first.

[3] "The Land of Moab," p. 46.   [4] *Ibid.*, p. 51.

at his disposal, and has left a graphic picture of the locality, which renders much detail in this place unnecessary.

Shortly after camping, we descended through the jungle separating the park-like region from the great plain of sand and mud, which is liable to inundations when the sea is in flood, and which is largely covered by the prostrate trunks of palms and other trees and plants which have been carried down by the torrents from the mountain valleys. It was the intention of Major Kitchener to measure a base line for triangulation along this nearly level plain, but it was found that the mud and slime were too soft in many places to admit of this being done with any approach to accuracy. He and Mr. Armstrong had, therefore, to content themselves with triangulating, and taking magnetic bearings, on known points.[1] On returning to our camp in the evening, we were entertained to a prolonged chorus between the dogs of the village and the jackals of the thickets ; while the discharge of distant guns amongst the hills, which we were informed came from the Haiwatats, announced the proximity of the foes of our present protector, Sheikh Ali.

The nocturnal noises of Es Safieh were indeed, to our unaccustomed ears, almost appalling. It is the custom of the cocks at this village to crow *after* sunset ; and up to about bedtime the air was resonant with their voices. To these were added the barking of the dogs and the long shrill cries of the jackals. No one who is not a sound sleeper should pass a night at Es Safieh ! About midnight I was awakened by the most strange and appalling noises. At first I thought we were about to be attacked by the Bedawins ; but on listening for a little, I distinguished the peculiar high-pitched dismal cry of the jackal, mingling with the howling of the village dogs. The whole jackal population of the adjoining thickets and valleys seemed to have congregated around our camp, and to be holding council whether or not to make a raid on us. As, however, we all arose in safety in the morning, it is to be presumed they came to the conclusion to postpone the attack, at least for this night. It was one to be held in remembrance by us ; the place at the time seemed a sort of pandemonium.

Considering the position of our camp unhealthy, I ordered it to be moved further inland from the jungle, and to one more open to the air, as well as more distant from the village. The spot was surrounded by open groves of small trees, of which several species of acacia and the

---

[1] It has been found as a result of this survey that there is considerable error in the form and position of this part of the Dead Sea as given in the maps.

zizyphus were the most abundant, generally growing in picturesque clumps, with narrow glades between. The cultivated fields of the Ghawarneh spread around; and beyond, the river descending from the Wâdy el Hessi flowed between the plains and the mountain slopes, and bounded the cultivated lands towards the east. The grand mass of Jebel es Somrah, with its adjoining heights and deep ravines, formed the background at a distance of two or three miles; and from its ever varying colours, according to the position of the sun's rays and the time of day, formed an object of unwearied study to us during our long detention at Es Safieh. This mountain is remarkable for the interest attaching to its geological structure. Its base is formed of very ancient volcanic materials, consisting of successive beds of trap, porphyry, "ashes," and agglomerates—penetrated by numerous dykes, and dipping at a small inclination towards the north.

Upon this volcanic platform the horizontal courses of the Desert Sandstone formation repose, breaking off in great cliffs, and forming the flanks of the mountain to an elevation of about 3,000 feet above the base; finally, the sandstone itself is surmounted by an escarpment of limestone, which extends upwards into the table-land of Moab. It will be seen from the above description that this volcanic formation is of more ancient date than that of the Desert Sandstone, and consequently has no connection whatever with the present structure or formation of the valley.

FIG. 15.—GORGE OF THE W. EL HESSI.

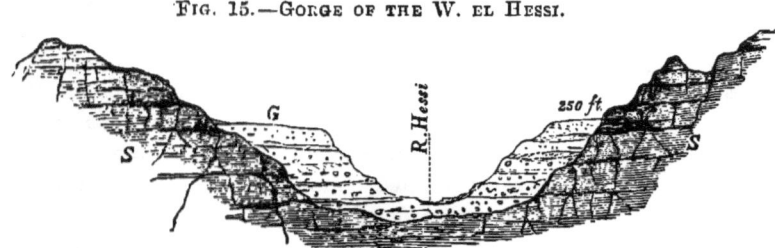

S Cliffs of red sandstone enclosing terraces of gravel, sand, and shingle (G) of the ancient Salt Sea (Bahr Lut), through which the valley of the River Hessi has been channelled out.

The southern flank of Jebel es Somrah terminates along the deep gorge called the Wâdy Salmoodh, the sides of which are in some places flanked by great beds of gravel rising to a level of 600 feet (by aneroid measurement) above the surface of the Salt Sea. These gravel beds may be observed running up the sides, not only of this valley, but also those of the Wâdy el Hessi, and through them the present river channel has been cut down, sometimes to a depth of over 200 feet. There can be no doubt, from their position and the level of their upper surface, that these beds of gravel are portions of the ancient floor of the sea, when the waters stood over 600 feet higher than at present, and that they were once physically connected with the terraces which line the southern and western sides of The Ghôr. In both cases the level of the upper surface is almost the same ; though the materials differ, as might be expected, considering the very different formations which line the sides of this great depression on either hand.[1]

The Ghawarneh. —It is only due to the people of this tribe to state that after they had satisfied their very natural curiosity by an inspection of our camp on the day of our arrival, we were not troubled with their presence any further, except when they brought poultry, eggs, or flour for us to purchase. On returning from our excursion up the Wâdy Salmoodh we had a good opportunity of observing the habits and mode of agriculture of this industrious people.

I had taken as my guide for the day Sheikh Seyd, the village chief, who, mounted on his pony, led the way going and coming. We crossed a briskly flowing stream of rather muddy water, brought down from the Wâdy el Hessi by an artificial conduit—like a "mill race" of our own country—by means of which the fields are irrigated, and the people and animals of the village supplied with water ; we also noticed men engaged in ploughing, and others fencing the fields with zizyphus and other prickly branches.

On our return through the groves we were surprised at the large herds of camels, numbering in all probably two hundred, and in good condition. The males were sometimes of great size and nearly white. They were browsing in groups on the trees and shrubs, and every evening they were driven from their feeding ground homewards in a long procession. These animals must be a source of considerable revenue to the Ghawarneh, as the price of a camel varies from £5 to £10, or even more. There were several young foals amongst them. In addition to the camels the Ghawarneh possess cattle (generally used for ploughing) as well as flocks of sheep and goats, and during our stay of ten days we were regaled with fresh cows' milk for breakfast. From the cultivation of the ground

---

[1] I only touch on this interesting topic here, reserving fuller details for another volume.

supplies of wheat, maize, and durra are raised, together with indigo and cotton. The women were generally busy with household duties, or engaged in tending the flocks of sheep and goats ; while the children might often be noticed playing various games on the ground adjoining the village. On the whole it was pleasant to see for the first time on coming from the desert evidences of industrious habits amongst an Arab tribe.[1] As a consequence, however, of their comparative wealth they are subjected to heavy exactions on the part of the sheikhs and people both of Kerak and of Petra, and while we were camped at Es Safieh we were told that a demand had come from the former for a sum of £120 in payment of annual tribute ; a demand which there was no possibility of resisting without the risk of ruin. This poor people are in effect the wheat between the upper millstone of Kerak and the nether of Petra.

The day after our arrival at Es Safieh we received a polite message from Ibn Mudjelli, the Sheikh of Kerak, to the effect " that he was the friend of travellers" (as any one might know from his treatment of Canon Tristram[2] and his party !) and that he would send horses and mules to enable us to pay him a visit in his highland fortress ; moreover, that for our sakes he would not attack Sheikh Ali, with whom (as before stated) he was at deadly feud. We replied that we were much obliged for his courtesy, but had made arrangements for proceeding forthwith to Jerusalem. Perhaps this was a little more than we had a right under the circumstances to say. It is true we had despatched messengers to the Holy City for horses and mules, but we knew not whether they had been able to deliver their message, and consequently whether the horses were on their way to our relief. We hoped the morrow's light might see them arrive—a hope destined to disappointment. Instead of our escort from Jerusalem we had an unwelcome visit from the bandits of Petra, who came up to our camp next day brandishing their spears and demanding money. This demand we felt bound to resist even at some risk ; and being unsuccessful with us they proceeded towards the village to quarter themselves for the night on the Ghawarneh, whom they ordered forthwith to kill a sheep for supper ; and, as no news had

---

[1] If indeed they are Arabs. It is possible they may belong to the fellahin, or cultivators of the ground, throughout Palestine, whom Captain Conder considers, with great probability, to be the descendants of the inhabitants of the country at the time of its conquest by the Israelites.

[2] "Land of Moab," p. 84, et seq.

come from Jerusalem, we retired to our tents that night with spirits far from cheerful.

Next day, Wednesday, 19th December, we made excursions in several directions in search of objects connected with the topography, geology, and natural history of the remarkable district in which our lot was for the time cast. Accompanied by Sheikh Seyd, I examined the volcanic rocks along the flanks of Jebel es Somrah, consisting of irregular beds of felstone, porphyry, and agglomerate, with strata of finer volcanic tuff. From the flanks of this mountain I had an extensive view across The Ghôr, and the waters of the Salt Sea, as far north as the Lisan, the remarkable promontory which divides this sea into two unequal portions. I was impressed with the fact, when surveying its blue, still, waters from this point, that there is nothing about the appearance of the sea, or of the surrounding hills, to lead one to suspect that its surface is 1,300 feet below that of the Mediterranean ; and it is therefore not surprising that this physical fact should have remained so long unrecognised by travellers. It is only when one looks at the face of the aneroid, and observes that the index hand has passed away beyond the highest (ordinary) reading of 31°, and points to the very lowest in the opposite direction, that we become conscious that we are under extraordinary atmospheric pressure, and only to be accounted for by the inference that we have descended far below the level of the ocean.[1] The climate of The Ghôr at this time of year does not feel much warmer hat we had been accustomed to in the Wâdy el Arabah ; in fact, during one day of our sojourn at Es Safieh we had a hailstorm !

On returning to the camp I received the unwelcome tidings that a rigid quarantine had been established by the Turkish authorities for all travellers coming from the direction of Egypt and the Haj Road at Akabah, and that all such travellers were obliged to proceed to Gaza to put in a term of fifteen days in the quarantine station. It was, therefore, quite possible that our messengers might have been captured on their road to Jerusalem and sent off to Gaza, in which case our prospects would be far from enviable.

Next morning (Thursday, 20th December) we rose with the hope of soon hearing the tinkling of the baggage mule bells coming across the marsh to our relief, but hour after hour elapsed and no such sound greeted our ears. It was tantalizing to look across the blue waters of the Salt Sea

[1] Ordinary aneroids are not graduated for reading depressions much below that of the level of the ocean.

to the mysterious salt mountain, which is connected by the traditional name of " Jebel Usdum " with the doomed " cities of the plain," and find ourselves unable to give it a personal examination during the time at our disposal. We thought (it must be confessed) of the letters from home lying for us at Jerusalem, of the possible anxiety of friends who might have expected us within the walls by this time, and of the diminishing prospect of spending Christmas at the birthplace of the Saviour.

In the afternoon, however, our Arab messengers arrived : they had succeeded in eluding the guards, and had faithfully delivered our letter to the agent of Messrs. Cook and Son. They produced a letter in reply to say—that " the horses and mules would be with us without fail and without delay ?"—not at all, my dear reader. You have not lived in the East or under Turkish rule! The reply was, that on receipt of our letter the agent had got horses and mules ready, had then applied to the Pasha for an escort, and had been peremptorily refused. Orders were issued that, before proceeding to Jerusalem, we must undergo quarantine for fifteen days at Gaza, and that the muleteers would also be obliged to undergo a similar detention at our cost, should they leave the city. The agent had then represented the case to Mr. Moore, Her Majesty's Consul, who sent us a kind letter expressing his sympathy, and stating that his efforts with the Pasha to have the orders set aside were ineffectual, as they (the orders) really came from Constantinople. Under these circumstances Messrs. Cook's agent came to the conclusion *not* to send the mules and horses till further orders ; a conclusion that practically consigned us to imprisonment for at least another five or six days, and possibly for a much longer period.

Our feelings at this news " may be better imagined than described," to use a familiar phrase. Christmas at Jerusalem was now out of the question ; letters from home indefinitely postponed. Indeed, our exit from The Ghôr seemed also indefinitely postponed ; and our only consolation was that our friends at Jerusalem were not ignorant of our fate ; and it seemed that it was entirely in their hands whether we were to be left as prisoners amongst the Bedawins till all our money, provisions, and hope were exhausted. Under these circumstances we applied to Sheikh Ali, to ascertain whether he could escort us across to Gaza along the direct road by Ain el Melh and Beersheba. This, however, he positively refused to do ; and we had again to fall back on our Arab messengers, and await the result of a second letter to the agent, with instructions to forward the horses immediately, in order that we might proceed to Gaza to undergo the term of quarantine.

We had on the previous day despatched a second Arab, who had engaged for 20 dollars to take a letter to Consul Moore ; but, much to our annoyance, he returned to us at breakfast time stating that he was sick ; and, throwing down the money and letter, refused to go. This was another day lost. But our former messenger, Hassam, again volunteered ; and, taking up the money and depositing the letter safely in the folds of his dress, departed, with a large supply of good wishes for a successful journey on our part.[1]

Having now a prospect of several days stay in The Ghôr, we determined to put the time to the best account in exploring more thoroughly the objects of interest around us. We visited the remarkable ruins described by Tristram, lying at the foot of the hills about two miles to the east of Es Safieh, and known as Khasa el Hassa (or Hessi), and of which he says " We have probably here merely the remains of a Roman village in the more peaceful days of the early empire."[2] While here I proceeded to put into practice a mode of observing the landscape which I first learned some years ago in North Wales. Laying my head on the ground and lying on my side, I viewed in this position, first, the line of the mountain crest and then the wooded slopes of The Ghôr, with the plain and hills beyond. The effects of colouring when seen in this manner are generally surprising, and often beautiful. In this case, all the colours of the mountain sides, the grey and brown of the limestone above, the red and purple of the sandstone, and the dark grey and brownish-red of the volcanic basis were seen to be blended and harmonised in a manner quite peculiar, and differing from the effect when seen in an erect position. There was thrown over the whole landscape (as it were) a halo of mystery. The softening and blending of the tints were of a kind which a Claud or a Turner have attempted to portray on canvas. My companions were no less struck with the effects than myself.

A bath in the River Hessi terminated the day's ramble.

---

[1] It is right that I should state that Mr. Hart more than once volunteered to carry a message to Jerusalem for the horses ; but, knowing something of the risk he would have to run in traversing a wild and unknown region, inhabited for some distance by Bedawins of ill-repute, I felt unable to give my consent to his generous proposal.

[2] *Supra cit.*, p. 48.

On Saturday, 22nd December, we deemed it desirable, on economical grounds, to dismiss the greater number of our Arab attendants, only retaining, at a greatly reduced expense, the services of Sheikh Ali and a small guard, till our mules should come from Jerusalem. Let me here do justice to our Bedawin attendants. At the first, on starting from Akabah, we formed (as previously stated) but a low estimate of the Alowîn, and of their mental and physical capabilities. They were for the most part inferior in stature and in personal appearance to the Towâra, from whom we had parted; and at first there was great difficulty in getting them to perform the duties of loading the camels, taking down and setting up tents, drawing water, and other daily occupations. Gradually, however, they got accustomed to their work, and more expeditious in performing it. We also began to find that there were with them, as in all communities, differences of character and acquirements: that, while some were lazy and untrustworthy, others were active and entitled to our confidence. They were generally cheerful, pleasant fellows, trying to anticipate our wants, honest to the last degree, and grateful for little kindnesses;—at least for a time. There were amongst them several young men of handsome features and good proportions, and in their gait there was a certain ease and grace of motion, evincing great activity and power of endurance. Their clothing was similar to that of the Towâra, except that it was inferior in quality and they wore the khefeyeh[1] instead of the turban. Such were our Alowîn guards.

As regards the general character of the Bedawins there is much difference of opinion. By some they are regarded as treacherous in the extreme; others (such as the late Rev. F. W. Holland, who had had much experience and intercourse with them) seem to have entertained a very different opinion of them.[2] My own opinion, based, it must be confessed, upon a comparatively limited experience, is favourable; nor does the fate of Palmer and Gill alter my opinion, as this lamentable event arose from circumstances quite exceptional. In recently traversing the district near to which this tragedy occurred, Major Kitchener stated that the Arabs everywhere expressed their detestation of the foul deed, and

---

[1] This is a cloth, or shawl, sometimes of silk, folded back and bound round the head by a double fillet of coloured cord. The ends hang down the back, or are gathered into folds round the neck and chin, and fastened by little tassels into the fillet. It is thus a protection against either heat or cold.

[2] See *Quarterly Statement*, P.E.F., April, 1884.

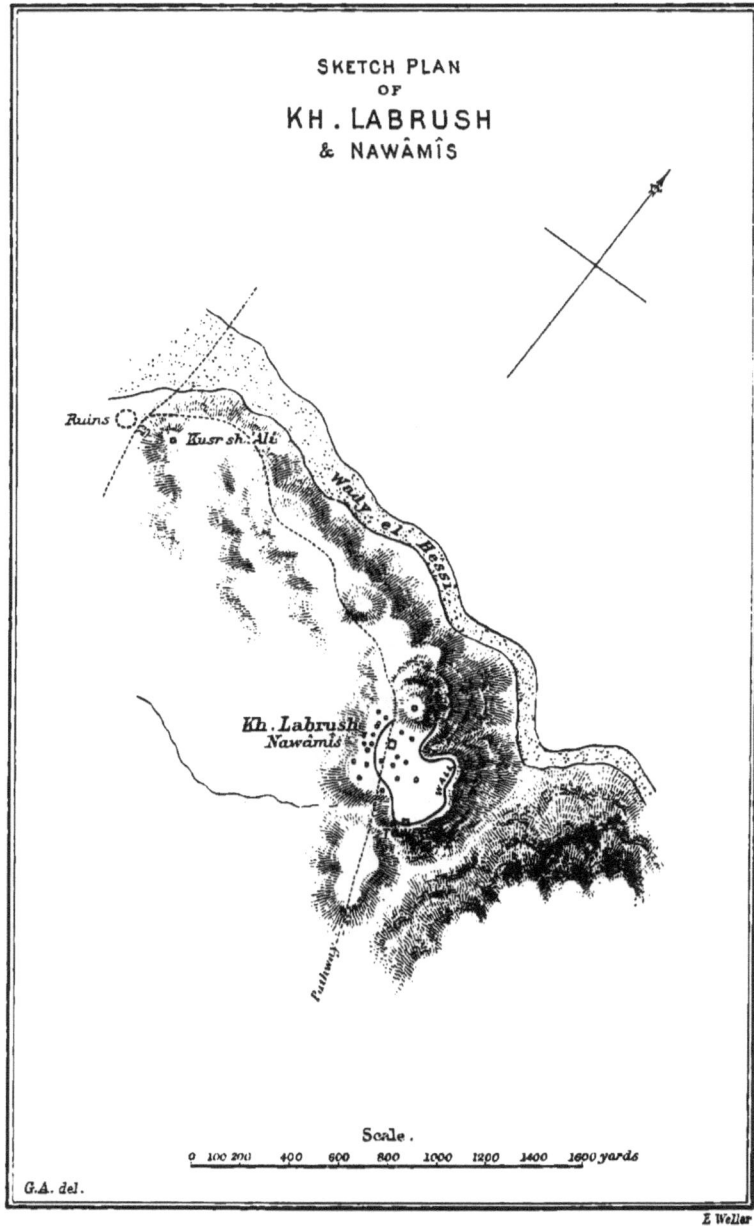

SKETCH PLAN
OF
KH . LABRUSH
& NAWÂMÎS

Ruins

Kusr sh. Ali

Wady el Bessi

Kh . Labrush
Nawâmis

Pathway

Scale .

0   100 200   400   600   800   1000   1200   1400   1600 yards

G.A. del.

E Weller

their admiration of the gallant Englishmen who entered the Desert subsequently and captured four of the murderers. There is one vice, at least, common amongst the inhabitants of the British Isles, which amongst the children of the Desert is unknown. Water, milk, or coffee are their only drinks, and as Mahomedans they are free from that temptation which amongst nominal Christians has brought ruin and misery into many a home ; and amongst the aborigines of America and other countries has carried off whole tribes when they have come in contact with the " white man." There can be no question regarding the wisdom of the prohibition of intoxicating drinks in the case of the Arabs. Amongst a people whose food is so scanty, and who live under a sub-tropical sun, alcoholic drinks would have been utterly destructive had they been indulged in. The Arab's simple diet is his best safeguard against disease, and when ill the herbs of the Desert are generally sufficient for medicinal purposes. There are, in truth, many qualities in him to admire ; such as his abstemiousness, power of endurance under fatigue, fidelity to a stranger when under contract, natural politeness of manner, and (perhaps to a small degree) capability of personal attachment. If he is fond of money, and in doing right looks for pecuniary reward, he is not different in this respect from people of more civilised countries.

Ruins of Lebrusch.—On returning one evening from an excursion up the mountains bounding the Wâdy el Hessi, Mr. Hart announced the discovery of " an ancient city," or something of that kind ; and, at his request, we all determined to visit it on the following day. The position of these remarkable ruins is several hundred feet higher up the mountain side than those described by Canon Tristram, and about a mile from them on the south side of the valley. It was a lonely and wild spot, the haunt of the ibex,[1] which we reached after a stiff climb. The ruins consist of a series of circular enclosures of rough stone (stone circles), running along the edge of a limestone terrace for a distance of 300 yards, and accompanied by a rude wall, behind which the rocks formed a low ridge. Towards the southern end the enclosures take the form of a rampart of stone work, extending about 400 yards, and at the end of the hill it turns up towards the crest of the ridge for 200 yards further, so as to form a wall protecting the interior.[2]

---

[1] Close to this Mr. Hart had come upon three of these animals, which are seldom seen except in very unfrequented spots.

[2] The ridge is formed of the " Wady Nasb limestone," which we here discovered in the centre of the sandstone formation. It is fossiliferous.

Several circular enclosures were found inside the ramparts, and about the centre of the whole structure was a hollow reservoir. The position commands an extensive view of The Ghôr, and all the approaches to the valley. Some of the circular enclosures had evidently been covered in, but their form seemed to forbid the supposition that they were tombs. Various conjectures as to the nature and use of this series of structures were hazarded by the members of our party, but no two were identical. It was a case of *tot homines quot sententiæ*. For myself, I came to the conclusion that this spot had been the camping ground of an army;—but of what nation or period we had no clue. A plan of the hill has been made by Major Kitchener, and drawn for me by Mr. Armstrong (Fig. 16).

On descending from the ruins for the last time down the mountain side, we were treated to a display of the gorgeous colouring characteristic of the eastern side of The Ghôr, when lit up by the slanting rays of the western sun. The evening had been cloudy, and some rain had fallen. Suddenly the sun burst forth through a gap in the clouds, and lighted up the cliffs along the northern side of the valley with tints of surpassing richness and brilliancy. The red colours of the sandstone cliffs, and the yellow tints of the sandy terraces below, brightly illumined where the rays descended directly upon them, gradually faded into the deep purple tints of the higher altitudes and recesses of the mountains ; and high above, the mountain tops were shrouded in heavy cloud, in which was set "the many-coloured bow of heaven." We might have lingered long to watch this wondrous display of natural colouration ; but the sun was nearing the horizon, and it was not a region in which it was desirable to be caught under darkness. We regarded the scene as a parting salutation from Moab to its visitors.

The days following (Friday and Saturday) had new surprises, and new disappointments, in store for us. We had sent off a third messenger (as has been seen above) to Jerusalem, with positive orders for Mr. Cook's agent to send horses and mules forthwith, to convey us away from our prison-house amongst the Arabs, and we awaited the result with some hope that the messenger would reach his destination on Saturday evening, 22nd December, and that by Tuesday the animals would arrive at our camp. In the afternoon of Friday, a Bedawin arrived, bringing a letter from a party of excursionists, consisting of the American Consul, Mr. Merrill, and a nephew of General Gordon, who had been on a visit to his uncle at Jaffa, and was making a tour of a few days, accompanied by an escort, along the shore of the Salt Sea, near Jebel Usdum. In this letter (which was addressed to Major Kitchener) it was stated that our messenger had shown them our letter to Cook's agent, and that on their return to Jerusalem on Christmas Eve they would leave no stone unturned towards getting us out of The Ghôr, and released from quarantine ; *also that our Arab had been sent on his way to Jerusalem.* All this seemed very promising ; because, should our messenger not arrive, our friends would be able to deliver our message on reaching the Holy City. The reader may, therefore, imagine our disappointment on beholding our Arab back again in the camp the next day ! We were all absent at the time in various directions. Bernhard Heilpern was taking a nap ; and, on awakening, could scarcely credit his senses when he beheld Hassam seated at the fire and conversing with Sheikh Ali. The question arose whether some sinister influence had again been at work to prolong our stay, and Heilpern's suspicions fell on Sheikh Ali, who was making money by our detention. When questioned why he had returned, Hassam merely replied that he had heard from some other Arab that we were about to start for Gaza, and had thought it useless to proceed further ;—so here he was again. Thus were two days lost to us, and I began to feel that " hope deferred which makes the heart sick."

The Sheikh, at Heilpern's request, administered chastisement to his retainer, not a very severe one certainly, and for the third time Hassam was depatched to Jerusalem with the letter. We never saw him again, though we understood he reached the city and fulfilled his errand.

Christmas Eve.—This afternoon brought with it tidings, not from Jerusalem, but from Cairo, the first we had received from the outer world for six weeks. In the afternoon four Arabs of the Hawatat tribe on camels, headed by ·a sheikh, arrived in our camp bearing a letter addressed to me by Sir Evelyn Baring, Her Majesty's Consul-General, to inform us of the defeat of General Hicks' army in the Soudan, and stating that some anxiety had been felt concerning us on the part of our friends both in England and Egypt ; as the news of the disaster might have occasioned a hostile feeling amongst the Arabs towards Europeans. The letter was intended to put us on our guard should we perceive any symptoms of such feeling. The Arab party had tracked us step by step from Suez to Jebel Mûsa, thence to Akabah, and then to this spot ; and being well mounted, they had accomplished the whole distance in twenty days. We felt grateful to the Consul-General for his consideration ; and we were by no means sorry to have an addition to our party of four dependable Arabs, whose head Sheikh in Cairo was "to be held responsible for our safety." The messengers were accompanied by a small party of "the hawks" of Petra, who said we must now retrace our steps back to Akabah, as "the infidel dogs" had been defeated. We replied that we were now in the territory of the Sultan, and were in daily expectation of an escort of soldiers from Jerusalem. We added, also, for their information, that although it was an Englishman whose army had been defeated by the Mahdi, the army itself was composed of poor cowardly Egyptians who had run away and left their officers to be killed, and that if the Egyptians did not know how to defend their country, an English army would be sent to put matters straight. This view of the subject appeared to have a wholesome effect, as "the Petra hawks" went off to the village of the Ghawarnehs for the night. We ordered a sheep to be prepared for the entertainment of the Arabs from Cairo, who took up a station behind our camp.

Christmas Day in the Wilderness amongst a people who love not the Saviour's name, and are governed by laws little in harmony with those He came to proclaim! Still, even amongst these strange scenes, we can lift up our hearts and say, "Glory to God in the highest ; on earth, peace; good will towards men." It was not to be our lot to celebrate this Christian anniversary at the birthplace of the Messiah ; but, for myself, I had rather spend the day here in the Wilderness, than be a witness to the grotesque and childish ceremonies which are annually enacted by the Greek and Latin Churches in Bethlehem, and which have brought discredit on the Christian name.

I had passed a night in which sleep was banished or disturbed by gloomy thoughts. The cries of the jackals and the barking of dogs repeated at intervals caused a cold chill to permeate my frame. The lines I had learnt somewhere when a youth *would* recur in spite of myself, "Nec spes erat salutis, nec redeundi domum." What if they should be prophetic ! But the bright sunshine of the morn succeeded the deluge of rain and hail of the previous day, and helped to dispel these gloomy forebodings. The river which drains the Wâdy el Hessi had risen, and the distant roar of the torrent was audible from our camp. A thought occurred to me which rendered me uneasy for a time :—might not the River Jeib, swollen by the same rains, render our camp inaccessible from the opposite side of The Ghôr, and thus cut off our succours should they be on their way to us from

Jerusalem ; or cut off *our* retreat by the only door now left? This supposition, however, I was relieved to find, on consulting Sheikh Seyd, was
not borne out by experience, as the Jeib is nearly always fordable, and
falls rapidly after rains have ceased.

After breakfast I sallied forth with Armstrong to examine the ruins
described by Canon Tristram, about two miles from our camp. We
found a considerable extent of ground occupied with them, and the walls
which had enclosed the village on two sides. We also noticed fragments
of two or three unfluted columns to which Tristram refers, and large
quantities of broken pottery along with pieces of green glass. The pottery
had glazed surfaces and rude patterns ; but of the age of the village or
town we could form little idea. As we were returning we found ourselves
in front of a large party of Arab " free-lances," which induced my companion and myself "to put the best leg foremost ;" though of course
only at a walking pace ; and after a stiff trudge over the fields, and a
scramble through a thorny hedge, which we performed with the best grace
we could muster, we were not sorry to see before us the white tents,
which we reached very much " blown." There was nothing to have prevented these men from carrying us off to their mountain prison had they
felt inclined to do so ; at the same time it is probable they did not con-
template any such outrage.

In the evening a crowd of Arabs surrounded the tents, and by way of
a Christmas entertainment, Laurence produced a little galvanic apparatus,
and proceeded to operate on our visitors in the usual way, by joining hands
or plunging them into the water of a tub into which the ends of the wires
were inserted. It was amusing to watch the expression of face and
gestures of these wild men when engaged in this performance. They
behaved very much like school boys at home on like occasions—jumping,
grinning and laughing when they felt a "shock," and evidently much
astonished at the wonderful English magician who had come amongst
them! This little entertainment put them all in good humour ; so much
so, that after it was over they came back to request that it might be
repeated.

The dinner was the event of the day ; and we endeavoured on this
occasion to preserve home traditions as far as the circumstances would
allow. Abu Miriam was not unequal to the occasion. For a time we
forgot the Wilderness and the hawks of Petra, and thought only of home
and our relatives, separated from us by a distance of 3,000 miles ; and we

knew that they were thinking of us as spending the day within the walls of Jerusalem. A penultimate bottle of claret was produced from the "cellar," in which the memory of absent friends was duly honoured ; and, as a conclusion to the feast, Hart produced a plum cake of home manufacture, specially reserved for this occasion. Such was the evening of Christmas Day as observed in The Ghôr in the year 1883, by a party of deserted Englishmen !

On the evening of the day following Sheikh Arari, of Wâdy Mûsa, came into our camp on a visit to Sheikh Ali, and I took the opportunity of making his acquaintance. The interview was of some interest to us from the fact that he is supreme over all the chiefs of the district about Petra and the mountainous region extending to Kerak and the shores of the Salt Sea. The interview was witnessed by parties of his own retainers on the one hand, and of the Ghawarneh on the other ; and I determined to take the opportunity of pleading the cause of these quiet and oppressed people.

Sheikh Arari is a man of about forty-five years, of a countenance somewhat Israelitish, and quite devoid of any sinister expression. We both remained standing in the open air ; and after the usual salutations and expression of pleasure on my part at making his acquaintance, the following conversation took place.

Sheikh Arari expressed his regret that some of his followers had given us annoyance the evening before we left our camp at the head of The Ghôr, but reminded me that after he had given his promise (to Major Kitchener) that we should not be further disturbed this had been faithfully kept.

I replied that I was quite aware of this, and thanked him for his consideration.

Sheikh Arari then said he was friendly to English travellers, and did not wish they should be put to any annoyance while passing through his territory.

I replied that English travellers were always ready to pay what was just and reasonable to the sheikhs through whose territories they happened to travel ;—but nothing more. Arari replied he did not wish them to pay more than that.

I then said the Ghawarneh are our friends and hosts. We are camping on their ground, and we wish them to be fairly and kindly treated ; that they ought to be paid for whatever was got from them (slight murmurs amongst Arari's attendants), which I feared was not always the case. [1]

Arari replied that the Ghawarneh were also his friends; that he would not allow them to be ill-treated, and that they (Arari's people) always paid for what they got. [2]

Knowing this to be a slight stretch of the truth, I replied that the Ghawarneh were a peaceful people, cultivating the ground, and raising crops of corn, tobacco, and other produce, which are necessary for the Bedawin; and that if they should be driven away by oppression they (the Bedawin) would have no means of procuring necessary supplies; therefore it was their interest to protect them. We then parted with expressions of goodwill, and with the hope on my part that this interview may not have been without some benefit to our oppressed friends.

While I was writing the above an Arab came into the camp with the good tidings that he had seen the mules and horses approaching from the opposite side of The Ghôr, and that they would be here before sunset. This intelligence was received with a general cheer from our party, and I slipped a dollar into the hands of the bearer of the good news. Orders were issued to prepare for an early start on the following day.

Some time after, and (as the Arab had stated) before sunset, a muleteer rode into the camp, and was welcomed by Bernhard Heilpern, who recognised an old friend from Jerusalem; others soon followed, and presently some thirty horses and mules were gathered round our camp, accompanied by a very ancient sheikh, already known to most of our readers—Sheikh Hamzi, of Hebron, [3] whom Major Kitchener immediately recognised.

We now learned that notwithstanding it had been represented to the Pasha of Jerusalem that we had been for over a month in Turkish territory, and all in perfect health, we were again ordered to proceed to Gaza for quarantine of fifteen days. An additional evidence of the hostility of the Turkish authorities was their refusal to send a guard of soldiers, and it was only on the strong representations of our Consul that on the

---

[1] This was not a surmise on my part, but a notorious fact.

[2] This is, perhaps, literally true, but as I was informed the mode of barter is, that the Arabs offer about one-fourth of the value of the article, and the Ghawarneh dare not refuse the offer.

[3] Tristram's "Land of Israel," 2nd edition, pp. 195, 352, &c.

following day we were joined by a guard of four mounted soldiers, who had to travel day and night to reach our camp.

It was clear we were regarded by the authorities with suspicion as in some way connected with "the Jordan Valley scheme"; and it was probable that our protestations to the contrary, conveyed to the Turkish government through Sir E. Baring before we left Cairo, only tended to confirm their impressions; and, all things considered, it must be confessed that appearances were against us!

The diversion of our course towards Gaza, with the prospect of captivity for fifteen days was, it must be confessed, a great disappointment to us. We were thus deprived of the opportunity of visiting the western shore of the Salt Sea beyond Jebel Usdum and about Ain Jidi (Engedi) as we had intended. Moreover, our letters, which must have been lying for us at Jerusalem for several weeks, had not been sent by the muleteers, and some days had now to elapse ere we could receive them. Still, we were again about to go forward after a detention in The Ghôr of eleven days, and we could not but esteem "the passage of our weary steps as foil wherein to set the precious jewel of our home return." We had much of interest still to see, and the march to Gaza would enable us to make a geological traverse of Southern Palestine.

It now appears that we did not get out of The Ghôr at all too soon. I learn, through Major Kitchener (letter dated Abbassiyeh, March 21), that Sheikh Arari of Petra is at war with Ibn Mujelli of Kerak, and the battleground is doubtless the neighbourhood of Es Safieh. Had this war broken out when we were there our position would not have been pleasant. As neutrals we should have been regarded by both parties with suspicion; and possibly have been treated as *they* treat the Ghawarneh.

The evening was spent in preparation for the morrow's march. The important question of the proper amount of bakhsheesh for Sheikh Ali and his retainers had to be decided, as well as the sum to be presented to Sheikh Seyd as "ground rent" during our encampment. The former question was the more difficult of the two; because it was certain Ali placed a high value on his services over and above that previously arranged, a value much in excess of our estimate. Finally, we agreed to give him 30 mejedies (about £5), and the money having been tightly bound up in a little parcel was entrusted to me to be slipped into his hands when bidding him farewell next morning.

CHAPTER XIV.

MARCH FROM ES SAFIEH AND JEBEL USDUM.

THE morning of Thursday, 27th December, saw our deliverance from the enforced captivity of The Ghôr. We were up before daybreak, for we knew that we had a long day's march before us, and much to see on the road. The baggage was distributed amongst the mules, and we selected our riding horses; and so well was everything done that by 8 a.m. we were in the saddle, and headed by Sheikh Seyd, as guide to the passage across the slimy plain, we were wending our way amongst the thickets of Es Safieh. We were a merry party; light of heart as boys leaving school for the holidays. Our cavalcade consisted of 30 horses and mules, the four camels which had come from Cairo, and were now to return through part of the way with us, and four mounted soldiers who had arrived by forced marches from Hebron during the night. We took farewell of Sheikh Seyd at the edge of the marsh, and bent our steps towards the foot of Jebel Usdum—that mysterious tabulated hill we had so often contemplated from the eastern side of The Ghôr.

Having halted for a litte, we commenced to examine the cliffs of Jebel Usdum, and to penetrate some of the caves which open into their sides. These caves give egress to the torrents which issue forth after rain, and along their walls the rock salt is constantly melting. Hart and Laurence scrambled up to the summit of the cliff, and for the first time the upper surface of this remarkable saliferous plateau was examined by a European.[1] The difficulties of both reaching and traversing its upper surface are considerable, owing to the holes and fissures by which the strata are penetrated. Mr. Hart informs me that the upper surface is composed of shales and marls with gypsum and selenite, much broken, and not consolidated. They do not at all resemble the limestone strata of the Cretaceo-nummulitic formation, of which the adjoining table-land is

---

[1] Tristram describes the face as "quite impracticable," "Land of Israel," p. 326; and Lartet speaks of it in similar language, "Voyage d'Exploration," vol. iii.

composed, and with which they are grouped by Lartet. There are also fine sandy bands with pseudomorphs of salt crystals, all indicating lacustrine conditions.

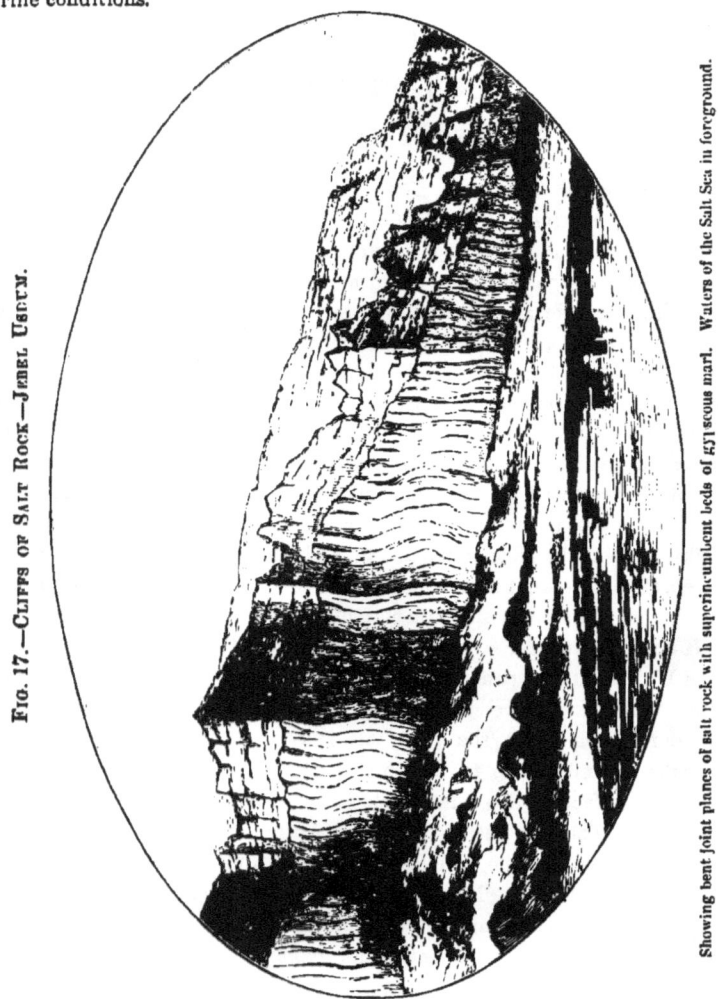

FIG. 17.—CLIFFS OF SALT ROCK—JEBEL USDUM.

Showing bent joint planes of salt rock with superincumbent beds of gypseous marl. Waters of the Salt Sea in foreground.

At the cave I examined, immense masses of the rock salt had fallen down quite recently; and further north, where the rock is traversed by vertical joint planes, there have been large dislodgments of the sides of the cliff, supposed to have been due to an earthquake ; while the rock-salt unsupported by the firmer sides, has been bent along the faces of the joints by the superincumbent weight of materials. This remarkable phenomenon is represented in the adjoining sketch. Fig. 17.

The lower part of Jebel Usdum is formed of solid bluish rock-salt, which reaches a thickness from 30 to 50 feet, and this is capped by beds of marl, salt, and gypsum ; while below the rock-salt are beds of gravel, shale, and laminated sandstone, often crushed out and lying in heaps at the base of the cliffs. There was no doubt in the mind of myself, or of any of our party, that this salt mountain is a portion of the ancient bed of the Salt Sea, and the elevation of its upper surface, 600 feet above the waters of the sea itself, confirms this view.[1]

Mr. Hart furnishes the following account of the upper surface of this hill :—

"On Thursday, the 27th of December, when passing under the eastern base of Jebel Usdum, *en route* from Es Safieh to Gaza, it occurred to me that the salt cliffs of that unique eminence did not look by any means so inaccessible as writers had led me to suppose. Choosing a point about half-way in its length on the steep eastern face, I scrambled up the rock-salt and white powdery marls which partly covered it for about 200 feet ;—my friend, Mr. Reginald Laurence, following me ; after that there was no further difficulty. The solid mineral salt appeared to cease at about 100 or 150 feet, and the remainder of the elevation was a cap of marl. The salt is cut and broken into all sorts of glacier-like crevasses and ugly black holes visible for another hundred feet or so. A slip down one of these treacherous caverns, where ice is replaced by glittering salt, and snow by white marl, would produce a well-preserved museum speci-men for future naturalists. The marl is here scooped out by water action into blocks and beds and mounds of dust, often half concealing the pits. After a while the cracks are filled (at least as I passed over them I hoped so), and in about a mile I reached the base of the inner ridge, the highest point of which my aneroid gave me at 600 feet above the Dead Sea. In

---

[1] M. Louis Lartet states the thickness of the rock salt to be 20 mètres, and that the summit is formed of chalky limestone with bands of flint, belonging to the Cretaceo-nummulitic formation. In this view I am unable to concur ; and possibly, if M. Lartet had been able to examine the summit himself, he would have arrived at a different conclusion.

many places this marl, the ancient floor of the Dead Sea, is solidified into calcareous crusts and blocks of various degrees of consistency; and frequently crystals of selenite, in stellate patches, from 1 to 3 inches across, of a pale brown colour, lie on the surface. The central ridge is about 200 yards from the western edge of Jebel Usdum, and forms its axis, lying north and south magnetic. An easier descent would bring one down to an inner wâdy, sloping north and south from a central height of about 400 feet above the Dead Sea, or 200 below the summit. Thus this mountain of salt, or rather of marl with a foundation of salt, is completely isolated. Its length is about six miles. It would be easy to ascend Jebel Usdum from either end, or from the inner wâdy between it and the limestone declivities of Judæa about a mile beyond. The summit corresponds accurately with the height of the conspicuous marls all round the southern base of the Dead Sea. I estimated their levels in Wâdy Arabah, and in two or three places in the ravines, and on the cliff sides to the east and south-east of our encampment in The Ghôr near Es Safieh, and their upper limit always lay somewhere been 600 and 650 feet.

"From the plateau on the summit of Jebel Usdum there descends a gully to the north, which one would imagine it would take a wider watershed to form. Down this we descended, Laurence having joined me on the top, by a cutting through deep smoothly-sliced walls of marl, white and unspeakably dusty. Often these are finely and beautifully laminated with great regularity, showing the ancient planes of deposition. No trace of organic matter could be detected in them. Nevertheless, at the very summit almost, were the burrows of a small rodent (I believe the porcupine mouse *Acomys dimidiatus*, Gray); and a solitary sparrow-hawk, perched on the highest point, was hardly induced to make room for me. A couple of tamarisk bushes reminded me of botany, and about six other species of plants, all of the Desert type, were noted in the upper hundred feet. As we descended straggler after straggler appeared in the dry watercourse; and by the time we reached the wide Muhauwat Wâdy at the north-west corner of Jebel Usdum, some forty thirsty feverish grey weeds had put in their appearance. Here our successful little detour was somewhat marred by finding we had caused our comrades alarm, and our ever-watchful guardian had been induced to send Bedawins to scour the country for us. We availed ourselves of the delay by a swim, or rather wade, in the Dead Sea, an experience which I shall ever recall with a pious horror of smarting eyes and inflamed scratches."

While exploring the shores of the Salt Sea, I saw evidence which convinced me that its waters are still receding. A terrace of gravel stretches from the base of the salt cliffs outwards towards the margin of the sea to a distance, in some places, of 30 yards ; it then abruptly terminates in a descent of about 5 feet to the line of drift wood which marks the upper limit of the waters. That the gravel terrace was originally the bed of the Salt Sea does not admit of a doubt, so that since it was laid dry the waters have fallen to the extent (5 feet) above indicated. The formation of this terrace must be of very recent date, but *that* may be over a thousand years. When the waters covered the terrace they washed the base of the cliffs of the salt mountain, which they do not now appear to be ever able to reach.

We lunched on this terrace by the shores of the sea, in which some of our party were courageous enough to bathe. My aneroid marked 32° 1', which, according to the determination of the Ordnance Survey, would mean for that day 1,292 feet below the level of the Mediterranean.

Leaving the shores of the Salt Sea, and the northern extremity of the Jebel Usdum, we crossed the stony bed of the Muhauwat, which sometimes sweeps down from the interior, and is joined by that of the Zuweirah, so that the combined effects of these torrents is to cover an area of about half-a-mile with great piles of shingle and large blocks of limestone and chert. Here it was that Canon Tristram started a herd of twenty-two gazelles; but we were not so fortunate.

As the sun was now approaching the horizon, and we had done a good deal in the way of exploration, we would gladly have camped at the base of the hills to the north of Jebel Usdum, but the time at our disposal did not permit of so leisurely a progress. Our stations had been arranged beforehand, and our mules with the tent-equipage were far in advance ; it was therefore necessary to press onwards, and we turned our horses' heads up the bed of the Wâdy Zuweirah, along which the only practicable path to Beersheba and Gaza lies. The pathway through the windings of this ravine was steep, and often difficult, owing to the slippery surface of the limestone ledges ; but our good steeds never lost their footing. Often the walls of rock, constructed of beds of limestone and dark chert,[1] rose high above our heads, while the terraces of marl, sand, and gravel, belonging to the ancient Salt Sea bed, might be observed clinging to the sides of the older formation, and running up the branching ravines to a level of about 600 feet above the waters of the Salt Sea. It was clear from the relations

[1] Chert is a silicious stone often found in limestones, and like flint is very hard.

of these two formations that this deep glen had been hollowed out before it had been invaded by the waters of the sea. At a subsequent period these rose to a level of about 600 feet above the present surface ; and while wearing down the walls of the valley allowed the beds of marl and gravel by which the valley itself was partially filled up to be accumulated ; when again the waters fell away, and receded to their present level, the torrent channelled out its bed chiefly through these softer materials, which, by their lighter colours as well as by their composition, can be easily distinguished from the older limestone strata.[1]

We passed the interesting ruins, described by Canon Tristram, and referred by him to the period of the Crusades,[2] though referred by Dr. Robinson to the Saracens, and continuing our course ultimately attained to the upper surface of the table-land. The sun was now setting, and we had yet several miles of broken country to cross before reaching our camp in the Wâdy el Abd. It soon became pitch dark ; but fortunately two of our Arabs from Hebron were well acquainted with the path, which they tracked with wonderful sagacity ; while our horses managed to keep their footing, even when sliding down into a rocky ravine, the floor of which was quite invisible, at least to my eyes ; or when climbing some slippery bank. Mile after mile was traversed in the darkness, and yet no kindly light gleamed forth amid the encircling gloom to indicate the place of our camp. At length, as we were beginning to fear we had lost our way, or had passed the camping ground in the darkness, Gordon appeared on the top of a bank holding a lantern and pointing out the way. On arriving we found ourselves inside a stony glen, the floor of which had to be cleared of stones before the tents could be pitched, and nothing was prepared for our reception. Cold and weary with a march of twelve hours or more, we went down to join our Arab escort, who, seated around their fires, were preparing the evening meal. They politely welcomed us, spread their sheepskins on the ground for us to rest on, and then proceeded to prepare coffee for us ere partaking of any themselves. After awhile our tents were got ready, and throwing ourselves on our beds " tired nature's sweet restorer—balmy sleep," soon came to our relief.

The next morning we were up and off betimes, and we continued our ascent towards the table-land by a path which wound along the

---

[1] A drawing showing the relations of the ancient deposits of the Dead Sea to those of older date at W. Suweirah is given by Lartet, " Voyage d'Exploration." Plate II.   [2] " Land of Israel," p. 356.

sides of the limestone hills, sometimes crossing ledges of bare slippery rock, on which our horses had much ado to keep their footing. In some places the rounded form of the hills, the close herbage, and the numerous sheep-tracks running along the sides, reminded me of the chalky downs of the South of England ; and we noticed several flocks of white sheep and black goats of the Jáhálin Arabs pasturing on the fresh grass and tender herbs which the recent rains were causing to spring up. On reaching the summit we noticed a large cairn a short distance to our left, on which Major Kitchener had planted his theodolite ; and, assisted by Mr. Armstrong, was taking bearings on several prominent points and objects which here came into view. We were now at an elevation of about 3,500 feet above the Salt Sea, and consequently we were in a commanding position for a view in every direction. Far below, towards the east, was the deep depression of The Ghôr, holding in its spacious lap the blue waters of the Salt Sea. Beyond the hills and table-land of Moab, and towards the south-east, the green oasis of Es Safieh, which had sheltered us for so many days. The whole surroundings of the sea, except the northern end, lay spread out before us like a map. *There* was the Lissân, projecting far into its waters from the eastern side, its white surface glistering in the morning sun. Far away towards the south were seen the range of hills bordering the Wâdy el Arabah, and conspicuous amongst the several heights rose the conical summit of Mount Hor. At our feet the limestone hills resembled a continuous sea of ridges and furrows, tumultuously thrown together, and presenting every variety of brown, yellow, and light green shades amongst the hollows, while the dark brown beds of chert imparted definite form and outline to the ridges and scarps. The white table-land of Jebel Usdum, deeply scored and furrowed, was just visible behind the darker cliffs of limestone to the south of our position. The cairn on which we stood was of large dimensions, about 50 feet in diameter, circular in form, and constructed of large blocks of chert. The centre was hollow and about 10 feet in depth ; it probably marks the grave of some great chief.

We camped for luncheon on the rolling plains of " The Wilderness of Paran," which, if the hollows were cultivated, might produce abundant crops of wheat and other grain. The only inhabitant now is the Jáhálin shepherd and his flock, and a few wild animals. In some places the herbage was freckled over with multitudes of little white snails (*Helix seetzeni* and *H. vesialis*), covering the ground and climbing up the desert-plants, which appeared as if sprinkled with snow. Along with these were a few specimens of a shell in form like a small *Trochus*, of a brown colour, and the whorls handsomely sculptured (*II. tuberculosa*). I presented the specimens to Mr. Hart for description. The plains are entirely treeless—neither tree nor shrub are to be seen for miles; nevertheless, the ground was green with herbs, small plants, and grass; and amongst them could be distinguished, even at this early season, cyclamens, a pretty little marigold, and a mallow in much esteem with the Arabs as a vegetable. Flocks of small birds, such as larks, wagtails, starlings, green plover, and pin-tailed grouse, abounded, and imparted somewhat of life to the otherwise desolate landscape. In the afternoon we pitched our tents at Tel-el-Milh, the Moladah of the Bible,[1] where water is always to be found. From the reference to Moladah, Beersheba, and other cities with the villages thereof, it seems evident that the tract of country, through which our road towards Gaza lay, had been largely inhabited both before and after the Captivity;—but how great is now the change! Of the works of man little remain but a few wells, which fortunately preserve the names of the original sites, together with the foundations of stone walls, or small mounds of stone, bricks, and pottery. The physical features alone remain; the hills, valleys, river channels, and brook courses are probably much as they were in the time of the prophet Nehemiah, or even earlier. The patriarchs and prophets gazed on the same hills, valleys, and plains that we do now; and in reading the sacred records we recognise the careful accuracy of the references to these phenomena on every hand. There is, as it seems to me, some satisfaction in this reflection; and in surveying the landscape one is tempted to recall the pathetic lines of Sir Walter Scott, as applied by him to the natural scenery of his native land—

> " It seems to us of all bereft,
> Sole friends thy hills and vales are left;
> And thus we love them better still,
> E'en in the extremity of ill."

The wells of Tel-el-Milh are sunk about 60 yards from the river bank —one shallow and dry, the other deep and containing water. They are of excellent construction, built throughout of hewn blocks of limestone in regular courses; the depth to the water I estimated at 60 feet. The edge stones are deeply grooved by the ropes of men who have drawn water

[1] One of the outpost cities of Judah towards Edom (Josh. xv, 26; Nehem. xi, 26).

therefrom during a period of perhaps three thousand years ; and in an outer circle round the well are ranged nine large stone troughs for cattle to drink out of. These are supported in position by little piles of stones.[1]

We arrived at Beersheba early in the afternoon of Saturday, and pitched in the vicinity of "Abraham's Wells," which, like those of Tel-el-Milh, are sunk a few yards from the river's brink. The reason for this

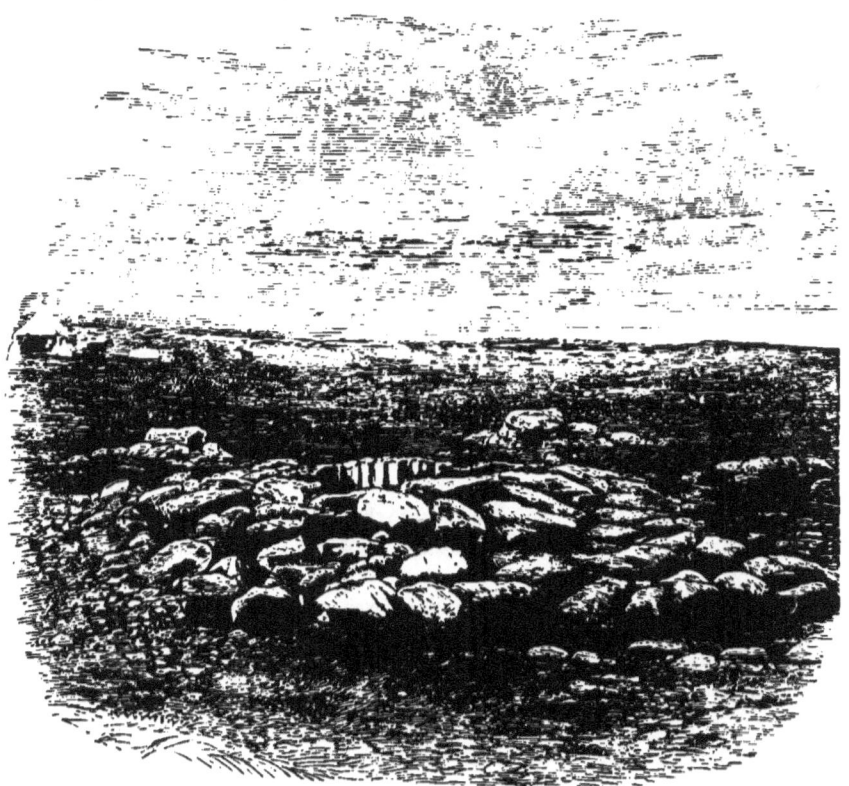

FIG. 18.—ABRAHAM'S WELL, BEERSHEBA.

is obvious. The well-sinker knew that the chances of a constant supply were greatest in the low ground which borders a river's bank, and that the water from the river itself would find its way by percolation into the well. Yet are the wells themselves at a sufficient elevation to prevent

[1] For a picture and account of these wells, see "The Land of Israel," p. 374.

the river water, which is generally turgid, from getting *direct* access to the water of the wells. In the selection of the sites, as well as in the execution of the work, there has, therefore, been displayed both judgment and skill; while it must have been a work requiring both strength and perseverance to hollow out of the hard limestone rock, of which this region is formed, wells of such depth and excellence of construction. Captain Conder states that the depth of the larger well is over 45 feet, lined with rings of masonry to a depth of 28 feet, and he made a discovery which, as he remarks, was rather disappointing, namely, that the masonry is not very ancient. Fifteen courses down, on the south side of the large well, he found a stone with an inscription in Arabic on a tablet dated 505 A.H., that is, in the twelfth century.[1] This discovery, however, does not throw any doubt on the antiquity of the wells themselves, but may only refer to the date of their restoration from a state of previous dilapidation.

Beersheba and its surroundings have been so often described that it is not my intention to dwell further on this most interesting locality. It was a reward of many a day's toil to stand on the spot where dwelt the Father of the Faithful; to drink of the same well of which he drank; and to look upon the same scenes which, day after day for several years of his eventful life, met his gaze. The history of the Patriarch becomes on this spot a vivid reality.

We had now reached the southern margin of the tract included in the Ordnance Survey Map of Western Palestine.[2] All the way between Tel-el-Milh and Bir es Sebâ (Beersheba) the country is strewn with ruins of walls and foundations of buildings, showing how thickly it was once inhabited. Now, the land is "desolate, almost without inhabitant;" for during the fourteen miles of march between these places, we only twice fell in with human beings: on one occasion a Bedawin; on the other, fellahin ploughing with their camels.

The pressure on our time, the expense consequent on our detention in The Ghôr, and prospective detention in Gaza, forbade the idea of the usual Sunday rest; we therefore pressed on for another day's march to Tel Abu Hareireh, a distance of about fifteen miles. The country we traversed consisted of an undulating plain, over the sides and hollows of

---

[1] "Tent Work in Palestine." New edition, p. 246.

[2] The district about Tel-el-Milh and Beersheba was surveyed by Captain Conder and Major Kitchener, assisted by Serjeant Armstrong, who, with the exception of the first, were now revisiting the scene of their former labours.

which was spread a deep covering of loam of a very fertile nature; while from time to time horizontal beds of white chalky limestone cropped out along the sides of the valleys. The district is extensively cultivated by the Terabin Arabs, and by little parties of fellahin, who annually squat down for the season between sowing and reaping, living with their families in tents pitched in sheltered spots. Here the camel is largely used for ploughing, one camel being equal to two oxen, and the tall gaunt form of "the ship of the desert" might often be seen against the sky-line moving slowly along in front of the plough and the plougher. This was a kind of work at which some of us had not hitherto seen the camel employed. The extent of ground here cultivated, as well as all the way to Gaza, is immense, and the crops of wheat, barley, and maize must vastly exceed the requirements of the population. In fact, large quantities of agricultural produce raised in this part of Palestine are annually exported from Jaffa and other towns; and as we approach the western seaboard the cultivation improves, till about Gaza, El Medjel, and Jaffa, it attains a degree of excellence scarcely surpassed by that of Italy, France, or England.

We camped by the side of a running stream at the foot of Tel Abu Hareireh, on which is placed the tomb of the distinguished personage of that name. Our dragoman, Ibraham, who is a great authority on all matters connected with "the Prophet," informed me that Abu Hareireh was one of the "companions" of Mohammed, and a great scribe and commentator on the Koran. How he came to die, and be interred in this out-of-the-way spot, is a point on which my informant was unable to throw light. The spot, however, was of other interest to us, for here we came into contact with a new geological formation, hitherto, as I believe, unrecognised, but which occupies an extensive area stretching through the land of Philistia northwards to the base of Mount Carmel. This formation consists of rather hard yellow calcareous sandstone, traversed by joint planes similar to those of the limestone. I was unable anywhere to observe a junction between the two formations, but judging by the general position of the strata throughout this part of Palestine, there can be little doubt that the sandstone is newer than the limestone of the central plateau, which dips towards the west and passes below the sandstone in the direction of the Mediterranean sea-board. (See Geological Map.)

In the position and relations of these two sets of strata, we have, as it seems to me, an explanation of the features of Western Palestine. It is now generally known that the whole of the interior table-land of Judah, and of Ephraim, is formed of exceedingly hard beds of limestone. In the centre of the table-land the strata reach their highest altitude, and are in a nearly horizontal position; but along the western slope they dip westwards, as may be seen in the sections along the Jaffa and Jerusalem road at Bab-el-Wâdy, east of Ramleh.[1] At the western margin of the table-land, which, commencing at Tel es Sherîah on the south, ranges northwards by 'Arâk el Menshiyet, Kezâzeh, Ramleh, Ludd, Kalkilieh, and El Marâh to the sea at Mount Carmel, the limestone gives place to the yellow sandstone. This latter being of a much softer character, and having been denuded from off the upper surface of the limestone plateau, it has also been deeply worn down along the tract of Philistia, and the Plain of Sharon; in consequence of which, this tract is much depressed, and is at a lower level than that formed of the limestone beds. As regards the geological age of the sandstone formation, my impression is, that it forms an upper member of the Eocene Tertiary series, and that it was accumulated beneath the waters of the sea, under conditions somewhat different from those which prevailed during the deposition of the Cretaceo-nummulitic limestone.[2]

Another object of interest which attracted our notice in the Wâdy es Sheriah, when camped at Tel Abu Hereirah, was the presence of beds of calcareous sand and gravel, containing numerous shells of varieties now living in the Mediterranean, including species of the genera *Pecten*, *Cardium*, *Ostrea*, *Dentalium*, *Turritella*, and species of *Echini*. The aneroid showed that we were here about 200 feet above the level of the Mediterranean, so that we could not doubt we had again before us a portion of "the 200 feet raised beach," which we had seen along the shores of the Gulf of Suez, and to the north of the Gulf of Akabah. We subsequently noticed this raised sea-bed at intervals all the way to Jaffa, where its presence is marked by a sandy or gravelly terrace, containing numerous sea-shells, amongst which *Pectunculus violascens, Purpura hemi-*

---

[1] This is very well represented by Lartet in the "Coupe hypothetique de Jaffa á Shihan," *supra cit.*, Plate II.

[2] We examined this rock at Jaffa, Yazûr, Yebnah, Gaza, and other places, but were unable to discover the presence of fossils. It seems to be represented in Egypt by Schweinfurth's "brauner kalksandstein" of the upper Eocene period. ("Ueber die Geol. Schichten d. Mokattam b. Cairo." "Abd. a. d. Zeit. d. Deuts. Geol. Gesellschaft." 1883.)

stoma, Murex brandaris, and *Columbella rustica* are the most abundant forms.[1] This sea-beach runs up the valleys, and occupies the plains, of Western Palestine along the sea-board to a level of about 200 feet, as in the valley below Tel Abu Hareireh.

On the last day of the year 1883 we parted with our colleague, Major Kitchener, who had arranged to return to Cairo, and thus escape detention in quarantine at Gaza. His departure was greatly regretted by us all. He had proved a most agreeable companion during our journeyings of nearly two months, while his knowledge of the Arab customs and language, and his skill in dealing with the Bedawins, proved of much service to the Expedition. Assisted by Mr. Armstrong, Major Kitchener had worked unsparingly, and under many difficulties, owing to the necessary rapidity of our movements, in order to produce a correct outline map of the district we had traversed between Mount Sinai and Southern Palestine. The necessary observations had now been made; and there was, therefore, no necessity that he should accompany us further, much less that he should subject himself to the restrictions of a quarantine detention. He, therefore, made arrangements with the four Hawatat Arabs, who had arrived when we were camping in The Ghôr, to return with them to Cairo, though by a road probably never before traversed by an Englishman; and ere we struck our tents for the day's march into Gaza, Kitchener, mounted on his little horse, and accompanied by his four Arabs on their camels, crossed the Wâdy es Sheriah, and taking a south-westerly line of march, made for Ismailia, which he ultimately reached in safety.[2]

Our march towards Gaza lay over an undulating country, generally covered deeply with loam, and extensively cultivated by the Terabin Arabs, whose camps we frequently passed. Numerous small plants were unfolding their petals under the influence of the warm sunshine, and amongst others the scarlet anemone (*Anemone coronaria,* Lin.), so rich and beautiful in colour that on seeing it for the first time I involuntarily exclaimed, "Surely this is the 'lily of the field'!"—a view in which Mr. Hart concurred.[3] Numerous bulbous plants overspread the ground,

---

[1] The first-named is by far the most abundant, as it is on the sea-shore at the present day. The other forms are much rarer, and are given by Lartet, *supra cit.,* p. 170.

[2] The distance was about 140 English miles, and he was everywhere well received by the Arabs whom he happened to meet.

[3] On referring to the "Teacher's Oxford Bible," I find the scarlet anemone

but had not yet come into flower; and occasionally we came upon the leafy tuft of that peculiar plant, the mandrake (*Mandragora officinalis*), supposed to be the same as that mentioned in Genesis xxx, 14, with its purple bell-shaped flowers concealed within the interior of its "primrose-like" leaves.

About noon we reached Khurbet el Baha, an artificial mound, marked on the Ordnance Survey Map, about 120 feet across at the base, and 30 feet high. It is covered by broken pottery and pieces of slag, and commands an extensive prospect over the plains. Here we set up our luncheon tent and rested for a while. Just as we were preparing to remount our horses, an Arab Sheikh, gorgeously arrayed, with two attendants, and spear in hand, rode up towards our tent, and after the usual salutations, we inquired of him to what tribe he belonged. He replied, "I am Sheikh of the Tihyaha. All the lands you see around (waving his hand proudly) we have taken from the Terabin, who have gone further south to the country of the Azâzimeh." After a little more conversation he bid us farewell and rode away. This Sheikh was certainly the finest representative of an Arab chief I had seen. What he had mentioned referred to a contest which had raged for several years between the Tihyaha and the Terabin tribes about the ownership of a tract of land in which the former were the victors. The Government were obliged ultimately to interfere; and, having sent a body of soldiers with guns into the district, compelled the Sheikhs of the respective parties to come to terms, the Terabin being obliged to surrender a portion of their territory.

Shortly after starting, a herd of fifteen gazelles crossed our path in open order some distance ahead of us. It was the largest herd I had seen; and it was a beautiful sight to see these graceful animals bounding across the plain; of course, no one was prepared for this, and the gazelles passed unmolested by us. Coming to the foot of a low ridge which our path crossed, and from which we expected to get a sight of the Mediterranean and of Gaza in the foreground, we put our horses into a gallop, which, to do them justice, they were always ready to go in for. On reaching the summit, we had an extensive prospect. Gaza, our future prison, lay at the other side of an extensive and fertile plain, which swept

mentioned as most probably that with which our Lord contrasted the raiment of King Solomon. Canon Tristram entertains a similar view.

away from our feet for several miles ; beyond, was the broad blue streak
of the Mediterranean, our pathway to Europe and home ! Gaza itself
looked inviting ; charmingly situated on a low range of hills amongst
palm-trees and olive gardens, while numerous flocks of sheep and goats,
together with herds of cattle, were pasturing at intervals upon the plain.
The sight of the sea raised our spirits, notwithstanding the prospect of
imprisonment. Cantering along we passed a picket of soldiers belonging to the quarantine, and soon were winding our way through the
gardens and hedgerows of cacti towards the sand-hills on the west of the
city, where arrangements had been made by Bernhard Heilpern, who had
preceded us, for our encampment. To the last we had flattered ourselves
with the hope that our friends in Jerusalem had succeeded in getting a
remission of the order for our imprisonment, and that Heilpern would
have good news for us upon our arrival. But no ! On the contrary, orders
had come that we were to put in our fifteen days at Gaza. Amongst
other letters was one from the British Consul, Mr. Moore, confirming the
tidings, and recommending that, as he was unable to effect our release, I
should telegraph to Lord Dufferin, the British Ambassador at Constantinople, asking his intervention on our behalf. This I lost no time in
doing ; and, as will be seen in the sequel, had an immediate reply of the
most friendly kind. The delay to this extent would have proved a serious
loss of time as well as of money, as we should have had to pay for, and
support, not only ourselves, but our muleteers, and even our guard of
soldiers, of whom three were placed as sentries round our camp. We
estimated that, for the whole time, the cost would amount to £150, or
possibly more.

We found our tents pleasantly situated, beneath a small grove of locust
trees, tamarisks, and sycamores, in a hollow, bounded on one side by
gardens, and on the other by sand-hills which stretched towards the sea-
shore, and formed an excellent protection from the westerly winds. From
the sand-hills behind our tents we had a good view of Gaza and the
district towards the east, but the sea was completely hidden from our
view. The Rev. Mr. Schapira, of the Church Missionary Society, was
waiting to receive us, and to offer us every assistance in his power, and
during our stay we were indebted to him for numerous friendly offices.
A budget of letters and papers, the first we had received since leaving
Suez, gave us abundant occupation for the rest of the day, and we awaited
with some equanimity the result of our application to Lord Dufferin.

CHAPTER XV.

AMONGST THE PHILISTINES.

New Year's Day, 1884.—This day was spent in camp, writing letters and sending telegrams. Mr. Schapira came early to the camp, to wish us "a happy new year," and brought a copy of the *Standard* of the 9th December, which was very acceptable. Shortly afterwards came the medical officer of quarantine, mounted on a pony, with an attendant. He was an Italian, and spoke his own language, or French, with great volubility. We endeavoured to impress upon him the absurdity of keeping our party in durance, as it was six weeks since we left Egypt, and, therefore, we might be presumed to be perfectly free from the taint of infection. He replied that his orders to detain us were imperative, and that the quarantine regulations were "international." That it did not matter how long we had been out of Egypt, and that he could only release us if we gave him our word of honour that we had not come from that country. He congratulated us on our healthy appearance, and expressed his regret at the necessity for keeping us in quarantine for fifteen days ; and wished us "good-bye," remarking that he "must return home to dinner." He then formally declared us in quarantine, and rode away. Two additional sentries were placed round our camp, cutting off our outlet to the sand-hills, which the day previous we had been allowed to ramble over.

Early in the morning of Wednesday, 3rd January, a telegram was received from Lord Dufferin, stating that he was doing all in his power to obtain our release from quarantine. This was good news, and we all felt grateful to his lordship for so promptly complying with our request. Shortly after, the medical officer again arrived, bringing newspapers, copies of the *Revue des deux Mondes,* and desiring special introductions to each member of our party. He then presented us with a bottle of wine, another of excellent Trieste beer, and wished us—"adieu."

On Saturday morning, the fifth from our entrance into Gaza, our eyes were gladdened by the sight of the doctor, accompanied by Mr. Schapira, making their way towards the camp. A wave from Mr. Schapira's hand was the first intimation of our release, and a telegram from Lord Dufferin was handed to me intimating the immediate prospect of this event. This I read out, and a cheer for his lordship burst forth from all the party. I immediately telegraphed our thanks, and also expressed to Mr. Schapira our gratitude for his friendly offices. Orders were given to prepare our horses for a ramble through and around Gaza, and my son returned to the city in company with the doctor, Mr. Schapira, and Bernhard Heilpern, to square up accounts—a most unpleasant transaction, as it afterwards proved.[1]

On Sunday, 6th January, after prayers in the tent, we left our camp at Gaza, in the forenoon, so as to reach El Medjet by the evening, on our way to Jaffa. Winding through the hedgerows of prickly pear, we entered an extensive forest of very ancient olive-trees, some of great size and girth, and some of which may have been at least a thousand years old. All along our way on the right the land was extensively cultivated, and numerous teams of oxen or camels were turning up the fallow ground. On the left, however, a different scene presented itself. The high sand-hills, under which we had camped at Gaza, continued all along, advancing inland or retreating towards the coast, but on the whole a continuous feature all along the sea-board of Philistia.[2] These enormous accumulations of fine sand, being driven by the westerly winds, are constantly advancing towards the east; swallowing up lands, gardens, farms, and even villages, in their resistless progress. They thus constitute a serious source of danger, and a constant menace to such towns as Gaza, El Jora, Ascalon (now partly buried in sand), Esdúd, and Yazúr, which are situated near their borders. It is well known, in fact, that ruins of the ancient Gaza are now lying buried beneath the sandhills;

[1] The early release of our party proved a great disappointment to the doctor, who, notwithstanding his attentions above stated, really expected to make a very handsome thing out of us—five Englishmen. Owing, however, to Mr. Schapira's interference we were not allowed to pay more than was legally due, amounting to 53½ dollars, the sum originally demanded being 20 dollars for each of the five travellers, and 10 to 15 dollars for each of the attendants and muleteers. They also wanted us to pay for the use of our own tents, and for the custody of our baggage which we had in the camp!

[2] The sandhills are clearly marked on the Ordnance Map of Western Palestine.

L

and, as this city had a port named Majuma as late as the sixth century of our era, which has now disappeared, it is quite possible that the ancient city, which it cost Alexander the Great such an effort to take, may have been swallowed up, and that the present site may be much more recent. The only place where I observed a barrier to the progress of "the irresistible destroyer," was along the banks of the Wâdy-el-Halîb, where for some distance the sand appears to be swept away by the waters of the river as fast as it enters its channel. On the eastern bank the country was free from sand.[1]

Towards evening we pitched our tent in an open space outside the walls of Medjet (Migdol Gad, one of the towns given to Judah, Josh. xv, 37) amidst cultivated fields, gardens, and olive groves. Some of the olive-trees are of large size, and hollow in the interior; one which I measured was 19 feet in circumference at 4 feet from the ground. Hart measured others of even greater girth. The district around is the raised sea-bed, and in the loam and sand occur numerous shells, especially those of the *Pectunculus glycineris*.

It was with extreme regret that we were unable to visit Ascalon, which lay several miles to the west of our road, but time did not permit. The reader, however, will have less cause of regret owing to the excellent description of this most interesting city given by Captain Conder.[2] In the course of the following day we passed through another of the five cities of the Philistines, Ashdod (Asdûd), standing on two hillocks surrounded by gardens; and in the afternoon we camped for the midday meal at Yebna (Jabneel, Josh. xv. 11). It is remarkable how slightly the old Scripture names have changed, and consequently in traversing this interesting country our thoughts are from time to time carried back to the wars of Israel with the Philistines, and the eventful histories of David, of Saul, and of Sampson. The huge form of Goliath of Gath rises before our eyes; and at some distance to the right of our

[1] On the origin of these remarkable sand-hills, I shall have a good deal to say when I come to deal with the geology of this part of the country. I may here briefly state that I consider the sands to have been previously derived from the disintegration of the sandstone of Philistia, and their accumulation by the winds to be consequent on the elevation of the coast-line and the sea-bed.

[2] "Tent Work in Palestine," p. 281. The author states that the sands are advancing year by year, and having climbed over the southern walls are destroying the fruitful gardens on that side of the city.

line of march we could see the great valley on either side of which were
drawn up in martial array the armies of the Philistines and "the hosts
of the Living God," and where the stripling laid the monster giant low
with a stone from the sling. The road we were travelling had often felt
the tramp of armies. Here the hosts of Assyria and of Egypt had
passed and repassed. Later on, those of Alexander, of the Romans,
the Crusaders, and last of all, of Napoleon Buonaparte. The country
along which we wended our way was excellently cultivated, and often
formed of rich brown loam many feet deep. Camels and oxen were
busy in the fields, or passed us laden with agricultural produce, while
large herds and flocks of cattle and sheep covered the pasture lands. The
land is cultivated by the fellahin ; and, if any of them are descended from
the race of the giants, I can well believe it, as they are for the most
part men of good stature, if not of gigantic proportions. All along our
road to the left, the desolating sand-hills might be seen—sometimes at a
distance rising in steep slopes, threatening to bury the country at their
feet. In one spot, a short distance south of Yazûr, the sandy avalanche
had descended the hillside, and had partially covered the gardens and
park of some important householder (apparently in the position of a
"country gentlemen" at home), and it seemed only a question of time
when the house itself would be entombed ; some fine trees, which had
originally decorated the grassy slopes of the adjoining park, were now
rising out of a surface of sand. At length, after passing the suburbs of
Yazûr, we emerged towards evening on the high road from Jaffa to
Jerusalem. It was a new experience to tread on a paved or "metalled"
road, and to meet a waggonette carrying passengers. For two months
we had been traversing pathless wastes, or following tracks of animals,
sometimes scarcely perceptible ; but we had not till now trod a carriage
road, nor witnessed any vehicle in the form of a stage coach. We felt
that we had now left the desert and its people behind, and were coming
in contact with Western civilisation ! This feeling was intensified when,
after winding along lanes in the suburbs of Jaffa, bordered by groves of
orange and lemon trees laden with fruit, we found ourselves within the four
walls of "the Jerusalem Hotel," and were able to stretch our limbs on a bed
under cover of a roof, and to rest after a ride of thirty English miles. Perhaps it was ungrateful not to feel in boisterous spirits at the change in our
surroundings which we had experienced ; but, truth to tell, camp life had
become, not only familiar, but pleasant to us ; and our feelings at changing

it for one of a more civilised kind were not altogether those of unmixed pleasure.

Time did not admit of a prolonged stay at this interesting old city, but only of a visit to the beach, the fountain, and "the House of Simon the Tanner."[1] A natural breakwater of calcareous sandstone projects outwards into the Mediterranean from the ancient walls at the south end of the town. Outside this all large ships are obliged to cast anchor ; and passengers as well as cargoes have to be received and discharged by means of boats, which frequently have to breast a heavy surf. The rock is seen under the lens to be composed of comminuted shells, pieces of coral, and other marine forms ; and it appeared to me to be of recent formation, raised into the air when the whole sea-bed was being elevated. A similar formation of shelly limestone appears still to be in process of consolidation along the shore further towards the north, where it is quarried just under the sands at the margin of low water. The shells of which it is formed are those which strew the shore in immense numbers, chiefly those of *Pectunculus glycineris.*

A similar formation has been recognised by Drs. Hedenborg and Lartet as occurring at other points of the coast of Palestine and Syria, as, for example, at Tyre and Sidon, and they attribute its position at, or near, the surface, to the recent slow elevation of the sea-bed, which may be still in progress.[2]

Having made a circuit of the town, and paid off our dragoman Ibraham and his assistant, we mounted our horses early in the afternoon in order to proceed to Ramleh, where we proposed to break the journey by passing the night on our way to Jerusalem. The hotel at Ramleh, like that at Jaffa, was kept by a German Lutheran, and was clean and comfortable. A pretty little gazelle was the playmate of the family, and we felt grateful to the German nation all round, who send settlers to Palestine in order to provide "gasthausen" for weary travellers. Ramleh is a village pleasantly situated amongst gardens, and groves of olive-trees, sycamores, and carob-trees. Its lofty tower rises high above the surrounding country, and is a work of great skill and excellence ; both Christians and Moslems claim the honour of having erected it, and if we are to believe the inscription over the door, the honour is due to the latter. Ramleh is a town of

---

[1] The traditional "House of Simon the Tanner" overlooks the breakwater ; it is now used as a small mosque.

[2] "Voyage d'Exploration de la Mer Morte," Vol. III, chap. x, p. 198, &c.

comparatively modern date, founded in A.D. 716 by 'Omayyad Khalif Suleimân,[1] but at a distance of only two miles to the north, on the old road to Jerusalem, is the village of Lydda (Lud), the name of which is dear to every reader of the New Testament, the home of Æneas. We are told that Lydda was nigh to Joppa,[2]—that is just twelve miles,—and thither the messengers from Joppa were sent to hasten the steps of the Apostle to the deathbed of Dorcas. Like Ramleh, Lydda is surrounded by extensive olive-groves, and seems a pleasant spot.

The road from Jaffa to Jerusalem is not one of the best in the world, but it is the best in Palestine. It is repaired when there is a prospect of the visit of some foreign prince or potentate. Not far out of Jaffa we passed a large number of men busily engaged in breaking stones for repairing the specially bad places, and near Ramleh we found them laying the stones on the mud and (will the reader credit the fact?) rolling them with segments of marble, or granite, columns which may have adorned some ancient palace, temple, or theatre! On seeing this desecration one might well exclaim—

" Sic transit gloria mundi !"

On leaving the courtyard of our hotel next morning I was shocked to behold, for the first time, a group of lepers, who, lining the wayside on either hand, plaintively called on the "hawajahs" for bakhsheesh, and holding out their hands approached unpleasantly close to the horses. Except on the Bethlehem road outside the walls of Jerusalem I nowhere else saw any persons afflicted with this incurable disease. An excellent hospital for the reception of these unhappy beings has been established outside Jerusalem by the liberality of Germans and English. It is presided over by a pious German, who has devoted himself to the duty of attending on the patients, who are well cared for when within the walls. Unfortunately, however, for society, seclusion of lepers is not compulsory, and thus the disease, which is hereditary, is perpetuated. Under the circumstances, of which I was fully informed,[3] it is a crime against society to give alms to the lepers of Palestine.

On leaving Ramleh the sky was cloudy, and rain was falling; but as we proceeded the weather improved, and our ride was full of interest. About

---

[1] According to Baedeker, "Palestine and Syria," p. 133.

[2] Acts ix, 36.

[3] By our conductor, B. Heilpern.

noon we came in view of the Valley of Ajalon, renowned in Jewish history, stretching away to the northwards till lost amidst the hills; and shortly after, we halted at Bab-el-Wâdy (the mouth of the Valley) for the midday meal. Here the table-land of Central Palestine rises from the plain, and the glen itself, hollowed out of sheets of limestone, affords a field of great interest to the botanist. As we ascend it gradually expands in breadth ; and the olive-trees, which line the brook-course, gradually spread over the sides of the glen, and ultimately rise to the hill-tops, so as to cover, as with a forest, the whole surface of the country. Hart soon found abundant occupation amongst the shrubs and plants which lined the ledges of the limestone rocks, or had obtained a footing in their fissures or on their sides. They were for the most part evergreens, approaching in character those of the south or west of Europe and the British Isles ;—or, perhaps, rather those of the Jura hills and the borders of the Alps. One could recognise a large-leafed barberry, an arbutus, a dwarf oak with large acorns (*Quercus pseudo-coccifera*, Desp.) a *Poterium spinosum*, and several prickly shrubs. A pretty little cyclamen, a large daisy, and a "bachelor's button" peeped out here and there from under the bushes. To make the surroundings more homelike *there* were our robin redbreast and a blackbird flying about, and coming as confidingly close to us as they are wont to do in England when unmolested. On ascending to the top of the long valley, and turning a point of the road, we were able to look back through a gap in the hills, and we could see far below us the plain of Ramleh and Lydda, and in the distance the blue waters of the Mediterranean.

Our road for many miles wound along the sides of these bare limestone hills, or overlooked the very deep ramifying valleys which penetrate far into the central table-land. The scenery was most peculiar, and differing from any I had seen elsewhere. The absence of natural forest trees in valleys, which one would suppose were peculiarly fitted for their presence, together with the scarcity of verdure, cannot but strike the eye even of the most cursory spectator ; while on the other hand, where labour had been bestowed in cultivating these stony valley sides, the results were evidently most successful ; as, for instance, in the vicinity of Lôba and Kastal. At length, on reaching a bend in the road on the verge of the spacious Wâdy Suleiman, we noticed a little hamlet perched on the hill-side to our left, and marked by three small white domes. "That," said Bernhard Heilpern, "is Kûlonieh, in all probability the village of Emmaus;[1] it is just the distance of a 'sabbath-day's journey' from Jerusalem." So now we were for the first time approaching the scene of the Saviour's converse with the disciples when about to leave our world, and in a few minutes we should be treading the very road which had been pressed by His footsteps. I felt that the place was to me holy ground.

We recollect Cowper's lines :—

> " It happened on a solemn eventide,
> Soon after He, who was our Surety, died,
> Two bosom friends, each pensively inclined,
> The scene of all those sorrows left behind,
> Sought their own village, busied as they went
> In musings worthy of the great event.
> They thought Him, and they justly thought Him, one
> Sent to do more than He appeared to have done—
> To exalt a people, and to place them high
> Above all else, and wondered He should die!
> Ere yet they brought their journey to an end,
> A stranger joined them, courteous as a friend,
> And asked them with a kind, engaging air,
> What their affliction was, and begged a share.
> Informed, He gathered up the broken thread
> And, truth and wisdom gracing all He said,
> Explained, illustrated, and searched so well
> The tender theme on which they chose to dwell,
> That, reaching home, 'the night,' they said, 'is near,
> We must not now be parted—sojourn here.'
> The new acquaintance soon became a guest,
> And, made so welcome at their simple feast,
> He blessed the bread, but vanished at the word,
> And left them both exclaiming, ''Tis the Lord!'"

Full of such thoughts we pressed onwards along the rugged road towards the sacred city, and entered its gates just before sunset.

[1] Conder, "Tent Work in Palestine," p. 140.

CHAPTER XVI.

JERUSALEM, BETHLEHEM, AND SOLOMON'S POOLS.

WE were very kindly received by the friends of the Palestine Survey in Jerusalem, including H.B.M. Consul, Mr. Noel T. Moore ; the American Consul, Dr. Selah Merrill, Dr. Chaplin, Dr. Sandreczky, the Rev. A. H. Kelk, and Mr. Schick. Preparations were set on foot for a visit to Bethlehem and the Pools of Solomon, the Jordan Valley, and Jericho. Meanwhile we examined the quarries and rock-exposures in the vicinity of the Holy City.

The geological structure of the district is sufficiently simple to be explained within a short compass. Jerusalem itself is built on a platform of nearly horizontal strata of limestone, bounded in every direction except the north by deep valleys, along which the beds occasionally crop out in gently sloping courses. The valley along which the plateau terminates on the east is the Wâdy Sitti Mariam, or Valley of Jehoshaphat ; that on the west is the Wâdy Rahâbi, or Valley of Hinnom, and these two unite to form the Wâdy-en-Nâr, or the Valley of the Kedron, which follows a somewhat irregular course towards the south and east till it enters the Salt Sea south of Râs Feshkah. The Valley of Jehoshaphat is 204 feet in depth under the Mosque of Omar, and is bounded on the east by the Mount of Olives, which at Kefr-el-Tûr reaches an elevation of 2,683 feet above the level of the Mediterranean.[1] The hills to the outside of the valleys are somewhat higher than the Jerusalem platform, and thus, as has been often remarked, bear out the beautiful simile of Psalm cxxv, 2. They are composed of similar calcareous strata, and have a slight dip towards the south in the direction of the general drainage of the country. The valleys are therefore due to erosion facilitated by the solvent action of water containing carbonic acid gas ; the present streams, however, are only periodical and intermittent ; and it is probable that the remarkably deep valleys of the table-land of Palestine, as well as the

---

[1] As determined by the Ordnance Survey.

principal physical features, were hollowed out and sculptured at a time when the amount of rainfall was much greater than at present, and when these valleys and ravines formed the channels of swift perennial rivers. It is impossible to suppose that such deep and precipitous ravines as that of the Kedron at Mar Saba, and of the Cherith near Jericho, can be due to the action of the little rills that from time to time creep along their beds.[1]

Viewed on a large scale the limestone table-land of Judæa forms a great arch, near the centre of which is situated the capital of the country. As we have already observed, the general dip of the strata on entering the table-land at Bab-el-Wâdy is westward ; but as we ascend towards the higher elevations in an easterly direction the strata become flatter, and at length, at Beit Nakuba, they assume a nearly horizontal position. This continues as far as Jerusalem, where the beds begin to slope gently towards the south, and on passing by Bethany, and onwards along the road to Jericho, we find the dip to take a strong easterly trend, until close to the margin of the Jordan Valley, where they again approach the horizontal position. Over the whole of this region the depth of soil is exceedingly slight, and the solid framework may be clearly seen. Where the beds are horizontal they crop out along the sides of the deep glens and profound ravines in courses and ledges, the upper surfaces of which support a little reddish soil and a vegetation of small plants, but capable when cultivated of being turned to excellent account. The rock itself presents considerable variations in character as well as colour. Around Jerusalem it produces not only a solid and durable white building stone, but marbles of red, pink, and yellow colours capable of receiving a fine polish. In other places it is mottled, veined, or pure white. The upper beds, which occur in the direction of the Jordan Valley, contain numerous bands of dark chert (or flint); and where the strata are contorted, these bands, which are exceedingly hard, stand out on the hillsides and describe curiously curved lines and patterns which may be seen from considerable distances. All these strata, whether calcareous or silicious, are of organic origin, and were deposited below the waters of the sea during the Cretaceous and early Tertiary periods.

[1] I refer here to a period which may be termed "the Pluvial period" for this part of the world, which is represented by the "Glacial" and "post-Glacial" epochs of Britain and Europe. We have already seen evidence of a former Pluvial period in the Sinaitic Desert.

Dr. Fraas, in his geological map of the environs of Jerusalem,[1] shows that the strata consist of the following in descending order :—

1. Craie blanche (white chalk). Senonien, D'Orb.
2. Etage supérieur des Hippurites (locally called "Misseh").
3. Etage inférieur des Hippurites (locally called "Melekeh").
4. Zone des Ammonites rhotamargensis. Senonien, D'Orb.

The above strata are of Cretaceous age, but in the upper Hippurite limestone Dr. Fraas found nummulites, from which it would appear that there is a passage in this region from the Cretaceous into the lower Tertiary strata. Mr. Etheridge, also, identifies the uppermost strata of the Mount of Olives as of nummulitic Tertiary age.

The beds of the upper Hippurite stage ("Misseh") have yielded the large blocks used in the ancient structures of Jerusalem, such as those of the Wailing Place of the Jews, which have been extracted from the quarries near the Damascus Gate. They also yield the blocks used for ornamental purposes and works of art at the present day.

Sir Charles Wilson has shown that the reservoirs, sepulchres, and cellars under, and around, the sacred city are hewn out of the softer beds of the lower Hippurite limestone ("Melekeh") underneath the firmer and more durable marble beds of the upper zone. But, throughout Palestine and Arabia Petræa, the Cretaceous and Tertiary limestones are so intimately connected that it would be impossible, without a long and detailed survey, to represent on a geological map their respective limits.

It is not my intention in this place to inflict upon my readers my views regarding the sights and objects, sacred or secular, real or pretended, with which Jerusalem abounds, though I may have a little to add on some of these topics further on. I shall, therefore, restrict myself to the personal narrative of our Expedition down to the time when we bid farewell to Palestine and Syria.

From Jerusalem as a centre we had arranged to make excursions, southwards, to Bethlehem and the Pools of Solomon, and eastwards, to the Jordan Valley and Jericho, after which we were to proceed on horseback through North-Western Palestine, to visit the Sea of Galilee ; and crossing the country to Hâifa and Mount Carmel, to proceed northwards along the coast to Beyrût, from which we should leave for Europe. Events beyond our control prevented the accomplishment of the last stage of our programme, as will be seen in the sequel.

[1] Published in 1869.

January 12*th.*—We left Jerusalem early for the Pools of Solomon, and passing through the Jaffa Gate, proceeded southwards by the Hebron road, if such it could be called, as it is in many places in a semi-chaotic condition, rendering an occasional *excursus* into the fields alongside desirable or prudent. Everywhere along our route there were signs of improvement, barren spots being reclaimed and cultivated, fields enclosed and cleared of stones, and olive groves planted on the hill slopes. At length, after a ride which tried the mettle of our little horses, and sometimes the patience of the riders, we reached the brow of the valley in which are situated these remarkable reservoirs.[1] They are supposed to be referred to in Ecclesiastes ii, 6, but though the statement, "I made me pools of water," is a general one, there is little reason to doubt that these pools are included therein. The aqueduct which originally connected these reservoirs with the city has been partially cleared by Colonels Wilson and Warren, and is capable of being again utilised for the purpose. I was informed that the Baroness Burdett-Coutts, some time ago, offered at her own expense to have the water from the Pools re-introduced into Jerusalem, where it would have afforded a permanent and abundant supply of excellent spring water. Permission had, in the first instance, to be obtained from the Pasha, who replied, "Very well, give me the money and I will have the work done." To this her ladyship replied, "Thank you, but I fear if I hand you the money I shall never see either it or the water. If I have the work done, I shall employ English engineers and English workmen to do it, and entrust the supervision to Captain Wilson." This difficulty, however, was ultimately got over ; but a fatal obstacle was raised by the Turkish authorities on the question of distribution of the water and the permanent management,[2] so that the desire of this noble-hearted lady to confer a permanent benefit upon the inhabitants of the city, Mohammedans as well as Christians, has been frustrated through Turkish obstinacy ! The cost was estimated at thirty thousand pounds sterling.

[1] A good account of these pools and the gardens lower down the valley is given by Tristram, "Land of Israel," p. 403. The plan of the conduits is accurately laid down on the maps of the Ordnance Survey of Jerusalem.

[2] Lady Burdett-Coutts desired that the water should be introduced by the high-level aqueduct, which would have entered at the Jaffa Gate and sufficed for the wants of the higher parts of the city; the Turkish authorities, however, insisted on the low-level aqueduct being used, which would have left a large portion of the city unbenefited. The existing sources of supply are most impure.

The Pools, by whomsoever constructed, are certainly of great antiquity, and of excellent workmanship. They are still in remarkably good preservation, and could easily be put into perfect order. Their construction at this spot is doubtless due to the existence of a fine spring of water, which is still utilised for the supply of Bethlehem, to which place it is conducted by a culvert which runs along the side of the valley with a gradual downward slope. On descending the hill by the large Turkish castle which has been built close to the upper pool, the unusual sound of running and falling water saluted our ears. The spring rises in the limestone hills above the pool to the northwards and enters the pool by an underground culvert which may be examined by means of a ladder giving access thereto a few feet below the surface. The aqueduct was repaired and lined with pipes by the Crusaders, after which it again fell into ruin, but was opened and explored by Colonels Wilson and Warren. There is a fall of about 400 feet towards Jerusalem.[1] On our way down the valley towards Bethlehem, we noticed ancient terraces which had doubtless once been fruitful vineyards or olive-yards; and on turning the angle of the valley towards the left, we beheld at our feet "the Gardens of Solomon," neatly laid out over the bed of the valley, and extending, according to Canon Tristram, for more than two miles in all, from the little village of Urtas. This spot was first reclaimed and cultivated about thirty years ago by Mr. Meshullam, a converted Jew, who settled down here with the object of proving that the land if cultivated was capable of producing a rich return to the cultivator. Soon after some fellahin followed and settled by his side; Germans followed, and patch after patch was brought under culture, and now the whole valley has been converted into a series of well-tilled gardens, producing vegetables for the Jerusalem market, besides numerous fruit trees, such as those of the apricot, peach, almond, fig, and pomegranate. The hillsides are also being banked up into terraces for the growth of vines and olive-trees. It can scarcely be denied, after viewing the pretty picture of a garden valley, that Meshullam has succeeded in demonstrating that the vales of Palestine are capable of becoming as fruitful as in former ages, if only persevering industry be applied to the work of reclamation.

Following a pathway, along which the aqueduct is carried, we turned another angle of the valley, and came in sight of Bethlehem as seen from the south; the City of David and the birthplace of the Messiah.

[1] The dimensions of these pools are given by Tristram and Baedeker.

Bethlehem is now altogether a Christian town, and has a thriving and progressive appearance. The top of the ridge on which it is built is covered by substantial stone houses, while the valleys around are clothed with verdure, and planted out in extensive olive gardens. Terrace succeeds terrace from the bottom to the summits of the hills, which are steep-sided, and require to be thus laid out in order to afford footing to the plants. The work of construction must have been labourious, and brings to mind some of the vine terraces along the banks of the Rhine. Through these olive groves our pathway lay; and having climbed to the summit of the hill we entered the city, and after winding through narrow streets and passages, we at length found ourselves in front of the Franciscan Convent adjoining the Church of the Nativity. Here we were admitted by a brother who recognised our conductor, Bernhard Heilpern, and after a short consultation we were shown into the Guest Hall, where lunch, which we carried with us, was spread. Here we partook of the Convent wine, grown on the spot, which was good; and of the Convent coffee, which was better!

After lunch we proceeded to visit "the Holy Places," and the interior of the church. It was strange to see a Turkish soldier keeping guard while service was proceeding in the Greek portion of the building; but since 1873, when an attack was made by the Greeks on the Romans, a guard is always present to keep the peace between the rival Christian sects at the birthplace of their Founder, the Prince of Peace. The disgraceful riot referred to above, and the scenes of violence which annually take place at Christmas round the site of the Nativity, are little calculated to impress Moslems with a reverence for Christianity.

Leaving the town, and having passed numerous workshops, where the hum of industry was everywhere to be heard, we turned a little off our road to visit the "Well of David," and observe the extensive prospect from this position. Here we had a view of Bethlehem from the northern side, where it is best seen. Between our position and the City of David lay a wide valley, sloping downwards in the direction of the Jordan depression and partially laid out in gardens, terraced vineyards, and olive groves. On the opposite side the stone and arched buildings cover the sides and summit of the ridge, terminating with the Church and Convent of the Nativity on the left. Turning eastwards, and looking down the valley, we recognised the deep depression of The Ghôr by the haze which rises over the hollow; and beyond was the table-land of Moab, bounded by sides deeply furrowed. At a distance of about four miles from Bethlehem, and on the opposite side of the valley amongst the hills, is a remarkable elevation with the form of a truncated cone, planted on a nearly level platform, on which Herod the Great erected his summer palace, and also his tomb. Its ancient name was Herodium ; its present, Jebel Fureidîs. Captain Conder states that this cone is surrounded by a circular wall, on which are four round towers.[1] Under this is the remarkable Cave of Khureitûn, generally supposed to be the "Cave of Adullam,"[2] but this is a view in which Conder does not concur.[3] We may suppose, however, that while David lay in concealment, and his enemies, the Philistines, held possession of Bethlehem and its approaches, the newly anointed king cast longing eyes towards the city of his birth, and the well of whose cool waters he had doubtless drunk when a boy. Parched with thirst and weary of life, "hunted like a partridge on the mountains," he exclaimed, "Oh that one would give me drink of the water of the well of Bethlehem, that is at the gate !" Hearing this exclamation of their king, the three valiant captains, at the risk of their lives, brake through the line of the Philistine guards and drew water from the well. But here the nobility of David's character was strikingly shown. Notwithstanding his thirst, and the ardent longing for water to cool his tongue, he pours out the water on the ground, exclaiming, "Shall I drink the blood of these men which have put their lives in jeopardy" for my sake ? How such an act must have endeared David to his soldiers. As one stands by the well, and looks down the valley, the whole scene becomes a vivid reality.

This day's excursion enabled me to get a good idea of the character of the country south of Jerusalem, and of its geological conformation. It consists of beds of limestone, white, yellow, or reddish, sometimes chalky, and with bands of chert. The strata undulate slightly in various directions.

[1] "Tent Work in Palestine." New edition, p. 152.

[2] 1 Chron. xi, 15.

[3] Nevertheless, the spot where David was at the time of the narrative, called "the hold," could not have been far distant from Bethlehem.

CHAPTER XVII.

JERICHO AND THE JORDAN VALLEY.

OUR next excursion was to Jericho and the banks of the Jordan. We left Jerusalem early on Monday morning, 14th January, and crossing the valley ascended the Mount of Olives, passing the Garden of Gethsemane, and the village of Bethany, the home of the young Sheikh who accompanied our party, and whose father is lord paramount of the district we were to traverse. I took a great fancy to this young fellow from his appearance and conduct. He was slight of build, sat his horse gracefully, and was always polite and ready to oblige. It is unnecessary for me to attempt to describe the well-known road from Jerusalem to Jericho ; no parable is better known than that of which the scene is laid here ; and, one may add, no example is more rarely followed than that of the Good Samaritan !

The hills which bound the valley are much of the nature of the chalk downs of the South of England. From Bethany onwards towards the Wâdy-es-Sidr they consist of limestone, sometimes chalky, and dipping steadily eastwards. We are now on the eastern side of the great arch of Central Palestine, as we were on the western side when ascending towards Jerusalem from Ramleh. On approaching the Wâdy-es-Sidr, however, we find that the strata become contorted; and on crossing the brook, the cause of this disturbance of the beds becomes evident, in the occurrence of a mass of volcanic rock, which has here been intruded into the limestone, and has to a great extent altered and calcined the rock itself. This volcanic rock is of a red colour, variegated with yellow and white ; it is soft, and resembles "Domite" in general character, except that I could not recognise any crystals of mica, hornblende, or other minerals. It seemed to me, that we have only here the upper surface of a deep-seated mass, where it has come in contact with the limestone, so that we have no opportunity of judging of its characters as they would appear if observed at some depth. Its presence at the surface is due entirely to denudation, and it again breaks out under the Khan el Ahmar, where the limestone beds are contorted and calcined.[1]

As we were resting under the rocks near the Khan, a large party of Russian pilgrims, mounted on donkeys and ponies, arrived on their way to receive baptism from the Patriarch of the Greek Church in the sacred waters of the Jordan. They presented a strange spectacle—their pots and pans for cooking, their little stores of food and clothes fastened on the pommels of their saddles—all chattering briskly and pressing onwards to reach the hospitable roof of the Greek Convent (which stands in the midst of the Jordan Valley) before nightfall. We were pretty well mixed up with these pilgrims for the most part of our way, which did not tend to our own gratification, or facilitate observation on the natural phenomena around us. At length, towards evening, we found ourselves on the brink of the Wâdy Kelt, one of the deepest ravines in Palestine, generally considered to be "the Brook Cherith that is before Jordan," where Elijah was fed by the ravens.[2] As Conder says, the whole gorge is wonderfully wild and romantic. It is bounded by vertical cliffs of limestone in nearly horizontal courses several hundred feet in depth, and hollowed into caves, the abode in past times of Anchorites. The bottom of the gorge is lined with tall canes, and the water, which rises in a spring amongst the mountains, nearly four miles from the spot where it debouches on the plain of Jericho,[3] is probably perennial, even during the longest droughts. Terrible, therefore, must have been the drought in the days of Ahab, "when the brook dried up, because there had been no rain in the land."

At a bend of the road near the mouth of the Kelt we found ourselves overlooking the plain of Jordan. The pilgrims gave a shout of joy as they beheld the object of their long and toilsome journey. A vast expanse of green and brownish tints stretched from our feet away to the distant hills of Moab; and in front, amongst the groves and gardens of Gilgal,

---

[1] This rock is noticed by Tristram, "Land of Israel," p. 200, as also the occurrence of the "wavy undulations and folds" of chert; but surely not "irrespective of the stratification"?

[2] 1 Kings xvii, 3. The term is 'Oreb (*Corvus umbrinus*), but it has been suggested that by the word in this passage is meant the Arabs. I confess to a preference for the usually received interpretation. The life of Elijah was one dependent throughout on the miraculous interposition of God; and this was only one amongst many miracles.

[3] Conder, "Tent Life in Palestine," p. 211.

rose the huge pile of the Greek Convent, where the travellers were to rest.

To the extreme right we could get a glimpse of the northern lip of the Salt Sea; and to the left, looking across the deeply worn channel of the Kelt, were the mounds of Jericho rising from amongst gardens, and lying near the foot of the stupendous cliffs of Jebel Karantul, which here bound the plain of the Jordan. Over the whole scene was spread a lurid haze, indicative of the grand thunderstorm which was to burst upon us during the night.

Descending by the steep pathway into the plain, we turned our horses' heads towards the left; and crossing the Kelt pushed onwards towards the mounds of ancient Jericho, where our tents had been pitched, by the side of the warm and copious spring of Ain es Sultân. The site and surroundings of ancient Jericho have often been described, and it is unnecessary for me to say much on the subject.[1] It is a spot of great interest, where baths, aqueducts, roads, and mounds of pottery attest its former importance. The source of this is, without doubt, to be found in its magnificent springs, both of tepid and cold waters. These impart verdure to the soil; and for sanitary purposes were, as we know, highly prized, especially in Roman times. Jericho was the city of palm-trees, of which none now remain; but the constant supply of running water, combined with the intense heat, causes the gardens of Gilgal, close by, to produce lemons and oranges, bananas, castor-oil plants, besides melons, figs, and grapes. Sugarcanes were extensively cultivated down to the time of the Crusaders, and the ruins of the sugar-mills formed a prominent object on the hill above our camp.

Our tents were pitched a few yards below the Sultan's Spring, which issues forth into an ancient basin of hewn stone. The temperature of the water is 84° Fahr.,[2] and the stony bed of the brook is thickly strewn with the dark purple shells of several species of molluscs. Our camp was at an elevation (by aneroid) of 520 feet above the Salt Sea, and on the margin of a terrace which stretches for several miles towards the banks of the Jordan. A second terrace of gravel may be observed on both sides of the limestone ridge on which were erected the sugar-mills; this terrace is 630 feet above the same datum, and seems to represent

---

[1] The account in Murray's Handbook is excellent.

[2] According to Baedeker; but only 71° Fahr. as determined by Mr. Laurence, of our party.

the principal terrace which borders the southern margin of The Ghôr, to which Jebel Usdum belongs. According to Tristram, the surface of the lower plain is formed of mud and silt, containing fresh-water shells of the Jordan and its tributary streams, of which *Melanopsis prærosa* and *M. Saulcyi* occur in this locality; and lead him to the conclusion, that within a comparatively recent geological period, the whole lower valley has been exposed to fresh-water floods from the upper Jordan, where these shells abound.[1] When crossing the Cherith Valley, on our way to the banks of the Jordan on the following day, we searched the marly and gravelly banks for remains of shells, but without success; we were then about 275 feet above the surface of the Salt Sea.[2]

At about a mile from the banks of the Jordan, we descended about 40 feet on to a lower terrace, a little over 200 feet above the same datum. The materials are of white marl, encrusted with saline matter, and they break off in a succession of little plateaux with symmetrical banks, descending to the alluvial plain which borders the river, and which sustains a dense growth of trees, shrubs, and reeds—the haunts of the wild boar. Altogether, between the escarpment of Jebel Karantul, which bounds the valley of the Jordan on the west, there are three well-marked terraces, which have successively formed the bed of the ancient inland sea, namely :—

The Upper Terrace, with an elevation of	630 to	600 feet.	
The Second Terrace	„	520 „	250 „
The Third Terrace	„	200 „	130 „
The Alluvial Plain, liable to floods	90 „	0 „	

All these terraces, except perhaps the upper, have doubly sloping surfaces, both towards the centre of the valley, and towards the Salt Sea, so that the levels taken along one line would not correspond exactly with those taken along another. The upper terrace only slopes towards the centre of the valley, as its upper surface corresponds almost exactly with the terrace of Jebel Usdum, and the other old sea margins, near the southern end of The Ghôr.

---

[1] "Land of Israel." 2nd edition, p. 221.

[2] This is probably the same terrace described by Tristram near Ain Jidi, consisting of " chalky limestone and gravel " mixed with shells of existing species at a level of 250 feet above the Salt Sea waters. This terrace slopes upwards into the valleys which open out on the plain. (*Ibid.*, p. 281.)

[3] The elevations, as determined by the aneroid, are only approximate.

On arriving at the fords of the Jordan, which have been so often described as to require but little notice here,[1] some of our party prepared for a plunge into its turgid waters, with, I fear, less reverent thoughts than the ardent pilgrims we had fallen in with the day before. The stream is about 50 yards from bank to bank, which are clothed with tamarisks, willows, and tall reeds.

While we were having lunch on the grassy terrace, some Greek or Russian pilgrims came down from the convent to bathe, and it was an amusing, if not very edifying, sight to watch their performances. From the delicate manner in which they entered the stream, it might be inferred that bathing was not a pastime in which they often indulged ; and as some of them, at least, probably recollected that they would not again have so excellent an opportunity for fleshly purification, they proceeded to a very systematic course of washing, aided by a good lather of soap !

I was surprised to observe the water of the Jordan so turgid that it reminded me of the waters of the Nile, or of some streams descending from glacier valleys. It is well known that streams which issue forth from lakes, as is the case with the Jordan, are generally clear, as the mud is deposited in each instance over the bed of the lake itself. The Rhone may be cited as an illustration. Entering the head of the Lake of Geneva, charged with mud from the Alpine glaciers, the suspended matter subsides, and the waters issue forth at the lower end clear as crystal. Such, I supposed, would be the case with the Jordan ; but, as I am informed, though the river issues forth from the Sea of Galilee as a clear stream, it flows along between muddy banks, so that its waters become more and more impregnated with silt, till on entering the head of the Salt Sea they resemble those of the Nile at Cairo. The temperature of the water was 61° Fahr. ; that of the air 72° Fahr., in the shade about noon.[2]

On our way back from the Jordan, both we and our horses were unanimous as to the excellence of the ground for a trial of speed, so giving them the reins we were soon flying over the ground neck to neck. It required neither whip nor spur to make our little steeds show their mettle, for they were ever ready for the course, and none liked to be beaten. Gordon's horse proved, I think, to be the fastest ; Laurence's

[1] See Tristram's graphic picture, and more graphic description, of crossing the fords, " Land of Israel," p. 523, et seq.

[2] As determined by Mr. Laurence.

next; but we were all very nearly matched. We reached our tents in the evening, well satisfied with our day's ramble.[1]

[1] The great, almost only, danger from a gallop in this country, is due to the burrowing animals, such as moles, jerboas, &c., and the rider has to keep a sharp look out to prevent his horse putting his foot into one of the holes. A lady whom we met on board the steamer at Beyrût was thrown from her horse which had stumbled in consequence of a mole burrow.

CHAPTER XVIII.

RETURN TO JERUSALEM BY MAR SABA.

NEXT morning we left Jericho on our return journey by Nebi Mûsa and Mar Saba. For several miles after again crossing the Kelt, our way ran along the base of the escarpments of limestone which form the western margin of the Jordan Valley. The beds of limestone are here largely interstratified with dark chert, and are often contorted; but the general dip is westwards, from the plain into the hillside. An excellent section of the strata is shown in the W. Jorif Guzel, three miles south of the Kelt. After passing this, we struck up the deep gorge of the W. el Kueiserah. This valley introduces us into a country of smooth chalky downs, traversed by deep ravines, sometimes covered with grass, but generally bare and white. Here amongst the beds of limestone occur others, consisting of dark shales and bituminous limestone, which, as it is compact and takes a good polish, is manufactured into vases, cups, dishes, and ornaments by the artizans of Bethlehem and Jerusalem.

The Cities of the Plain.—If any of our friends expected that we should discover the ruins of Sodom or Gomorrah, they will be disappointed. I might add that we also failed to discover Pharaoh's chariots in the Red Sea! Both were equally probable, or impossible. As Captain Conder has well observed, it ought not to have been expected that ruins of such antiquity would remain to the present day; and the remarks which I have hazarded regarding the rapid disintegration of the native rocks apply with even greater force to ruined walls of an antiquity of nearly four thousand years. From the description in the Bible, I have always felt satisfied that these cities lay in some part of the fertile plain of the Jordan to the north of the Salt Sea, and to the west of that river; and when visiting the ruins of Jericho, and beholding the copious springs and streams of that spot, and how applicable to it would be the expression "that it was well watered everywhere,"[1] the thought occurred, May not the more modern city (ancient Jericho) have arisen from the ruins of the Cities of the Plain? A period of over four hundred years intervenes between

---

[1] Gen. xiii, 10.

the destruction of these cities and the first mention of Jericho.[1] There seems to be nothing improbable in the supposition that, at some period during this interval, the materials may have been utilised in the erection of the latter city ; even as those of the older Jericho were utilised (as we may suppose) in the construction of the more modern city of the same name, built by Hiel the Bethelite, 534 years after.[2] But of this second city, which, according to Eusebius, was destroyed by the Romans during the siege of Jerusalem, how little even now remains ! Nothing, in effect, but the foundations and tanks.

Amongst these hills has been erected the huge mosque of the Nebi Mûsa (Tomb of Moses), where the remains of the prophet are supposed to lie ;—in defiance of all history. Thus we have had the name of the prophet of Israel "cropping up" no less than four times during our pilgrimage : first, at Ayun Mûsa, near Suez ; then at Jebel Mûsa (Mount Sinai) ; again at the Wâdy Mûsa (or Valley of Petra) ; and, lastly, at Nebi Mûsa, on the western side of the Jordan ! It is certain the prophet of Israel never came here ; and exceedingly improbable (as it seems to me) that he ever entered the Valley of Petra. The place, however, is worthy of honour, as there are excellent wells in the valley below, from which, as we passed, damsels were drawing water, and readily allowed us to slake our thirst at their pitchers.

After crossing another ridge we descended into another glen, the Wâdy Mukalik, by a path so steep that it was found desirable to dismount and lead our horses. At the bottom we found ourselves in the dry bed of a mountain torrent amongst nearly vertical cliffs of gravel, clinging to the sides of the older limestone strata. Here we rested, partly to allow the baggage mules to come up with us, and we watched with some curiosity to see how they would manage to scramble down the almost precipitous path with their ponderous loads. Wonderful indeed was the strength, skill, and sagacity they displayed in supporting their loads, choosing their footing, and scrambling down the banks. All arrived safely at the bottom ; and, after a rest, commenced the as nearly steep ascent of the opposite bank. Next to the mountain road from the Wâdy Kuseibeh to Petra this was the most difficult road we had yet travelled in the East.

[1] Compare Genesis xix and Numbers xxii, 1.

[2] 1 Kings xvi, 34. The city of Jericho mentioned in connection with our Lord's ministry was a third city, or village, probably situated where is now the modern village of Er Riha.

The Wâdy Mukalik is of much interest from the fact that it once formed the bed of an ancient lake, probably at the time when the waters of the Salt Sea rose about 600 feet above their present surface. When first we came in sight of the valley there appeared in the centre of a circular range of limestone hills a flat terrace of lighter coloured material, through which numerous deep channels had been cut by torrent action. On descending into one of these it was found that the terrace is formed of sand, marly gravel, and boulders, more or less rudely stratified, and terminating against the marginal banks of limestone, which rise in some directions several hundred feet above the surface of the terrace. The only outlet is the narrow gorge in the direction of the Salt Sea plain ; and it is easy to conceive that when this plain was filled with water to the level above indicated the waters of the lake basin were banked up ; but that as those of the Jordan Valley were lowered, the channel communicating with them became deepened, until ultimately the lake itself was drained. It is not improbable there may be other lake deposits of a like description amongst these hills.

I was unable to observe any good evidence of the unconformity between two sets of limestone beds to which Canon Tristram refers when describing this tract of country. The appearance to which he alludes is probably due to the plications and contortions into which the strata have been thrown ; so that, when seen on the side of a hill, or of a valley, the upper portions of the same beds are not parallel to those below, and in fact recline at a considerable angle from them. All along the district, from the entrance to the Wâdy-el-Kueiserah to that of the Kedron near Mar Saba, the strata are much disturbed, and their contortions are often visible from long distances on the chalky downs, owing to the scantiness of the herbage, and the occurrence of numerous bands of dark chert. These bands enable the eye to follow the planes of bedding, with their numerous curves and foldings on the sides of the chalky downs, and the effect is often very striking.

We camped at noonday for luncheon near the borders of an extensive undulating plain. It was usually our practice at such times to loose the horses and mules and let them feed on the pastures—in some cases fastening the head by a halter to one of the legs. Generally the animals were easily secured when wanted ; but on this day the horse which Bernhard Heilpern bestrode, having gained his liberty, and rejoicing in getting rid of a tolerably heavy load, showed a marked preference for the pleasures of freedom over the duties of the saddle. Several times he was driven up towards the tent by one of the muleteers, but no sooner was an attempt made to seize his halter or his mane than tossing his head he would turn round and bolt !

Having watched this manœuvring for a little, and having mounted on my own more tractable steed, I put him in pursuit of the runaway. After an exciting chase I managed to turn his head towards the tent, and to drive him up towards a long rope held at either end by the muleteers in readiness to throw round him; but just at the critical moment he would turn and be off again, I in hot pursuit. Others now joined, and for the space of about half-an-hour our steeds were galloping over the plain after the fugitive ; and we thus gained some idea of the excitement of lassoing wild horses in the pampas of South America ! Our young Sheikh also joined, and we soon left the chase to him. It was amusing to watch the display of horsemanship ; and [the graceful curves, windings, and retrogressions through which he put his Arabian, but he was no more successful than ourselves ; the fugitive was not to be caught just yet ; and as time was wearing on, and we had still a long ride before us, we left the horse to his fate ; for we well knew that when we had all started he would rejoin his companions. And so it proved. We had not proceeded more than two or three miles when, on turning round, I perceived Heilpern cantering after us, and doubtless his steed had to pay dearly for his escapade.

The road to the entrance of the Kedron Valley was in some places difficult in the extreme, and with less trustworthy horses than ours would have been even dangerous. Rising at one moment over steep banks of broken rock it would then descend along slippery slopes, or skirt the sides of a precipice where a false step would result in precipitating horse and rider to the bottom. The hills were often formed of alternating beds of chert and limestone folded and waved ; and there were interesting examples of the process of the formation of ridges and scarps by atmospheric agency. This was specially remarkable along the southern slopes of El Muntar, where the harder cherty strata form the crests and upper surfaces of the ridges, and from their dark hues contrast remarkably with the white chalky limestones which enclose them above and below. Towards evening we reached the road which winds along the deep gorge of the Kedron, and shortly afterwards our tents, which we found pitched in a rocky glen behind the Convent.

The remarkable gorge of the Kedron at Mar Saba has been often described. Like that of the Kelt it is a water-worn channel of the Kedron when in flood, carried down through nearly vertical walls of limestone to a depth of about 400 feet from the upper surface of the country.[1] Tristram mentions the occurrence of a fossiliferous bed of *Hippurites liratus*. It occurs at a depth of 82 feet from the surface, and indicates the Cretaceous affinities of the strata. With the exception of this bed of characteristic fossils the limestone is remarkably unproductive of organic remains. The depth of this channel, with its dry bed, is one of the many indications one meets with in Palestine, that at a former period fluviatile action was much more effective than at present. The channel owes its existence entirely to water action, and there is no evidence of any " rent " or fissure running parallel with its course. The only fissure (or fault) is that which crosses the gorge transversely at its northern entrance. This fault ranges in a due east and west direction, with a " downthrow " on the northern side, by which the white chalky beds on that side are brought into contact with the yellowish limestone of the Mar Saba gorge which belongs to a lower geological horizon. On crossing the fault the dip of the beds is northwards, but they afterwards become flat, and then dip towards the south. On approaching the Valley of Hinnom, by the Kedron Valley, the marble beds of the Jerusalem plateau rise from below the white chalk, and crop out in the cliffs of Aceldama.

We returned to Jerusalem on Thursday evening, the 17th January, and made preparations for our final journey through Northern Palestine (as we hoped), upon which we intended to set out early on the following Monday. We little anticipated the disappointment which was in store for us !

Our traverses from the shores of the Salt Sea to Gaza, and again from Jaffa to Jerusalem and the Jordan Valley, together with our excursions to Bethlehem and Solomon's Pools, had enabled us to obtain an approximately complete knowledge of the general features of the country and of its geological structure, and we looked forward to a further *reconnaissance* northwards to the shores of the Lake of Galilee, and thence across to Mount Carmel and onwards to Beyrût, to enable us to complete our geological survey of the whole country;—but this was not to be, as my narrative will show.

[1] Tristram, *supra cit.*, p. 264, &c. There is an excellent engraving of this gorge in " Picturesque Palestine."

CHAPTER XIX.

SNOWED UP IN JERUSALEM.

By Saturday evening all our preparations for an early start on Monday morning were concluded. We had taken leave of our friends, made our last purchases in the shops and bazaars, sorted our baggage, a large portion of which was entrusted to Mr. Clarke, the agent of Messrs. T. Cook and Son, for direct transmission to England. The horses and baggage mules had also been secured, and Bernhard Heilpern was again to act as our conductor as far as Beyrût. The length of the journey was estimated for fifteen days.

On the following day we attended Divine Service in the English church, and we retired to rest expecting to be on our way soon after daybreak; but it was not so to be! At the time appointed Heilpern knocked at our doors, saying, "You need not stir, gentlemen, we are snowed up; travelling is impossible!" So it was! The wind had shifted to the west, increasing to a gale, and with it came a heavy snowfall, which did not cease till the whole country was covered to a depth of 2 feet and upwards. Such a fall had not occurred for five years. During the whole of Monday the storm raged furiously, accompanied by snow and rain, and during that night Laurence's thermometer registered four degrees of frost (28° Fahr.). But we resolved to wait for a day or two longer in hopes of a change of wind and a rapid thaw such as sometimes happens in these parts. Our hopes, however, were not destined to be realised. The air continued bitterly cold up till Tuesday evening, and little progress was made in thawing the snow even during the noonday sun. All traffic, even by road, was stopped; the postman to Jaffa was obliged to halt at "half-way house," and the telegraph wires were broken. On Wednesday morning, seeing that further delay would be useless, arrangements were made for a return to Jaffa in order to catch the Austrian Lloyd's steamer on the following Friday; and I despatched letters to the Secretary of the

Society, and to relations at home, to announce the termination of our Expedition.[1]

Our hotel at Jerusalem, however comfortable it may have been in warm weather, was far from being so in winter with snow on the ground. The upper part being open to the air affords a good supply of oxygen, where it is very much needed, but also admits snow or rain without stint. Fuel also began to run short ; it had not been thought necessary to lay in a large store, and the daily supplies were cut off; so that at length we were obliged to have recourse to old boxes, or other useless lumber, wherewith to feed our stoves. Still, Jerusalem under snow had its attractions. The howling of the dogs at night ceased for the nonce ; what became of these wretched animals during this period I could not make out—they must have had a bad time of it ! It was pitiable to see the inhabitants, sometimes barefooted, or thinly shod, and clad in apparel fit only for the summer months. To protect the head and neck seemed their chief cause of anxiety ; and these parts of the body they enveloped in thick shawls ;—the wearers seeming to care little for the feet and legs. The market-place in front of the hotel, usually the scene of a noisy crowd bartering for fruit, vegetables, firewood, and other necessaries, was tenantless. Snow covered the whole country in every direction, rendering communication difficult or impossible ; while a most bitter wind caused all who could do so to keep within shelter. By Wednesday, however, the wind fell, and a rapid thaw set in, so as to lead us to expect that by the following day we should be able to accomplish our journey of forty miles to Jaffa. I took the opportunity of ascending to the roof of our hotel for a last look over the sacred city, and the surrounding country. The scene was most striking. So clear was the air, that the snow-clad plains of Moab and Jebel Attarus, though at a distance of thirty miles, were quite distinct ; as were also the glens and promontories descending therefrom on to the Valley of the Jordan. The snow lay still undisturbed in the sheltered spots, and ice was on the surface of the Pool of Hezekiah below us ; the well-known solitary palm flung its plumes into the cold air, high above the buildings, bravely

---

[1] I need scarcely observe that in a country where there are no roads, only mountain paths, travelling on horseback and camping at night with thick snow on the ground was not practicable ; but, even had this been the case, it would not have been possible to make observations on the geology, or on the natural history of the region traversed.

defying the ungenial elements : under no circumstances could a better view be obtained.

Looking away in the far distance, towards the table-land of Moab, past "the green domed mosque," and through the deep depression of the Kedron Valley, the upper terrace of limestone, and the lower of sandstone of a faint reddish hue, were clearly discernible ; while the sunlight brought out in relief the bold headlands and ridges, and cast into shadow the deep furrows and glens which descend into the Jordan valley along the Land of Gilead on its eastern side. Amongst these, the cliffs bordering the gorge of the Wâdy Zerka Maïn were the most prominent. It was truly astonishing how objects so distant could be seen so plainly. I was able to distinguish even the bands of colouring of the sandstone cliffs at this distance, which was over twenty-five miles in a straight line !

Withdrawing our eyes from these distant points, we observe how truly the hills are said to "stand round about Jerusalem," in almost every direction, except the gorge of the Kedron which forms the natural outlet for the waters which descend, on the one hand, from the Valley of Jehoshaphat, and on the other from the Valley of Hinnom. Looking across the valley towards the east, there lay the Mount of Olives, crowned by its mosque and minaret, from the summit of which we had enjoyed so extensive a prospect on the morning of our descent into the plains of Jericho, crossed by the road from Bethany, and recalling an event ever memorable in Christian annals. Below, towards the right, the little Garden of Gethsemane, shaded by its ancient olive-trees, and decorated with flowers. In our immediate front is the beautiful dome of the mosque of Omar, standing as a stately monument over a spot once the "Most Holy Place" of the children of Israel, now regarded as sacred by Jew, Moslem, and Christian alike ; a little beyond, the Church of El Aksa, built over the ancient approaches to the Temple of Solomon. Around, extends the spacious court of the Temple, white with unmelted snow.

Looking across the domes and flat-roofed houses, crowded together, and beyond the Damascus Gate towards the north, there may be observed a low, flat-topped hill, usually covered with grass, now with a sheet of snow ; and breaking off in the direction of the city wall in a cliff of limestone rock. A cave, known as "Jeremiah's Grotto," where the prophet is supposed to have dwelt when penning the Book of Lamentations, has been hewn in the face of the cliff. The hill is the property of a Sheikh, and its summit is used as a Moslem burying, ground. Unprofaned by any structure, secular or sacred, this platform "without the Gate," and overlooking the city from the north, as Olivet does from the south, is now generally regarded as Mount Calvary. For myself, I feel confident that this is so; and I am happily spared any necessity for adducing arguments in favour of this view, after those which have been so clearly stated by Captain Conder.[1] Seen in certain directions, the rocky platform bears a not unfanciful resemblance to a skull, which may have given to it the name of "Golgotha." It lies beyond the gates of the city;[2] and an ancient Roman road has been discovered to lead from the precincts of the temple in this direction—probably that by which the Saviour was led to Calvary. No determination carries with it more interest, or certainty, than that of the place of the Crucifixion. It is exactly on the opposite side of the city from that of the Mount of Olives, where the Lord first "beheld the city and wept over it."[3]

Such is the scene which presented itself on the day previous to our departure—one of indescribable interest rather than of beauty; but so rich in the memorials of the past, that no scenic beauty could enhance the interest in the mind of the Christian traveller.

Having taken leave of our friends, we left Jerusalem on Friday morning, 25th January, for Jaffa, in order to catch the Austrian Lloyd's steamer which was to touch at that port, on her way to Constantinople.[4] Snow covered the country all the way to the entrance of the Bab-el-Wâdy. We passed a carriage imbedded in the snow drift, which had been left behind, horses and passengers having proceeded onwards to Jerusalem. The storm had made much havoc amongst the live groves; and notwithstanding the Government prohibition against cutting firewood, abundance of this material had been provided by the power of the winds, especially amongst the older trees. As we rode over the plain of Ramleh, the early flowers were already beginning to decorate

---

[1] *Supra cit.*, p. 195, *et seq.*, and still more recently by General Gordon.

[2] The present wall is stated to have been built by Agrippa, about ten years after the Crucifixion, to enclose the surburbs north of the city, but the Church of the Sepulchre was probably inside the former wall. (*Ibid.*, p. 195.)

[3] I have again referred to this interesting case of recent identification further on page 190.

[4] Mr. Armstrong remained behind, in order to complete the drawing of the map of the Arabah Valley, and to complete some business connected with the Palestine Survey. He returned to London a few weeks later.

the fields, amongst which the brilliant scarlet anemone, and the delicately tinted dwarf iris, were the most conspicuous. We wound our way to the Jerusalem Hotel, amongst the orange and lemon groves, heavily laden with ripe fruit, which the rigorous enforcement of quarantine in the Mediterranean ports was causing to rot on the ground. For a few pence we purchased a small hamper of these delicious fruits for use on our voyage ; but it was clear that, at this late period, it would be utterly impossible to send to market one half of the magnificent crop which was blooming on the trees, and bending with the weight of fruit their branches to the ground.

CHAPTER XX.

HOMEWARD BOUND.

NEXT morning, having made all arrangements with the agent of Messrs. Cook and Son, and bid a warm farewell to our trusty conductor, Bernhard Heilpern, we sailed from the Jaffa roads, and cast anchor off the port of Beyrût.

On reaching the deck of the steamer, on Sunday morning, our eyes were charmed with the view of the mountain range of the Lebanon, the snows of which were glistening in the sunlight, and from below which the well-wooded slopes, channelled and furrowed by many a glen and ravine, descended to the sea. In front lay the spacious and busy city of Beyrût, with its little harbour, far too little for the requirements of so important a port. To the right rose conspicuously the fine buildings of the American Protestant College, which is doing such excellent work in the education of the Syrian youth.

Early in the afternoon, accompanied by my son, and Dr. Selim, of Gaza, who had kindly constituted himself our guide, I called on the Rev. Dr. Bliss, Principal of the College, who received us most kindly, and arranged to show us the museum the day following. I then went to pay my respects to Mr. Aldridge, H.B.M. Consul-General of Syria, who was also most friendly; and invited us to lunch with him the next day. After this I took a ramble over the city, under the guidance of Dr. Selim, visiting the excellent School for the children of Druses, kept by Miss Taylor. Here I saw about twenty nice little girls, who looked very happy, and evidently much attached to this devoted lady, whose cheerful and loving care could not fail to win their affections. After they had sung some hymns, both in English and Arabic, I gave them a little address, which Miss Taylor interpreted to them, and took leave of the good lady who has devoted her life to this useful work.

The day following I made the acquaintance of Dr. Post, Head of the Surgical Department of the College and Hospital of St. John, and after inspecting the geological collection, proceeded with Dr. Bliss to lunch at the Consulate. The afternoon was spent in an excursion, kindly arranged for me by Dr. Bliss, into the borders of the Lebanon, during which I had an opportunity of examining the remarkable conglomerate of Lokandel el Motram, about three miles from Beyrût, which Dr. Bliss has very properly recognised as a portion of the old bed of the straits which ran up the valley to the east of the ridge on which Beyrût is built, and which at that time must have existed as an island. This old sea-bed reaches levels varying from 120 to 150 feet above the present sea-level.[1]

Having thus made the acquaintance of the capital of Western Syria and its surroundings under very favourable circumstances, we returned on board our ship, and in the evening weighed anchor, and steamed westward towards the coast of Cyprus. Gradually the shadows deepened, and the snow-clad Lebanon and the dark headlands of the Syrian coast faded from view, and only the waters of the Mediterranean bounded the horizon as the darkness of night set in.[2]

We returned home by Cyprus, Smyrna, Constantinople, and Varna; and when resting for a short time in the capital of the Turkish Empire, I took the opportunity of calling on Lord Dufferin, in order to express, in person, the thanks of myself, and of our party, for his prompt and effective services in procuring our release from quarantine at Gaza. His Excellency received me in the most friendly manner, and I shall ever retain a pleasant recollection of my interview with this distinguished representative of the British Empire in the East. We were greatly favoured by the weather in our passage through the Dardanelles and the Black Sea; but I could well understand how in rough weather the landing at Varna must be both difficult and dangerous. We reached Vienna by "the Oriental Express" train on February 7th, and on the morning of the 13th of the same month touched again the shores of "Old

---

[1] I regretted much not having time to visit the waterworks of Beyrût, the construction of which was carried out under the direction of my valued friend, the late W. J. Maxwell, C.E., acting as representative of the firm of Sir J. MacNeil and Son. The water is taken from the Nahr-el-Kelb, which issues forth from an underground channel in the mountains explored by Mr. Maxwell and described by Rev. J. Robertson in "Good Words," November, 1875.

[2] At Beyrût we bid farewell to Messrs. Hart and Laurence, who had arranged to make a bold attempt to see Damascus and Baalbec, notwithstanding the deep snows which covered the country. This they happily succeeded in doing, as the "French road" to Damascus had just been cleared.

England." On hearing of our arrival in London, Mr. Walter Besant, whose courtesy and desire at all times to meet our wishes I am happy to have an opportunity of acknowledging, summoned a meeting of the Executive Committee of the Palestine Exploration Fund, at which the Chairman, Mr. Glaisher, presided; and from one and all we received a most hearty welcome. A few hours later, and I was on my way homeward by the Irish Express to receive another welcome from those on earth most dear to me, just four months since I had bid them farewell.

CHAPTER XXI.

SUMMARY OF SCIENTIFIC RESULTS.

I PROPOSE to give here a summary of the scientific results of the Expedition; reserving for a future work, which will be devoted to this subject fuller details on the several heads here referred to, and which I hope will be completed in the course of the year 1885. I do not wish it to be supposed that the work done by the members of our Expedition was always new, and altogether original. Several men of science of great eminence—amongst whom the names of Russeger, Fraas, Lartet, Vignes, together with those of investigators connected with the Palestine and Sinaitic Surveys, will always hold a prominent place—had previously entered this field. The members of the Expedition have had the advantage of their labours, and it would have been culpable on their part either to neglect or ignore them. On the contrary, we have endeavoured, I trust with proper acknowledgment, to utilise the observations of our predecessors in this wide field of research, which is every day receiving fresh accessions of explorers.[1] The results, then, are as follows :—

1. A complete triangulation of the district lying between the mountains of Sinai and the Wâdy el Arabah, together with that of the Wâdy el Arabah itself, bounded on the west by the tableland of the Tîh, and on the east by the mountains of Edom and Moab. This was entirely the work of Major Kitchener, and his assistant, Mr. G. Armstrong (formerly Sergeant-Major R.E.). An outline survey along the line of route was also made, and has been laid down in MS. on a map prepared by Mr. Armstrong on the same scale as the reduced Map of Palestine, viz., $\frac{3}{8}$ inch to one statute mile, or $\frac{1}{168960}$.

2. Some important rectifications of the borders of the Salt Sea, and of the Gulf of Akabah, were also made.

---

[1] Amongst the most recent contributions to the natural history of this part of the globe may be mentioned Tristram's " Fauna and Flora of Palestine," and C. and W. Barbey's " Herborisations au Levant, Egypt, Syrie, et Mediterranée " (Lausanne).

3. A geological reconnaissance along the line of route through the districts of Sinai, Akabah, and the Wâdy el Arabah, including the following particulars :—

(a) Collections of fossils from the Wâdy Nasb Limestone ; additions to those already made by Mr. Bauerman and Colonel Sir C. W. Wilson. These fossils (which are being examined by Professor Sollas) go to show that this limestone is of Carboniferous age. The Wâdy Nasb limestone was found to continue over a considerable region north of Mount Sinai, and was again recognised amongst the mountains of Moab on the east side of the Salt Sea in the Wâdy el Hessi. As this limestone rests upon a red sandstone foundation, this latter may also be assumed to be of the same geological age, and therefore cannot be the representative of the "Nubian Sandstone" of Rosiere, which (as Professor Zittel has shown) is of Cretaceous age. I propose to call this formation, therefore, "the Desert Sandstone." It forms, with the limestone, a strip along the borders of the ancient rocks of Paleozoic, or Archæan, age, and is about 400 feet in average thickness ; the base is generally a conglomerate.

(b) Above the Wâdy Nasb limestone is another sandstone formation, of which a large portion of the Debbet er Ramleh is formed. It is laid open in the Wâdies Zelegah, Biyar, &c., and along the mountains of Edom and Moab. Out of this rock have been hewn the ancient temples, tombs, and dwellings of Petra and the Wâdy Mûsa. It stretches along the southern escarpment of the Tîh plateau, and forms the base of the limestone cliffs along the margin of the Wâdy el Arabah as far north as Nagb es Salni. This sandstone formation is soft, red, or beautifully variegated. It is (in all probability) of Cretaceous age, and, if so, the true representative of the "Nubian Sandstone" of Russeger. It will thus be seen that there are two red sandstone formations, one below, the other above the Carboniferous limestone of the Wâdy Nasb.

(c) The geological structure of the Wâdy el Arabah was examined throughout a distance of 120 miles from south to north. That it has been hollowed out along the line of a main fault (or line of fracture and displacement) ranging from the eastern shore of the Salt Sea to that of the Gulf of Akabah, was clearly determined. The position of the fault itself was made out and laid down on the map[1] in six or seven places ; one being about ten miles north of Akabah, another near the watershed,

----

[1] The map used was an enlarged plan from Smith and Groves' Ancient Atlas (J. Murray).

in which places the limestone of the Tîh (Cretaceo-nummulitic) is faulted against the old porphyritic and metamorphic rocks, as illustrated by the section across the Arabah Valley, given in a previous page (p. 77).

There are numerous parallel and branching faults along the Arabah Valley, but there is one leading fracture running along the base of the Edomite Mountains, to which the others are of secondary importance ; this may be called "the Great Jordan Valley fault." The relations of the rocks in The Ghôr and Jordan Valley have already been shown by Lartet, Tristram, Wilson, and others, to indicate the presence of a large fault corresponding with the line of this remarkable depression, and the author considers the fracture he has observed in the Arabah Valley to be continuous with that of the Jordan.

(d) The ancient rocks which form the floor either of the Desert, or Nubian, Sandstone formations, consist of granite, gneiss, porphyries, and more rarely of metamorphic schists—together with volcanic rocks, consisting of agglomerates, tuffs, and beds of felspathic trap. The author is disposed to concur with Dr. Lartet in considering the gneissose and granitoid rocks to be of Archæan (or Laurentian) age, as they are probably representative of those of Assouan in Upper Egypt, which Prof. Sir J. W. Dawson has recently identified with those of this age.[1] The granites and porphyries are traversed by innumerable dykes of porphyry and diorite both throughout the Sinaitic mountains and those of Edom and Moab ; and the author considers it probable that the volcanic rocks which are largely represented along the bases of Mount Hor, and of Jebel es Somrah near Es Safieh, are contemporaneous with these dykes. As far as the author was able to observe, none of these dykes penetrate the Desert or Nubian Sandstones, and, if so, they may be considered of pre-Carboniferous age. The upper surface of the ancient rocks was originally extremely uneven, having been worn and denuded into ridges and hollows, previous to the deposition of the Desert Sandstone ; over this irregular floor the sandstone strata were deposited.

4. The occurrence of terraces of marl, gravel, and silt, through which the ravines of existing streams have been cut at an elevation (according to aneroid determination) of about 100 feet above the level of the Mediterranean, was taken to show that the level of the Salt Sea (Bahr Lut) at

---

[1] Dawson has shown, however, that there are two metamorphic series in Upper Egypt. *Geol. Magazine*, Oct., 1884.

one time stood about 1,400 feet higher than at present. These beds of marl were first observed at the camp at 'Ain Abu Beweireh ; they contain blanched shells of the genera *Melanopsis* and *Melania*. The beds of marl were observed to be enclosed by higher ground of more ancient strata in every direction except towards the north, where they gently slope downwards towards the borders of The Ghôr, and become incorporated with strata of the 600 feet terrace.

5. The author concurs with Dr. Lartet in thinking that the waters of the Jordan Valley did not flow down into the Gulf of Akabah after the land had emerged from the sea ; the disconnection of the inner and outer waters was very ancient, dating back to Miocene times.

6. The occurrence of beds of ancient lakes—consisting of coarse gravel, sand, and marl, amongst the mountains of Sinai, and in the Wâdy el Arabah, where now only waterless valleys occur, taken in connection with other phenomena, have impressed the author with the conviction that the former climatic conditions of Arabia Petræa were very different from those of the present day. Such terraces have been observed by Dr. Post in the Wâdy Feirân, and Colonel Sir W. Wilson in the Wâdy Solaf, and by the author in the Wâdies Gharandel, Goweisah, Hamr, Solaf, and Es Sheikh or Watiyeh. It would appear that, at a period coming down probably to the prehistoric, a chain of lakes existed amongst the tortuous valleys and hollows of the Sinaitic peninsula. The gypseous deposits of Wâdy Amarah and of 'Ain Hawareh are considered to be old lake beds, and Mr. Bauerman has observed remains of fresh-water shells (*Lymnæa truncatula*) and a species of *Pisidium* in " lake or river alluvium " of the Wâdies Feirân and Es Sheikh ("Quart. Journ. Geol. Soc.," Vol. XXV, p. 35).

7. The author considers it probable that these ancient Sinaitic lakes belong to an epoch when the waters of the Mediterranean and of the Red Sea rose to a level considerably higher than at present ; and when, consequently, there was less fall for the inland waters in an outer direction. The evidence of a submergence, to a depth of at least 200 feet, is abundantly clear in the occurrence of raised beaches or sea beds with shells, corals, and crinoids, of species still living in the adjoining waters. The raised beaches of the Mediterranean and Red Sea coasts have been observed by the officers of the Ordnance Survey, and by Fraas, Lartet, Schweinfurth, Post, and others. They were observed by members of the Expedition at the southern extremity of the Wâdy el Arabah, and shells

and corals were found round the camp of the 3rd December at an elevation of about 130 feet above the Gulf of Akabah.

These ancient sea beds are represented in the Egyptian area by the old coast-line of 220 feet, discovered by Fraas along the flanks of the Mokattam Hills above Cairo, and recently described by Schweinfurth. (Über die geol. schichtungliederung d. Mokottam bei Cairo ; Zeit. d. Deuts. Geol. Gesel, 1883.) The period in which the sea rose to this level may be stated in general terms as the Pliocene, but it continued downwards till more recent times ; and the author believes that at the time of the Exodus the Gulf of Suez reached as far as the Great Bitter Lake (*Quarterly Statement*, April, 1884). It is scarcely necessary to observe that throughout the longer portion of this period of submergence Africa was disconnected from Asia.

8. The Miocene period is not represented by any strata throughout the district traversed by the Expedition. The author considers that in this part of the world the Miocene period was one of elevation, disturbance, and denudation of strata ; not of accumulation. To this epoch he refers the emergence of the whole of the Palestine, and of the greater part of the Sinaitic areas, from the sea, in which the Cretaceo-nummulitic limestone formations were deposited. To the same epoch also he considers the faulting and flexuring of the strata is chiefly referable ; and notably the formation of the great Jordanic line of fault, with its branches and accompanying flexurings of the strata—which are very remarkable along the western sides of The Ghôr. These phenomena were accompanied and followed by extensive denudation, and the production of many of the principal physical features of the region referred to.

9. The evidences of a Pluvial period throughout this region are to be found (a) in the remains of ancient lake beds, (b) in the existence of terraces in the river valleys, (c) in the great size and depth of many valleys and gorges, now waterless except after severe thunderstorms, and (d) in the vastly greater size of the Salt Sea (or Dead Sea), which must have had a length of nearly 200 English miles from north to south, at the time when its surface was at a higher level than that of the Mediterranean at the present day. The author considers that this Pluvial period extended from the Pliocene through the post-Pliocene (or Glacial) down to recent times. As it is known, from the observations of Sir J. D. Hooker, Canon Tristram, and others, that perennial snow and glaciers existed in the Lebanon during the Glacial epoch, the author infers

that the adjoining districts to the south of the Lebanon must have had a climate approaching that of the British Isles at the present day ; and that, in a region of which many parts are over 2,000 feet in elevation, there must have been abundant rainfall. Even when the snows and glaciers of the Lebanon had disappeared, the effects of the colder climate which was passing away may be supposed to have remained for some time, and the vegetation to have been more luxuriant down to within the epoch of human habitation. The author's views generally coincide with those of Theobold Fisher, as extended by him to a much wider area (Studien über das Klima der Mediterranean Lander," Peterman's Mittheilungen, 1879).

10. The author considers that there are reasons for concluding that the outburst of volcanic phenomena in North-Eastern Palestine in the region of the Jaulan and Hauran, &c., has an indirect connection with the formation of the great Jordan Sea of the Pluvial period. The presence of water in considerable volume is now recognised as necessary to volcanic activity, and the author submits that this interdependence was brought about when the waters of the Lake stretched as far north as the little Lake of Hûleh. These waters, under a pressure of several hundred feet, would find their way into the interior of the earth's crust along the lines of the great Jordan Valley fault, and of its branches, and thus supply the necessary "steam power" for volcanic action. The period when the volcanoes of the Jaulan and Hauran were in action appears to have ranged from the Pliocene through the post-Pliocene to the beginning of the recent ; when, concurrently with the falling away and partial drying up of the waters of the great inland sea, the volcanic fires became extinct and the outpourings of basaltic lava ceased to flow.

If these views are correct, it would seem that during the Glacial epoch, Palestine and Southern Syria presented an aspect very different from the present. The Lebanon throughout the year was snow-clad over its higher elevations, while glaciers descended into some of its valleys. The region of the Hauran, lying at its southern base, was the site of several extensive volcanoes, while the district around, and the Jordan Valley itself, was invaded by floods of lava. A great inland sea, occupying the Jordan Valley, together with the existing comparatively restricted sheets of water, extended from Lake Hûleh on the north, to a southern margin near the base of Samrat Fiddân in the Wâdy el Arabah of the present day, while numerous arms and bays stretched into the glens and valleys of Palestine and Moab on either hand. Under such climatic conditions, we may feel assured, a luxuriant vegetation decked with verdure the hills and vales of Palestine and Arabia Petræa to an extent far beyond that of the present ; and amongst the trees, as Sir J. D. Hooker has shown, the cedar may have spread far and wide.

11. The author has not thought it necessary to go into the question of the origin of the salinity of the Salt Sea, as this question is now fully understood. He is obliged to differ with Dr. Lartet in his view of the origin of the salt mountain, Jebel Usdum,[1] which he (the author), as also Mr. Hart, regards as a portion of the bed of the Salt Sea, when it stood about 600 feet above its present level. This level exactly corresponds to that of the terraces, both along the south and east of The Ghôr, formed of lacustrine materials. The upper surface of Jebel Usdum was examined by Messrs. Hart and Laurence, of the Expedition, but previous explorers had considered the sides inaccessible.

12. The author concurs with previous writers in considering that the Cretaceous and Tertiary periods succeeded each other over this region (at least as far as the marine deposits are concerned) without any important physical disturbances ; in consequence of which the limestone formations of these periods are in physical conformity and are generally incapable of separation without prolonged and detailed examination. It seems probable, however, that while the Nummulitic limestones predominate in the Egyptian and Nubian areas, those of the Cretaceous period were more fully developed over the area of Arabia Petræa and Palestine.

13. A complete series of meteorological observations, consisting of maxima and minima readings of the thermometer, and levels of the barometer, were made by Mr. Laurence, and will appear in the scientific work to follow.

14. A series of photographic views were taken by Dr. E. G. Hull, and a selection from them will be published.

15. A large collection of plants, and a smaller of animals, was made by Mr. H. C. Hart.

---

[1] Lartet regards the strata of this mountain as belonging to the Nummulitic period.

CHAPTER XXII.

SOME REMARKABLE SITES CONNECTED WITH BIBLICAL HISTORY VISITED BY THE EXPEDITION.

ADVANCES in the identification of most of the places connected with the Exodus, and with early Christian history, are being daily made, and I propose here to deal with a few cases which have come under my own immediate notice (with one exception), and to offer some observations upon them. They are as follows :—

1. The Passage of the Red Sea by the Israelites under Moses.
2. The Giving of the Law from Mount Sinai.
3. Kadesh Barnea and Mount Hor.
4. The Site of Calvary.

Making three illustrations from the Old Testament, and one from the New.

1. *The Passage of the Red Sea by the Israelites.*—From the earliest period of history Egypt was connected with Asia by a narrow neck of land occupying a position to the north of the present Great Bitter Lake Over this neck lay the road connecting the capital of the Pharaohs at Tanis, or Zoan, with the East by way of Philistia on the one hand, or, again, by the way of Shur, or finally by the way of Elath, at the head of the Ælanitic Gulf.

By the first of these roads, leading into Philistia, the Israelites could have reached the Promised Land within the shortest time ; but, enfeebled and dispirited by long captivity, they were forbidden to face the warlike inhabitants of Philistia, and on reaching the neck they were ordered by the Lord to turn southwards, and in this direction they continued their march till they found themselves confronted by the sterile mountain range of Jebel Attâkah, flanked by the waters of the Red Sea on the east, and pursued by the army of Pharoah on the north and west. That the place of the passage called " Pi-hahiroth before Baal-Zephon " was in the neighbourhood of the present town of Suez, at the head of the Gulf, there can be little doubt. The locality, as suggested by Dean Stanley, was probably in the vicinity of Ajrûd, the halting-place of the Mecca pilgrims. Now, to the north of the Gulf of Suez, and extending a distance of ten statute miles to the Bitter Lakes, there exists at the present day a neck of land, across which the Israelitish host might have marched into the wilderness of Etham on their way to Mount Sinai, and over which the army of Pharaoh, with its chariots, would probably have been unable to follow; at any rate (if the conditions had been the same then as now) there would have been no necessity for the performance of a miracle in dividing the waters of a sea which at the present day does not exist. Here is a difficulty; arising from the impossibility of reconciling the Scriptural narrative with observed physical phenomena.

It seems to me, however, that the explanation is sufficiently clear to any one who considers that ever since the Pliocene period down to very recent times the land has been gaining on the sea over the area which was the scene of these events. At the Pliocene period the whole of Lower Egypt and the borders of the Mediterranean were submerged to a depth of (at least) 200 feet below the present sea-level, and since that period the land has been slowly rising. It is not too much to assume that at a period of four thousand years ago the process of elevation had not been completed to its present extent; and that, in consequence, the waters of the Gulf of Suez stretched northwards into the Bitter Lakes, forming a channel, perhaps of no great depth, but requiring the exercise of Almighty Power to convert it into a causeway of dry land in order to rescue the chosen people from their impending peril. The levels taken for the Suez Canal show that a depression of about 25 feet would suffice to bring the waters of the Gulf of Suez into the Bitter Lakes; and this submergence would still leave the neck to the north of the Bitter Lakes in the position of land such as we know it to have been in the time of the Pharaohs, and which formed the line of communication between Egypt and the East. In this way, as it appears to me, we may bring the Bible narrative into harmony with physical phenomena.

2. *The Giving of the Law from Mount Sinai.*—The claims of the different mountains of the Sinaitic peninsula to be that from which the Law was delivered to Israel have been carefully analysed by one who knows the topographical details perhaps better than any other Englishman, Colonel Sir Charles Wilson,[1] who gives his decision in favour of Jebel Mûsa, or

[1] "Ordnance Survey of Sinai," p. 140.

Moses' Mount—a decision which must be accepted as final. It has been shown in detail by this author, that all the requirements of the case as described in the Bible are met in their minutest details, if we accept Jebel Mûsa as the "Mount of the Law." In this view the late Professor Palmer concurred.[1]

This mountain rises to an elevation of 7,363 feet, and at its southern end the grand precipitous cliff of Rás Sufsâfeh, reaching an elevation of 6,937 feet, rises directly from the plain or wide valley called the Wâdy er Rahah, with a front of 2,000 feet. This plain contains 400 acres of convenient standing ground ; while at its further extremity it opens out into the wide valley of Es Sheikh, which would easily afford camping ground for the people with their flocks and herds. Here then we have all the requirements for the events related during the sojourn of the Israelites. We may well suppose that Moses was called up to be with Jehovah on the higher summit of Jebel Mûsa, while the people watched his ascent from the plain and from the slopes of the mountains. Sir Charles Wilson lays special stress on the position and character of the cliff of Rás Sufsâfeh. Nothing can be more graphic than the description of this noble, precipitous mass of granite, as the mountain which "may be touched." Its almost sheer rise from the plain lends force to this description, while it afforded facilities for marking off its sacred precincts from trespassers.

One other point may be noticed. In the vicinity of this mountain group are several perennial springs and six streams affording cool and delicious water throughout the year. They derive their sources from the snow which, for a few weeks in winter time, caps the upper heights of Jebels Mûsa and Katarina. One of these streams descending along the Wâdy Sh'reich was probably that into which Moses cast the dust of the Golden Calf.

The late eminent Astronomer Royal, in his attempt to trace the events connected with the journeys of the Israelites to purely natural causes, has advanced the view that the thunderings and lightnings of Sinai were caused by the outburst of volcanic forces. If such had been the case we might have expected some evidence of volcanic action, or of a modern volcanic mountain, in this neighbourhood. Jebel Mûsa, however, together with all the mountain groups forming the southern extremity of the

[1] "The Desert of the Exodus," pp. 55, 99, and 102. I cannot by any means accept Mr. Baker Greene's views of the identity of Mount Sinai with Mount Hor.

Sinaitic peninsula, consists of granitic and metamorphic rocks of immense geological antiquity ; nor are there any traces of recent volcanic products.[1]

3. *Kadesh Barnea and Mount Hor.*—The position of Kadesh Barnea, a locality for ever memorable in the history of the Israelitish wanderings, has been a question of controversy amongst geographers down to the present day. According to the sacred text it was eleven days' journey from Horeb (Mount Sinai) by way of Mount Seir,[2] and it was, also, immediately to the south of the borders of Canaan,[3] and not far from those of Edom or Mount Seir. From this description, Kadesh Barnea might lie either along the western border of the Wâdy el Arabah, or at some distance further west amongst the valleys of the Tîh. Accordingly, the spring called Ain el Weibeh, discovered by Dr. Robinson, at the base of the cliffs which form the bounds of the Arabah Valley, has been identified by some writers as the site of Kadesh.

A more recent determination, and one in which I am disposed to concur, is the valley and spring of 'Ain Kadeis, which lies about thirty-five miles to the west of the Arabah Valley, amongst the limestone hills of the Tîh. This identification was first made by the Rev. John Rolands, and is ably supported by an American writer, Dr. Trumbull, in a recent work,[4] written after a personal visit to the spot.[5] Under this identification, the camping ground of Kadesh Barnea was probably reached by the route suggested by the Rev. F. W. Holland, and which was also followed throughout a great part of its course by our own Expedition. Mr. Holland supposes that the Israelites, after leaving Jebel Mûsa (Horeb), marched northwards, and after traversing the grand gorge of the Wâdy el Watiyeh, turned to the east along the valleys of Zillegah and El Ain. Turning northwards they entered the region of the Tîh, by the Wâdy el Atiyeh ; and then proceeding onwards across the great plains of limestone reached their halting-place at Kadesh Barnea. The whole distance would be about 150 miles (English), and for eleven days would be at the rate of nearly fourteen miles per day.

That Kadesh Barnea must have been a place of note in the days of the

---

[1] It is too much to suppose that Moses was exposed during forty days to the fury of a volcano in active eruption !

[2] Deut. i, 2.

[3] Numb. xxxiv, 4.

[4] " Kadesh Barnea " (1884).

[5] The spot had also been visited by the Rev. F. W. Holland.

W. Jaifeh.

J. Moraifig.

J. Aneiqah.

FIG. 19.—WÁDY KADEIS AND WÁDY JAIFEH.

W. Kadeis.

A. Johnson, delt.

The supposed site of Kadesh Barnea. (*From a sketch by the late Rev. F. W. Holand, May 13th, 1878.*)

Israelitish wanderings cannot be doubted. The name Kadesh means " holy " or "sacred," and we must suppose that there was ordinarily an abundant supply of water giving a claim of sanctity to the spot. Owing, however, to some cause not stated, but probably that of a prolonged drought, the flow of water failed during the second visit of the Israelites, previous to their march to the Promised Land ; and the Lord commanded Moses and Aaron to assemble the people before the rock facing the camp, and to speak to the rock, that it might give forth water for the people and their cattle.[1] Instead of speaking to the rock, Moses struck it with his staff twice, and having failed to sanctify the Lord in the eyes of the children of Israel, he and Aaron were condemned to die before entering the Promised Land. The account here seems to agree with the topographical features of the Wâdy Kadeis, as given in rather glowing language by Dr. Trumbull. From the base of a limestone cliff jutting out into the valley, a stream of water bursts forth which spreads fertility over a considerable area till gradually absorbed into the porous bed of the valley. Mr. Holland has also described the place, stating that there are three springs : two on the hillside, and one in the bed of the valley, and from the sketch he has left it may be inferred that at the junction of the Wâdies Kadeis and Jaifeh there is extensive camping ground.[2] (Fig. 19.)

On leaving Kadesh the Israelites marched eastwards towards the borders of Edom, and encamped at the base of Mount Hor, while awaiting the reply of the King of Edom to the request of Moses for permission to pass through his country on the way towards the Land of Promise. This route was circuitous ; but it may be presumed that the Israelites, having thirty-eight years previously been smitten before the Amalekites and Canaanites,[3] were permitted to circumvent their enemies by the way of Edom, Moab, and the Jordan Valley. They, therefore, appear to have marched eastward to the head of the W. Kadeis, crossed the limestone plain, and descended into the great valley of the Arabah, by the W. Ghamr, or one of the other branches. Having crossed the Arabah, here about ten miles wide, they continued their course toward the base of Mount Hor, and camped at the western base of the mount, in the wide valley called W. Abu Kuseibeh, which was the site of our own camp

---

[1] Numb. xx, 8.
[2] *Quarterly Statement*, January, 1884.
[3] Numb. xiv, 44.

while we visited Petra and Mount Hor, between the 8th and 10th of December, 1883.

In its name Jebel Haroun (Aaron's Mount), Mount Hor retains the memory of that event which forms so melancholy a chapter in Jewish history. The identification of J. Haroun with "Mount Hor, by the coast of the Land of Edom" (Numb. xx, 23), has been disputed by Dr. Trumbull, but (as it seems to me) on insufficient grounds. He suggests Jebel Madurah, an isolated hill near Ain Kadeis, as the real scene of Aaron's death. Dr. Trumbull has doubtless seen Jebel Madurah, but if he had visited Jebel Haroun he would have been aware how completely this conspicuous elevation fulfils the requirements of the narrative. The language, "that the whole congregation journeyed from Kadesh, and came unto Mount Hor," appears to indicate an interval of perhaps several days' march from the time of their departure from the one, till their arrival at the other. It may also be presumed that, as Moses was permitted to view the Land of Canaan from Mount Nebo, Aaron was permitted to do so from Mount Hor. In both these respects Jebel Haroun meets the requirements of the case. The summit of Mount Hor, rising as it does about 4,580 feet (as determined by Major Kitchener) above the Mediterranean, or 5,875 feet above the level of the Salt Sea and The Ghôr, affords a commanding prospect of the great valley of the Arabah, and the borders of Seir, of the depression of The Ghôr, itself, and of the tableland of Southern Palestine; and we may well suppose the eyes of the high priest of Israel were allowed to rest themselves upon the hills of Judea, ere he resigned his priestly robes, and prepared himself for his resting-place, perhaps in the little cave which is covered by a Mohammedan shrine, whose white walls are visible to the traveller for many a mile around.

4. *The Site of Calvary.*—One of the most recent identifications in or about Jerusalem is the site of Calvary, the topographical details of which have been very clearly elucidated by Captain Conder.[1] Attention has up till recent times been diverted from this determination by the assumption that the site of our Lord's Crucifixion is beneath the roof of "The Church of the Holy Sepulchre," which occupies a position nearly in the centre of the modern city. The labours of the officers of the Palestine Survey, and others, have not only succeeded in exploding the

---

[1] "Tent Work in Palestine," p. 195, &c.

claims of this locality, but also in fixing the real site, as it seems to me, beyond the pale of controversy.

If there is any fact clearer than another, in reference to the place of the Crucifixion, it is that the spot was outside the walls of Jerusalem. As the Apostle puts it, both figuratively and actually, "Jesus suffered without the gate,"[1] and as there was a garden at the place of the Crucifixion containing a tomb,[2] it is tolerably certain the spot was beyond the suburbs of the city. The traditional site, on which the church of the Crusaders stands, was either inside the second wall, as may be inferred from the description of Josephus, who says that it stretched from the Gate of Gennath *in a circuit* to the angle of Fort Antonia, or it must have been in close proximity thereto ; and, consequently, fails in either case to answer to the language of St. John xix, 20, that the place was "nigh unto the city." As has been pointedly remarked, the language of the Evangelists seems to imply that the procession, on leaving the Prætorium, passed, not through the city, but outside it.[3] Now from the relative positions of the Prætorium and the traditional site, the procession would have had to wind its way along the side of the second wall, instead of outwards towards the country.

But beyond the second wall stretched at that time the populous suburb of Bezetha, which was enclosed about ten years after the Crucifixion by Agrippa's third wall, and it is extremely unlikely that the Crucifixion and entombment would have been permitted in the midst of suburban residences.

We are obliged, therefore, to look outside, and beyond, those limits for a position which would answer the requirements of the several narratives, which are all quite consistent with each other. Calvary was clearly an elevated site, affording space for a large assemblage of spectators ; it was some distance from the city walls, and from ordinary habitations ; it was by the wayside leading into the country ; and was within easy reach of the Prætorium, or Herod's Judgment Hall, which occupied the north-west angle of the Temple area.[4] All these requirements are met by

---

[1] Heb. xiii, 12.

[2] John xix, 41.

[3] Matt. xxvii, 31; Mark xv, 20; Luke xxiii, 26; John xix, 17.

[4] In the excellent Map of Ancient Jerusalem in the Biblical Atlas and Gazetteer the plans are well shown, but the position of the spot now identified is better shown in the map of the modern city.

the site described by Captain Conder, which is one accepted by (I believe) the intelligent European residents of Jerusalem,[1] and it is one which, after having visited and carefully considered it, has satisfied my own mind.

On passing through the Damascus Gate, which leads out from the north side of the city, we turn to the right by the road which follows the course of Agrippa's wall ; and at a distance of about one-fourth of an English mile we find ourselves in front of a platform of limestone, breaking off with a slight scarp in the direction of the city. The face of the scarp is perforated by a cave, known as "Jeremiah's Grotto," and seen in a certain direction this prominent knoll has an appearance not unlike that of a skull ; hence, possibly, the name "Golgotha." More probably, however, the locality was a place of interment ; for it is known that the great cemetery of Jewish times lay to the north side of the city, and therefore in the neighbourhood of the Grotto of Jeremiah. A Mohammedan cemetery occupies a portion of the platform, and an Arab Sheikh has pitched his tent at its base. Here, undesecrated by any building, sacred or profane, stands in its naked simplicity the natural platform on which was erected the cross of the Saviour. From this position, with outstretched arms, He embraced the city over which He had wept when first He had viewed it from the Mount of Olives. The position of the first and last view are almost exactly opposite each other. And, as if to place the identification of the spot beyond controversy an ancient Roman causeway has been discovered stretching in the direction of Herod's Gate, which, passing through Agrippa's wall, opens out almost in front of the platform ; we can scarcely doubt it was that along which the procession moved after leaving the Prætorium towards the place of Crucifixion. Amongst all the objects referable to the time of our Lord, none seems to me more clearly genuine than that I have now described as the site of Calvary.

Such is a brief account of some of the localities (with the exception of Ain Kadeis) visited by the members of our Expedition.

[1] Amongst whom may be mentioned the British and American Consuls and Dr. Chaplin. General Gordon, in his notes on Palestine, takes the same view, and Canon Tristram has reminded me that he has also for some time held this view.

CHAPTER XXIII.

EXPLANATION OF THE GEOLOGICAL MAP.

SINCE this volume contains a Geological Map, it may be expected that I should offer some explanatory observations upon it.

Every good Geological Map ought to explain itself. It ought, in fact, to tell its own story regarding the features of the country it represents, and the rocks and formations of which the region is constructed ; and if every person was acquainted with the principles of geology, and had been properly instructed in the plan according to which Geological Maps are prepared, no explanation would be required. With a Geological Map of any district before him, and one also showing the features of hill and dale, mountain and valley, an observer would receive a correct idea of the physical structure of the whole region. He would be able for himself to determine what were the older, or newer, formations : in what way they were disposed one to the other ; and, also, be able to form some idea regarding the distribution of land and sea at past periods. Such a map would speak to his mind regarding past physical events as distinctly as a piece of written music, when placed before a musician, conveys to *his* mind what would be the character of the composition if reproduced on an instrument.

Unfortunately the sublime science of geology has only as yet a limited number of cultivators. Its truths have as yet only been revealed to the favoured few ; but the day will doubtless come when the study of geology will be considered as essential to a good education as is the study of geography or history. It is now admitted that geology is the basis of geography ; and it cannot be questioned that the physical history of any country has had an important bearing on the history and character of its inhabitants ; so that, in order properly to understand the latter, we ought not to neglect the investigation of the former.

O

In no country has this statement a fuller illustration than in the region over which the little Geological Map accompanying this volume extends. The present habits, and much of the past history, of the inhabitants have been moulded on the physical characters of the various parts which are the direct outcome of their geological structure. The mild patient character of the Egyptian cultivator befits the nature of that wide alluvial tract of fertile land which is watered by the Nile, and is one of the most recent tracts reclaimed from the sea.[1] The mountainous tracts of the Sinaitic peninsula, formed of the oldest crystalline rocks of that part of the world, have become the abode of the Bedouin Arab, the hardy child of nature who has adapted himself to a life in keeping with his wild surroundings. The great tableland of the Tih, less rugged and inhospitable than the mountainous parts of Sinai and Serbal, supports roving tribes, partly pastoral, and gradually assimilating their habits to the fellahin of Philistia and of Palestine, who cultivate the ground and rear large flocks and herds.

A review of the past history of these regions would probably show a still more intimate connection between the character and habits of the various peoples and the physical features of the country than those even of the present day; but it is not necessary that I should do more than allude to them here, in order to enforce my statement that the connection between their characters and habits may be traced largely to the nature of the country, and this again back to its geological structure. I therefore pass on briefly to explain the meaning of the various colours which have been used in the construction of the map.

It will be seen that the map embraces a large area, extending from the banks of the Nile on the west to the mountains of Edom and Moab on the east, and from the southern extremity of the Sinaitic peninsula on the south, to the mountains of Lebanon on the north. It includes the entire Jordan Valley, and the long continuous depression of the Arabah Valley till it becomes submerged beneath the waters of the Gulf of Akabah.

The oldest rocks occupy the greater portion of the Sinaitic peninsula, as well as the mountains bordering the Gulf of Akabah, and extending northward along the eastern side of the Wâdy el Arabah. They are coloured deep purple and pale pink on the map; and consist of granitic,

---

[1] Coloured deep green on the map.

gneissose, and schistose rocks, amongst which have been intruded great masses of red porphyry, dark greenstone, and other igneous rocks in the form of dykes, veins, and bosses. These rocks are probably amongst the oldest in the world, and are representative (at least in part) of those in Upper Egypt at Assouan (Syene) from which the noble monoliths of ancient Egyptian art have been hewn.

Two isolated masses of the granitic and sandstone formations occur amongst the limestones of the Tíh, and were discovered by Mr. Holland; but details regarding their relations to the newer strata are wanting.[1]

After these ancient rocks had been consolidated they were subjected to a vast amount of erosion, and were worn into very uneven surfaces, over which the more recent formations were spread; first, filling up the hollows with the lower strata, and ultimately covering even the higher elevations as the process of deposition of strata went on.

The oldest of these formations is the red sandstone and conglomerate, which I have called the "Desert Sandstone" formation. It is coloured blue on the map, and forms a narrow strip along the margin of the old crystalline rocks.[2] It is capped by the fossiliferous limestone of the Wâdy Nasb, which shows it to belong to the Carboniferous period—in fact, to be the representative of the Carboniferous Limestone of Europe and the British Isles. It is also found east of the Arabah Valley and amongst the mountains of Moab east of The Ghôr.

This is succeeded by another sandstone formation coloured yellowish brown, and more extensively distributed than the former. It belongs to a much more recent geological period, namely, the Cretaceous; and is the representative of the "Nubian Sandstone" of Roziere, so largely developed in Africa, especially in Nubia and Upper Egypt.

This is succeeded by the Cretaceous and Nummulitic Limestone formations, which occupy the greater portion of the map, forming the great tableland of the Tíh, from its western escarpment to the borders of the Arabah Valley, and stretching northward throughout the hill country of Judea and Samaria into Syria and the Lebanon.

On the east of the Jordan Valley the Cretaceous Limestone forms the tablelands of Edom and Moab; as far north as the Hauran and Jaulan where the limestone passes below great sheets of basaltic lava coloured

---

[1] *Quarterly Statement*, Palestine Exploration Fund, Jan. 1884.

A portion of this tract is taken from the Ordnance Survey of Sinai.

deep pink. The Cretaceous Limestone is coloured yellow, and represents the Chalk formation of Europe and the British Isles.

The Nummulitic Limestone is represented by a buff colour; but the boundary between the two limestone formations is intentionally indefinite, as it could only be determined with accuracy by a careful and detailed survey and examination of the whole region. Outlying patches of the Nummulitic Limestone occur in Palestine, and are taken from M. Lartet's map; but it is probable that the formation is much more largely represented than is shown on either of those maps. The two formations, although belonging the one to the Secondary, the other to the Tertiary, periods, are very closely connected in Palestine as far as the mineral characters are concerned, though the fossil contents are perhaps altogether different.[1] Both also contain beds and bands of flint or chert.

The Cretaceous Limestone underlies nearly the whole of the Jordan and Arabah Valleys, though concealed by more recent deposits, and is broken off along the line of the great Jordan Valley fault against older formations. This has been explained in a previous page (p. 76), and need not further be insisted on. But it is entirely owing to the presence of this leading line of fracture and displacement, and the subsequent denudation of strata, that this great valley exists, and that the eastern side is so mountainous and characterised by such grand features of hill and dale.

These limestones pass under a newer formation of calcareous sandstone in the direction of the Mediterranean. To this formation I have applied the name of "Calcareous Sandstone of Philistia," as it forms nearly the whole of that country, or at least is its foundation rock. It is probably of Upper Eocene age, and appears to be represented in Egypt by the sandstone formation ("Nicolien Sandstein" of Zittel) with fossil trees found overlying the nummulitic limestone of the Jebel Mokattam, near Cairo. It is coloured deep brown on the map.

The formations next in order approach more nearly those of our own time, and range from the Pliocene period downwards. They consist of raised beaches and sea-beds along the coast, and of lake beds in The Ghôr and Jordan Valley; they are coloured a light shade of green.

[1] Dr. Zittel states that although there is no definite line of division between the Cretaceous and Nummulitic formations of the Libyan Desert, the fossils of each formation are entirely different. It is probably the same in Arabia Petræa.

The volcanic lavas of Northern Palestine and the district bordering the Jordan Valley are coloured deep pink; their geological relations to the other formations have already been pointed out in a previous chapter. The sandy and gravelly tracts are shown by engraved dots.

It is much to be desired that the central portions of the Tih should be traversed in several directions by competent geologists. From the notes recorded by Mr. Milne and the Rev. F. W. Holland it may be inferred that there is more variety in the stratification of that region than is generally supposed; and that a somewhat detailed *reconnaissance* would bear interesting results.

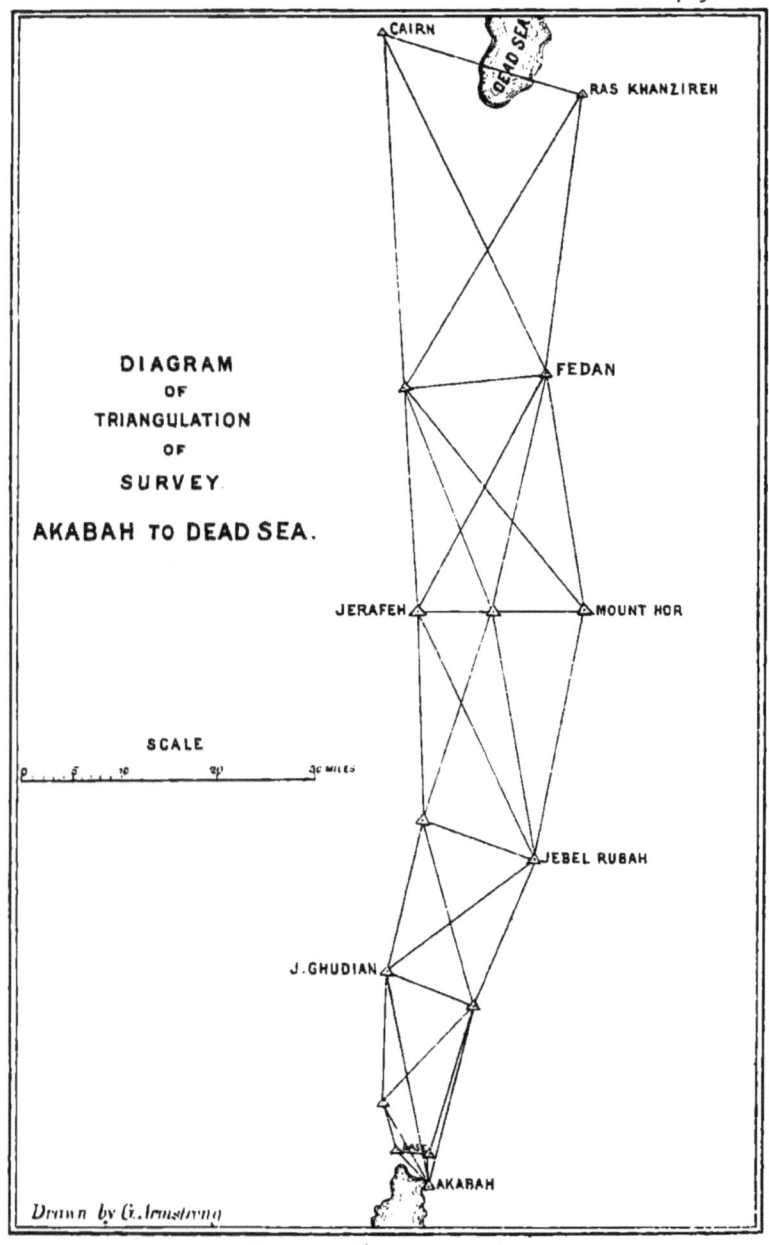

DIAGRAM
OF
TRIANGULATION
OF
SURVEY

AKABAH TO DEAD SEA.

SCALE

CAIRN

RAS KHANZIREH

DEAD SEA

FEDAN

JERAFEH   MOUNT HOR

JEBEL RUBAH

J. GHUDIAN

AKABAH

Drawn by G. Armstrong

APPENDIX.

MAJOR KITCHENER'S REPORT.

On the 10th of November, 1883, the party left Suez for the camp at Ayun Mûsa. I was able to compare chronometers at the Eastern Telegraph ship on the way out of the harbour.

The small oasis called the Ayun Mûsa has been fully described in guide books, and Baedeker gives an enlarged plan of the locality with the heights of the springs in detail.

The place consists of a few springs of limpid but brackish water, small pools with gardens of palms and tamarisks around them, as well as beds of vegetables and culinary herbs.

These gardens are kept by a Frenchman and some Arabs, who have provided summer-houses for the convneience of those who resort thither from Suez to enjoy the fresh desert air.

They form the market gardens from which the vegetable supply of Suez is principally drawn. There exists also a solitary pool upon the top of a neighbouring hill of sand, having one single palm beside it.

While camped there I went over my stores and instruments, and took some astronomical observations to see that all were in proper order for the start.

On the 12th November, camp was moved to Wâdy Sudur; the route was over an open plain by the sea-shore with a line of cliffs supporting the Tîh plateau, about ten miles to the east. Torrents from these cliffs had covered the ground in many places with rocks and boulders. These torrents are extremely short-lived, coming down in force when any rain falls, and drying up almost as quickly. When it ceases, they spread themselves over the plain in many shallow channels, covering a large area with stones and *débris*. One had come down Wâdy Sudur about ten days before, and the traces of wet mud, &c., were still visible over the plain. This wâdy has become famous for the tragedy enacted in August, 1882 when Professor Palmer, Captain Gill, and Lieutenant Charrington were murdered here.

I obtained from an Arab of the Haiwat tribe a story of the murder which I have never seen published in any account of it. I give it merely for what it is worth : Arabs, as everybody knows who has had to do with them, have a remarkable facility for making up a story to meet a supposed occasion.

This was the story in the Arab's own words :—

" Arabi Pashi, directed by the Evil One—may he never rest in peace !— sent to his lordship the Governor of Nakhl to tell him that he had utterly destroyed all the Christian ships of war at Alexandria and Suez ; also that he had destroyed their houses in the same places, and that the Governor of Nakhl was to take care if he saw any Christians running about in his country, like rats with no holes, that the Arabs were to finish them at once. On hearing this news, a party of Arabs started to loot Ayun Mûsa and Suez. Coming down Wâdy Sudur they met the great Sheikh Abdullah and his party ; they thought they were the Christians spoken of by Arabi Pasha, running away, so they surrounded them in the wâdy. But the Arabs ran away from the English, who defended themselves in the wâdy ; all night they stopped round them, but did not dare to take them till just at dawn, when they made a rush on them from every side and seized them all.

" The Arab Sheikh, who had come with the party, ran away with the money. The Arabs did not know Sheikh Abdullah, and did not believe his statement, and when he offered money, his own Sheikh would not give it, so they believed that the party were running away from Suez, and they finished them there. Afterwards the great Colonel came and caught them, and they were finished at Zag ez Zig. May their graves be defiled ! "

Such is the story I heard, and there seems to me to be some amount of truth in it.

Colonel Sir Charles Warren's energetic action in the capture and bringing to justice of the perpetrators of the crime, has created a deep impression, and I consider that the whole peninsula is for foreign travellers now as safe as, if not safer than, it was previously. While on this subject I may mention that I found Professor Palmer's death everywhere regretted deeply by the people, and his memory still warm in the hearts of his Arab friends in the country. Many of them came unsolicited to ask me if I had known him, and to express their sorrow at his loss.

From the length and breadth of Wâdy Sudur I should imagine it must drain a considerable area on the Tîh plateau. The existing maps appeared to me to be wrong after Sinn el Bisher, or Jebel Bisher, as the true scarp appears to recede considerably. I was unable, however, to prove these points, but if a map were made of this part it would probably show considerable variation of the existing plans.

The tract after Wâdy Sudur passes over more rolling country to Wâdy Gharandel, where we camped for the second night; the wâdy flows between banks, and is of considerable importance, and drains an extensive country broken up by high hills; on the edge of the Tîh scarp there are springs and some trees in the valley.

Wâdy Gharandel forms the boundary of the Ordnance Survey, so that from this point to Jebel Mûsa the map was complete. I was able to sketch in some features on the border of the finished Survey while passing.

Our route led through Wâdy Hamr, Wâdy Nasb, Wâdy Kamîleh, from which Armstrong and I visited the temple at el Sarâbît el Khâdim.

The sandstone columns and tablets are in many cases in an excellent state of preservation, and the hieroglyphics were in many cases almost as sharp and perfect as when first cut; others were very much weathered, some tablets 7 feet 6 inches high, by 2 feet wide, and 1 foot 6 inches thick, and rounded at the top like the Moabite Stone, appeared to me to deserve a better fate than being left to perish from the effects of the weather and the vandalism of the Arabs. Excavations here would, I think, reveal many interesting points connected with the Egyptian occupation of this country at the time of the Exodus. I noticed that the artist had been inspired by his surroundings; engraving the ibex in different positions to form ornamental patterns round the hieroglyphic inscriptions. There were several stations on the surrounding hills where tablets stood, similar to the one described; but these have been mostly thrown down and broken up.[1]

[1] The following description of Sarâbît el Khâdim is given by the late Professor Palmer, in his book, "The Desert of the Exodus."

"Although only 700 feet in height, the ascent of Sarâbît el Khâdimis is by no means easy.

"A scramble over a rough slide of loose sandstone at the upper end of the valley, a treacherous sloping ledge of rock overhanging an awkward precipice, and a steep ravine which brings into play all one's gymnastic capabilities, leads to an extensive plateau broken up by many deep ravines and rising knolls. On one of the highest of these last is a heap of ruins—hewn sandstone walls, with broken columns, and numerous stelæ, in shape like ordinary English gravestones,

On the morning of the 18th I took observations with the theodolite from Zibb el Baheir (a trigonometrical station of the Ordnance Survey),

standing or scattered at irregular intervals about the place, the whole being surrounded by the *débris* of an outer wall.

"The building consists of two temples, apparently of different dates—one constructed entirely of hewn stones, the other formed by two chambers excavated in the rock at the easternmost end, and having a walled continuation in front. In the largest of these chambers the walls show signs of having been once completely covered with hieroglyphics, though a great portion have now scaled off; at the upper end is a small niche, probably the altar, beside which is carved a figure in bas-relief. Another niche is seen at the right-hand corner, and in the centre of the chamber is a pillar, cut in the solid rock and covered with hieroglyphics. Some of the hieroglyphics in this cave still bear traces of the paint with which they were formerly ornamented—emerald green inside the characters, with a red and black band above and below.

"The cornice of the wall which forms the continuation of the temple is ornamented with a pretty pattern, and fragments of Egyptian coping lie around the entrance.

"The *stelæ* above mentioned, as well as such of the walls of the building as are still left standing, are covered with hieroglyphics, and amongst them may be remarked the *cartouches* of many of the earliest Egyptian kings.

"The purpose of these monuments was for a long time enveloped in mystery, but the researches of Professor Lepsius and other learned Egyptologists have shown that they were connected with the working of copper mines in the neighbourhood, and that the temple was probably that in which the miners and their guards worshipped the national gods of Egypt.

"The mines themselves were first rediscovered by Mr. Holland, during a previous visit to the peninsula, and were carefully examined by the Expedition on this occasion; they exist in great numbers in the neighbourhood of the temple, and several of them contain beautifully executed hieroglyphic tablets.

"From the inscriptions and cartouches found there, it is evident that the mines were in full working order at the time of the Exodus.

"There is another means of access to the ruins of Sarâbît el Khâdim, by a ravine rather higher up the main valley, which involves a less toilsome climb; but as it also necessitates a walk along a narrow sloping ledge of rock, with a terrific precipice beneath, I cannot recommend it to the traveller unless he feels confident in the possession of a sure foot and a steady head.

"The name Sarâbît el Khâdim signifies 'the Heights of the Servant,' and the place is said by the Arabs to have been so called from a black statue, representing a 'servant or slave,' which was removed 'by the French' during their occupation of Egypt. Amongst the ruins we noticed a pedestal, which might have served for the base of such a statue; and I have since seen in the British Museum a beautifully executed female foot, carved in black stone, which formed part of the collection of curiosities found by the late Major Macdonald in this very spot.

over the district to the north-east through which we were to pass, also into Jebel el Watiyeh, on the edge of the Ordnance map, which was formed into a trigonometrical station by observing with the theodolite from it, subsequently observing from Jebel Musa. I was thus able to fix many points in the country we were about to survey from a very extended base of Ordnance survey work.

On the 22nd November we left the surveyed country at El Watiyeh, and I made a detour by 'Ain el Akhdar, which I was able to fix; the spring is of good water, and is perennial, with a few palms and other trees hidden in the corner of the valley. I then made my way across low-lying hills at the foot of outlying scarp, to the Wâdy Zelegah, where camp was pitched.

" It is not unlikely that amidst the antiquities in the Louvre, the remaining portion of the ' Khâdim ' from Sarâbît may yet be found.

" The hieroglyphic inscriptions from Magharah range from Senefru of the third Egyptian dynasty to Thothmes III, of the eighteenth line; those of Sarâbit el Khâdim end with Rameses IV, of the twentieth, after which period the mines and temples were abandoned. No inscriptions have been discovered at Sarâbît of kings who reigned between Thothmes III and the twelfth dynasty, nor any after the twentieth. They occur rarely and after long intervals after Rameses II.

" One of the principal tablets at Sarâbît el Khâ·lim refers to a certain Harur·ra, superintendent of the mines, who arrived there in the month Phamenoth, in the reign of some monarch not mentioned, probably of the twelfth dynasty. The author of the inscription declares that he never once left the mine; he exhorts the chiefs to go there also, and ' if your faces fail.' says he, ' the goddess Athor will give you her arms to aid you in the work. Behold me, how I tarried there after I had left Egypt,—my face sweated, my blood grew hot, I ordered the workmen daily, and said unto them, there is still turquoise in the mine and the vein will be found in time. And it was so; the vein was found at last, and the mine yielded well. When I came to this land, aided by the king's genii, I began to labour strenuously. The troops came and entirely occupied it, so that none escaped therefrom. My face grew not frightened at the work, I toiled cheerfully; I brought abundance—yea, abundance of turquoise, and obtained yet more by search. I did not miss a single vein.'

" Another inscription runs :—' I came to the mines of my lord, I commenced working the Mafka, or turquoise, at the rate of fifteen men daily. Never was like done in the reign of Senefru the justified.' These and the frequent recurrence of tablets representing the various kings triumphing over and slaying their foreign captives, will enable the reader to judge of the nature of the mines and the manner in which they were worked by their Egyptian discoverers."

Next day our road led down Wâdy Zelegah, which bends towards the east, about a mile from the camping ground ; and where the bed of the valley opens out Armstrong came across a stone circle almost buried in the sand, the top of the stones only being visible. Striking across to the eastern side of the valley, where a detached piece of rock stands conspicuously out, he found some Arabic inscriptions and a lot of figures, chiefly animals, rather roughly carved out on the face of the rock. The valley, though bounded by steep cliffs, has an open, level, and wide bed, which is one of the principal features of the wâdies in all this region, making the passage of even very mountainous districts easy for animals and even possible for wheeled traffic. No valley of importance joins the wâdy from a continuous line of high hills with cliff, cutting off all communication up that side.

Camp was pitched at the end of this range of hills opposite the broad mouth of Wâdy Biyar, where there is an open space with an isolated hill in the centre. Wâdy Abu Tareifeh here comes in from the south-west, joining Wâdy Ughelim from the south, and flows into Wâdy Zelegah ; the valley here takes the name of Wâdy Biyar, and after a few miles turns to the north at a point where there are some nâwamîs.

These nâwamîs are small round circles of stones, some of them built up into a dome shape, having a small entrance on one side ; they are a great deal too small for human dwellings, and they are not, as far as one can judge, tombs. They occur in many places in the peninsula, and are generally in groups ; there are usually some traces of ruined walls about. The entrance is not in any particular direction ; the stones are small, and have not any appearance of having stood from very remote antiquity. I have never seen the question of their origin satisfactorily explained.

While travelling subsequently through the country to the south-east of Gaza on my way to Ismailia, I noticed the Arabs cultivating the ground extensively ; they live, of course, entirely in tents, and the barley they grow is sent in to market, but the chopped straw is made up into numbers of small heaps on the ground and covered with earth, forming little domes exactly like the nawâmîs. There are few stones on the Gaza plain, and little earth to spare in the wâdies of the peninsula. I would suggest that they are stone houses of the Arabs when they cultivated these wâdies, probably not very long ago. I saw no traces of cultivation now, but there are many places that would repay the labour well ; and, as far as I can judge, nawâmîs are usually found not far from some spot of this sort.

Figures cut on the rock in Wady Zelukâ

Copied by G. Armstrong

The walls in the neighbourhood are the traces of the enclosures round the tents. I know that much has been written about these nawâmîs, but having no books of reference with me I submit this opinion with diffidence.[1]

[1] The late Professor Palmer, along with Mr. Drake, visited these nawâmîs and groups of many others, and gives the following remarks in his book, "The Desert of the Exodus."

Professor Palmer thus describes them :—

"Shortly after passing 'Ain el 'Elyâ (Râs el 'Ain) we came to a group of nawâmîs, those quaint beehive huts of which I have before spoken.

"They stood on the hills to the east of the wâdy, and were more perfectly preserved than any which we had hitherto seen in the peninsula.

"They consisted of two detached houses, on separate hills, and a group of five on the side of a higher eminence. The first two had been used as Arab burial-places; but of the second group at least three out of the five were apparently untouched.

"Their dimensions average 7 feet high by 8 feet in diameter inside. They were circular, with an oval top, the construction being precisely the same as that of the nawâmîs in Wâdy Hebrân, but the perfect condition in which they have been preserved exhibits in a much more striking degree the neatness and art of their builders. In the centre of each was a cist, and beside that a smaller hole, both roughly lined with stones; these were covered with slabs of stone, over which earth had accumulated.

"Some human bones which we found in the cist at first led us to the conclusion that they were tombs; but the small size of the cist, and the evident fact that they had never contained perfect skeletons, proved the idea to be erroneous. In the smaller cist the earth showed signs of having undergone the action of fire, and, in one or two, small pieces of charred bone and wood were found. The doors, which are about 2 feet square, are admirably constructed, with lintel and doorposts. All the stones used in the construction are so carefully selected as almost to give the appearance of being hewn, and those in some of the doors have certainly been worked, if not with any instrument, at least by being rubbed smooth with other stones.

"A flint arrow-head and some small shells were found in one of the nawâmîs. They are evidently dwelling-houses; but I must leave to those who are better versed than I am in the science of prehistoric man the task of determining to what race they once belonged; the remains are certainly some of the most interesting which I have met with in the East. The country all around is covered with them, every hillside having some remains of nawâmîs upon it; but, owing to their exposed position, they have none of them been preserved in so perfect a state as those just described. Close by the nawâmîs were some stone circles. There would seem to have been a large settlement of these people in the neighbourhood of 'Ain el 'Elyâ.

"The word nâmûs is not known beyond Sinai, the Arabs in other parts of the desert calling them merely gusûr, or castles."

After three miles the valley turns again abruptly to the east, and at the corner are the important springs of Râs el 'Ain (called 'Ain el 'Elya by Professor Palmer), surrounded by palm-trees ; the water is good and plentiful, forming a small stream running towards a narrow passage (Es Sûk) in the granite hills ; this does not at all prepare the traveller for the grand gorge he has a few steps ahead of him. On entering Es Sûk the cliffs close in on both sides, forming every combination of turn and bend, and running up to about 800 feet with sheer precipitous sides ; every turn increases the height and grandeur of the gorge, while the small stream keeps the place cool and green with many plants and shrubs. Careful traversing had to be adopted through the gorge, which extends four miles.

Camp was pitched beyond the gorge, where another spring occurs called 'Ain el Akari, watering a small patch of reeds and palms. I had to observe from several high points on either side of the gorge in order to carry on the continuity of my observations.

On the 26th camp was moved. After passing through narrow valleys surrounded by granite hills, the road emerged opposite Jebel 'Aradeh, a high mountain of white limestone, which had to be ascended for observation. In the open portion of the valley there is a well of good water, having a perennial supply, called Bir es Saura : it occurs in a small cave. This well was said to belong to the Terabîn tribe of Arabs, but I could not find out that any of them ever came here, and it is certainly detached from their main possessions to the north and west of Nakhl.

The broad valley up which we travelled changes its name frequently as it passes each locality : thus in a few hours it becomes Wâdy 'Aradeh near the Jebel 'Aradeh, Wâdy 'Attiyeh opposite the tomb of the Sheikh of that name, and Wâdy Herteh at Jebel Herteh where we camped.

To the west of Wâdy Herteh the country is much broken up by small hills and valleys. The valley itself is large and open. After bending to the east and passing between some hills it again changes its name and becomes Wâdy el Hessy, which name it retains to its source. There is a small well in Wâdy Hessy, called 'Ain Hamâti, with a scanty supply of water.

The route continues in Wâdy Hessy, which gradually opens out on to an extensive plain ; crossing the plain to the north the watershed is reached : it is formed of low hills with a descent of a few hundred feet to a lower plain on the north. On the west is the range of hills called Turf er Rukn, running out into the plain as far as the Haj road, ending in abrupt cliffs. A broad valley leads away to the north called Wâdy Shiah, joining eventually the Wâdy Jerafeh, and thus falling into Wâdy 'Arabah and the Dead Sea. To the east of this valley are the granite hills of Jebel Humra jutting up in innumerable sharp peaks. The Derb el Haj runs immediately south of the Jebel Humra, through an open plain which is bounded on the south by a line of cliffs running east from the watershed. We passed along the plain and camped above the Nukb, or descent to the Gulf of 'Akabah.

The Derb el Haj descends about 2,000 feet to the plain of 'Akabah, by a carefully constructed road ; the rock had to be considerably excavated in places, and bridges span the watercourses when necessary. A carriage could be driven down the descent without much risk ; the road winds down a steep hillside for the first mile, and then descends by a valley through granite hills to the plain below. Before descending I had to make a long detour in order to obtain a good station to observe from, and I was fortunate in finding a point from which I had a splendid view of the Wâdy 'Arabah, which became afterwards one of my trigonometrical stations when passing up the valley.

The Admiralty Survey does not correctly give the form of the head of the bay, which is not so pointed as shown. At the lowest part of the valley the soil is soft and loamy ; the remainder of the broad bed is sand and *débris* from the hills.

The castle of 'Akabah is an extensive, but ruined, building situated close by the sea-shore on the eastern side of the bay, and is surrounded by a few wretched hovels and extensive groves of palm-trees along the shore. It is the abode of an Egyptian Governor, who has a few soldiers at his disposal, and is considered an important station on the Egyptian Haj road. There is practically no trade in the place, as ships never come there. The bay contains sharks and numerous other fish.

'AKABAH TO THE DEAD SEA.

The party had to remain three days at 'Akabah, while arrangements were being made with Sheikh Muhammed Ibn Jhad, of the 'Allawin Arab tribe, to take us up the Wâdy 'Arabah.

During this period I was fully occupied measuring a base line on the plain and starting the triangulation of the valley. I was also able to survey some portion of the shore line and hills about 'Akabah, which were not correctly laid down on the Admiralty plan. I measured the base line

completely across the valley : its length was 233·86 chains. A point close
to the castle of 'Akabah was observed for the vertical angles, and the
system employed for extending the triangulation up the valley can best
be seen from the attached diagram of triangulation (p. 199). The Sheikh
Muhammed Ibn Jhad declared that he could only take us as far as Petra,
and that from there we should be obliged to strike across country to Gaza.

On the 3rd December we left 'Akabah, shortly followed by another
party, who had been sent out by some company to ascertain the height of
the watershed above the sea, by a line of levels from 'Akabah.

About a mile from the north-east corner of the bay Armstrong observed
a number of small mounds similar to what are usually found on old sites ;
fragments of pottery of various colours are found, and an old wall of
masonry is seen cropping out here and there.

The general features of the valley are well known. On the east are
the bold granite mountains of Midian, intersected by valleys that have
thrown out a mass of *débris* into the main valley, forming a semicircular
fan-like ramp up to the mouth of each wâdy ; these are very marked, and
when seen from the opposite side of the valley have a very curious effect.

On the west limestone cliffs form a continuous scarp, broken at places
and intersected by granite upheavals ; very few important wâdies join the
valley on this side, although there are naturally many small ones from the
scarp itself. Camp was pitched near Ed Deffieh, some brackish pools of
water in the muddy slime that formed the lower portion of the valley;
some rain that had fallen while we were at 'Akabah increased the difficulty
of passing this sticky mud.

Next day we passed Wâdy el Mânei'aieh, flowing from the west, and
forming a picturesque recess in the scarp of the western side of the valley,
with a granite outbreak closing the entrance. The limestone scarp then
continues regularly. I had to visit a high prominent point upon it, to
take observations, and from here for the first time I saw and observed
Mount Hor. The ascent of the scarp was a stiff climb of 1,500 feet.

Camp was pitched near the border of the marsh of Et Tâbâ.

Et Tâbâ is a considerable marsh of mud and rushes, extending the
whole width of the bed of the valley. There is a passage round it on
either side ; the western one leads by 'Ain Ghudyan, while the eastern road
passes 'Ain Tâbâ, where there are palm-trees, and pools of water and reeds ;
to the north of the marsh begin the blown sand dunes with a few scattered
palms.

At the north-west extremity of the marsh a spur runs out from the western scarp for three miles, and under it is the 'Ain Ghudyan ; there is a pool of water, and several wells giving a plentiful supply of good water.

I found the foundations of a rectangular building, about 20 yards square ; there were also tracks of ancient lines of wells converging from the hills on to the 'Ain, and an Arab graveyard that has been noted before. I saw no traces of a Roman road.

To the north of 'Ain el Ghudyan the centre of the valley is choked with sand, leaving a passage on either side.

The hills on the east decrease in height, giving place to limestone and sandstone hills, joining a high range in the background called Jebel Serbal ; the scarp on the western side continues regularly with no wâdies of importance breaking through ; there are several minor valleys. Camp was pitched at the mouth of one of those, called Wâdy Galaita.

Next day I had again to ascend to the top of a prominent point on the western scarp near Wâdy el Beiyaneh, from which a good round of angles were observed ; just below the point there appeared to be a small water-shed ; the water channel from the eastern side comes across the valley and flows to the south down the western side, while the valleys from the hill I was on appeared to me to flow north ; it was so late and dark when I got down from the point I was on, that I was not able to examine this point as closely as I should have liked, but my impression was that there is a small depression in the valley here which does not drain south, unless when a considerable flow of water from the north filled the depression, causing the water to overflow.

The western scarp falls away after the high point near Wâdy Beiyaneh, forming low rolling hills with large openings, through one of which the main road turns westward over the lowest portion of the watershed.

Camp was pitched in the centre of the valley, at the mouth of Wâdy Heyirim, four miles south-east of the lowest point of the watershed.

To the south-east of the camp Wâdy Gharandel joins the Wâdy 'Arabah ; this valley breaks through a narrow and romantic gorge, and has a good supply of water at 'Ain Gharandel, situated some distance up the valley.

Next day I made an excursion to the west, surveying the low hills and the lowest portion of the watershed, which is on an open plain dividing Wâdy 'Arabah from Wâdy Jerafeh, flowing north from a south-westerly direction after the opening to the low watershed. A low line of cliffs

P

running north-north-east commences on the western side of Wâdy 'Arabah, separating it completely from the Wâdy Jerafeh; I walked along these hills, called Er Rishy, until I reached the watershed of the main valley at the mouth of Wâdy Huwer, flowing from the east. This watershed is 320 feet nigher than the other, and is the commencement of the great valley flowing south up which we had come.

The watershed is curiously formed—just at the mouth of this wâdy, part of the waters of which run north and part south. Those running north are joined by several wâdies from the Mount Hor range, and after passing the end of the low range of hills separating the valley here in an easterly direction, join the big valley of Wâdy Jerafeh or Wâdy el Jeib.

Armstrong found a ruined building in the valley. It measured 102 feet square, with well-cut drafted masonry. The building did not appear to date prior to Saracenic times—very probably one of the old road stations on the highway to 'Akabah.

Camp was pitched in Wâdy Abu Kusheibeh.

The eastern hills here recede, leaving a sort of amphitheatre in front of Jebel Harûn, the Mount Hor of Scripture, which rises magnificently in the centre. There is a mountain of white limestone immediately south of Mount Hor, over which it towers and gains by the contrast of its dark red hue over the white. Looking thus at Mount Hor from the south it appears to rise in several pinnacles, the highest of which is surrounded by a glistening white dome covering the tomb of the patriarch Aaron.

The scenery is exceptionally fine, and I do not consider former writers have exaggerated the grand appearance of Mount Hor; the brilliant colours of the rocks have been remarked by all travellers, but surpassed what I expected to find.

As I had been observing into the dome of Mount Hor for some time I was very anxious to complete my observations by obtaining a round of angles from there. Next morning therefore an attempt was made to go up without warning the Arabs, as had been done by Palmer and Drake; but this was frustrated, as I expected, by the Arabs having heard of our coming, and being on the alert. Two parties of our size travelling up Wâdy 'Arabah cannot do so without being remarked and making a sensation. We, however, penetrated up the valley leading to Petra for some distance, and noticed remains of terraces and some buildings on the slope.

We camped at the mouth of the wâdy that evening, and next morning was spent in discussion with the Arabs as to the amount for which they would take us to Mount Hor and Petra. As we could not come to terms, camp was moved in the afternoon towards the Wâdy 'Arabah and pitched in Wâdy Harûn. The Arabs then gave way and acceded to the terms we had stipulated for. Next morning we started before daylight and returned to the ruins we had visited before ; from thence we ascended by a steep zig-zag path to a saddle on the Mount Hor range. Passing along a slightly descending ridge we soon came to the base of a mountain rising from the ridge : this is Mount Hor, being actually from this side a mountain on a mountain, though, from the north the descent is much more precipitous to a far lower level. Unfortunately, the morning was exceptionally hazy, so that it was difficult to distinguish surrounding features.

An old path, similar to that on Jebel Mûsa, with worn steps made out of boulders at difficult parts, led up the mountain to another level space or platform, from which the highest peak rises abruptly. Passing over some ruined arches on an ancient cistern or building, the path leads up steeply by steps cut out of the rock itself to the summit, where there is the usual little round dome on a square building covering the tomb of the patri-arch Aaron. Looking inside, one saw the usual carpet covered cenotaph, with some ostrich eggs hanging over it—all in an uncared-for condition. We had to wait some hours on the summit owing to the mist which hung in dense clouds about us until 12 o'clock, when it partially cleared, and I was able to take some observations which were necessary for extending the triangulation to the north. After observing, we made our way rapidly down to Petra, and were able to visit the ruins and the more important tombs. There was no time to make a thorough investigation, but I was able to verify the accuracy of Laborde's plan of the place, and was much struck with the stupendous works in rock-cutting that had been under-taken and executed with the nicest accuracy ; also with the immense number of tombs, the ornamentations being as fresh and clear as when first cut, particularly those at Pharaoh's treasures. The colours of the rocks are wonderfully variegated, and most brilliant ; red to purple and blue are the most predominant colours, and these are set off by a cold grey background of limestone hills.

The ruins and tombs would doubtless well repay a thorough investigation.

It was dark when we got to the pass we had come up at dawn in the morning, and we reached camp about 9 P.M. after a long day.

Arrangements having been made with the Sheikh of our party to take us to the Dead Sea next morning, we started down the eastern side of Wâdy 'Arabah instead of crossing to the opposite side, as we should have done had our original route to Gaza been maintained.

I went across myself in order to take observations from the other side of the valley, as well as to survey the detail. The valley is here about ten miles broad ; the main water channel runs down the western side, and takes the name of Wâdy el Jeib with the main course alongside.

The hills on the western side are low, and much weathered, being of a soft, easily disintegrated limestone. It was late when I found the camp on the eastern side of the valley, and under the circumstances of camp moving continuously along the eastern side of the valley, I was compelled to give up attempting to do the western side, as it was quite beyond the power of myself and camel. I regret therefore that there is here an unsurveyed gap in the work.

Camp was moved next day to 'Ayûn Abu Werideh, or Buweirdeh ; it was impossible to find out the exact name, as the Arabs themselves were divided on the subject. I am inclined to think Buweirdeh is the correct name. It is almost impossible to collect the correct nomenclature when travelling so rapidly through a country, with Arabs from a different district ; and though I took every means in my power to determine the names definitely, I am not at all confident that in all cases I have obtained the correct names, or nearly as many as might be collected by a more prolonged visit to the neighbourhood. A good deal of blown sand from sand dunes in the valley lead up to the springs which break out in several places from some soft loamy soil in the valley, and form several small streams full of reeds, tamarisk, bushes, and palms, &c. ; the water is slightly brackish.

Near the springs Armstrong observed terraces of an old town of considerable extent. There are numerous little mounds of artificial appearance ; fragments of coloured pottery abound. The foundation of a building is seen, the stones having a very old and time-worn look, and portions of an aqueduct, level with the ground, are traceable from one of the springs leading to the site.

Next day I was able to obtain good observations from Samrat Fiddân, from which the Lisan in the Dead Sea was clearly visible.

A considerable perennial stream of water runs down Wâdy Fiddân, only losing itself when the valley opens on the plain of Wâdy 'Arabah. Doubtless the plain, east of Jebel Fiddân was a most fertile garden in former times

Example of Bedouin tribe Marks and Arabic Inscriptions in Wâdy Ghuweir.

and it would take very little to make it so again. I have rarely seen a
spot more suitable for every sort of culture, yet it is now a barren waste,
and until the Arabs of this country are placed under some control it
doubtless must remain so. The wooded mountains to the east about the
ancient Dhana form a picturesque background ; the ruins of this town,
I was informed, were as interesting as those at Petra, with carving in
rocks, &c.

Camp was pitched near the mouth of Wâdy el Weibeh, and I was
extremely glad to find that a day's halt was to be made in this locality.

Next day, by starting early, I was able to visit the western side of the
valley, a distance of twelve-and-a-half miles ; I observed with theodolite from
a trigonometrical station on the hills beyond Wâdy Jeib, and was able to take
up the survey again on that side, thus making the gap unsurveyed as small
as possible. Owing to the want of knowledge of the locality by my guide,
I was unable to visit 'Ain Aeibeh, which I had much wished to do.

Armstrong explored the country towards the east, and found, six miles
north-east of Fiddâu, the ruins of a small town in a valley, surrounded by
bold and precipitous cliffs ; the ruined walls are from a foot to 3 feet
high, the stones roughly squared, and of no great size ; some black heaps
resembling slag heaps point out that very probably ancient mines may be
found in the neighbourhood. A path leads from Wâdy 'Arabah to this
valley, crossing the watershed into Wâdy Ghuweir, where it joins, leading up
the valley in a south-easterly direction, a beaten and well-worn track : this
was probably the pilgrimage road from Gaza to Mecca. Lower down in
the wâdy (Wâdy Ghuweir) are numerous springs of sweet water trickling
out of the bed of the wâdy ; and in a narrow gorge the rocks are literally
covered with Bedouin tribe marks, Arabic inscriptions, &c., the work of
pilgrims on their way to Mecca.

Next day was unfortunately extremely hazy, and for the three following
days it was impossible to distinguish the western side of the valley at all.

We were not able to proceed a full day's march owing to the intrigues
of the Arabs.

Camp was pitched at Ed Debbeh close to the descent to the ghôr. We
passed a large ruined tank and remains of several buildings at the mouth
of the Wâdy Utlah ; these remains appeared to me to be of no great
antiquity, and to date from after Crusading times. There is little doubt
that all the eastern side of the valley was once a most fertile district,
the streams of water in each valley being used to irrigate gardens and

extensive cultivation, instead of running to waste on the hillsides, as shown by the remains of terraces which still exist almost perfect in many cases.

I heard many stories of the ruins and interesting country that lie to the east, which formed the ancient land of Edom, and I was frequently told that Wâdy Mûsa or Petra is not the most extensive ruin in that district.

The descent to the ghôr was down a sandy slope of 300 feet, and the change of climate was most marked, from the sandy desert to masses of tangled vegetation with streams of water running in all directions, birds fluttering from every tree, the whole country alive with life : nowhere have I seen so great and sudden a contrast.

The principal Sheikh of the Huweitât Bedouins, Sheikh 'Arâri, was camped close to the bottom of the descent, and he came out with some mounted men to meet us.

The country ruled over by Sheikh 'Arâri includes nearly the whole of ancient Edom, from Jebel Serbal to the ghôr where the Bedouins were camped ; he is chief of the Bedouins who do not cultivate the ground. There are also several other small tribes of fellahin Arabs who cultivate the ground, and also acknowledge him as their chief ; these fellahin are more difficult to deal with than the Arabs themselves, having no law, and acknowledging no government. The only way to deal with them would be through Sheikh 'Arâri, who is a very respectable Sheikh, and to whom they have to pay tribute. The 'Allawin Arabs under Sheikh Muhammed Ibn Jhad rule the country to the south of Jebel Serbal and to the east of the Wâdy 'Arabah ; they are closely allied to the Huweitât Arabs, and originally they say they were all one tribe. Even now the 'Allawin call themselves sometimes Huweitât ; they are under the Egyptian Government, and are employed to protect the Haj road south of 'Akabah. Another branch of the same Arabs is the important tribe of Egyptian Huweitâts under Sheikh Ibrahim Ibn Shedid, whose influence extends over the tribes as far as 'Akabah.

These three Sheikhs rule over a very vast country ; they are closely related by marriage, as the Arab Sheikh is very particular that his wife should be of noble blood, i.e., of the family of the Sheikhs. They also recognise that they were originally of one tribe, although they are now completely independent of one another.

The next most important tribe is the Ma'azi Arabs; they rule over the mountains of Kerak, which they are said to have taken from Sheikh 'Arâri's

Huweitât tribe. They say they are very numerous in the far East, and the three sections of the Huweitât all complain of the pushing nature of the Ma'azi on their frontiers. There is a large settlement of Ma'azi Arabs in Egypt, extending from Suez southwards along the Red Sea shore as far as Kosseir.

These Arabs everywhere have a bad character for thieving ; they are divided up under numerous Sheikhs, and are continually making raids on the Arab tribes round them ; they are generally very poor.

The only other two tribes of importance in this region are the Terabin and the Teiyâhah ; the latter are divided into two sections, the Teiyâhah and the Azazimeh. For many years the south country has been in a disturbed state, owing to the war going on between these two tribes ; the dispute was about the boundary of the tribe lands near Bir es Seba. Peace has now been obtained by the internal divisions of the Teiyâhah, a portion of whom have gone over to the Terabin, the remainder having no heart to continue the conflict, although it may break out at any time.

The Teiyâhah have no friends or allies in any of the tribes around them, and have a feud with the great Huweitât family. The Terabin, on the contrary, are at peace with their other neighbours ; they cultivate the ground extensively about Gaza, and are closely allied to the Huweitât of Egypt. They bear a good character, and are a rich tribe.

The Terabin rule the western portion of the south country, the Teiyâhah having the eastern portion as far as Wâdy 'Arabah.

The Haiwât are a small tribe occupying the country about the Haj road ; they are ruled by Sheikh el 'Ayân Mismeh, who has his camp generally about Bir etu Therned. Men of this tribe were the principal actors in the murder of Professor Palmer and his companions ; they are a poor tribe, under the influence of Sheikh Shedid of Egypt.

Camp was pitched in the Ghur el Feifeh, near Wâdy Tufihel, and next day we moved on to the Ghôr es Safieh, where the Ghawarneh were encamped. These are a wretched race of fellahin, who cultivate the Ghôr es Safieh, and are pillaged by the Huweitât from the south, the Ma'azi from the east, and the Teiyâhah from the west. They are the same race as those that occupy the ghôr at Jericho.

They were actually engaged in ploughing up their ground, which is well watered by the streams from Wâdy Safieh. Notwithstanding the constant blackmail they have to pay to different tribes they seemed to be well to do, and I believe make a good deal in trading with the Bedouins in barley, wheat, beans, &c. Owing to various causes we were obliged to stay in the Ghôr es Safieh until the 27th December.

The south end of the Dead Sea is formed of extensive mud flats of a very slimy character. The recent rains had doubtless contributed to the soft state of the mud, but the natives told me it was never hard. It was almost impossible to reach the edge of the water of the Dead Sea through the mud. A line of driftwood had been thrown up a considerable distance inland, forming a shore line almost half-a-mile south of the water's edge.

I found it was quite impossible to measure a base line through this slime, and the dense vegetation of the ghor left no open space available. After several attempts I was obliged to relinquish the idea; this I regretted very much, as I found the portion of the Dead Sea to the south of the Lisan had been very inaccurately delineated on previous maps, and the Lisan itself had to be moved considerably, as will be seen on the plans.

I took several observations into the trigonometrical station on our old survey of Palestine, and was able to connect my triangulation up the Wâdy 'Arabah from 'Akabah in this way with very satisfactory results. The diagram of triangulation and plans will show the observations that were taken, and how the connection was established principally through the observations subsequently taken from a cairn on Râs Zuweirah.

Overlooking the ghôr on the eastern side, just above the ruins of some modern mills at Kusr Sh. Ali, Mr. H. C. Hart, in his botanical rambles, found some very interesting ancient remains at a place called Khurbet Lebrush. These remains consisted of a large number of nawâmîs, some of which were in a wonderfully perfect state of preservation. These nawâmîs are dotted about thickly over the site without any plan, and the openings in them having no especial direction; a few loose stone walls near some of them have the appearance of having been thrown up recently round tents. Enclosing the greater number of these nawâmîs is an ancient wall following the contour of the hill for a quarter of a mile; only the foundations remain, but they were of massive undressed masonry, of apparently remote antiquity. Inside the wall there are the ruins of an oblong building of similar masonry, very probably an ancient temple; unfortunately the remains are so ruined that it is impossible without considerable labour to thoroughly explore or measure this monument: only one corner could be determined, the remainder being covered by heaps of massive stone blocks.

There are several other heaps of ruins and large cairns of stones inside the enclosure, but these are all detached and do not appear to be the remains of a town. I could see no extensive remains of buildings such as are found in ancient sites in Palestine.

The wall ran nearly north and south, and at the southern end there are the remains of what was probably a tower ; traces of the wall can then be seen following the hillside for a considerable distance, and enclosing the hill. The nawâmis are not all inside the wall, and appear to me to be of more recent construction. An apparently old roadway leads through the ruins, and crossing a saddle of the hills leads up to the high hills on the east.

The remains appear to me to be those of a very ancient site, subsequently used by the Arabs as a camping ground. I could find out nothing from the Arabs about these remains, though they are well known.

The view from here overt he gorge of Es Safieh to the north is very fine ; the various and brilliant colours of the rocks are most marked ; cliffs of a bright rose colour line the stream, alternating with yellow, dark red, and purple.

The ruins in the Ghôr es Safieh appear to be all modern ; there is a large reservoir and several ruined mills, all of Arab construction.

A track across the mud flats leads to the base of Jebel Usdum, the mountain of salt, on the western side of the valley. I found that this mountain had to be considerably altered in shape and position to what it has been shown on existing maps. It is almost detached from the surrounding hills, and descends abruptly in cliffs to the Dead Sea shore. It reaches a height of 600 feet above the Dead Sea, and is broken and cracked by many fissures. All round the ghôr there is a border of the same marly hills, more or less washed away, and extending for some distance up the valleys.

On the 27th December we passed round the Jebel Usdum by the seashore and followed a road leading up the Wâdy Zuweirah. The road leads up a winding ravine in the bare limestone hills that extend all along the west side of the Dead Sea.

A picturesque Saracenic castle, now in ruins, is perched on an isolated hill in the centre of the valley, defending the pass from an enemy advancing from the east.

An ingenious loophole has been cut in the rocks on the opposite side of the valley in advance of the castle, from which the valley is entirely commanded.

After the castle the road ascends steeply by zigzags to a pass, after which the country is more level, but continues to ascend as far as Râs Zuweirah.

Camp was pitched after dark in Wâdy el 'Abd, where there is a small supply of water. The water supply in these wells is very limited.

Next morning I was able to obtain a valuable round of observations from the cairn on Râs Zuweirah, at the top of the ascent. The cairn itself was apparently a very ancient landmark or tumulus, and is seen prominently from all the country round.

Passing over some rolling hills through very open country, with a few ruins distinctly marked by the verdure around them, we encamped on the edge of our former surveyed work at Tel el Milh. The following day we marched to Bîr es Seba, and from there to Tel abu Hareireh, all in the published Map of Palestine.

At the latter place I left the party, and with four Arabs of the Egyptian tribe struck across country by a southern road to Ismailia The rest of the party proceeded to Gaza.

I was greatly assisted in my work by Mr. George Armstrong, late Sergeant-Major R.E., who has had a vast amount of experience in surveying in the East for the Palestine Exploration Fund, and without his aid I should not have been able to arrive at nearly as satisfactory results on this expedition.

The means of surveying adopted was, 1st : In the Mount Sinai work taking a broad base over twenty miles long on Sir Charles Wilson's surveyed country ; positions were fixed by observation, and a chain of observations were kept through to 'Akabah.

2nd. At 'Akabah a base line was measured, and the former work connected with it. A triangulation was then extended up the Wâdy 'Arabah until, at Râs Zuweirah and Kusr Sh. Ali, it joins on to the old triangulation of Palestine proper.

The attached diagram of triangulation will show the number of points observed.

The plans will show full details of the work done. Heights were obtained up the Wâdy 'Arabah by vertical angles.

The total area triangulated and surveyed in the above manner in the two months employed is roughly 3,000 square miles.

Owing to the rapid passage of the party through the country, and the impossibility of getting guides with local knowledge, the names are not, in my opinion, in every case reliable, although I took every opportunity to check them by local information as much as possible. Many more names could also be collected by a more lengthy stay in the country.

I had the names written down in Arabic, so that the spelling is as correct as possible; but I have reason to believe the localities were not always correctly shown.

TEL ABU HAREIREH TO ISMAILIA.

On the 31st December I left Tel abu Hareireh with four Arabs of the Huweitât tribe of Egypt that had been sent to us at the Dead Sea with a letter from Sir E. Baring describing the disasters in the Soudan.

The rest of the party went on to Gaza to undergo quarantine.

As the El Arish road was well known, I determined to march direct on Ismailia, thus striking out a new line, and passing through much more interesting country. One of my party, Abu Suweilim, had been employed by Sir C. Warren in hunting the murderers of Professor Palmer, and was one of the most energetic useful Arabs I have ever met : he had been the road we were about to take fifteen years before; the others did not know the road at all, and were of the usual Bedouin type, lazy and greedy.

Passing over a plain of cultivated ground, with numerous Arab tents, the inhabitants of which were busily employed in ploughing, and which had been already surveyed, about one o'clock I came to Wâdy Fara; this is a large and deeply cut wâdy, and contained a good deal of water. Just below the crossing there is a prominent mound called Tel el Fara, and before descending there are some traces of ruins and foundations of buildings called Kh. el Fara, but nothing of importance was left. An hour beyond the valley is a well-known tent called El Khudra, where for the last ten years a merchant from Gaza has traded with the Arab tribes, and doubtless does a good business, as many of the Arabs dare not show themselves in Gaza. The trader was a Bulgarian, and was so delighted at hearing his native tongue spoken that he would take no pay for the provisions of coffee, dates, and a saddle-bag I bought ; he said he often had dangerous times with the Arabs, but that he bought a protection from the most powerful of the neighbourhood, and always obtained restitution of anything stolen.

We pushed on over open country until dark, when we made our camp fire on an open plain with a number of Bedouin's fires blazing round us. I was passed as Abdullah Bey, an Egyptian official journeying back to Egypt after having been to Jerusalem, and although it was only begun for that little while, I thus revived the name borne by a much more distinguished traveller, the great Sheikh Abdullah, and although it was only stated to stop the curiosity of the Arabs we met, I soon found I was called nothing else.

At dawn we were up, and after feeding the camels and getting some coffee brewed we were ready to start at 8.30. During the whole journey I never could manage to get started much before this hour, as the Bedouins require some time to get the night chills out of their bones ; the nights were certainly very cold and damp. Our track after crossing a plain struck a road coming from the north-west, and after rising a slight hill the country gradually became more and more sandy, all signs of cultivation gradually dying out, and the continual climbing up and down the sand dunes being most fatiguing and monotonous. At 12 o'clock the track changed direction to south-west, down an open valley amongst sand dunes called San'a el Men'aî, and we camped in a little valley surrounded by the sand. Next morning the route was continued over sand dunes, and we came early to a considerable pool of rain-water called El Khubara ; it is formed by the soil of Wâdy Abyad being turned by the Arabs into an old valley bed which is now closed, and they informed me it was kept full all the winter by rain-water coming down the wâdy. A few minutes further on is the first big valley since Wâdy Fara ; it is called Wâdy el Abyad, Wâdy Khubara, and Wâdy ez Zayik, and runs with a broad bed through the sandhills to the north-west; there are many tamarisks and bushes along its course. Here we stopped for an hour to bake bread, and then leaving the valley crossed over more sandhills which seemed interminable. At last the country opened out, and after passing over some very broken ground we arrived at Wâdy el 'Arish.

The valley runs in a deeply-cut bed with mud banks ; it is here about 80 yards wide. There was a pool of rain-water in a bend of the valley, which my guides informed me covered a well called Bír el Mujdebbah, and if my guides' account was true, that water could be got here all the year round ; this is the only perennial source on this road as far as Ismailia.

After Wâdy el 'Arish the country opens out into a broad plain with an isolated small range of hills called Jebel el Bena in the centre. To the north there is a sandy covered range called Riza Anizeh, and to the south the high hills of Jebel Helah ; a track leading away to the south-west between Jebel Bena and Jebel Helah through an open plain, led, I was told, to Suez. Here camp was pitched.

Next day we passed close under Jebel Bena on the north side over a stony plain called Ragadda ; the hills were formed of nummulitic limestone, and appeared perfectly dry and bare ; the wide open plains were very flat and bare of vegetation, with the exception of a small amount of the usual desert shrub. It was a great relief to get clear of the sand dunes, which ended close to Wâdy el 'Arish.

On reaching the end of Jebel Bena the high range of Jebel Yelek appeared to the south-west, and the long range of Jebel Mugharah flanked the valley on the north ; an open plain up which we travelled led between these two, and our track ran close under the Jebel Mugharah. I was told there was a cave in the interior of these mountains which contained a perennial supply of water. The hills rose abruptly from the plain, and appeared to be of the same formation as the nummulitic range of Jebel Bena. In some places the strata were much bent and contorted. At nightfall we reached a ruined well called Bîr el Hemmeh, which contained a small quantity of stagnant water which had a very unpleasant smell.

Next morning we passed a small ridge formed by a volcanic outbreak of trap rock, and shortly after the sand began to appear again. In a few hours we reached the watershed of the valley ; the sand had increased to high ridges and hills, through or over which we had to find our way. The watershed was flat, another open valley leading away to the west with Jebel Felleh on the south, and a continuation of the Jebel Mugharah range on the north. We camped on the sand near a prominent top called Jebel el Urf, which forms a landmark on this road.

Next morning we crossed the low ridge under Jebel el Urf, and passing down a sandy valley at noon we came to a flat of mud which formed the end of the valley, a barrier of sand having been thrown up and thus stopping up the valley completely. Crossing this ridge an immense extent of sandhills appeared as far as the eye could reach. I do not think I have ever seen so desolate and dreary a country : nothing but ridge after ridge of sand dunes for an immense distance. The wind blew a strong gale from the west, sending the sand up into our faces so sharply that the camels would at times hardly face it. This wind lasted, unfortunately, until we reached Ismailia, and was very trying to the whole party.

We camped under a sandhill and had a very cold and windy night. Next morning it was found we had no water. The Arabs are always most improvident about water, and require continual watching ; during the night they had used up the last drop, and in the morning said they could not go on without a fresh supply, as there was no chance of water before Ismailia, and they did not know how long it would take to get in.

They said they could find rain-water in Jebel Felleh. I, however, insisted on going on, and with some difficulty got the camels under way. Two of my Arabs had been lagging behind for some time, so one of the Arabs and myself went back and drove up the camels; the two Arabs were sulky and deserted; however, we got the camels all right. Pushing on through a blinding storm of sand over hill and valley, with only the compass to guide us, at 4 P.M. I saw Lake Tumah, and skirting the shore reached the ferry over the canal at dusk. I had some little difficulty in getting the party across the canal, and was not sorry when I reached comfortable quarters in Ismailia.

H. H. KITCHENER.

THE SECTION OF THE WÂDY 'ARABAH.

THE Wâdy 'Arabah extends from the head of the Gulf of 'Akabah to the south end of the Dead Sea, and is 112 miles long.

The width of the valley at the foot of the hills, from 'Akabah to near the lowest point of the watershed, averages about six miles.

A series of low ridges, called Er Risheh, of about 150 feet above the plain, run obliquely across the valley at this point, forming a length of ten miles. Opposite Mount Hor the valley widens out to thirteen miles, and gradually narrows in to six miles at the south end of the Dead Sea—the same width as that at 'Akabah. The sectional line is drawn from the Gulf at 'Akabah, through Wâdy 'Arabah, representing the lowest depression, to the southern end of the Dead Sea, and continued to the northern end, where the river Jordan enters, showing the depression of the Dead Sea, and that part of Wâdy 'Arabah below the sea level of the Gulf of 'Akabah.

The lowest point of the watershed (660 feet above Gulf of 'Akabah) is computed to be forty-five miles from 'Akabah, and twenty-nine miles farther north the sea level point is reached.

The sketch of the outline of the hills on the eastern side of the valley is given relative to the calculated heights as noted.

Those on the western side (not shown on section) range about 1,900 feet above sea level.

GEO. ARMSTRONG.

INDEX TO NAMES.

HARRISON AND SONS, PRINTERS IN ORDINARY TO HER MAJESTY, ST. MARTIN'S LANE.

www.ingramcontent.com/pod-product-compliance
Lightning Source LLC
Chambersburg PA
CBHW030640030726
47497CB00006B/1874